# PLOTS WITHIN PLOTS

Katrina Steiner's advisors, her grand-aunt General Nondi Steiner and Mandrinn Tormano Liao, observed her as she twirled a platinum paper knife between her fingers.

"If the vote were held tomorrow, who would be the First Lord of the resurrected Star League?" asked Nondi Steiner.

Tormano thought a moment. "The Precentor Martial is clearly grooming Victor to lead the Star League Defense Force that is attacking the Clans. Who possibly could be better than him?"

Katrina smiled. "If my brother Victor is leading the force, he will have to go with it and fight in the battles that come."

Nondi's eyes became slits. "Why give him a chance to return to the Inner Sphere as the man who conquered the Clans?"

"Because it will allow the rest of us to define his role when he returns. If he goes away, he cannot rule the Federated Commonwealth. We must go over the files for all of the delegates if I am to be elected as First Lord. I want every need met and noted. When I am nominated First Lord of the Star League, I want the sense of gratitude in knowing that everyone has decided I deserve that honor."

Tormano bowed his head to her. "I think you will find your brother rather stiff competition."

Katrina laid the paper knife down carefully. "I've handled Victor all my life. I will see to his downfall myself."

# BATTLETECH®

## Twilight of the Clans II:

# GRAVE COVENANT

## Michael A. Stackpole

A ROC BOOK

ROC
Published by the Penguin Group
Penguin Books USA Inc., 375 Hudson Street,
New York, New York 10014, U.S.A.
Penguin Books Ltd, 27 Wrights Lane,
London W8 5TZ, England
Penguin Books Australia Ltd, Ringwood,
Victoria, Australia
Penguin Books Canada Ltd, 10 Alcorn Avenue,
Toronto, Ontario, Canada M4V 3B2
Penguin Books (N.Z.) Ltd, 182–190 Wairau Road,
Auckland 10, New Zealand

Penguin Books Ltd, Registered Offices:
Harmondsworth, Middlesex, England

First published by Roc, an imprint of Dutton Signet,
a division of Penguin Books USA Inc.

First Printing, September, 1997
10  9  8  7  6  5  4  3  2

Series Editor: Donna Ippolito
Cover art by Roger Loveless
Mechanical Drawings: Duane Loose and the FASA art department

 REGISTERED TRADEMARK-MARCA REGISTRADA

BATTLETECH, FASA, and the distinctive BATTLETECH and FASA logos are
trademarks of the FASA Corporation, 1100 W. Cermak, Suite B305, Chicago,
IL 60608.

Printed in the United States of America

This book is dedicated to Ian Anderson and Jethro Tull.

This is my twenty-second novel, all of which were written with music playing in the background. Jethro Tull is always part of the playlist. During the writing of this novel I got to see Jethro Tull in concert. Music is magic and Ian Anderson is a sorcerer.

The author would like to thank the following folks for their contributions to this book:

Jordan Weisman, Bryan Nystul, Randall Bills, Jill Lucas, Bill & Nina Keith, Donna Ippolito, and Robert Thurston for their story direction, editing, and error-trapping.

Loren L. Coleman, Robert Thurston, Blaine Pardoe, and Tom Gressman for their books leading into and out of this one.

My father, Dr. J. Ward Stackpole, for medical consults on the traumas and diseases mentioned herein; John-Allen Price for the continued loan of Galen Cox; Mark Herman for explaining Entropy-based Warfare to me; and especially Mike Pond-smith for his generous donation to charity for his appearance in this book.

Jennifer Smith and Laura Gilman of ROC for their tolerance of my scheduling difficulties.

And, as always, Liz Danforth for living through the insanity of my putting this book together.

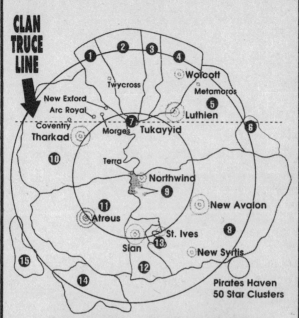

**CLAN TRUCE LINE**

① ② ③ ④

Twycross ⦿ Wolcott

Metamoros

New Exford ⑤

Arc Royal ⦿ Luthien

Coventry Morges ⑥

Tharkad Tukayyid ⑦

⑩ Terra

Northwind ⑨

⑪ New Avalon

Atreus ⑧

St. Ives ⑬

Sian ⓬ New Syrtis

⑮

⑭

Pirates Haven
50 Star Clusters

# MAP OF THE INNER SPHERE

1 • Jade Falcon/Steel Viper, 2 • Wolf Clan, 3 • Ghost Bear,
4 • Smoke Jaguars/Nova Cats, 5 • Draconis Combine,
6 • Outworlds Alliance, 7 • Free Rasalhague Republic,
8 • Federated Commonwealth, 9 • Chaos March,
10 • Lyran Alliance, 11 • Free Worlds League,
12 • Capellan Confederation, 13 • St. Ives Compact
14 • Magistracy of Canopus, 15 • Marion Hegemony

Map Compiled by COMSTAR.
From information provided by the COMSTAR EXPLORER SERVICE
and the STAR LEAGUE ARCHIVES on Terra.

© 3058 COMSTAR CARTOGRAPHIC CORPS.

# BOOK 1

## Congress of Treachery

# = 1 =

**Triad National Cemetery**
**Tharkad City, Tharkad**
**District of Donegal, Lyran Alliance**
**30 September 3058**

The moist breeze wending its way through the labyrinth of monuments in the Triad National Cemetery dragged on Victor Ian Steiner-Davion. The premature arrival of spring had reduced September's normal blanket of snow to islands of white floating in muddy oceans. The bright green of new leaves and grasses peeked out, seeking sun. The early spring had created a general feeling of well-being that was greatly in evidence on the media broadcasts the Prince had caught while his DropShip burned toward the planet.

*One good frost and it all dies.* Standing before his mother's memorial, Victor felt immune to the spring fever infecting Tharkad. Her death had come as a result of power grabs by just two Inner Sphere nobles. And now Victor had come to Tharkad to participate in the Whitting Conference, where dozens of Inner Sphere nobles would make still more power grabs. The conclusion that things would be a disaster was all but inescapable.

Victor frowned. *Things will only go bad if you allow them to go bad.* He shifted his shoulders and winced at the aches he felt. Most of them, he knew, came from the grueling trip from Coventry to Tharkad. JumpShips were capable of tearing a hole in the fabric of reality, allowing them to move instantaneously from point to point, up to thirty light years at a jump. Tiring though they were, those jumps didn't bother him so much as had the high-G DropShip burn in to Tharkad. *Being as small as I am, laboring under more than one gravity is a chore.*

He managed a smile. That hadn't stopped Kai or Hohiro from beating up on him. He fingered the fading bruise around his right eye. He'd gotten it after failing to pick off a rightcross delivered by Hohiro Kurita. *I saw it coming, but couldn't do anything about it.* Though chagrined about getting a black eye, he was also proud of it.

Too much of his life had become politics and appearances. He accepted the necessity of such things, but politics still grated on him. It struck him as completely ludicrous that he could be forced to take a position far more extreme than he ever intended to carry out, just so he could later compromise with opponents, finally getting what he wanted in the first place. The time and effort wasted in those games could be better spent actually getting things done.

Setting up the Whitting Conference was a prime example of the waste politics caused. Fourteen weeks earlier, on Coventry, he had proposed building a united force to take the war to the Clans. Within two days his sister, Katherine, Archon of the Lyran Alliance, had offered to host the conference on Tharkad. In doing so she had assumed the burden of organizing the meeting, inviting the leaders of the Inner Sphere and, quite deftly, positioning herself to be seen as the unifying force for the future of the Inner Sphere.

Victor acknowledged that she'd played her part well and that her orchestrations had dictated his actions. Though Coventry was less than ninety light years distant from Tharkad—a trip he could have made inside three weeks—there'd been no reason for him to show up before the first of October, the date Katherine had chosen for the conference to start. Victor had remained on Coventry along with his staunchest allies, putting their troops through training exercises.

Though the delay had annoyed him, the time spent training on Coventry had not. The insulation and isolation from life that Victor often felt vanished as he spent as much time as possible in the company of his troops. For the first time since his ascension to the throne of the Federated Commonwealth, he actually felt he had a grasp on the concerns of ordinary citizens.

He'd also taken the time for personal training. Victor had always been fit—blessed with the Steiner metabolism that prevented him from piling on the kilos—but physical inactivity had begun to sap his strength. He began a program of exercises, then supplemented it through kendo training with Hohiro and learning aikido with Kai Allard-Liao. In return he'd found an old grizzled sergeant who was willing to teach the royals the intricacies of boxing.

*And Hohiro learned a lot faster than I wanted him to.* Victor shook his head, wondering for a moment what his mother would have said about his black eye. She'd have been concerned, but would have smiled and told him it was good he was getting more exercise. *She always knew what to say to make someone feel good.*

He looked down at the dancing, cavorting fire of the eternal flame at the granite base of the monument. Unlike countless other statues memorializing his mother scattered throughout the Federated Commonwealth, this one lacked a physical representation of Melissa Steiner-Davion. And yet it had something of her. Its blocky stone strength was like the foundational strength she had provided to the union of the Federated Suns and the Lyran Commonwealth when she'd wed Hanse Davion thirty years before.

Victor bowed his head. He knew he should drop to his knees to offer a prayer for his mother, but the chilly moat the spring thaw had created around her gravesite had already soaked the hem of his long, steel-blue greatcoat. Since most of the citizens of the Lyran Alliance—the name his sister Katherine had given to the Lyran half of the Federated Commonwealth after she seceded—believed he had murdered his mother, his kneeling in a puddle before her grave would probably look to them like the wild behavior of a killer suddenly overcome with remorse.

He crossed himself and offered a brief prayer for the repose of Melissa Steiner-Davion's soul. He took a deep breath, then nodded toward the granite tomb. "What you and father built thirty years ago has dissolved in the two years since your death. Were you alive, uniting the Inner Sphere to face the Clans and destroy them would have easily been possible. Now I just hope the chance to destroy the Clans won't be bickered away."

A flicker of movement near the entrance to the cemetery caught his attention. Looking down through the gravestones, he saw a trio of black hoverlimos vaporizing puddles on the cemetery roadway as they sped toward him. The lead and rear limos had flashing lights playing against their windscreens while the middle vehicle—the largest of them all—moved between its escorts with a certain serenity.

From behind him he heard the click of his own hoverlimo's door opening. Victor turned and held up a hand to restrain the icy-eyed man emerging from the limo. "No need to be anxious, Agent Curaitis."

"Given who is in that vehicle, and what she has done to obtain power, is there a reason I shouldn't be anxious?" Curaitis was one of the few people who knew the truth about Katherine.

Victor thought for a moment, then nodded. "You have a point there."

The black-haired bodyguard closed the vehicle's door and remained standing beside it. Victor knew better than to expect further comment from the intelligence agent. *The man makes a rock seem talkative.* Besides, the approaching limos now had Curaitis' full attention.

The lead limo veered off, allowing the larger one to come to a stop barely ten meters from the nose of Victor's limo. The gull-wing door in the back third hissed and swung up. Victor saw movement in the darkened interior, then his sister emerged, unaided, and stalked toward him.

*You never change.* Taller than him, Katherine emphasized that by wearing knee-length white boots with spike heels. Her white sable coat hung down to the tops of her boots and was matched by the furred hat perched on her head. Her long, golden-blond hair played over the shoulders of the coat as her steady, long-legged stride brought her closer.

She gestured lazily toward him with a gloved hand. "Good afternoon, Victor."

"And you, *Katherine*." He made certain to pronounce every syllable of her name with care and precision. Though she had taken to calling herself "Katrina," Victor refused to acknowledge the change. Katrina Steiner had been his grandmother, an Archon and undoubtedly the shrewdest and most powerful woman ever to rule one of the Successor States of the Inner Sphere. For his sister to have usurped Katrina's name and image seemed a crime to him. "I'm surprised to see you here."

"Are you?" Her ice-blue eyes held his stare defiantly. "I missed you at the spaceport."

"Ah, so that was *you*." Victor gave her a slight smile and let his gray eyes show the venom he kept from his voice. "I should have realized you were sending a welcoming committee, but I really wanted to come here before I did anything else."

She stopped at the other side of the monument. "Easing a guilty conscience?"

"Guilt? Over what?"

Katherine smiled coldly. "You missed her funeral. You didn't care to make it."

Though Victor had thought he was ready for this encounter with his sister, her remark still got past his defenses. Not knowing at the time of their mother's death that Katherine was his enemy, he'd let her make all the funeral arrangements. Since their mother had been blown apart by a bomb, having her lie in state until all her children could gather was not really an option. Katherine staged the funeral almost immediately, and Victor alone among her children had been unable to arrive in time.

"I wanted to be there, Katherine, but there are times when the demands of leadership prevent us from doing what we want to do."

Katherine allowed herself a throaty little laugh. "Ah, yes, what were you doing then? Preparing to chase after some Clan bandits?"

"They were a threat to the Inner Sphere and the truce."

"No, Victor, they were your chance to play soldier one more time." Katherine opened her arms wide. "Look around you, Victor. This cemetery is full of people who were seduced by the lure of BattleMechs. Six hundred years ago 'Mechs were created to rule the battlefield. Three centuries ago Aleksandr Kerensky took the Star League Defense Force away from the Inner Sphere because he feared the Battle-Mechs that had hitherto been used to protect life would become instruments of its destruction, and he was right. For three centuries wars raged among the Successor States, with leaders mounting up in 'Mechs to win glory for themselves and some tiny piece of an entropic universe for their realms. Then Kerensky's people returned to show us just how destructive a 'Mech can be."

Katherine toed Melissa Steiner's grave. "Even our mother

was caught up in that MechWarrior mystique. She gave birth to Yvonne, took over as Archon from her mother, then announced she would become a BattleMech pilot. She became obsessed with these ten-meter-tall engines of destruction. She even went so far as to pursue a course of study at the Nagelring, all because it was traditional for an Archon to be a pilot, a warrior—though history shows that being a warrior is in no way related to being a leader."

She peered down her nose at him. "*That* is a lesson you still need to learn, Victor."

Victor's blue-flecked, gray eyes narrowed. "I doubt it's a lesson I could from you, Katherine."

"I could teach you much, Victor."

"Oh, I'm sure of that." Victor fought to keep his voice even and his anger in check. He had evidence, very strong evidence, that his sister had conspired with Ryan Steiner to have Melissa murdered. *I don't have the proof I need to expose you, Katherine, but Curaitis says it won't be long in coming. Then I will teach you a lesson—one concerning justice.*

He raised his chin. "I'm not certain I want to learn the lessons you could teach me."

His reply seemed to take her a bit by surprise. "You spend too much time playing warrior, Victor. It's not good for your realm."

"If I'd not played warrior on Coventry, you'd be a Clan bondswoman right now."

Katherine's cheeks flushed crimson at the idea, and for the barest of moments Victor thought she might actually thank him for stopping the Clans at Coventry. "Oh, what you did at Coventry was interesting, Victor. Your decision to allow the Jade Falcons to flee without punishment has played well with the public. Although I've heard some say it was your fear of public reaction to your cowardice that kept you from showing up here until the day before the conference."

"Not that you think that."

"Not at all, Victor. I think you had your reasons for delaying."

Victor nodded. "I did. In fact, my delay came from something you did teach me."

"Oh?" Vanity pulsed a spark into her blue eyes. "What was that?"

"I learned how to make an entrance." Victor folded his arms across his chest. "I waited for everyone else to arrive first, then I came, along with my troops. And then I went at once to my mother's grave, to pay my respects. And look who came to me! I'm sure your rushing to my side will also play very well in the media, Katherine."

She took a step toward him and he thought for a moment that she would slap him. Instead she reached out with her left hand, letting her fingertips linger at the edge of his jaw. With her thumb she traced the outline of the bruise around his right eye. "Oh, Victor, you think you've won this one, don't you? I hope you don't bruise easily because I think you will find this conference very battering. I set the agendas, I guide the discussions, I run the whole thing. If you don't play by the rules I lay down, you'll be left in the dust. It's as simple as that."

He shook his head slowly to make her pull back her hand. "No, Katherine, it's not going to be that simple. You know very well that the leaders of the Inner Sphere haven't come here to entertain you or let you play the queen, but to find a way to destroy the threat of the Clans. If you interfere with that, if you stand in the way of what must be done, *your* realm will bear the brunt of the Clan retaliation. And *then,* sister dearest, the people of the Lyran Alliance will wish they had a warrior as their leader again, because only a warrior will be able to save them."

He took a step backward, then tossed her a brief salute. "By the way, I'm appropriating Bifrost Hall at the Nagelring while I'm here. It will provide me with the facilities I need."

Katherine's eyes half-lidded. "And it is convenient to the ComStar compound."

"And the Luvon Foundation, which is where Morgan Kell and Phelan will be staying."

Katherine's eyes widened slightly. "I did not invite them."

"I know. I corrected your oversight." Victor walked to his hoverlimo, but turned back toward her before getting in. "You're right that being a warrior doesn't necessarily confer the skills needed to be a good leader and ruler. It also doesn't bar one from picking them up."

Katherine snorted derisively. "What you should be asking yourself, Victor, is whether you can pick them up fast enough."

"Perhaps, Katherine. Or maybe it's you who should be

wondering if you can prevent me from doing so." He gave her a cold smile. "If you can't, you'd best make sure I'm pointed at an enemy because you don't want me coming after you."

# ═ **2** ═

*Kerensky Sports Centre*
*Strana Mechty*
*Kerensky Cluster, Clan Space*
*30 September 3058*

**K**han Vladimir Ward of the Wolves strode up the grassy slope from the DropShip *Lobo Negro,* seeing the Clan capitol world with new eyes. He looked out over the vast expanse of green fields beneath a purple sky streaked with thin, lavender clouds and watched warriors racing back and forth playing lacrosse. He recalled the game well; the sweat, the competition, the hitting, and the degrees of finesse that separated the adequate from the truly talented.

The last time he had played on these fields had been more than seven years before. A faint smile came to his lips as he remembered the person he had been. He had thought himself nearly complete, the product of a superior breeding program that had created him to be the greatest warrior ever known to humanity. He still had no doubts about the success of the breeding program, but with seven years of perspective he realized that superior steel, unforged, unshaped, and untempered does not a keen blade make.

*In those days my ordeal had only just begun.* He wondered what the person he had been would think of him now. The rank of Khan would come as no surprise, of course, though the events that had led to his election would have been beyond imagining seven years ago. *My path to power has been twisted, to say the least.*

He recalled his last game on these fields. He had always been an excellent athlete and that match had been no exception. At the half, Phelan, the Inner Sphere foundling, had joined the game, but only now could Vlad admit that Phelan had showed talent, defeating opponents even though it was his first time playing by Clan rules. *Back then I saw him as an obstacle to be battered down and blasted aside.* Yet Phelan had prevailed against his opponents. He had even pointed out to Vlad that they could accomplish great things when they worked together instead of opposing each other.

*That was a clue I should have grasped, but I did not see it.* That Phelan was an enemy and a threat to the very nature of the Clans could not be denied then or now, but he was not an obstacle. If anything, Phelan was a challenge, a whetstone to ever make Vlad sharper. *We can never work together, Phelan, but only strike against each other so I may become all that I am destined to be.*

*And strike against each other we will.* Their previous clashes had been merely the prelude to an even grander drama that would continue to play itself out in the future. Each of them was now a Khan of the Wolf Clan, though Vlad's Wolves had rejected those misguided fools who had followed Phelan into exile in the Inner Sphere. There, Phelan had set himself up to oppose Clan aggression, further laying the groundwork for the conflict of the future.

Of course, Vlad allowed, this outcome surprised no one, but his fellow Clansmen did not see the significance of other events. Unbeknownst to any of the other Khans on Strana Mechty, Vlad had met and formed an alliance with Katrina Steiner, the Archon of the Lyran Alliance. Some months back she had ventured into Clan space hoping to reach the Smoke Jaguars and ally herself with them. By sheer fortune, her ship had fallen into Vlad's hands, and they had met for the first time. In their time together he had managed to convince her that he was a far better choice of confederate. Their mutual hatred of her cousin Phelan had strengthened the bond between them.

Vlad's face flushed as Katrina came to mind. The very same genetic engineering program that gave the trueborn Clan warrior his martial superiority had also severed the connection between sexual intimacy, progeny, and the strong emotional ties that bound freebirth families together. Because all young trueborns were raised in sibkos with as many as a hundred others, their emotional ties were to their sibmates. At puberty they were allowed to begin exploring their sexual desires and drives, and it was done with others in their sibko. Coupling became a gift between comrades, a joining of equals, not part of some mating ritual.

But Vlad had reacted to Katrina Steiner as to no other woman before her. She kindled in him primitive, even primal feelings that could not be dismissed as simple lust. He could not deny how intense was the attraction and even dared name what he felt love. It did not matter that the idea of love was scorned by members of the Clan warrior caste. He himself had scorned it once. But no more.

*Others are only warriors. I am Vlad of the Wolves.*

"My face would burn with shame, too, Vlad, were I you and bold enough to come to Strana Mechty." The voice lashed at him, breaking his reverie. It was a woman's voice, and one he recognized. "Games are for children, not warriors."

He forced a smile as he turned to face Marthe Pryde, Khan of the Jade Falcons. Tall and slender, with her black hair worn short, her skin showed a touch of the grayish hue that came with extended space voyages. Her blue eyes, despite the red tingeing them, were as full of fire as he remembered. "Oh, was that *your* DropShip following mine down to the planet?"

She folded her arms over her chest, drawing the green jumpsuit tight at the shoulders. "That little race, I had assumed, was at the instigation of our ship captains. But that is not the game I had in mind."

Vlad ran a hand over his dark hair, smoothing it back from the widow's-peak. "Which game, then, were you chastening me for?"

Marthe's features sharpened. "On Coventry you sent me a message threatening to take over six worlds in my occupation zone. You did that to torture me because you knew the forces the Inner Sphere had massed against me on Coventry were evenly matched against mine. If I withdrew to deal with the threat you posed, I would be dezgra in the eyes of the Clans. If I did not withdraw, both sides in that battle would have been shattered."

Vlad forced a smile that tugged at the scar running from

his left eye down to his jawline. "I do not see that as a game—merely an effort to distract you from your normal ruthless efficiency."

"I recognize that, Vlad, and even applaud it." Marthe graced him with a slight nod. "The game to which I refer is your treating with the enemy. You could only have learned of my mission on Coventry and the opposition I faced through contacts with the Inner Sphere. And do not try to tell me that Phelan Kell provided you the information. Even if he did not hate you, passing such information would have jeopardized his friends and he would never do that."

Vlad pursed his lips, then nodded slowly. "So you accuse me of using intelligence I gathered from the Inner Sphere against you. You have proof of my source, *quineg*?"

Marthe frowned heavily. "No."

"Good, because you would be wrong." Vlad met her stare and kept his voice even as he manufactured a simple lie. "The Inner Sphere believes in the free reportage of what they call news. Some initial reports leaked out of Coventry before the Inner Sphere shut them down. I merely had people on my occupied worlds who intercepted the transmissions and I drew the logical conclusions from them."

He could see she did not believe his explanation, so he pressed on. "It is just as well that Khans do not allow themselves to spread unsubstantiated rumors. Were this not the case, I might be given to wondering aloud exactly *where* you got all of the warriors that cycled through the fighting on Coventry. I know I have been forced to recruit from some of my lower castes so I can move garrison troops to front-line units. Though I have heard of no such effort by you, I have to assume that is what you have been doing."

Marthe lifted her chin defiantly. "You may assume that until you have proof to the contrary."

"I have no such proof, nor do I intend to seek it." Vlad's eyes narrowed. "Nor do I intend to let others seek it."

Marthe's brows arrowed together for a moment. "Why not?"

*Yes, an investigation could be your undoing, Marthe, but this is not the time for that.* Vlad turned and pointed to the largest building in the center of Strana Mechty's capital city. "In the Hall of Khans we have more immediate problems than what we could do to damage each other. Neither of us has recovered from our recent war to avoid Absorption by another Clan."

"We would eviscerate any Clan who sought to take us over."

"Agreed, but that would make the Clans even weaker, *quiaff*?" Vlad held his right hand out toward her, palm up. "You and I, the Jade Falcons and the Wolves, do not agree on much other than the Crusader philosophy. It is our destiny, our right and duty, to retake the Inner Sphere and reestablish order. Absorption will not aid this cause. Allowing two of the more dedicated Crusader Clans to die will not further it."

Marthe blinked her eyes as if disbelieving what she was hearing. "Are you suggesting an alliance between us, *quineg*?"

"Aff, an alliance. Your distaste for politics is well known. I agree that politics is beneath a true warrior, but it allows us to fight battles here, in the Grand Council, that then don't need to be fought by our warriors. We can preserve them for the true battles of the future."

"Despite your vulgar speech, I find truth in your words."

"I beg your forgiveness of my use of contractions, but they seem to underline the urgency of what we will be facing in there." Vlad closed his hand into a fist. "We cannot allow our Clans to be destroyed."

"Because, if we do, you cannot be elected ilKhan."

Vlad allowed himself a little laugh. "I do not want to be ilKhan." *At this time.*

Marthe arched an eyebrow. "No?"

"No. The next ilKhan will not complete the crusade. He will not take Terra."

She tapped her lower lip with an index finger for a moment. "Why do you think this is so?"

"The next ilKhan will be working hard to prove he is not Ulric. He will do none of the things Ulric did or would have done."

Marthe Pryde smiled. "And he will forget that despite being opposed to the Crusade, ilKhan Ulric Kerensky did the most of any Clan Khan to succeed at taking the prize. Interesting. There may be something to this theory of yours."

"There is. Think of it, Marthe: the crusade was undertaken by Khans who had never fought against the Inner Sphere. They had never fought the sort of massive campaign required to succeed at taking Terra. Among them, Ulric was a visionary, which accounts for his success. Mark my words— the Crusade will be completed by Khans who have passed through the fire and survived the crucible of the invasion."

Her eyes half-closed. "Which means you believe the task will fall to you?"

*Of course.* "Or you, or another who will rise up from the ranks." Vlad again stabbed a finger toward the Hall of Khans. "If we stand united, we will have a chance to see the Crusade reach its conclusion."

Marthe studied him for a moment, then nodded. "I agree. Do not think this means I trust you or that I will not strike at you if I believe doing so will benefit my Clan."

"Your words mirror my thoughts exactly, Marthe Pryde." Vlad returned her nod. "This is an alliance of convenience only—our convenience. That it will cause many others discomfort, well, that is collateral damage at which we can rejoice."

# ≡ 3 ≡

*Bifrost Hall, The Triad*
*Tharkad City, Tharkad*
*District of Donegal, Lyran Alliance*
*1 October 3058*

**V**ictor Steiner-Davion found himself holding his breath as he waited for Hohiro Kurita to make his move. The heir to the throne of the Draconis Combine knelt barechested at one end of the gymnasium's shuffleboard court. Hohiro wore a katana thrust through the broad gold sash circling his middle. His shoulders rose and fell with a final breath, then he was off.

Rising in one smooth motion, he freed the sword from its scabbard. The flashing steel blade swept out and around to the right, exploding a red, helium-filled balloon hovering at head-height. Hohiro continued the spin and let the blade drop half a meter. He came around and bisected another balloon with a pop. Another step forward and he slashed straight down with an overhand blow that shattered a small wooden block Morgan Hasek-Davion had lofted through the air toward him.

Half the wooden block skittered across the floor and bumped up against Victor's right foot. The Prince looked down at it, noticing how cleanly the katana had sheared through the pine cube. "Nice. Very nice."

Hohiro smiled proudly all the way up into his brown eyes. "*Arigato*, Victor-*sama*. Now it's your turn."

Victor winced. "You're a tough act to follow."

"Come on, Victor, you can do it." Kai Allard-Liao finished tying a green balloon to a short string so it would hang at about chest-height. His gray eyes sparked playfully. "You can't tell me you'll let the heir to the Dragon show you up."

Victor frowned. "He's had a lot more practice at this than I have. I'm playing his game, so I expect to lose."

The other man working on a red balloon cleared his throat. "I hesitate to point out, Highness, that when Hohiro indulges in boxing, he beats you at *your* game."

"Very funny, Jerry." Victor shook his head and walked toward the shuffleboard court. "Why don't you just hold that balloon instead of making smart remarks? I might miss, but your beard is looking a bit scraggly . . ."

Jerrard Cranston finished knotting the line onto the balloon, then stepped back. "Considering that this beard is the only flimsy disguise I have to keep your sister from recognizing me, I think I'll stay clear of that katana, thanks. Not that I don't trust your ability to trim my beard with it, Highness."

Victor knelt. "I think I liked you better before my sister let you die." He looked over at where Cranston stood between Hohiro and Kai. "But that's a discussion for another time." Even though Bifrost Hall was constantly being swept for listening devices and had, so far, proven clean, there was no need to be free with secrets.

*If Katherine knew Jerry Cranston was really Galen Cox, she could easily conclude I had evidence linking her to my mother's murder. She will certainly come to that realization some day, but she mustn't learn what I know until the time is right. Her access to that information, and her ability to respond to it, will have to be contained and channeled so she cannot cause too much trouble.*

Victor looked up at the balloons and at the older white and red-haired man who was ready to toss a block out for him to cut. The Prince nodded at Morgan Hasek-Davion, indicating his readiness to begin. He flexed his hands, listened to ligaments pop, then drew in a deep breath.

Victor knew the exercise inside and out, but he hadn't taken to it like Hohiro. The problem was that he kept breaking it down into parts and building it back up again instead of just flowing through it. *It has parts, but they're like notes in a song—each one is part of the continuum.* With that realization his ability to encompass the problem seemed to expand. He slowly exhaled and the world around him faded as he focused on his task.

*Now!* He came up on his right foot first and pulled the katana free of the scabbard as he started his turn toward the first balloon. The katana's slightly curved blade ripped through the red balloon, opening a jagged gash in its curved surface. Victor continued his spin, the sound of the balloon bursting almost unnoticed next to the pounding of his heart.

He corrected his aim as he came around to attack the green balloon Kai had hung in place. Victor saw that his blade was coming in too low, so he brought it up slightly. The katana's razored edge sliced cleanly through the balloon's neck. The knotted string fell toward the floor as the rapidly deflating green blob jetted into the air.

Victor tried to ignore its whirling flight-path and the flatulent staccato that accompanied it as he turned to slash at the block, but he could not. The flaccid green streak arced down toward Morgan just as the wooden block leapt up from his fingers. The Prince tried to track one, but saw the other. His overhead cut nicked the block, but missed the balloon entirely.

Furious with himself, Victor sank to his knees, allowing his momentum to slide him forward, and rehomed the blade without looking or giving the task much thought. The echoes of the balloon's dying raspberry faded with the snickers he heard from the trio on his right and the mild chuckle from Morgan on his left. Mortification flushed his face, and the faint plop of the green balloon hitting the floor underscored his humiliation.

Then the sharp sound of a pair of hands clapping killed it. Victor thought at first that one of his companions offered the applause in gently mockery, but it did not trail off the way such a false accolade usually did. The clapping remained strong and steady and cut off the laughter from Victor's friends. *Who? What?*

Victor turned as he rose to his feet and saw a man with Asian features standing in the gymnasium's doorway. Even though Victor had not seen him for seven years—years that had leeched color from his hair and also scored the flesh at the corners of his mouth and brown eyes—there was no mistaking the man or how much his son, Hohiro, resembled him.

The Coordinator of the Draconis Combine continued his applause and even let the hint of a smile play across his lips.

Victor immediately executed a formal bow, then deepened and held it for an instant longer than he would have for Hohiro. He knew countless people in the Federated Commonwealth might have read that gesture as subservient—*and high treason*—but he offered it out of respect and specifically out of gratitude for the Coordinator's gesture. Then he straightened and marveled at how Theodore Kurita managed to match his bow in depth and duration so effortlessly.

"*Konnichi wa,* Theodore Kurita-*sama.*" Victor forced himself to enunciate the words, knowing his Japanese was as flawed as his swordsmanship. "I wish you had been spared this exhibition."

Theodore shook his head. "Why? You honor my son by your close attention to the lessons he has taught you, and you honor the Combine by your willingness to learn about our traditions such as the Way of the Sword."

"Yes, but I hardly showed respect to *kenjitsu* or my *sensei* with that display." Victor cracked a smile. "Your applause was polite, but I think the laughter of my friends was more suitable."

Theodore gave Victor a curt nod. "Your cut at the second balloon was inexact, but it was not what I applauded. There, at the end of the exercise, despite your distraction and humiliation, you resheathed your sword without hesitation, without thought. The presence of mind you demonstrated in doing that is something few raised outside our society, or that of the Capellan tradition, ever attain."

Victor let his mind replay what he had done. He hadn't thought, he had just acted. He had rehomed the blade because that was the right and appropriate action. The idea of cursing or throwing the sword down in frustration had not occurred to him. Without realizing it, he had completed the exercise, and had even returned the blade to its scabbard without cutting himself—something he had done several times before under much less pressure.

Theodore smiled. "There are times, Prince Victor, when knowing how to return a weapon to its scabbard is more important than knowing how to cut with it. Anyone can cut and kill, but knowing when cutting and killing is not necessary, that is a milestone on the path to true wisdom."

"Thank you, Coordinator. I would like to think the road I

travel is one where wisdom can be attained." Victor opened his hands. "I believe you have met my companions." Victor nodded to his cousin. "Kai Allard-Liao."

Theodore bowed toward Kai. "The Champion of Solaris. You were most kind to my daughter during her sojourn there."

"Retired champion, Coordinator." Kai returned the bow. "And hosting Omi was a pleasure."

Victor pointed to the man on his left. "Morgan Hasek-Davion."

"We met on Outreach, Coordinator."

"As well I recall, Marshal Hasek-Davion."

After Theodore and Morgan exchanged bows, Victor turned toward Jerrard Cranston. "And this is my intelligence advisor, Jerrard Cranston."

Theodore bowed toward Jerry. "I am pleased to make your acquaintance, Mr. Cranston. My intelligence has a file on you that is most complete, but hardly conveys the true nature of the man."

Cranston smiled as he returned the bow. "We all have our secrets, Coordinator, and reasons to keep them."

"Indeed."

Victor was fairly certain Theodore knew that Jerrard Cranston had once been Galen Cox. Hohiro knew it, but Hohiro had spent more time with Cox on Outreach seven years ago than his father ever had, making the deception rather transparent for him. The Prince did not mind Theodore knowing the truth, but Theodore's comment about his intelligence apparatus suggested that his people did not know Cranston's secret. It did not seem unreasonable to Victor that the Coordinator might want to keep the information from his own intelligence personnel, primarily because it gave him something with which to impress or castigate them, but the idea that he might find value in being able to do that surprised Victor. *The Combine operates by rules I don't think I will ever understand.*

The Coordinator raised his hands. "I did not come here to interrupt your lessons, Prince Victor, but when Hohiro told me you would be here, I decided to come to speak of matters that are best kept away from prying eyes and hungry ears."

Kai cleared his throat. "I could stand getting a cold drink, if you will excuse me. Anyone else?"

The Coordinator shook his head. "You should stay, Kai

Allard-Liao, and you Marshal and even you, Mr. Cranston. What I say here you will doubtless learn from the Prince, and I have no reason to not want you to hear my words from my lips. What I say this afternoon may not be for public consumption, but it is not to be denied, either."

Theodore glanced down for a moment, as though gathering his thoughts. "First, I wish to express to you my sorrow at the loss of your mother and father. I knew him better than I did her, but I respected them both. Hanse Davion, the Fox, was a major source of anxiety for the Combine, and if not for incredible luck, I would be your vassal. Your mother, Melissa Steiner-Davion, amazed me with her ability to undercut factional fighting by appealing directly to the people over whom she governed. The future of the Inner Sphere was darkened when their lights were extinguished."

Victor swallowed past the lump in his throat. "Thank you, Coordinator. Your daughter Omi was most kind and gracious in attending my father's funeral and in expressing your regrets over my mother's death. I know both of them respected you, and it would have pleased them to know the sentiment was shared."

"The second matter I wish to mention is not one steeped in grief." Theodore's head came up and a smile spread across his face. "Your study of *kenjitsu* with my son, and your studies of Japanese, please me very much. Your father knew only one aspect of the Combine. He knew us as enemies who could and would fight as fiercely as anyone else. He knew us as the murderers of his brother. As much as he might respect us, anger and fear also insulated him from understanding us. From his perspective, we were simply a warrior people with whom he was at war.

"You, through your friendship with my son"—Theodore hesitated for a moment—"and my daughter, have access to the attainment of a better understanding of us. Your father looked at the symbolism of the sword and saw it as an embodiment of our martial intent. He knew of, but never fully comprehended, the greater significance the sword holds in our culture. The sword, and the right to wear two of them, separates nobles from commoners. It is a weapon of war, but as you know, is one that can only be wielded successfully after being studied and pursued with discipline. Similarly, the art of forging a sword requires study and discipline. In this, swordsmanship and the crafting of swords become a paradigm for all of the Combine."

Victor slowly nodded. "The Combine demands discipline and hard work from its people to facilitate the strengthening of the state. In my realm we use private enterprise—the profit motive—to motivate people. We stimulate compassion by offering rewards. Our system works well, *if* the profit in a situation can be recognized; otherwise things do not get done."

"And among us, these unprofitable things are done because they are a societal duty." Theodore's smile slackened slightly. "There are trade-offs, but these traditions form the core of our existence. And with the Clans a constant threat to our border, discipline and order have their value, even at the cost of creativity and freedom.

"Your father would have understood all this the way he understood martial law and the need for order. He would not see it as you can, as part of a whole. Your father pursued a grand plan of liberating the Combine from the oppressive nature of our regime, as if my father was as mad as Maximilian Liao—no offense intended, Kai."

Kai shook his head. "My grandfather's madness was not inherited by my line, so I am not offended."

*"Domo arigato."* Theodore's eyes narrowed. "Your father would have tried to liberate us from that which defines us. The Combine is not like the Clans—we are not a machine that stamps out warriors. We are a society that reveres the Way of the Warrior because of the discipline and the service that warriors give to us. They keep us safe and they provide an example of selfless duty to society."

Victor smiled. "Yet Hohiro has told me of the poetry and art they also create—though I don't think you'll find me ruining a perfectly good piece of rice-paper by splashing ink over it."

Hohiro laughed. "There is always haiku."

"True, but I was raised here on Tharkad, with German as my primary language, *ja*?" Victor frowned lightly. "In German there are words that would use up the syllable allotment for a haiku, and have syllables left over. Not my art form."

"It matters not that you have yet to find your personal avenue of expression, Victor. It only matters that you realize there is room for you to do so." Theodore folded his arms over his chest. "This provides you insights your father never really had a chance to attain. Despite that, however, your father was an intelligent and cunning man, which brings me to my third point.

"Seven years ago, on Outreach, all of the leaders of the Great Houses of the Inner Sphere gathered together as they do now, here on Tharkad. Back then, your father and I recognized that our internecine fighting could only hurt the effort against the Clans. We resolved, informally, of course, to refrain from attacking each other until the threat of the Clans was dealt with."

Victor nodded. "My father spoke to me of your agreement."

"Good." Theodore caught Victor's eyes. "I want you to understand that I intend to continue that agreement. Though I applaud this meeting and hope that the Inner Sphere will form a united front against the Clans because of it, we both know it is our two realms that will bear the brunt of the fighting. As long as we are united, we have a foundation for resistance."

Victor offered Theodore his hand. "I can only speak for my half of the Federated Commonwealth, but no troops of mine will attack the Combine while the Clans are still out there." The Prince's blue-flecked gray eyes narrowed. "In fact, I don't see troops under my command ever attacking the Combine."

Theodore shook his hand. "It is my profound wish that your vision of a peaceful future can be realized."

"As long as I'm in charge, it will." Victor nodded toward Hohiro. "He beats me with swords and he blacked my eye when we were boxing, so I know first-hand how tough Combine warriors are. Why would I send my people against them?"

Hohiro frowned. "You've been administering a nation, Victor. That doesn't give you the time Kai or I have to spend training."

Kai agreed with a nod. "And at that, you're coming on pretty fast and pretty strong. Your greatest asset, Victor, is that you learn well. Given enough time, you'll be giving as good as you get."

Hohiro laughed. "Then I'll be telling others how tough FedCom warriors are and using that to justify my refusal to spill blood needlessly."

Morgan Hasek-Davion cracked his knuckles. "I'd certainly be happy if more people shared the insights about the futility of old rivalries. I guess part of this conference should involve educating some of our counterparts about exactly that sort of thing."

The Coordinator bowed his head toward Morgan. "Indeed, that would be wise. Let our unity here make that our first task, then meld that effort into going after the Clans. Let them learn how valiant and fierce all the Inner Sphere's warriors are."

"That's a lesson that will take some teaching." Victor smiled and rested his hands on the hilt of his katana. "But it's one we'll drive home to them. And soon."

# ══ **4** ══

***Grand Ballroom, Royal Court***
***The Triad***
***Tharkad City, Tharkad***
***District of Donegal, Lyran Alliance***
***1 October 3058***

It was not until the welcoming reception for the delegates to the Whitting Conference had begun that Katrina Steiner realized that there was a problem with her playing hostess. Standing at the far end of Grand Ballroom, in the corner opposite the string quartet playing chamber music, she realized that it meant having to spend more time with these people than she had any desire to. *And I must smile all evening, even if I don't feel like it.*

Though she was indifferent to most of the individuals present—from the Hero of Coventry, Leftenant General Caradoc Trevena, to the plethora of Allard-Liaos accompanying Candace Liao—it was the ones for whom she felt contempt who garnered the lion's share of her attention. Those she could ignore she did, but there always seemed to be someone in her field of vision who irritated her.

Thomas Marik, Captain-General of the Free Worlds League, spun past on the dance floor with his new companion, the slender, petite Sherryl Halas. The dark-haired, hazel-eyed woman was the daughter of Christopher Halas, Duke of Oriente. The Halases were long-time supports of the Marik family, leading a substantial voting block in the Parliament, so

Thomas' courting her made perfect sense. And Katrina could not blame him. Marik had recently made overtures toward Katrina herself, but she'd simply left them unanswered. *Sherryl Halas is pretty enough to console him for not getting me.*

What angered her about Thomas was less his temerity in bringing the Halas woman to Tharkad than his audacity at courting someone who, except for her height, looked so much like his daughter Isis. Watching Thomas introduce Halas to the other delegates and squire her around set Katrina's teeth on edge.

*Too bad Sherryl doesn't have Isis' taste in clothes.* The woman was dressed for the occasion in pearls and black velvet, but the gown was several years out of date and it was the same one Katrina had seen her wearing in a holograph from some state function on Atreus. *Yes, the people of Oriente are known for being practical, but this borders on vulgar.*

Isis Marik, garbed in a simple gown of blue silk cut along classical Greek lines, was better dressed, but she found little more favor in Katrina's eyes. Isis had arrived on the arm of her betrothed, Sun-Tzu Liao, but had soon let him go his own way. She, in turn, successfully gathered a coterie of admirers from the various military staffs assembled for the conference. Isis laughed at their jokes, blushed at their compliments, and rather often reached out to touch one on the arm or shoulder, conveying her pleasure in this or that one's company.

Katrina almost admired the ease with which the young woman manipulated the men, except for two things. The first was Isis' brazen attempt to charm Morgan Kell. The grayhaired mercenary tolerated her ploys well enough, but was obviously immune. Isis, however, seemed unaware that he was invulnerable to her charms. Katrina knew he had nothing to offer the Marik girl, so why was she even wasting her energies on him?

Worse yet, in Katrina's mind, was the fact that Isis constantly monitored Sun-Tzu's activities. Any time she detected Sun-Tzu watching her, she would do something designed to kindle jealousy in his heart. The signs were plain for anyone to read, as was Isis' frustration that Sun-Tzu seemed not to notice. *She's not a stupid girl—her ability to charm soldiers and statesmen indicates that—but she should have Sun-Tzu wrapped around her finger by now.*

Sun-Tzu clearly had his hands full with other things. The cut of his embroidered silk Han jacket emphasized both his Asian ancestry and his tall, slender build. The green dragons that chased all the way up the sleeves of the gold jacket shimmered as the young Chancellor of the Capellan Confederation moved through the room. His expression remained unreadable when people stopped to speak with him, but his features sharpened as he stalked off in pursuit of his sister.

*I never did buy into that bumbling idiot act of his.* Katrina allowed herself a private smile. *Though I do believe his sister utterly and irredeemably mad.*

Kali Liao packed a lot of venom into a small body. She wore her reddish-brown hair piled high on top of her head, fixed in place with enough golden sticks to resemble a radio antennae array. Her sleeveless silken gown matched the color of her green eyes, had a high mandarin collar, and was slit to the hip on the right. It would have made Kali quite fetching, but her inability to master the art of walking in stiletto heels utterly destroyed the elegance she tried to project.

When Katrina greeted her, Kali had hissed a reply in Chinese. Though Katrina did not understand the words, the tone of voice and the look in Kali's eyes needed no translation. Not only was Kali a member of the brutal Thugee cult, but its members considered her an avatar of their goddess. The young woman apparently was so persuaded of her own divinity that she considered it unnecessary to be civil when dealing with inferiors. *Which would include most of the people in her realm, clearly.*

The three Kuritas from the Draconis Combine did their best to redeem the image of Asian dignity that the Liaos destroyed. Theodore, as always, exuded an aura of serene power. Distinguished and handsome, yet possessed of an intelligence that shone like a beacon in his brown eyes, he had a presence that demanded attention. Katrina easily saw why her father had considered Theodore a serious threat to the Federated Commonwealth.

His son, Hohiro, had inherited his father's good looks, but seemed to lack the strength of soul his father projected. The war against the Clans had not been kind to Hohiro. He had been imprisoned once by the Smoke Jaguars and then trapped behind the lines by the Nova Cats on another world.

If not for her brother's efforts, Hohiro would have been lost to the Combine forever—making his rescue another crime against the Federated Commonwealth for which Victor would some day have to pay.

Katrina watched Hohiro through heavily lidded eyes. *How much more pressure can he endure before he cracks?*

Omi Kurita, as always looking prim, proper, and gorgeous, hung back behind her father's shoulder. Katrina had gotten to know her three and a half years earlier on Arc-Royal and again on Solaris, the Game World. Katrina had liked Omi, and if not for the Kurita woman's peculiar taste in men, might have tried to make of her a close friend. *She guards the avenues to power in the Combine. Right now House Kurita is focused on the Clans, but that will not always be so. It's a pity she has fallen for my brother.*

Katrina broadened the smile on her face as Candace Liao came through the crowd to greet her. "Duchess, I am so pleased to see you." Katrina bowed to the older woman, then shook her hand. "I trust you find Elm House suitable accommodations for you and your entourage."

The older woman nodded carefully. "Quite suitable. Please convey my thanks to your Alpine Toy Manufacturing Corporation for outfitting that play room and the nursery. My grandson is thrilled with the toys, and the nursery is perfect for my granddaughter."

It hardly seemed possible to Katrina that Candace Liao was speaking of grandchildren when she hardly looked a day over forty. Katrina assumed the lack of gray hair was due to hair dye, and the file the Lyran Alliance's intelligence division kept on Candace suggested the paucity of wrinkles was due to cosmetic surgery. Katrina doubted that since she saw the hints of battle scars peeking out from beneath the short left sleeve on the Duchess' gown. *If she were vain enough to undergo surgery, certainly she would have had* that *problem taken care of.* Katrina believed Candace's generally healthful conditioning was due to a daily regimen of *t'ai chi chuan,* a practice she had learned from her late husband nearly thirty years before.

Candace smiled, her gray eyes full of intelligence and charm. "You know my son, of course."

Katrina offered Kai her hand. "It is good to see you again, Kai. I still remember watching you defend your title on Solaris. It was quite thrilling."

"You are most kind, Archon." Kai politely raised her hand to his lips and kissed her knuckles. "I remember your visit quite well."

"Archon? Please, Kai, I thought we knew each other well enough that such formality could be dispensed with." *You're enough of an ally of my brother to refuse to call me by my grandmother's name. It's very convenient to have such a simple litmus test for loyalty.* Katrina allowed her eyebrows to rise. "And this must be your wife. I am Katrina Steiner."

The black-haired woman on Kai's arm shook Katrina's hand with a firm grip. "Deirdre Lear. Pleased to meet you, Archon."

"The pleasure is mine. You've kept your name—but then you are a doctor, aren't you? Do you still practice?"

"Not at the moment. I . . ."

Katrina pressed a hand against her own breastbone. "Oh, forgive me. You just had a child, didn't you? A daughter."

Candace nodded. "She's only six weeks old."

Kai glanced back at Katrina. "She is Melissa Allard-Liao, named after your mother."

"After my mother." Katrina hesitated a moment, then let her voice drop to a choked whisper. "That is a great honor."

Deirdre Lear smiled. "We thought so."

Katrina read something in the woman's blue eyes that made her uneasy. It added to her dislike for Lear's being able to regain her figure and slip into a fashionable black gown despite only being six weeks removed from giving birth. *Clearly Kai's feelings for my brother have colored Lear's feelings for me. Still, she is a mother and therefore has a weakness, her children.*

"Please, Dr. Lear, if there is anything you need while here on Tharkad, I would be offended if you did not ask me for it. If you and Kai want to get away for even an evening, I can arrange child care. It would be an honor, and no trouble at all." Another factoid from Deirdre's file came to mind. "And I know you have been coordinating public health and education programs in the St. Ives Compact. If possible, I'm sure your counterpart here, Dr. Wilson, would love to compare datafiles and even exchange educational materials—if you have time." Katrina underscored her offered with an open-faced innocence that clearly took Lear by surprise.

"I appreciate your offer, both of them, in fact." Deirdre smiled carefully. "Melissa is a bit young to leave alone right now, but I would happily meet with Dr. Wilson, at his convenience, of course."

"Very good, I will tell him." Katrina pointed toward the refreshment tables. "Please, enjoy the hospitality of the Lyran Alliance."

As the Liaos moved away, Katrina caught sight of her younger sister, Yvonne, and fought to suppress a sigh. Though several centimeters taller than Katrina and two kilos lighter—allowing her to make a stunning success of the gown Katrina had obtained for her—Yvonne seemed as awkward as Kali Liao was feral. At nineteen, Yvonne was pretty by anyone's standards, with the red hair and gray eyes reminiscent of her father and the smooth, fair complexion of Melissa Steiner-Davion.

*Yvonne, you must come out of your shell.* Katrina, who was seven years Yvonne's senior, had always viewed her as something between a living doll and a protégé, though the younger woman failed in the latter department. She did allow Katrina to dress her up and make her beautiful, but she acquiesced mostly because of the futility of trying to argue Katrina out of something she wanted. Katrina knew her sister gave up without giving in, but that did not terribly bother her. *If you don't have enough spine to stand up to me, I can't use you, but you also can't be used against me.*

Back beyond Yvonne, Victor stood in conversation with Leftenant General Trevena and the tall man who had escorted Yvonne all the way from New Avalon for the conference. Tancred Sandoval towered over Victor by at least twenty centimeters and had a ruggedly handsome set of features that made Victor look rather boyish. Tancred's amber eyes proved to be his most striking feature. The color reminded Katrina of cats and their eyes, a connection strengthened by Sandovals fluid grace and, from the holovids she'd seen, his skill in the ancient art of fencing.

The sudden appearance of Phelan Kell eclipsed Katrina's view of Sandoval. Despite the formality of the situation, or perhaps in spite of it, Phelan had chosen to wear Wolf Clan leathers. The gray leathers clung to his body more tightly than the slinkiest of gowns on the vainest of women at the gathering. Katrina had to admit that her cousin had the powerful build to wear such outrageous clothes to great advantage, though she did not find him particularly attractive. *Not that it's not a nice package, but the eyes spoil it.*

Unadulterated disgust pooled in Phelan's green eyes. "Archon Katherine, how kind of you to invite me and my father to this reception. I am pleased that our invitation to it did not vanish the way our invitation to the Conference did."

"Khan Phelan, you *are* still a Khan, aren't you?" Katrina struggled to keep her voice even. "Surely you do not question the wisdom of not inviting an enemy to a conference whose sole aim is ridding ourselves of that same enemy."

"Not at all, though that hardly explains why my father was not invited." Phelan smiled coyly. "And, Katherine, I cannot believe your intelligence people forgot to mention that I and my people are at war with the Clans ourselves. The enemy of my enemy is my friend."

"I hardly thought you would characterize yourself as my *friend*, cousin."

Phelan gave her a quick nod. "Very good, Katherine, very good. I had forgotten how quick-witted you could be."

"Not a good thing to forget, Phelan."

"Agreed." Phelan's eyes narrowed. "I just hope you use your brains for the good of the Inner Sphere, to unite it instead of shattering it."

"Oh, it is my intention to bring the Inner Sphere together, Phelan, you can count on that." Katrina gave him a sly smile. *And when I do, there will be no place for people like you in it, dear cousin. You can rest assured of that.*

# ═══ **5** ═══

**Grand Ballroom, Royal Court**
**The Triad**
**Tharkad City, Tharkad**
**District of Donegal, Lyran Alliance**
**1 October 3058**

Victor Steiner-Davion nodded agreement with Tancred Sandoval. "You're right in pointing out that the Japanese emphasis on using the blade's edge—versus the European emphasis on the point and lunge—is a major distinction between the styles, but there's more to it than that."

"This I understand, Highness." The Baron of Robinson gave Victor an easy smile. "I've heard the theory advanced that Japanese-style swordsmanship is somehow more of a pure art than ours. Granted, fencing is a sport and even my specialty of epee is stylized, but it seems that comparing fencing with *kenjitsu* is unfair. Kendo is apparently as restricted as fencing and, therefore, more apt ground for comparison."

Victor caught a mixture of amusement and pride in Tancred's reply, which struck him as appropriate. The Sandoval family had long been the leaders of the Draconis March—the part of the Federated Commonwealth with the longest border and bloodiest history of conflict with the Draconis Combine. *Some Draconis Marchers would claim coal was white because a Kurita said it was black, but Tancred has his chauvinism more under control than that.*

"Then if fencing and kendo are more correctly compared with each other, what does the Western tradition have to match *kenjitsu*?"

Tancred smiled. "I believe Doc can answer that better than I can."

Victor turned to his military advisor. "Care to give it a go?"

Doc Trevena nodded, flicking a finger against his over-sized nose before he began. "In Japan, the design of the katana appeared very early and was modified very little down through the ages. What the Japanese did was to perfect a weapon, then continue to refine the technique for fighting with it to a high art."

Victor nodded. *"Kenjitsu."*

"Yes, Highness." Doc Trevena frowned for a moment, letting his brown-eyed gaze drift toward the ground with concentration. "In Europe, the sword underwent constant refinement. The weapon changed and developed new fighting styles around it. The introduction of the rapier, for example, caused a revolution in swordfighting techniques in Europe that transformed everything inside a generation. As a result, we have no art of swordfighting akin to *kenjitsu* because we have no solid, centuries-long tradition of fighting with the same weapon."

Tancred pressed his hands together, fingertip to fingertip. "So, let me ask the question begged by your explanation, Doc. Which method of fighting was better?"

Doc Trevena shook his head. "Apples and oranges, really. The only troops to fight against both samurai and European knights were the Mongols, and they pretty much pounded whoever they faced. Their fights against the samurai showed that the Japanese style of fighting was inbred and ritualized—it worked well against others playing by the same rules, but the Mongols didn't play by *any* rules. Against Arab and European forces the Mongols used their superior mobility and tactical sense to great advantage. Tactical maneuvering was pretty rudimentary in those days, though the world's three best tacticians of that age were contemporaries: Genghis Khan, John Lackland of England and Saladin. It would have been fascinating to see any of the three of them pitted against the other."

Tancred winked at Victor. "I see why he is serving as your military advisor."

"He knows his stuff."

"Forgive me, my lords, if I bored you." Doc's face wrinkled with consternation. "The tactical team I've assembled has been working on the most comprehensive breakdown and analysis of tactics and warfare since reliable records were being kept. We're running all sorts of simulations—for example, if Genghis Khan had been in charge of the Russian forces in 1941, the Germano-Russian conflict would have been over a lot sooner."

"Does that carry with it the assumption that Stalin's purges of the officer corps never took place, or were greatly reduced?" Yvonne Steiner-Davion stepped into the conversation between her brother and Tancred. "My reading on the subject suggests that a lack of competent leadership plus an advancement beyond prepared defenses was what led to the initial catastrophe for the Soviets—as they were called during that period of history."

Doc blinked away surprise. "We certainly had to allow for the Mongol philosophy to be reflected by the unit commanders, so, in effect, we blunted the purges. Even so, having and using mobility proved effective in lessening the devastating effects of the Nazi drives forward."

Yvonne raised an eyebrow. "And what if your simulation was run with the winter showing up later and not being nearly as severe?"

Doc winced. "The Trans-Siberian Railway would serve Brats and Alt on the runs from Himmlergrad to Adolphvostock."

Victor frowned as he looked up at his sister. "I thought your course of study at the New Avalon Institute of Science was pre-law."

"It is, Victor." She laid her right hand on his left shoulder. "That's what you want me to study, so that's what I'm studying. I do have electives, though, you know. And Tancred noted that if I overlap enough courses, I can pull down a Master's degree in history or political science with only two more years at the NAIS."

Tancred shrugged. "Her Highness told me she was getting bored at school. She's tested out for credit on most introductory courses and is really taking graduate level seminars already. Her average is two points short of perfect."

Victor gave his sister a sidelong glance. "It's not a perfect?"

Yvonne shrugged and let her shoulders slump. "There's a physical education requirement for graduation. I took a fencing course that Tancred was teaching and I barely passed."

The Baron of Robinson raised a hand to forestall any questions from Victor. "Your sister does lack a bit of physical coordination."

"She *has* kind of sprouted up in the last four years." Victor smiled. "Time was we could look eye to eye."

Yvonne blushed. "I'm sorry."

"Don't be. Nothing you could do about it." Victor shrugged. "Just because my portraits on coins are life-size . . ."

Everyone chuckled. Victor reached up and gave his sister's hand on his shoulder a gentle pat. "You're a good kid, Yvonne."

"Too good, I'm afraid, Highness." Tancred shook his head. "Other students were somewhat reluctant to attack her in duels, but she refused to take advantage of the openings they gave her."

"You ascribe to reluctance what can adequately be described as ineptness." Yvonne smiled apologetically. "Pinpoint accuracy with the tip of a meter's worth of steel may be your forte, Baron Sandoval, but it's not mine."

"You weren't that bad, Highness. If you had been, I'd have failed you."

A frown creased Victor's forehead. "I didn't know you were on the faculty at the NAIS, Tancred. I would have thought your duties in the Interior Secretariat would have kept you busy enough."

"My duties do keep me busy, but Kommandant Allyn Hasek is the coach of the fencing team over at the New Avalon Military Academy. We were on the 3038 Olympic fencing team together, back when we were both your sister's age and full of pride. We were rivals then and have been friendly rivals since. He goaded me into coaching the NAIS team, and to be able to coach I had to teach at least one class." Tancred smiled. "I did not need much convincing—I was tired of seeing the NAIS team getting trounced."

Victor replaced his frown with a smile. "Well, I'm tired of being trounced by Hohiro Kurita and Kai Allard-Liao in a variety of martial sports. Why don't you come teach us some fencing? You can even learn a bit about *kenjitsu* from Hohiro."

"I don't think that would be a good idea, Highness."

"Why not?"

Yvonne sighed heavily. "You forget, Victor, Tancred is from Robinson. His father commands the defenses of the Draconis March. There would be repercussions if he were seen socializing with Hohiro Kurita."

Tancred shrugged. "I know that's silly, but it's true. My people are still wary of the Combine, despite the last seven years of peace."

"And those seven years should continue, believe me." Victor nodded. "I tell you what—consider your presence with us a command performance. I'll take the heat for your being there. We'll work things out so that you're seen as upholding the pride of the Federated Commonwealth because I'm sure not." The Prince tapped the mouse on his right eye. "I could really use the help."

Tancred considered the request for a moment, then nodded. "Clearly I cannot refuse, so I shall not. And I very much appreciate your sensitivity to my situation."

"That's part of my job, isn't it?" Victor smiled and shook hands with Tancred. "I'll get our schedule communicated to you. Now, if the three of you will excuse me, I see some other people I have to speak with."

Victor withdrew from the circle and worked his way around to where Hohiro stood with his sister Omi. She wore a pink silk gown with short sleeves and a high collar, but loosely belted it with a blue cord that matched both the color of her eyes and the cyclone of embroidered stars that spiraled down her lithe body. Her black hair had been put up at the back of her head and held in place with a blue bow, but Victor barely noticed it because of the way her long neck had been exposed. He wanted nothing more than to plant kisses all over her neck and throat.

*If Tancred thinks teaching Hohiro how to fence will cause problems in the Draconis March, just imagine what my giving into my whims would do!* Victor shook his head as he approached the Kuritas, then he bowed. *"Komban-wa."*

Hohiro and his sister respectfully returned the greetings. "Good evening, Victor." Hohiro looked back over Victor's shoulder. "The red-headed woman, that is your sister Yvonne?"

"Have you not met her?" Victor glanced back at where Yvonne stood with Doc and Tancred. "I'd be happy to introduce you."

"I would be pleased to make her acquaintance, yes, but I

have known Doc long enough now to get him to introduce me." Hohiro smiled. "If you would do me the honor of accompanying my sister in my absence. . . ."

"The honor would be all mine, Hohiro. Beware, though. The other man is Tancred Sandoval." Victor smiled. "He'll be instructing us in fencing and he's quite good."

"And being from the Draconis March, he will be a bit wary of dealing with a Kurita." Hohiro nodded. "I understand. Thank you for the warning."

"The last thing I want for a brother in arms is a surprise." The Prince patted Hohiro on the back, then shifted over to take his place next to Omi. "And how are you this evening, Omi-*sama*?"

"Much better, now." Though only a small smile played across her lips, it came to full blossom in her sapphire eyes. "I am surprised you show no concern over my brother's desire to meet your sister."

"Should I be concerned?"

"Our father and mother were seven years married when my father was Hohiro's age, and they had two children by then." Omi looked across the room to where Doc was making introductions. "Pressure grows on Hohiro to look to the future and produce an heir for the Dragon throne. Your sister is not unpretty."

Victor frowned, standing on his toes to catch a glimpse of Hohiro. "You can't be serious."

"Why not? A generation ago the idea of a Davion and a Kurita marrying would have been unthinkable."

"Have opinions changed that radically in the Combine?"

"No." Omi shook her head with some finality. "But Yvonne *is* a Steiner, too. That's somewhat more acceptable."

Victor started to reply, then closed his mouth as Omi's giggle made it past her hand. He looked up into her eyes and couldn't keep a smile from his face. "You set that up with your brother, didn't you?"

She shrugged ever so slightly. "The idea occurred as you made your way over here. Please, do not fear. Your sister is safe with Hohiro . . ."

"I have nothing to fear from your brother, outside of a boxing ring, that is."

Omi reached up and stroked the side of his face. "I see that. It does not hurt?"

The similarity of her gesture to that of his sister Katherine struck Victor immediately, but their contrasts separated them easily in his mind. *Katherine went at the bruise as if it were a dirt smudge that could be cleaned off. Omi is far more gentle and caring.*

"It doesn't hurt anymore." Victor looked around. "Lots of prying eyes here. Would you care to join me for a walk in the garden?"

"I would be pleased to, but Tharkad's climate is a bit . . . I have yet to acclimate to it and despite the thaw, it is cold." Omi nodded toward the French doors leading out to the darkened garden. "No one else is foolish enough to have ventured out there."

Victor caught the secondary meaning in her statement. *And for you and I to leave together, unchaperoned, would be unseemly.* "You're right, of course, Omiko. Having grown up here I think of the weather now as wonderful, but I know not everyone would see it that way. Perhaps, as the conference continues, I will able to prove this to you."

"I shall cherish your efforts in this regard." Her eyes narrowed slightly. "And I would relish time well away from where I feel on display."

Before Victor could comment, Morgan Hasek-Davion and his wife approached them, smiling as they came. Kym clung to her husband's arm affectionately, momentarily reminding Victor of times when he had seen his parents together in similar settings. With Morgan in the black and gold uniform of the First Kathil Uhlans, and his wife wearing a gold gown trimmed in black, they made a matched set that seemed to Victor more elegant than any other couple present. White locks lightened her gold hair, just as traces of white streaked his red mane, but their eyes and smiles contained enough life to belie their fifty-five years.

"I hope I'm not interrupting, Victor, but Kym was saying she felt the reception hall was a bit crowded. I suggested we wander off and tour the gallery your grandmother maintained of bronzes." Morgan jerked his head back toward the stairs and the doorway behind them that led to the gallery. "The soldiers posted there said access was restricted."

Victor blinked. "They wouldn't let you enter?"

"No. I was thinking they could hardly refuse you." Morgan grinned easily. "Perhaps if you would like to show Lady Omi the bronzes, Kym and I could tag along."

Omi smiled briefly, then glanced down at the ground. "I

should enjoy seeing the bronzes, but I would not intrude upon the time you wish to spend with your wife, Marshal Hasek-Davion."

Kym reached out and touched Omi on the arm. "It would not be an intrusion. I recall very well feeling as if I were in a glass bubble when I first knew Morgan. At the time he was Hanse Davion's heir and the most eligible bachelor in the whole of the Inner Sphere—Hanse was betrothed to Melissa by then, you see. I always felt I was being gawked at, except when I was with friends. Touring the gallery with you and Victor would be being with friends and therefore delightful. In fact, if what Morgan has told me of the gallery is accurate, we could easily get lost and never see each other."

Victor looked up at Morgan. "I appreciate this effort, Morgan."

"Victor Davion, you can think I'm making this suggestion to allow you and Lady Omi to slip away, but that's because you underestimate how much I would truly like to show that gallery to my wife. You should know, after all, how much time we already spend apart, and how much time we are likely to be apart in the future." Morgan took Kym's hand in his own. "And you should know I've learned to relish what little time I have to spend with the woman I love."

Omi folded her hands together. "Victor, I see no way we can fail to assist them. To do so would be most ungracious and rude."

"As always, Omi, you are as wise as you are beautiful." Victor smiled at her. "Shall we ask your brother and my sister to join us?"

Omi cocked an eyebrow at him. "Hohiro has little interest in bronzes, I think. This deficiency should be corrected, but not tonight."

"No, not tonight." Victor waved toward the doorway with his right hand. "Please, if you will join me in the bronze gallery, it would be my pleasure, my extreme pleasure, to share its wonders with you."

# 6

**Grand Ballroom, Royal Court**
**The Triad**
**Tharkad City, Tharkad**
**District of Donegal, Lyran Alliance**
**3 October 3058**

**V**ictor looked about the room and marveled at how, in two days, his sister's people had transformed the Grand Ballroom of the Royal Palace into a meeting room. The delegation tables had been laid out in an octagon. Several rings of tables and seats on risers backed the main tables, creating an amphitheatre arrangement. Data terminals sat on all of the tables, the cables that linked them snaking down beneath the stands.

A dais and podium stood at the top of the octagon, leaving the speaker's back exposed to the staircase leading down into the chamber. Standards from each of the nations represented had been placed on the stairs to form a dramatic backdrop for the speakers, and a circle of holographic projection plates had been placed at the heart of the octagon so any data a delegate wanted to share could be displayed easily. Present in the room were enough security personnel from each nation that despite the speaker having his back to the entrance and stairs, he would hardly be vulnerable.

*Besides, all the attacks will be coming from within the octagon, not outside it.* To the podium's left was the table shared by ComStar and the Free Rasalhague Republic.

Prince Haakon Magnusson and the Precentor Martial were accorded equal standing despite the fact that Magnusson's nation had been all but overrun by the Clans and only continued its existence because of ComStar's victory at Tukayyid. ComStar had effectively established the seven remaining Rasalhague worlds as a protectorate and Magnusson's presence was really a courtesy.

Victor's table came next, and he was fairly certain his sister had seated him there so he and his delegates would have to turn in their chairs to face the speaker. It was no real hardship, of course, just one of those little inconveniences that made life annoying. *She wants me distracted, but she doesn't realize it will take a lot more than this to turn me from my purpose.* Victor smiled. *Of course, I am going to have to get Morgan Hasek-Davion to shift over to my left so I can actually see the podium.*

To the left of Victor's table came the one originally given over to the St. Ives Compact. Candace Liao and Kai Allard-Liao still had their places there, but Candace had graciously allowed Morgan Kell and his son Phelan to appropriate half of it. This gave the Arc-Royal Defense Cordon the status of a nation-state, something Victor was certain his sister would protest. Though the St. Ives Compact was not very big, and the Arc-Royal Defense Cordon had not seceded from the Lyran Alliance, the leaders of both groups were, along with the Precentor Martial, the most seasoned and experienced warriors on hand.

Beyond them, arranged to face the speaker's podium directly, was the Lyran Alliance table. Though made of identical blond oak and shaped just like all the rest, it look different somehow. Victor noticed that his sister's golden hair seemed to shine more brightly as well. Glancing up, he noticed a pair of pinpoint spotlights in the constellation of lights above. *The illumination is meant to suggest that Katherine is enlightened. I wonder if the lights will follow her to the podium, too?*

Thomas Marik and was seated at the table located to Katherine's left. Victor found it interesting that Isis Marik chose to sit with her father instead of her betrothed, Sun-Tzu. *There is doubtless something significant to all this. I'll have to ask Jerry what he makes of it.* Victor realized that Isis was really a cipher. He'd met her years ago on Outreach, but she'd always remained in the shadow of her father or fiancé.

Victor slowly smiled. *I wonder how she'd react if she knew that the man seated beside her is not her father, not the rightful heir to the Captain-Generalcy of the Free Worlds League?* Genetic tests run at the New Avalon Institute of Science had proved beyond a shadow of a doubt that the Thomas Marik leading the Free Worlds League was not a Marik at all. Though no one had been able to prove where the man had come from, Victor felt certain he was a double that ComStar had substituted for a dead or dying Thomas Marik after an assassination attempt in 3035. It was even possible that the real Thomas was still alive somewhere.

The irony of it was that the fake Thomas had turned out to be more effective than almost any true Marik before him, and under his rule the Free Worlds League had come into full flower as a power in the Inner Sphere. Isis' impending marriage to Sun-Tzu would unite the Free Worlds League with the Capellan Confederation, creating a huge nation and a deadly enemy for Victor's own Federated Commonwealth. *And giving them a bomb for a wedding present would probably be frowned upon.*

Directly across from the Federated Commonwealth's table sat the Draconis Combine's table. Hohiro Kurita flanked his father on the right and Narimasa Asano, now one of the Coordinator's closest advisors, sat at Theodore's left. Omi sat behind and above her father in the first row of the seats ringing the octagon. Victor looked up and thought he caught her eye, but he couldn't be certain since any number of other things could explain the trace of a smile on her face.

The Capellan Confederation table completed the octagon. Sun-Tzu sat there with Wu Kang Kuo, commander of the Harloc Raiders. They were the Liao unit that had been sent to Coventry, and their presence at the conference was by Sun-Tzu's invitation. Prior to Coventry, the Capellan Confederation had not committed troops against the Clans. Victor had found Wu to be an intelligent and thoughtful man. *Perhaps he'll be able to talk some sense to Sun-Tzu.*

Anastasius Focht, Precentor Martial of ComStar, mounted the dais and approached the podium. He stood tall and lean, unbowed by his years. His thick white hair contrasted with the black of the eye patch over his right eye. The other eye was a pale gray, and its gaze was cold but strong. The

Precentor Martial looked around at the assembled leaders and advisors, then smiled and, to Victor's eyes, seemed to pull himself up even taller.

"I call to order the first session of the Whitting Conference. I am, as you know, Anastasius Focht, Precentor Martial of ComStar. I have watched the Clans from both sides of the battlefield—first as the old ComStar's ambassador to them, and later as the defender of Tukayyid. The successful defense of Tukayyid earned us a fifteen-year truce, of which we have used up more than six years. This conference, or one like it, to discuss our common interests and concerns should have been held at that time. The delay is regrettable, but it is not a mistake from which we cannot recover."

Focht tugged at the sleeves of the light blue fatigues he wore, then smoothed down the golden mantle draped around his shoulders. The ComStar insignia of an oval with two elongated diamonds extending from the bottom had been worked of gold and set with hematite, then made into a brooch that held the mantle closed at his throat. Standing there, his rich voice filling the room, he seemed very deserving of his status as a legendary warrior like Aleksandr Kerensky.

"We know who the Clans are and whence they have come. Three centuries ago, when Aleksandr Kerensky used the Star League Defense Force to put down the Amaris coup d'état, he knew that the Star League was dead. The various member states had already begun to vie for dominance, each leader intent on reestablishing the Star League with him or herself at the head. Kerensky realized the nationalistic fervor being whipped up in the member states would destroy the SLDF, so he took them and fled from the Inner Sphere.

"The Exodus took the SLDF out of the Inner Sphere, but he could not cure his own people of their violence. Despite Kerensky's efforts, his followers eventually descended into war, and almost blew each other into oblivion."

Focht paused for a moment to let the horror sink in.

Victor shook his head. *What the SLDF did to itself the Inner Sphere's states did to each other, battering each other not quite back to the Stone Age, but cutting damned close to the Industrial Revolution.* It was only thirty years ago that a Star League-era memory core had been discovered and so many things stopped being referred to as *lostech.* Having been born *after* that discovery, Victor hadn't experienced the phenomenon of lostech so severely, but he knew that plenty of those sitting around him still remembered only too well what it meant.

"Aleksandr's son, Nicholas, took over for his father and conceived of a means by which the SLDF could be saved. He created the Clans and remade the SLDF society into one where warriors are the highest caste and the reason for the existence of all the other castes. The goal was to produce the most perfect warriors possible, which meant specialized breeding programs, brutal testing, and most resources being directed to weapons-system modification and development.

"Within the Clans there arose two factions: Crusaders and Wardens. The Wardens believed their job was to protect the Inner Sphere—they clung to the original purpose of the SLDF. The Crusaders, on the other hand, believed it was their duty to reestablish the Star League and punish those who had destroyed it. The Crusader faction grew in power over the years and finally led to the invasion of the Inner Sphere."

Focht nodded toward Victor. "Three months ago, on Coventry, Prince Victor Davion argued that part of the Clans' advantage over us was that they were fighting on our worlds, forcing us to defend targets of their choosing. We had lost sight of that truth despite the fact that the Federated Commonwealth and the Draconis Combine used it to defeat the Clans at Twycross and Wolcott, respectively. But we are blind no more, and have come together to create a united front against the greatest enemy ever to threaten the Inner Sphere. The time is now to take the war to the Clans."

The Precentor Martial held up two fingers. "To accomplish this we will need two things, two results of this conference. The first is a unified military force that will be tasked with taking the war to the Clans. On the agendas kindly provided by Archon Katrina you will note that we have scheduled military planning sessions in addition to these political sessions. The military planning group will report back to this body with its conclusions, though many of you will also attend them personally or via your military advisors.

"The second result we need is a political one. It is a decision that will require a consensus and will provide our military with a potent weapon against the Clans. Without it, our military operation can still take place, but its efficacy will be severely compromised. In that case the overall result we want—an elimination of the Clan threat—probably will not be achieved."

Focht looked around the room. "Our political objective is the re-establishment of the Star League."

Even though Victor had known that was coming, hearing the Precentor Martial say it was still a shock. *For three centuries, ever since Stefan Amaris tried to usurp the power of the Star League, every nation-state here has dreamed of placing its leader's arse on its throne. To be the First Lord of the Star League was an ambition that prompted my father to start two wars. Countless people died in the Succession Wars and now, for the Inner Sphere to survive, we will have to do bloodlessly what centuries of warfare could not achieve.*

"The reasons for reestablishing the Star League are simple and subtle, but no less vital. The Clans hearken back to the days of the Star League and do not recognize our authority because our ancestors destroyed the Star League. In reestablishing it, we undercut one of their basic assumptions about their mission and about us. As a unified Star League command, our military will carry with it an authority that it has not had before. The Clans, by opposing Star League troops, will be forced to question a mission they hold almost sacred. In losing to Star League troops, they will realize they have been beaten by a force that has more legitimacy than they do in the Inner Sphere."

Off to Focht's right, Sun-Tzu Liao stood. "Forgive my interruption, Precentor Martial, because I find what you are saying rather fascinating. However, before proceeding any further with this discussion, there is a procedural matter that *must* be dealt with."

He pointed across the octagon toward where Candace Liao and Morgan Kell sat. "How can we effectively plan the restoration of the Star League when we have people present who have no legitimate political standing? One might argue that the St. Ives Compact, by virtue of its twenty-nine years of pseudo-independence, deserves a seat here. The Arc-Royal Defense Cordon has no such history, has not even declared itself independent of the Lyran Alliance, *and* is led by a man whose son is a Clan quisling. Arc-Royal is harboring Clan Wolf, the Clan that has done the most damage to the Inner Sphere, and its Khan is seated behind his father, ready to relay details of what we are planning to his Clan masters."

Phelan Kell's mocking laughter cut through the buzz of conversation sparked by Sun-Tzu's remarks. "Precentor Martial, perhaps you can confirm for the Chancellor of the Capellan Confederation that, despite my affiliation with the Clans, I am not controlled by them. My people and I are Wardens through and through, and fought a war against the Jade Falcons that devastated them."

Sun-Tzu's jade-green eyes sharpened. "If they were so devastated, perhaps you can explain how they attacked Coventry?"

"I would rather remind the Chancellor that it was the advice of a Wolf, one of *my* Wolves, that led to the solution on Coventry."

"A solution," Sun-Tzu shot back, "that allowed Jade Falcon troops to flee the planet unmolested."

Victor frowned in Sun-Tzu's direction. *You're doing wonders for reinforcing your image as an idiot.*

The Precentor Martial held up his hands. "Your argument concerning Phelan Kell is baseless, Chancellor. He possesses a wealth of information about the Clans without which the planning of any operation against them would be folly. I trust him implicitly and emphatically."

Thomas Marik narrowed his eyes. "I believe, Precentor Martial, that the Chancellor has a valid point concerning the seating of Morgan Kell at this council. Neither he nor his son were invited by our hostess, but by her brother. Morgan Kell's presence here is obviously a goad to anger her, though I should point out she is far too gracious to react to it. The fact remains, however, that Morgan Kell has no place here."

Victor stood. "Morgan Kell has more right to be here than half the delegates present. His Kell Hounds have fought the Clans in numerous battles, on numerous worlds. They were at Twycross and were part of the successful defense of Luthien. Arc-Royal itself was attacked by the Clans, and the Kell Hounds drove them off. And the Hounds were also at Coventry. You can argue the legitimacy of the ARDC all you want, but the fact remains that Morgan should be here."

Thomas opened his hands. "I would not deny the valiant effort the Kell Hounds have put forth in defending the Inner Sphere. Yes, we need his counsel, but in your strategy meetings, not the political discussions we will have here."

Before Victor could reply, Candace Liao stood and held up a silvery Kroner coin. "Let me settle this. Here, Colonel Kell, I wish to hire the Kell Hounds." She snapped the coin down on the table in front of him. "There, he is my advisor and has a place here."

Sun-Tzu laughed aloud. "Archon Katrina, please, have your architects back in so we can expand this hall. Each of us will now be flanked by the leaders of our mercenaries."

"No." Morgan Kell shook his head. He pressed a metal finger on top of the coin and slid it to his right, back to Candace. "The Hounds are not for hire. I came here, I accepted Candace's invitation to take my place here, because I have pledged all I am and all I have to guaranteeing the safety of sixteen worlds from assaults by the Clans. My purpose in creating the Arc-Royal Defense Cordon was not to split the Lyran Alliance, but to provide more direct control in an area that needed it, freeing the Archon to deal with problems elsewhere. If that is insufficient reason for me to be seated here, then I will go."

Victor turned his chair around, looked at Jerry Cranston, and jerked his head toward Morgan Kell. "Colonel Kell can back-bench me; he's not leaving."

Cranston nodded and started to make his way over to the St. Ives Compact table.

Candace Liao, still on her feet, rested her left hand on Morgan's mechanical right shoulder. "Enough of this nonsense. Morgan Kell, marry me."

Morgan blinked his dark eyes in surprise. "What?"

Candace's left hand tightened its grip. "I hereby give you the world of Warlock, making you a peer of my realm, but I know my nephew will protest that is not enough to allow you your place here. Therefore I ask you to become my consort. No one can gainsay your participation here if you accept my proposal."

Victor smiled, half in appreciation of Candace's ploy, but mostly at the shock on the faces of most of those seated at the tables around the room. In Candace's voice, in the fiery look she gave everyone else, Victor saw his father. *Hanse would have loved this. He'd even have offered to supply dishes for the wedding reception.*

Morgan's voice came low. "I loved my wife very much and it was Inner Sphere treachery that killed her."

Candace nodded. "And I loved my husband as well. The

same politics that killed your Salome killed my Justin. Together perhaps we can stop such insanity."

Morgan smiled, then half-closed his eyes. "I accept your proposal."

Sun-Tzu barked a harsh laugh. "This is a sham. You *mock* these proceedings!"

Candace slapped her right hand hard against the tabletop, and the resulting gun-crack sound startled Sun-Tzu into silence. Icy words filled the quiet, and though Candace directed them at Sun-Tzu, Victor could tell she meant them for everyone. "No, nephew, *I* do not mock these proceedings— you and your actions do. Have you not heard what the Precentor Martial has told us? Only by uniting can we prevail. What I have done is not divisive, and only through such a shocking action can I make you see how important the task we have come together to perform truly is."

She looked down at Morgan. "Are my proposal and his acceptance of it desperate measures? Certainly, but if they are the least of the desperate measures we are forced to employ before the Clans are defeated, we shall all be fortunate indeed!"

$$=7=$$

**Royal Palace, The Triad**
**Tharkad City, Tharkad**
**District of Donegal, Lyran Alliance**
**3 October 3058**

**K**atrina Steiner sat back in her plush white leather chair and twirled a platinum paper knife between her fingers. "This first day did not go as anticipated, did it?"

Her two advisors looked at each other to determine who would answer first. The choice was made as it had been made countless times before: Tormano Liao let General Nondi Steiner, Katrina's grand-aunt, speak first. Katrina knew that wasn't so much courtesy as Tormano's desire to see how she herself would react to Nondi's words. *He still tells me what he thinks I should hear as long as it doesn't provoke my anger.*

Nondi Steiner wore her gray hair shoulder length, but it was gathered back into a small pony-tail so as not to obscure her uniform's epaulettes or the rank insignia riding on them. Katrina had always considered Nondi hatchet-faced, and her hard, gray-eyed gaze did nothing to dispel that image. *If she were not so loyal to House Steiner, she would be an enemy I would have to destroy.*

"There were surprises, Archon, but none that present real problems." Nondi struggled to lever herself from the depths of an overstuffed white leather chair. "The Precentor Martial's call for the reformation of the Star League was a bit premature, but he was smart in making that announcement at the start of things, I think. The battling to see who becomes First Lord should occupy the politicoes enough that the military folks will have little trouble planning the operation we need to mount. Though Focht said that the military planning was secondary to the political consensus, only someone as stupid as Sun-Tzu would believe it."

Katrina nodded slowly. "Do you concur, Mandrinn Liao?"

Tormano Liao balanced his stocky body on the arm of a chair like the one that had captured Nondi. His almond eyes and khaki fleshtones betrayed his Asian heritage, but the cut of his clothes was strictly contemporary. "I concur with General Steiner that only an idiot would believe what the Precentor Martial said. I do not think my nephew is stupid, however, and if she persists in believing in his foppish routine, we will regret it."

Nondi frowned. "He's a buffoon."

"He's the buffoon who has gained back a significant number of the worlds Hanse Davion took away thirty years ago. He may be immature, but he's not stupid." Tormano's dark blue eyes hardened. "Just because the Liaos have been defeated in the past does not mean they cannot win in the future. Our line has survived this long—as have the Steiners—and we shall continue to survive, perhaps even thrive."

Katrina smiled and tapped the synthetic top of her desk with the tip of the paper knife. "Mandrinn Liao has a point, Aunt Nondi. The Liaos can be very shrewd."

Nondi smiled. "Candace's maneuver was rather impressive."

Katrina's irritation quickened the staccato of the paper knife drumming against the table top. She had wanted to see Morgan Kell booted from the discussions from the moment Victor told her he'd invited the mercenary to the conference. She could not order him barred because she had already embraced his taking responsibility for the Arc-Royal Defense Cordon. To protest his action and attempt to bring him to heel could have resulted in open rebellion and secession, which she would not chance. Victor would have instantly recognized Morgan Kell's realm and then supported it, giving her brother another piece of her nation.

While she had resented Morgan's presence, his statement about why he had set up the Arc-Royal Defense Cordon had touched her. The Kells had always been strong Steiner loyalists. Morgan was a cousin of Arthur Luvon, Katrina's maternal grandfather, and, ages ago, had gone off on some magnificent adventure with the original Katrina Steiner. It seemed very right and proper that he would do what he did, and she almost felt ashamed for doubting him. *Perhaps his refusal to aid me when I asked for help last year was because he wanted to protect the Lyran Alliance against the Clans and did not want to be distracted from that task.*

Katrina slowly nodded. "It was shrewd indeed. Will they go through with it?"

"Morgan and my sister marry?" Tormano laughed sharply. "I can't see it happening. Then again, they would be a good match."

Nondi snorted with disgust. "They would deserve each other."

"What do you have against my sister?"

"Nothing, though she has been rather full of herself ever since she abandoned the Capellan Confederation and made her St. Ives Compact a ward of the Federated Commonwealth. I've had troops from all over the Lyran half of the Commonwealth serving down there. That world Warlock she gave Morgan is an iceball."

"I know. My family maintained a retreat on it where I learned to ski." Tormano folded his arms across his chest. "Still, General, I cannot understand your animus against Colonel Kell. After all he has done for the Lyrans over the years."

"My quarrel with him is old. He and his cousin helped my sister out during a difficult time in her life. That's all well and good, but Morgan and his brother and Arthur Luvon ended up having undue influence over Katrina." Nondi's gray brows arrowed together. "They softened her, took away her edge. If not for them, she'd never have sold her daughter off to Hanse Davion. And I say that, Katrina, knowing you were the result of that union. Proves there isn't a black cloud that doesn't have a touch of silver in the lining."

"Thank you, Aunt Nondi." Katrina gave her a smile and fought to keep the contempt from her voice. She thought it a wonder that Nondi's jealousy of Morgan's influence over the original Katrina Steiner didn't turn her whole body green. Nondi's anger with her sister—born of a sense of betrayal when Katrina began to listen to her husband more than she did Nondi—had prompted Nondi to ally with Katrina's political enemies at the beginning of her regime. Though Nondi finally came to her senses and made peace with her sister, she never forgave Morgan for the changes that had come over Katrina.

Nondi shook her head. "Morgan has always wanted to be a player. Back in the Fourth Succession War he conducted his own operations against the Draconis Combine. Seven years ago, when the Clans first attacked, he also helped host the conference on Outreach. He wants to be present during the political talks because he thinks he should be made First Lord of the Star League."

"Interesting insight." Katrina nodded thoughtfully. *Utterly insane and incorrect, but interesting anyway. You're a good general, Nondi, but no politician.*

"Indeed, Archon, it is interesting, but I think General Steiner is off the mark," Tormano said. "Morgan's stake in the political discussions is to keep them on track. I dare say that my sister Candace, the Precentor Martial, and even Prince Magnusson have the same goal. Each knows he or she cannot and will not be elected First Lord of the new Star League, but they see the importance of making the election happen."

"Much the position you find yourself in, yes, Mandrinn Liao?"

Katrina admired the way Tormano covered the sting of Nondi's question, revealing none of the pain it must have caused him. *It is one thing to have your ambition thwarted and yet another to be tweaked about it.*

"I would agree, General, except for one thing: I am a realist. Without having the Capellan Confederation's Celestial Throne between my ass and the cold stone floor, I could never be considered for that office. And the only way I could take the throne would be to murder my sister and my nephews and nieces. That will not happen."

Sparks ignited in Nondi's flinty eyes. "No, it would not. Kai Allard-Liao would cut you dead in no time."

"Yet one more reason for me to be content advising the Archon." Tormano's head came up. "You may consider me a mutant for it, but I do not have the Liao predilection for spilling the blood of my parents or siblings."

Katrina let the paper knife drop to the desktop with a clatter, killing the discussion. "I would prefer to return to a more fruitful avenue of analysis. Assuming there will be a new Star League that comes out of this, what should our goals be?"

Nondi's face hardened. "We must make certain our troops are not used as the mainstay of this military operation. We can't afford to have the majority of the blood spilled be ours. If we are left with a weakened military after all is said and done, Victor will turn on us and devour us."

Katrina smiled. "Good point and one worth remembering. I assume you will attend to those details in the planning sessions, and that you will keep me informed about all that goes on in them."

"Of course, Archon. Sharon Byran will be our representative there, and your wishes shall be communicated to her." Nondi's voice quivered a bit with uncertainty. "Was my answer not what you expected?"

"Oh, no, it was exactly what I expected you to say, which is why you are my military advisor." Katrina turned to Tormano. "If the vote were held tomorrow, who would be the new First Lord?"

Tormano furrowed his brows and thought for a moment. "I would put you or Victor at the top of the list, with Thomas Marik third. Assuming that some sort of rotating leadership is established, making you the initial First Lord would seem appropriate because you are hosting this historic meeting."

"Why is Victor in the running?"

"That, Archon, should be obvious." Tormano gave her a reproving look. "Victor led the coalition force at Coventry and came up with a plan that prevented bloodshed. As much as Sun-Tzu and others might protest that, selling a bloodless victory on Coventry has been much easier in the Free Worlds League and Capellan Confederation than trying to explain why troops died in defense of a Lyran world would have been. The Precentor Martial is clearly grooming Victor to lead the coalition force attacking the Clans, and if the resurgence of the Star League is meant to be a weapon used against the Clans, who better to lead the SLDF than the new First Lord?"

Nondi thumped a fist on the arm of her chair. "Victor will lead that force over my dead body."

Katrina frowned. "Why is that, Aunt Nondi?"

"Because, because Victor is . . . not right."

The Archon retrieved the paper knife from the desk and resumed twirling it. "You're not trying to say Victor isn't a seasoned warrior, are you?"

"Of course not. He's very good at what he does, but he's only got years of experience whereas he should have decades of it. We have people like that. Morgan Hasek-Davion, Theodore Kurita, Narimasa Asano, Sharon Bryan—there are plenty of people who could and should lead that taskforce before Victor."

"But, Aunt Nondi, you forget two important factors. First off, Victor has as much experience as anyone fighting the Clans. And second"—Katrina smiled carefully—"if Victor is leading the force, he will have to go with it. My brother will actually lead troops and undoubtedly fight in the battles that come. You yourself have pointed out that he is a threat to this realm, so why would we deny him any chance to get himself killed?"

Nondi's eyes became slits. "Why give him a chance to return to the Inner Sphere as the man who conquered the Clans?"

"Because the time it takes—and for all we know it could take decades—will allow others of us to define his role when he returns. If he goes away, he cannot rule the Federated Commonwealth. Who will he put in his place?"

"Unless your brother Peter resurfaces or Morgan Hasek-Davion does not go with the taskforce, I would guess he would give the job to Yvonne." Tormano hesitated, then nodded. "Yvonne, definitely. Your brother Arthur may be two years older than she is, but his studies indicate that he's not the best choice for the job."

Katrina saluted Tormano with the paper knife. "That's the kindest way I've heard it said that Arthur is more heart than brains, which is, unfortunately, true. Yvonne will present no threat to the Lyran Alliance. That means that while Victor is off destroying the major threat to this realm, and perhaps being destroyed by it himself, we'll be able to build ourselves up."

Nondi snorted. "You forget the Jade Falcons poised on our border. If Victor attacks them, they can attack us and force him into the sort of defensive war he does not want."

"I do not fear a Jade Falcon attack."

Nondi frowned. "No?"

Tormano coughed lightly. "What the Archon means is this, General—the greatest likelihood is that the war against the Clans is going to be launched from Lyran space and go against the Jade Falcons. If it does not, the Jade Falcons are hidebound enough that they will certainly rally to the defense of their home territories. Either way, they are not a substantial threat and the chance of their attacking us is minimal."

Katrina gave Tormano another abbreviated salute with the letter opener. *Nondi knows nothing of my alliance with the Wolves led by Vlad Ward. His forces will keep the Falcons off me, or between us we will grind the Falcons into bone meal. Nondi would go mad if she ever did learn of this agreement, so it is well that Tormano covered for me. He has his uses and, once again, proves that the Liaos are very clever.*

"I think, my friends, I see what we need to do to get things into the position we want—which would be *my* election as First Lord. First I need to speak with my peers and win them around to my way of thinking about who should be First Lord. I will also speak with Morgan Kell and smooth out our differences."

"That will be a waste of your breath, Katrina."

"Perhaps, Aunt, but it is my breath to waste."

The older woman clucked at her. "Listen, child, you are quite capable of charming your enemies, but not Morgan Kell."

*Who do you think I am, Nondi, a simpleton like Isis Marik? I learned how to wind people around my little finger by watching my mother in action. Theodore Kurita might have to order a vassal to commit suicide, but with a sigh and a wink my mother could have convinced whole crowds to kill themselves—and they would have done it thinking their lives had been fulfilled in the doing. No, Morgan Kell's feelings for the Steiner line make him vulnerable to my wiles.*

"I appreciate your caution, Aunt Nondi. I shall proceed with care." Katrina looked over at Tormano. "I want you to go over the files for all delegates. I want their every need met and noted. I do not want blackmail information, though I will take it. I want everyone to know that I've been seeing to it that they have only the distractions they want. I want that sense of gratitude so that when someone decides to honor me with nomination as the First Lord of the Star League, everyone else will decide I deserve the honor."

"I understand what you want, Archon, and I will deliver." Tormano bowed his head to her. "I think, however, you will find your brother rather stiff competition."

"Indeed. That is why I have you doing what you are doing, and Nondi what she is doing." Katrina laid the paper knife down carefully. "I've handled Victor all my life. I will see to his downfall myself."

# 8

**Hall of the Khans, Warrior Quarter**
**Strana Mechty**
**Kerensky Cluster, Clan Space**
**3 October 3058**

Vlad was surprised at the sense of awe inspired in him by actually being inside the Grand Council Chamber in the Hall of the Khans. He and fellow Khan Marialle Radick had been given seats in the rear of the semicircular room, in the highest of the rows. Beside them and before them the seats were empty—signifying the place once held by Clans that had since been absorbed or destroyed.

*My remade Wolves are the newest Clan, hence our having been put in our place.* Vlad would have taken this as an evil omen, but the Jade Falcon Khans Marthe Pryde and Samantha Clees had likewise been given seats in the back row, just across the staired aisle that led at one end to the chamber's double doors and, at the other, to the speaker's dais where Kael Pershaw was installing himself as Loremaster. Seated next to the Jade Falcons were the two octogenarian Khans of Clan Nova Cat. The seating arrangements, Vlad realized, were the result of maneuvering by Clan Khans who wanted to be in the thick of things during the discussions.

He didn't let his location worry him. The Clan Wolf banner still hung above his position, as did the various other Clan banners above the seats their Khans occupied. The seats he had been given were carved of granite like all the others in the room, padded with red velvet cushions and fronted by black marble tables streaked with white. *Each of the forty seats for Khans are identical, and so we are all equal here.*

That he felt *equal* with his fellow Khans, and not *superior,* surprised Vlad. He knew, deep down, that he was more than their equal. He fervently believed what he had told Marthe Pryde—leaders tempered in the battling with the Inner Sphere were the only leaders capable of completing the Crusade. He knew this to be the truth, but, at the moment, that all seemed rather tangential.

The sense of ceremony carried him beyond his sense of self. Each Clan Khan had come to the chamber clad in a formal uniform. The Ghost Bear Khans wore cloaks made of the pelts of their namesake animal, and other Khans wore and carried similar totems of their Clans. The gray leathers he himself wore were reminiscent of a wolf's coloration. The riot of textures, styles, and hues made the assembly of Khans a brilliant spectacle. The fact that he had never witnessed such a gathering prior to his elevation to the rank of Khan meant that he looked at everything through a child's eyes, and was impressed accordingly.

Each Khan also wore an enameled helm fashioned after the Clan's symbolic animal. Vlad's own helmet bore a snarling wolf face and erect ears. Marthe Pryde's sharp-beaked, big-eyed helm made her the avatar of her Clan's fierce falcon. The dorsal fin crest on the Diamond Shark helmets made their Khans almost as tall as Lincoln Osis of the Smoke Jaguars.

Kael Pershaw—a twisted creature who appeared to be more metal than flesh, more machine than man—hammered a gavel against the Loremaster's desktop at the head of the room. "I am Kael Pershaw and have been chosen as Loremaster for this gathering of the Grand Council. I hereby convene this conclave under the provisions of the Martial Code as laid down by Nicholas Kerensky. Because we exist in a state of war, all matters shall be conducted according to its provisions."

"Seyla," Vlad breathed reverently. He seated himself and fought the urge to pull his helmet off. *The symbol of the Wolf will frighten more of my fellow Khans than my face will.* He felt the tightness of his flesh where the scar puckered the left side of his face. *There is no reason to remind them that I have been weak before.*

Pershaw looked up at the assembly. "There is, this day, a matter most serious for your consideration. Khan Asa Taney of the Ice Hellions has proposed a Ritual of Absorption."

The Ice Hellion Khan rose from his position in the middle of the assembly, two rows down from Vlad, and laid his helmet on the table in front of him. The white helmet had been fashioned into the visage of the vicious pack predator of the planet Hector's tundra. The image looked ferocious, though Vlad and other Wolves had always denigrated it by calling it a rime-stoat. *And just like a weasel clan to suggest the Absorption.*

The large-headed Ice Hellion pilot smoothed his red hair into place. "It is with deep regret that I suggest Absorption, but there is no question that some of our Clans have suffered too much damage to continue to be viable. As we have always done, by absorbing one Clan into another, we preserved the genetic potential for our breeding program. I call for a Ritual of Absorption to prevent losses from which we cannot recover."

Ian Hawker, the fair-eyed and -haired Khan of the Diamond Sharks, unmasked himself and stood across from Taney. "I find myself concurring with this call for Absorption. Continuing the Crusade is of vital importance. We cannot afford to allow a dull edge on the blade we employ against the Inner Sphere. The time for Absorption has come."

Marthe Pryde doffed her helmet as she stood, but kept it under her right arm instead of setting it on the table. "Loremaster, in the previous two Absorptions, was the Ritual called for prior to the designation of a target Clan?"

Pershaw punched a request into the datapad at his desk, then shook his head. "The procedure Khan Taney is following is the tradition. There is nothing in the record to reflect, in a formal sense, that the choice of Clans to be absorbed was made before the vote was taken. However, Clans Widowmaker and Mongoose had suffered a number of reversals in the decade prior to the Ritual being enacted."

"Ah, a *decade's* worth of reversals. The failure of two breeding cycles." Marthe's tone was casual, but no one missed the implication.

*Two cycles of failure mean serious problems with their*

*breeding program. That is not the sort of problem the Wolves have had, and our reversals are merely a year old.* Vlad stood but kept his helmet on. "Perhaps Khan Asa Taney could be persuaded to define what it is that makes a Clan viable in his eyes."

The Ice Hellion smiled indulgently. "I would think viability is obvious. A Clan must be able to supply, train, and deploy troops of sufficient number and quality that they can defeat their enemies and win great victories. This is the purpose for which the Clans were crafted."

"I see." Vlad removed his helmet carefully and set it down on the table, with its snarling muzzle pointed toward the Ice Hellion. "Please, then, answer this question for me—would a Clan capable of mounting a two-hundred-light year penetration of the Inner Sphere, meeting and savaging the best troops the Inner Sphere has to offer be considered viable or non-viable to your mind?"

Taney frowned. "We are not discussing the Wolves' past victories, Khan Ward. You yourself severed your Clan's history from those Wolves, in any event. That is all ancient history—we are interested in current events and their ramifications."

"As am I, Khan Taney." Vlad looked over to his right. "The events I have described are those accomplished by the Jade Falcons since last a Grand Council met. The Falcons organized, trained, and armed troops that scythed through the Inner Sphere with incredible ease. They ripped apart some of the most seasoned troops the Inner Sphere has to offer."

Hawker snarled. "And then they fled from a force that was sufficient to give them a good battle."

Marthe started to reply to that point, but Vlad held up a hand to forestall her. "And do you know why she accepted *hegira* from the troops on Coventry?" He let the question hang in the air for a moment, allowing the word *cowardice* to surface in the minds of the other Khans, then he answered it. "She chose to accept their offer because she had discovered that I was massing troops to take some invasion-corridor worlds away from her. Why would she waste her troops against Inner Sphere forces that clearly had no belly for a fight when she could pit them against my warriors? She did what every one of you would have done, and in your hearts you know it."

Lincoln Osis got to his feet and rested a massive ebon

hand on top of the helmet he'd set on his desk. "Khan Ward's point is well taken. The Jade Falcons are obviously viable and even virile. The Wolves who fled to the Inner Sphere so fear them that they have allied themselves with mercenaries for protection. It seems clear that anyone suggesting an Absorption did not have the Jade Falcons in mind as a target."

Ian Hawker's expression sharpened. "Indeed, it would seem that there is but one Clan that is a likely candidate for Absorption."

Marthe Pryde looked out over the other Khans. "Do you meant to suggest that the Wolves are ripe?"

Taney nodded. "Your predecessors in the Jade Falcons thought so, though their attempt at doing that was misguided and bungled."

"Which is why my predecessors are dead."

"Granted. The fact remains that the Wolves have suffered significant reversals." Taney shook his head. "Not only did the war with the Jade Falcons tax them, but the Warden element of the Wolves removed itself, further weakening the Clan. We have a history of weakness there."

Marthe arched an eyebrow. "Do we?"

Taney blinked. "It is obvious, *quiaff*?"

"Neg, Khan Taney." Marthe showed teeth amid a shallow grin. "Did you not just tell Khan Ward that his Wolves were divorced from the victorious history of the other Wolves? How can his Clan have suffered reversals when it did not exist at the time those reversals occurred? Would you have the sons suffer for the sins of the fathers?"

Hawker waved her protest away. "It does not matter, Marthe, for the Wolves are a weak whelp."

"Weak, are they?" Marthe looked over at Lincoln Osis. "Which Clan is weaker, the Clan that wins a fight or the Clan that loses it? Seven months ago the Wolves successfully raided Kiamba. They took breeding stock from you, did they not, Lincoln? If defeating you did not prove their strength, certainly the seeding of Osis blood in their sibkos should make them strong, *quiaff*?"

Osis snarled and Vlad wanted to applaud. *You have eloquently returned the favor I have done you, Marthe.*

The Smoke Jaguar nodded slowly. "It is true that the Wolves mounted an extended raid through the Ghost Bear occupation zone and hit our world of Kiamba. They soundly defeated the troops we had there. Khan Ward did win bondsmen and breeding stock, but this does not mean the Wolves could not be a target for Absorption."

Vlad opened his arms. "I agree with the Smoke Jaguar Khan's analysis, and even that of Khan Taney, though I think neither of them has carried their analysis far enough. Asa Taney said that for a Clan to be viable it must be able to produce enough well-trained and well-armed troops to be able to stage operations and win victories. I would suggest that there is another level for the test of viability." He let his voice drop to a harsh growl. "That is this: for a Clan to be viable, it must also have the willingness, the heart, to actually find an enemy and attack."

Vlad pointed toward the Ice Hellion Khan. "For the last eight years the Jade Falcons and Wolves and other Clans have been fighting against the Inner Sphere. How many battles have you fought in that time, Asa Taney? Have you raided our homeworlds? You claim you are strong, but you do nothing to prove it."

Taney puffed his chest out. "I would be more than willing to provide Khan Ward with an analysis of the Ice Hellions' strength so he can read for himself how tough we are."

"Your datafile strength is worth exactly the energy needed to destroy the disk." Vlad leaned forward and leered down at the man. "If the Ice Hellions had any heart, you'd find a fight in which to prove yourselves."

"And I will fight your Clan if you are the target of the Absorption, Vlad Ward."

"Ha!" Vlad shook his head. "*If* the Wolves were made the object of the Absorption, the Ice Hellions would never win the bidding to take us over. The Ghost Bears or Smoke Jaguars or even the Jade Falcons would outbid you for us. The fact is that you and the other Clans not included in the invasion of the Inner Sphere have been left so far behind the rest of us that you could never absorb an invading clan. What we have learned fighting against the Inner Sphere has made us inherently stronger than you will ever be. If there is to be Absorption, it will not be an invading Clan that is gobbled up."

Straightening up, Vlad pointed to first the Falcon and then the Jaguar Khan. "Ask Marthe Pryde. Ask Lincoln Osis. They know that your secret dreams of absorbing an invading clan and thereby taking its place are folly. The only leaders capable of completing the Crusade against the Inner Sphere are those who have been tested in the crucible of combat. Surviving Tukayyid is a test any true leader must have passed. We have known victories and we have known defeats. It is only through these things that we have learned what must be done to defeat the Inner Sphere."

Lincoln Osis folded his bulging black arms across his chest. "Though I may find this Wolf's audacity and arrogance an annoyance, he has battle-won wisdom, for which there is no substitute. If there is to be an Absorption, I do not look forward to bidding against him for the right to absorb any of you."

Marthe laughed. "You betray your own arrogance, Lincoln, by assuming *you* would be competing with Vlad for the right to absorb another clan."

Vlad smiled and gave Marthe a quick nod. *Lincoln Osis came around quickly to the idea that only an invading Clan Khan could possibly lead us to victory in the Inner Sphere. He knows the Wolves, the Jade Falcons, and the Ghost Bears will not provide candidates against him, and likely the Nova Cats will also refrain from nominating one of their own. That leaves the Steel Vipers or the Diamond Sharks to oppose him, but neither of them were part of the original four invading Clans and their defeats on Tukayyid were positively embarrassing. By backing me, he positions himself to be elected ilKhan.*

Vlad smiled at Kael Pershaw. "Perhaps, Loremaster, it is time to call for a vote concerning Absorption."

Taney raised a hand. "In light of the cogent arguments against Absorption, I will withdraw my proposal."

Ian Hawker turned on him. "Have you no spine?"

Marthe laughed. "I believe Khan Taney has no appreciation for irony, for it would have been ironic had his proposal resulted in the Absorption of his Clan."

Khan Taney blushed purple. "I invite any of you to step into a Circle of Equals if you doubt my courage."

Vlad interlaced his fingers and bridged his hands, cracking his knuckles audibly. "Had I not recently slain an ilKhan, I would take you up on that invitation."

"Enough, Khan Ward." Lincoln Osis held a hand up. "There are matters of importance to be decided here, and killing off Khans will not hasten the decisions."

Vlad bowed his head. "You are right, of course, Khan Osis. My apologies."

The consternation on Lincoln Osis' dark face almost made Vlad smile. *When last we spoke, such an order from him would have provoked a sharp response from me, but here I acquiesce. He cannot believe his fortune at my deferring to him here. This is good. A confused enemy is a defeated enemy.*

Vlad looked over and caught Marthe Pryde watching him. *She, too, seems surprised at me. She hates politics, but I think she is mesmerized by it as well. A curious combination. One that bears watching in a foe . . . and in an ally.*

Kael Pershaw crashed his gavel against the table. "The matter of Absorption has been withdrawn. The next, most pressing item to deal with is the election of an ilKhan, but some procedural matters must be taken care of first. Some of you have not seen combat recently enough or have not tested out as a warrior recently enough to be recognized as warriors for the purpose of casting a ballot for the ilKhan. Once that problem is remedied, we can proceed."

Vlad folded his arms over his chest and looked down at the other Khans. *So, many of you are warriors in your dreams alone. It does not surprise me. What does surprise me is how you did not take warning from Elias Crichell's death for the same lack of standing. Have the Clans we left behind sunk so far or am I just risen so high?*

After a moment's thought, he answered his own question, and donned his helmet again to hide his smile.

# === 9 ===

**Royal Court, The Triad**
**Tharkad City, Tharkad**
**District of Donegal, Lyran Alliance**
**4 October 3058**

**V**ictor Davion sat back in his chair and looked up at the holographically projected agenda for the conference's first strategy planning session. The items on it seemed to him to be positively benign and hardly befitting a council of war. He had already made up his mind about the approach necessary to take on the Clans, but the Precentor Martial had correctly pointed out that the coalition leadership would have to be brought around to his way of thinking before they would agree to it.

*And agree to commit troops to it.* Holding the coalition force together was vital for two reasons. The first was that only by presenting the Clans with a united front would the Clans realize that piecemeal conquest of the Inner Sphere was not going to be possible. If everyone were not involved in the fighting, the recreation of the Star League would be shown to be a sham. Victor could easily imagine the Clans interpreting the new Star League as a trick meant to shame them, and it would be used as yet further proof that the Inner Sphere definitely needed to be conquered.

The second and more important reason everyone had to fight together was because none of them could afford to throw troops into the offensive if they also risked losing worlds in attacks by other states while their backs were turned. Victor was sure that both Theodore Kurita and his sister Katherine understood the true threat of the Clans, but he wasn't convinced Sun-Tzu might not view renewed war against the Clans as a means to expanding his own Capellan Confederation. Moreover, the military resources that would be needed to defeat the Clans were more than any two or three realms could provide.

*We hang together or we hang separately.*

A smaller room had been set aside for the military planning sessions. In normal times it served as a small theatre, with a podium set on a raised stage. The holographic projection units above the stage were focused so any images blossomed to life in front of the semi-circle of tables where the delegates sat. The old wooden floor and stairs to the stage creaked as the Precentor Martial made his way from the ComStar table to the podium.

Focht looked out over the assembled leaders and military advisors. "The purpose for our sessions here is to come up with a comprehensive plan that will allow us to take the war to the Clans. Lest anyone be of a different mind, it is important to point out that our discussions here are *military* in nature and are not dependent upon political considerations. We are coming up with the best plan we can possibly construct to drive the Clans off and end their menace. Any considerations that distract and deflect us from this goal should be left outside this room."

Marshal Sharon Bryan of the Lyran Alliance spoke up from her place. "Von Clauswitz noted that military action is the ultimate extension of politics, so how can we divorce it from politics?"

The Precentor Martial's gray-eyed gaze sharpened. "Von Clausewitz made that observation about Napoleonic politics and warfare, but his book was published well after both he and the phenomenon he commented upon had vanished. If you look at the history of warfare fought while his doctrine held sway you'd see that the empirical data fails to support his conclusion. Warfare is far too complex a phenomenon to fit into so simple a paradigm, especially when the forces unleashed in warfare are capable of sterilizing whole worlds.

"Please, harbor no illusions about what we will be discussing here. The Clans have, through genetics, technological development, and advanced training, created the most fearsome human military force mankind has ever seen. The fact that we have not been totally overrun shows that their advancement does not make them insurmountable and furthermore suggests that our warfare doctrines apply pressure to weaknesses in their armed forces."

Focht nodded at a man in a Federated Commonwealth uniform. The man's ebon skin spoke of his African ancestry, but his crisp and precise gait as he approached the podium attested to military upbringing and training. Victor knew that the man was one of Doc Trevena's analysts and Doc spoke highly of him. *For Doc to let him make this presentation means the guy has a lot on the ball.*

The Precentor Martial nodded at the man. "For those of you who have not met him, this is Dr. Michael Pondsmith. He is currently serving in the Armed Forces of the Federated Commonwealth as a Kommandant, though when not on active duty he is an instructor at the Sakhara Academy. His field of study is military history and quantitative analysis. His studies have found a model of warfare upon which we will build our assault, and we have asked him here to explain it to you. In this way we will all start with the same foundation. Dr. Pondsmith."

"Thank you, Precentor Martial." Pondsmith's voice came deep and rich, instantly commanding attention. "The model of warfare I have been studying is known as Entropy-based Warfare. It was developed by Dr. Mark Herman, a military analyst and designer of military conflict simulations in the late twentieth and early twenty-first century. It adds a third realm of conflict to the usually accepted dual-realm model of warfare. The additional material this theory addresses has been, at various times, dismissed as difficult to quantify or only marginally influential; but the fact is that this model applies very directly and significantly in facing a threat like the Clans."

Pondsmith hit a button on the podium's control panel and a yellow holographic circle appeared before the delegates. "Warfare modeling began very simply. One mode was taken into account, here represented by this yellow circle. It is lethality: the ability of troops to kill other troops and the effect of such power on the enemy. We all know—most recently from the Clan invasions themselves—that an enemy's ability to project lethality upon troops can make those who survive the attack crumble because of the horror and fear created by this projection of lethal force. For the longest time, lethality was the only element in warfare and, even up to the time of post-industrial military conflicts, it was the primary deciding factor in war."

Victor saw a red circle burn into the projection and overlap with the yellow one. It bore the legend "Disruption."

"As tactical considerations increased and became more necessary—because increased lethality and range accompanied military technological advances and increased the size of battlefields and wars—non-lethal and deceptive methods of causing problems for the enemy became valuable. If an enemy could be made to think you were going to attack at one place when, in fact, you meant to attack at another, his military might would be misplaced and wasted. Even keeping enemy troops on alert for an attack that never comes will have a serious effect on their ability to wage war.

"The overlap between lethality and disruption comes from the advantage gained when command and control units are destroyed, or supply lines are disrupted. By a very specific projection of lethality, a target that affects the enemy's ability to respond can be destroyed. Kill a messenger relaying orders to a unit and that unit never moves. Kill a commander and that unit has no brain. While these units are by no means taken out of the battle, they are less than effective in helping to prosecute it."

The black man pointed to the center of the room as a blue circle materialized and overlapped with the other two. "The Herman model adds in this third element: friction. It accounts for the damage done to a unit through wear and tear, both of maintenance necessary to keep it operational while on station and especially the problems caused by bringing the force to battle. Desertion, vehicle breakdown, taxing of fuel and food supplies, morale problems, and a host of other barely tangible factors fall into this realm. The green area of overlap between friction and lethality is known as maintenance attrition. It covers the inability of a force to repair damage and recover from a battle. The purple overlap between friction and disruption is called inertia and covers the damage done to a unit as it reacts to false threats and other deceptions.

"The central area there, where all three circles overlap is the crux of entropy-based warfare. What it says is this: if you make the enemy move where you want him to move, hit key command and control units so he begins to lose command cohesion, then you hit him hard enough to shock his troops—and it's vital that shocking occurs—the enemy's troops will crumble. They literally won't know why they are where they are, they won't know what to do, and they'll be faced with enemies against whom there is no defense. If war is hell," Pondsmith concluded, "entropy-based warfare is Satan's sauna."

Marshal Byran shook her head. "This theorizing is all well and good, and perhaps this friction allows quantitative methods to come up with numbers that match reality after the fact, but math isn't going to be what defeats the Clans."

"Agreed, Marshal Byran." Pondsmith leaned forward on the podium. "However, analysis of Tukayyid, the Coventry campaign, and even the Red Corsair's raids into the Lyran Alliance point out that EBW is directly applicable to the Clan threat. The Clans operate almost exclusively in the realm of lethality. On Tukayyid we saw that forcing them to fight a prolonged war seriously affected their ability to fight. Their profligate use of munitions is an example of friction—they could not continue to fight because they used up the materials needed to keep them in combat. Only the Wolves, by restricting the need for supplies, were able to obtain a substantial victory over the Com Guards in the conflict."

Wu Kang Kuo looked up from his place at the Capellan Confederation table. "Would I be correct in assuming, then, that operational and tactical considerations of our campaign are going to be focused on maximizing this friction damage to the Clans?"

Pondsmith frowned. "Since the Clans appear to be vulnerable to damage in this realm, that would seem to be a wise plan; but that consideration is something better addressed by others."

Victor stood. "Thank you, Dr. Pondsmith." He turned and let his gaze travel around the faces of his counterparts at their various tables. "The primary reason for presenting entropy-based warfare to you as the underlying doctrine of our campaign is because it points out the one serious reality we all have to face: this will be a *long* campaign. It may have taken the Clans only two years to seize all the worlds they have, but they've had five years to prepare defenses. Our campaign will have to push them back across a broad front, and it will not be easy."

Marshal Sharon Byran leaned forward at her place. "There's another way to end this invasion."

Victor raised an eyebrow.

Byran smiled. "We can strike at the Clan capital world, taking it and them out of the fight."

"And you know how to get there?" Victor gave her a hard stare. "I wasn't aware you possessed its location."

"I don't." Byran looked over at Phelan Kell. "But he does. He can lead us back to their lair. One strike, a coup de grâce, and we'll be done with this business."

Phelan's green eyes glittered coldly. "I will not lead you to Strana Mechty."

"Treacherous dog! Then what are you doing here?"

"I am here to help you defeat the Clans, Marshal Byran."

"Yet you protect them."

"No." Phelan shook his head adamantly. "I refuse to lead you to Strana Mechty for a variety of reasons, not the least of which is that I do not possess the data to get you there."

The Precentor Martial frowned. "You do not have a route to Strana Mechty?"

Victor saw pain wash over Phelan's face. *I think that's the first time I've ever seen him show weakness.*

Phelan stood slowly, with his head bowed. "When ilKhan Ulric Kerensky sent my taskforce into the Inner Sphere, he wanted to remove me from all temptation. He wanted me and my people in the Inner Sphere to serve as a brake on the rest of the Clans. He knew he was going to die, and he knew we would want to avenge him. To prevent this he took the extraordinary precaution of having the databanks of our ships purged of navdata for the Clan homeworlds. On top of that—to my knowledge—no complete map of that route exists. Way-stations and transit points provide the route to ships that are inbound."

Byran's dark eyes became slits. "I think you're lying."

"You have that luxury, Marshal Byran, but regardless, I do not have the data you want." Phelan's head came up. "Nor would I give it to you if I did. A single, long-range strike at Strana Mechty would only enrage the Clans and invite them to continue their war against the Inner Sphere. Without a campaign that shows we can meet them and defeat them, the Clans would dismiss such a strike as nothing more than lucky—and lucky it would have to be to get out there and back again while operational."

Victor nodded toward his cousin. "There's nothing more I'd like than to make a single strike that could stun the Clans, but if we view matters realistically, it means we're going to have to force them out of the Inner Sphere. It is my estimation that such a campaign will take a very long time—on the order of seven or more years, depending on how involved it becomes."

Wu raised a hand. "Define *involved*."

"How many of the Clans are we going to have to take on?" Victor shrugged his shoulders. "If we can prosecute this war by finding a way where we only have to pit ourselves against one of the Clans, we might be able to work through them more quickly."

Phelan nodded. "You must recall that the Clans themselves are split politically on the necessity of the invasion. The Crusaders believe the Inner Sphere must be liberated from those who have no claim to it, while the Wardens believe the purpose of the Clans was to save the people of the Inner Sphere from any threat—including themselves. If we choose a Crusader Clan to attack, we hurt Crusader credibility in the Clan Council. The Clans might be convinced to sue for peace."

Byran tapped a finger against her desktop. "But we would never accept peace without a complete Clan withdrawal from the occupied worlds, correct?"

The Precentor Martial stood and waved both Victor and Phelan back to their seats. "That, Marshal Byran, is a political question and will have to be settled by politicians. Our purpose is to address problems of troop readiness, transport, assignments, supply, and suitability for attacking particular targets. Where we will be fighting has to be settled by the politicians as well, but we must assure them that we can and will fight. We are the scalpel that others will use to carve the Clan cancer free of the Inner Sphere. It is up to us to determine how long that operation will take and how best to approach it."

Sharon Byran scoffed. "I think you'll find this war anything but surgical."

Victor met her contemptuous stare without flinching. "As long as the patient lives, Marshal, we've done what we need to do."

# ≡ 10 ≡

**Royal Palace, The Triad**
**Tharkad City, Tharkad**
**District of Donegal, Lyran Alliance**
**5 October 3058**

**K**atrina Steiner met Thomas Marik just inside the doorway to her office. She offered him her left hand by way of greeting, allowing him to use his strong left hand to meet her grasp rather than his scarred right hand. She read the surprise in his eyes at her action, but she refrained from letting anything but friendliness play through her smile. *I know it impresses him when someone remembers his preference for using his left hand—he considers them thoughtful and kind, which is the impression I wish to make.*

"I am so pleased you were able to join me this afternoon, Captain-General."

"I was most pleased to accept your invitation, Archon."

Katrina looked up and beyond him as the double doors to her white office closed. "Your companion will not be joining us?"

Thomas turned slightly to present his unscarred profile to her. "No, the Countess asked me to express her regrets, but she is shepherding my daughter about on an expedition through Tharkad City. I believe Isis was intent on enriching your economy, while Sherryl intends for her to see some of the points of cultural interest in the city."

Katrina waved Thomas over toward the white leather

couches bracketing a low glass and wrought-iron table. "Please, be seated. Can I get you some refreshment?"

"Right now, no, thank you." Thomas tugged at the legs of his uniform trousers as he sat down. The green uniform was trimmed with royal purple, but lacked the stripes, chevrons, and braid that should have adorned the uniform of a man of his rank. To Katrina the uniform seemed martial enough, but its lack of decorations reminded her of the plain nature of ComStar uniforms.

*As if I needed to be reminded that Thomas was once a ComStar adept and even now is considered to be the "Primus in exile" by many of the Word of Blake faction.*

She had chosen to wear a suit cut along soldierly lines, consisting of a bolero jacket, a tailored skirt, and riding boots that hugged her calves like a second skin. Cut from white wool and leather, the only color in the clothes came from the gold buttons and buckles. Her hair had been gathered back into a single golden braid that she let drape forward over her right shoulder like a snake.

"I'm sorry Countess Halas was unable to join us. She seems delightful, and I should very much like to get to know her better." Katrina took a seat opposite him. "I'm glad you have found companionship to comfort you for the loss of your Sophina."

Breath caught in Thomas' chest. Less than a year and a half ago he had lost his wife and had discovered, shortly thereafter, that his son and heir, Joshua, had died while undergoing medical treatment on New Avalon—the capital of Victor Davion's Federated Commonwealth. The blow had been crushing for Thomas. When he discovered that Victor was plotting to substitute a double for his son, Thomas had attacked the Federated Commonwealth and succeeded in reconquering the worlds Hanse Davion had won from his realm two decades before.

"Yes, I have been fortunate in that way, though Sherryl is the silver lining to a dark cloud."

"No one could replace your Sophina. I know that." Katrina forced herself to swallow hard. "I felt so sad for you."

"And I very much appreciated your message of sympathy at the time." Thomas stroked his jaw with his left hand. "And your decision to refrain from attacking my realm as I punished your brother's perfidy showed me your true nature."

"Victor is my brother, but I could never support such a devious and cruel deception."

"I sensed in you, then and now, a desire for justice." Thomas shrugged slightly. "I felt a kinship with you then that might have led to many things."

*So Tormano was right—you* were *interested in me as a consort.* Katrina smiled and toyed with the end of her braid. "There are things one does for political reasons, and things one does for personal reasons. I know it is unrealistic for me to hope that my life can be one where these things are separated, but I truly wish it would be so. The love of my life—Galen Cox—was slain because of politics. My mother died because of it and—no, I should not say it. . . ."

Thomas's gaze sharpened, but he covered his interest with a gentle nod. "I will respect your confidence, Katrina. What we say here is between kindred souls, not political rivals."

She let relief gush through her voice. "My mother was desperately unhappy."

"What?"

"Oh, I know, it is considered heresy of high order—blasphemy really—to suggest she was not hopelessly in love with my father. She was, of course, in many ways, but Hanse Davion was distant and all but unknowable to a woman of her youth. It's true that they did grow closer over the years, but she hated being used to extend Davion power over her people. Think of it—for a wedding present my father gave her a war. He slaughtered millions in her honor."

Thomas blinked several times while she spoke. "I had no idea."

"Very few did. I don't think my brother realizes it, really, and I don't know if he would care if he did. Too much Hanse's son, he is."

The Captain-General nodded quickly. "The Fox bred true in that one."

"Unfortunately."

"Do you think so?" Thomas frowned. "Though I never liked your father, if I could call him back from the grave and put him in charge of taking the war to the Clans, I would do so in a heartbeat. To mangle a saying, when your problem is a nail, the solution is a hammer."

Katrina nodded. "True, but politics and rulership of a nation are not problems that can be described as nails, are they?"

"No, statecraft is more an art than a skill."

"I find myself in a position, Thomas, where I must deal with the problems of statecraft without sufficient advice. I cannot speak with Victor because he hates me for breaking the Federated Commonwealth apart. Theodore Kurita has had his mind poisoned against me by Victor. Sun-Tzu Liao and I will never see eye to eye, especially since I employ his uncle as an advisor." She smiled hopefully. "You are the only person who seems worthy of trust, and you have the knowledge I need to make certain I am doing the right things."

The couch's leather squeaked as Thomas sat forward. "You honor me, Katrina."

"I merely state the obvious, Thomas."

"It is obvious to you, perhaps, but I never would have dared guess you trust me so."

*But you will now because this is the conclusion to which I wish you to jump.* "I trust you, Thomas, because we both have needs the other can fulfill." Katrina leaned to the left against the arm of the couch and crossed her legs. "I would not be surprised if your Sherryl Halas should soon announce that she is carrying your child. Please, don't look so surprised—I have nothing more than intuition to go by. You need an heir to supplant Isis and keep Sun-Tzu away from your throne, and Halas makes a suitable consort."

Thomas' dark eye sparkled. "She was not my only choice of prospective candidates to give me an heir."

"So I suspect." Katrina smiled. "Were my brother still the Archon-Prince of a united Federated Commonwealth, he might have offered me to you as a consort, hoping our child might be the vehicle for uniting our realms."

"It would be a powerful alliance, even now, Katrina."

"Agreed, but not possible at the moment, Thomas." Katrina met his gaze. "Were we to wed and merge our realms, we would be reduced from two votes to one in this Star League we are to form." Her smile tightened. "While I will not provide you an heir, I do believe I can help your new heir survive."

"How?"

"Tormano is constantly itching to strengthen his Free Capella Movement. Kai Allard-Liao is its leader now, but can you imagine him refraining from joining the war against the Clans? Hardly, and in the vacuum, Tormano will be able to exert more influence. His actions can bedevil Sun-Tzu and keep him off-guard."

"Focus his attentions elsewhere."

"Indeed, focus them away from your child." Katrina smiled. "In fact, I would be honored to let the Countess stay here for as long as she wished, both pre- and post-partum."

Thomas' face closed and his tone became formal. "You will forgive me, Archon, but I have already had one child enjoy your family's hospitality."

Outrage whirled up through Katrina. *How dare you think my offer a trick, you misshapen excuse for a man!* She wanted to lash out at him, but she held her rebuke in check. To cover herself, she raised a hand to her mouth, then sat forward and reached out to press his knee with one hand.

"Oh, Thomas, I did not think. Oh, how evil you must imagine me to be." Katrina translated her anger into horror and let it underscore her words with tremulous tones. "I merely thought that as difficult as it might be for Kali Liao to have her assassins in position on Atreus, it would be that much more difficult for them to strike here. Please, forgive me. I . . . I . . . I feel so horrid."

Thomas' left hand descended on hers, trapping it against his kneecap. "I choose to believe you were mistaken, Katrina. I truly do." An edge crept into his voice. "I want you to know, however, that any threat to my child will result in full retribution. I did not continue the war against your brother because it was your father's plan that he followed, but my restraint should not be taken as cowardice. I may be reluctant to fight, but that does not mean I cannot or will not fight."

"That is not a mistake I am in the least inclined to make, Thomas." Katrina slid forward on the couch, bringing her knees to the edge of the table, and straightened up as much as her trapped hand would allow. "I don't see a situation where I would want a hostage from you, nor one in which you would require one from me. With the border our nations share, we are already each other's hostages. If we should fight, we would be eaten up by the others, for the Clans would attack my realm and Sun-Tzu would attack yours. Once we had been ravaged, my brother and House Kurita would sweep up whatever the Clans had not devoured."

Katrina slipped her hand from beneath his as the pressure slackened. "Our only chance for prosperity, for survival, is for the two of us to work together. With me as your ally, you risk nothing by bringing Sun-Tzu to heel. Proper employment of your future son-in-law will position my brother where we need him, and Theodore will follow whatever plans most benefit his realm."

Thomas frowned. "Do you truly think so little of your brother?"

That question surprised Katrina and she only partially succeeded in covering her surprise. "Victor? It is not that I think so little of him, Thomas, but that I know him so well. He sees Sun-Tzu as his enemy, but he also sees him as a direct threat to his friend Kai. Victor is loyal almost to a fault and that loyalty blinds him. And, as you noted before, Victor is more of a warrior than a politician. Manipulating him is not easy, but it can be done."

Thomas slowly nodded his scarred face. "I cannot deny the logic of what you say. I'm not certain, however, that I like the idea of manipulating Victor."

"But you have said yourself that Victor is the best hope we have for leading the force that will destroy the Clans. Our informal alliance can guarantee he does the job to which he is most suited." Katrina allowed herself a throaty little laugh. "The fact that his preoccupation with the Clans will lessen the threat against our realms is merely a bonus."

Thomas pressed his hands together as if in prayer. "I believe, Archon, that our two realms will benefit greatly from our cooperation. It will all have to be sub-rosa, of course, but that is acceptable because what we are planning will benefit the Inner Sphere as a whole." Thomas smiled. "Does my quick acceptance of your offer surprise you?"

"I suppose it does. Your creation of the Knights of the Inner Sphere, with their emphasis on chivalry and justice, made me think that such dealing behind the scenes would not be so acceptable to you."

"In reality it is not. In a perfect society, this sort of power-brokering would not be necessary." The Captain-General's eyes hardened. "This is not a perfect society, and we will have to make decisions that cost mothers and fathers their children, much as I paid the price with my son. If secret deals will lessen that price, then I will deal. However much I wish it were unnecessary, it is not, therefore I will make the best of it."

He looked up and Katrina felt a chill go through her. The

face was a ruin, yet it seemed to glow with some inner fire. "Jerome Blake, whose words I studied when I was with ComStar, looked ahead to a golden age for humanity. That goal is one I wish to attain. It does not justify the means to reach it, but it does demand due diligence in its pursuit. In you, Katrina, I trust I have a partner in its attainment. For this reason, I work with you, but only for the benefit of all mankind."

"Your goal is my goal, Thomas." Katrina clasped her hands together over her heart. "A golden age"—*led by a golden woman*—"let no one stand in our way."

# ═ 11 ═

**Grand Ballroom, Royal Court**
**The Triad**
**Tharkad City, Tharkad**
**District of Donegal, Lyran Alliance**
**8 October 3058**

**V**ictor could feel the fatigue that had etched lines on the Precentor Martial's face ache from his own bones. The military planning sessions had broken down into long meetings spent comparing each military's official troop readiness and strength assessments with the facts and figures Jerry Cranston and Doc Trevena provided. By and large the numbers proved to be similar, though Sun-Tzu overestimated his new units and undervalued his House Warrior units.

The numbers and discussions had begun to lay the groundwork for making the coalition force a reality. Though Marshal Byran still detested the resolution of the conflict on Coventry, the other leaders, including Wu Kang Kuo and Sir Paul Masters of the Marik's Knights of the Inner Sphere, seemed to respect Victor's willingness to accept a victory that didn't cost soldiers their lives. Though no one dared imagine that the campaign against the Clans would be won so cleanly, all seemed to agree that the profligate waste of life was to be avoided at all costs.

The Precentor Martial leaned heavily against the podium as he looked out over the assembly of political leaders. "You have all by now received your own private reports on the course of discussions in the military planning meetings. As you know, our preliminary work has been to assess the troops we will be able to mobilize against the Clans. This new Star League Defense Force will be formidable, but the campaign will take time and a serious commitment of resources. Exactly how long it will take and how much in the way of personnel and materiel it will require cannot be accurately predicted at this point.

"Certain issues must be addressed before we can begin any substantive planning phases for our campaign. Were this a purely planetary campaign, tactical and grand tactical considerations would dictate where, when, and how we begin. Because we're looking at driving the enemy from an area comprising hundreds of thousands of cubic light years, the determination of where to begin can and must include political considerations. So, this is the issue I place before you: from where shall we launch our assault?"

Victor heard those words as solemn and serious, but judging by the speed with which his sister leaped to her feet, it seemed more as though she'd heard them as a call for bidding at an auction. It also struck him that what they were about to do would be much akin to the bargaining that preceded a Clan attack, and the irony of it brought a small smile. *We become more like the enemy and they like us.*

Anastasius Focht nodded toward Katrina. "Archon, if you wish to begin."

Katrina smiled and pointed toward the center of the room. A holograph slowly formed itself there. It showed the Lyran Alliance from the border with the Free Worlds League on up through the Jade Falcon Occupation Zone. The map extended far enough down to show Terra and the borders shared between the Lyran Alliance, the Draconis Combine, and the tiny Free Rasalhague Republic.

"I would submit to you, my peers, that the Lyran Alliance offers a superior venue for staging and launching our assault on the Clans. The front with the Jade Falcons is broad, but not so much so that our troop concentrations would be diluted. The Jade Falcon occupation zone is densely packed with worlds, which puts most combat operations only a single jump from the lines. An assault from the Lyran Alliance would liberate Alliance worlds, as well as worlds of the Free Rasalhague Republic."

Katrina pointed down at Terra, and the home of humanity began to glow. "As we all know, the stated objective of the Clan invasion is the taking of Terra. One of our first objectives can be to cut across the base of the Clan occupation zones, creating a buffer that will preclude their strike at Terra *and* take the pressure off the Free Rasalhague Republic."

She looked up, and a triangular area along the center of the line with the Jade Falcons popped up several centimeters from the rest of the projection. "This is the Arc-Royal Defense Cordon. Colonel Kell—Prefect von Warlock, if you will—has pledged his Kell Hounds and his son's troops to defending this area from Clan predation. If we do not attack from the Lyran Alliance, we will lose the use of these highly trained and deadly forces."

Morgan Kell stood at his place. "Forgive my interruption, Archon, but this last statement is not accurate. I have never said nor meant to suggest I would withhold my troops from fighting the Clans. When, in the past, you requested my help, it was for operations against *Inner Sphere* targets. I have refused to use my troops against Inner Sphere forces when the Clans are such a great threat. My people will fight where they are asked to fight."

Victor caught a flash of anger rippling over his sister's face, followed by a bit of surprise before she recovered herself. *She never expected Morgan to make that admission. She's seen him as a thorn in her side and, until now, she believed it was because he hates her. Now it seems that he only hated her choice of targets. This will give her something to think about, which is just as well.*

Katrina nodded toward Morgan as the mercenary seated himself again. "I very much appreciate that clarification, Colonel Kell. The fact remains that the preparations you have made for defending the Arc-Royal Defense Cordon could easily serve as the groundwork for the invasion force."

The Precentor Martial smiled down from his position. "Your points are well made, Archon, and your formal proposal is being downloaded to the noteputers of the staff personnel present. Coordinator, if you would care to address the assembly."

Clad in a dark suit that lacked any military decorations, Theodore Kurita stood. "The Archon has made a number of excellent points in her presentation. I would offer the

Draconis Combine as the staging site for the invasion for a host of different reasons."

He gestured toward the center of the room and a holograph of the Draconis Combine replaced that of the Lyran Alliance. It showed the kidney-shaped realm canted at a forty-five degree angle, with the Clan invasion zone occupied by the Smoke Jaguars and Nova Cats nestled against its interior curve. The holograph painted the Combine in shades of red and made the Clan zone gray. Beyond the Jaguars and the Cats, a far more slender Clan zone occupied by the Ghost Bears appeared in shades of light blue.

"The Combine has a number of superior benefits to offer our forces. First and foremost, security issues are less of a problem because the news media are a branch of the government. Many of you have decried this state of affairs in the past, but the simple fact is that by monitoring broadcast media the Clans might learn the nature of our military preparations here in the Lyran Alliance. Though the media is also a tool we can use to deceive them, true operational security can only realistically be obtained in the Combine."

A world glowed red in the heart of the gray zone. "This is Wolcott. It is a world the Smoke Jaguars failed to take from us, and in the bargaining that preceded the battle, they agreed to leave it alone if they failed to conquer it. We have been able to use Wolcott as a staging area for operations to harass the Smoke Jaguars. It gives us a secure forward base for attacks as well as for resupplying our forces.

"Archon Katrina noted that the worlds in the Jade Falcon zone are more densely packed, making movement between targets easier. This would also allow the Falcons to reinforce and resupply their troops more quickly. In the zone closest to the Combine we actually have fewer targets, which means we can concentrate our forces to the greatest effect."

Theodore's voice dropped slightly as his eyes tightened. "We also have reason to believe we might not be forced to attack the worlds occupied by the Nova Cats."

Thomas Marik's jaw dropped open. "What? Have you been negotiating with the Clans?"

Theodore held a hand up. "There have been overtures from the Nova Cats. As the Precentor Martial knows, the Nova Cats are different from the other Clans. They seem to be as much mystics as warriors—though they can be fierce fighters when they wish, as evidenced by the fighting the

Northwind Highlanders saw on Wayside V. The Nova Cats seem to place great stock in the visions experienced by some of their warriors and Khans. I gather there has been a vision showing a nova cat being mauled by a dragon, or some such, and this is prompting a detente."

Thomas Marik's eyes narrowed as he followed up his initial question. "What are you telling us, Theodore?"

"I am telling you that the Nova Cats apparently see another means by which their ends can be met. If there is a way to reach a compromise with them—and our talks have moved in that direction—I see it only to our benefit to continue pursuing such talks."

Katrina stared daggers at Theodore. "Are you suggesting you would be willing to allow a Clan to possess worlds in the Inner Sphere?"

"As those worlds are *mine* to do with as I see fit, certainly." The Coordinator shook his head. "I see no reason to buy with blood what I already own and can have ceded back to me peacefully."

Sun-Tzu laughed softly. "Your outrage at what Theodore would do is curious, Katrina, because you yourself have Clanners dwelling within your realm."

Morgan Kell snarled at him. "My son's people are Clanners in all but the most important aspect: their allegiance. I gather the Coordinator is making that same point concerning the Nova Cats."

The Precentor Martial held his hands up. "Please, let us realize that the Coordinator is merely suggesting that he has found a way to deal with a reality that we may all face—there are likely to be Clanners who remain on worlds we take back. It is very easy for us in this room to forget that for most people the conquest of a world means a change of faces on coins and new national anthems and holidays, nothing more. Just as our people did not flee the conquered worlds, neither will Clan people flee the worlds we take back. We have no way of knowing how many of them have come into the Inner Sphere, nor how many worlds have been reshaped according to Clan social structure, but we will be dealing with Clanners in the Inner Sphere for a very long time. This we know and this we should accept."

Victor stood at his place. "Precentor Martial, I think our discussion here is likely to break down very quickly unless we reframe it in a manner that focuses it on our objective:

finding a vector for attacking the Clans. Certainly my sister and the Coordinator of the Draconis Combine have made good arguments. There isn't one among us who wouldn't wish our subjugated peoples to be liberated first, but their liberation is not our primary objective."

"Pray do tell us what that is, Prince Victor," Sun-Tzu sneered. "Beside your aggrandizement, of course."

Victor refused to dignify Sun-Tzu's sniping. "Bottom line, for our campaign to work, *one Clan must die!* There can be no compromise, no faltering, no pulling back. If you study the history of the Clans, you know that of the twenty clans created originally, two have been absorbed into other Clans and the third, the Clan that goes unnamed, was wiped out to the last by the rest of the Clans. This complete and total destruction of a Clan is considered a monumental event in the history of the Clans. It shocks them and terrifies them. If we destroy a Clan, we will accomplish what only *they* have accomplished before. The death of a Clan will make us into their peers."

The Precentor Martial nodded. "Prince Victor's point is very well taken. The Clans respect power. We all agree that by pushing them back, we will show ourselves to be powerful. Choosing one Clan to attack and defeat will certainly send them a message."

Katrina frowned. "But attacking only one Clan will leave the rest of them free to attack us."

Victor shook his head. "The Clans are no more united than we are. If we go after one Clan, its enemies won't come after us. It's also important to reiterate a point Phelan made in our first strategy meeting: the Clans are divided along philosophical lines. The Crusaders populate the Clans that wanted and plotted the invasion. If we destroy a Crusader Clan, not only do we reduce the Crusader power block in the Clan Councils, but we cast serious doubts about the philosophy underlying the Crusader invasion."

"So, then, Prince Victor, what are our choices?" Theodore Kurita glanced at his aide, and a map of the Clan invasion zone replaced the one of the Combine. "The Nova Cats are benign and the Ghost Bears are not Crusaders. The Jade Falcons, the Wolves, and the Smoke Jaguars are Crusaders."

"That certainly narrows our choices down." Victor nodded toward the map. "The obvious choices would be the Wolves or Jade Falcons. Both were weakened by their recent war with each other, and there are reports that some worlds in the Jade Falcon zone have not yet been pacified after the Wolves liberated them."

The podium creaked as the Precentor Martial leaned forward on it. "The only difficulty I see with attacking the Jade Falcons is that the Wolves would likely snap up worlds, contributing to our victory, but lessening the impact we want to make. This move would, in effect, strengthen the Wolves and their standing in the Clans. Enhancing Vladimir Ward's position is nothing I would recommend."

Before Victor could offer his opinion on that point, Katrina stood. "It strikes me that our only choice is to attack the Smoke Jaguars. As my brother has indicated, both the Jade Falcons and the Wolves are weak, so attacking them might seem to be taking undue advantage. The fact that the major gains made during the invasion were made through the new Free Rasalhague Republic—no disrespect intended, Prince Magnusson—means the Clans attacked through the weakest member of the Inner Sphere. If we take on a more worthy opponent, then we will be morally superior to the Clans."

Candace Liao glanced past Morgan Kell and at Katrina. "You realize, Archon, that your endorsement of the Smoke Jaguars as a target is, in essence, a complete reversal of your earlier position. This would mean that your realm would not be the site of the assault."

"I do realize that, Duchess Liao, and you do not know how much it pains me to see my people subjected to tyranny and be unable to liberate them."

"You would be surprised, Archon, how much I *do* know about that."

Victor saw Sun-Tzu blanche at the ice-edged words from his aunt. "I would have to concur with my sister. The Smoke Jaguars seem to be the logical choice as our target. If we are fortunate, the animosity between the Falcons and Wolves will prevent either from becoming adventurous. Since neither is known to have much love for the Jaguars, presumably they will remain neutral during our attacks."

The Precentor Martial nodded. "I would also point out that the ilKhan at the time the invasion began was Leo Showers, a Smoke Jaguar. It is fitting that his Clan bear the brunt of the Inner Sphere's retribution."

Theodore Kurita looked around the room. "Is it decided? Are we all agreed that the destruction of one whole Clan is the price of our future, and that the Clan we will attack is the Smoke Jaguars?"

Katrina laughed lightly. "Your people will benefit from our wisdom, Theodore. It is decided."

Victor's eyes became slits. "Understand his questions, Katherine, because the Coordinator does not ask them lightly. Yes, we can agree on the Smoke Jaguars as our target, but do we all agree on their complete and utter destruction? When we are done, they will be driven from our worlds. Their symbols will be destroyed, their buildings razed. There will be nothing left of them."

Thomas Marik frowned. "You're not talking genocide, are you? Prisoners will not be slaughtered, will they?"

Victor shook his head. "No, we won't kill prisoners, we won't murder innocents, but we will murder the Smoke Jaguars. Their culture and that which makes them unique within the Clans will be erased. We'll absorb and reeducate what we can, but their original creations—and their home-world, if we can find it—will be nothing but a memory."

Haakon Magnusson smiled coldly. "The Clans have all but managed to do that with my Rasalhague Republic. I have no reservations about paying them in kind."

"This is not revenge, Prince Magnusson." Theodore Kurita posted himself up on his arms as he leaned forward. "The Clans were once part of us. They have rebelled and must be punished. We will punish them, but we must all agree to abide by this decision. Some people may consider our plan to be barbaric, but their opinions matter not at all because the Clans are the ones we must impress. If you cannot accept this responsibility, speak now or remain silent."

Victor looked around at the other delegates. Sun-Tzu fidgeted ever so slightly and Katrina seemed bored, but everyone else wore solemn expressions. Morgan Kell, Candace Liao, and Theodore Kurita—MechWarriors of note all—understood what was being asked of them. Haakon Magnusson had also been a warrior and accepted the burden placed on him almost too eagerly, as far as Victor was concerned.

Thomas Marik appeared to be wrestling with the most demons, but that didn't surprise Victor. Though the man was not truly a Marik—his imposture was known only to a handful of Victor's advisors and, presumably, by the double himself—he had been a member of the ComStar sect before taking the throne. He was an idealistic leader who had made a number of changes intended to soothe the infighting and constant hostilities among the people of the Free Worlds League. He had also formed the Knights of the Inner Sphere—some called it a private army but Marik claimed it was a new military order based on a noble view of combat. The strategy being advocated here directly conflicted with the aims he had for his nation and his dreams for the Inner Sphere. *And yet he has to see that this is the only way.*

Thomas slowly rose at his place, his scarred visage made all the more terrible by the sadness written on it. "What we are choosing to do is *evil.* There is no question about that, but it would be a greater evil to fail to oppose the Clans. I consider it a major personal failure that I cannot see another way to convince the Clans to leave us alone. They cannot be appeased, therefore they must be destroyed. With great reluctance I agree to this course of action."

One by one the leaders of the Inner Sphere nodded in assent. The Precentor Martial waited until the last of them voted, then he, too, agreed. "It is done. We will oppose the Clans with one massive campaign to be launched from the Draconis Combine. Its objective is simple: the Smoke Jaguar Clan will die."

# ═══ 12 ═══

Royal Palace, The Triad
Tharkad City, Tharkad
District of Donegal, Lyran Alliance
9 October 3058

With each step that took Phelan Kell and his father into Katrina Steiner's office, Phelan wished he'd accepted Victor's invitation to fence instead. *I'm sure we'll be doing fencing enough here as well, but I much prefer the sport when I can see the foils and know when a point had been scored.* Had Katrina's invitation for a meeting been for him alone, he would have refused, but he'd been included in an invitation to his father. Morgan had asked him to overlook the slight.

Phelan found the room blindingly white. He'd heard the office described by Katrina's loyalists as virginal and pure, but to him it seemed cold and sterile. *Less hospitable than the ice fields of Morges.* He smiled slightly at the thought. *That was the last time I saw combat, and I think I would rather be there than here.*

Katrina, clad in cashmere sweater and trim trousers as white as the decor of her office, waved the two men to a sofa and took a seat on the one facing them across a low glass table. Lying on the table were magazine disks of a half-dozen journals published on Arc-Royal or within the defense cordon. He didn't try to look closely at them to discern date and volume numbers, but he assumed they contained pieces on him, his father, and the Wolves. *Not all of them favorable, either, I imagine.*

"I wish to thank you both for joining me on such short notice. Can I offer you anything?" Katrina waved a hand toward the sideboard. "I even have some of the Irish whiskey from Connor Distillery on Arc-Royal that you used to send my grandmother."

Morgan shook his head. "Thank you, no." He looked around the room, a wistful expression softening his face. "The last time I drank Irish whiskey in here, this office was much different. Your grandmother was still alive and you were dressed in braces and bows. You were not much here in those days, since you were raised mostly on New Avalon."

"It is rather ironic, isn't it, that Victor rules a world where he did not grow up, and the same with me." Her blue eyes flashed at Phelan. "And even Phelan here had to leave the womb of the Inner Sphere before he could fulfill his destiny. Doubtless we could chat for a good long time about the chains of events that led to all this, but I have urgent matters I wish to discuss with you both."

Phelan got up from the couch and crossed to the sideboard. "What would those matters be?"

"I have misjudged you, both of you, and I wish to make amends." As Phelan filled a tumbler with cold water, Katrina leaned forward to his father. "What you said yesterday in the session made me see that I had been wrong about you. A year ago, when you refused my request for help, then created the Arc-Royal Defense Cordon, I thought it was an act of defiance. I realize now, of course, that it was no such thing."

Morgan nodded slowly. "At that time you, Thomas Marik, Sun-Tzu Liao, and your brother were all engaged in a conflict that was deflecting us from the primary threat to the Inner Sphere. If not for ilKhan Ulric Kerensky tearing through the Jade Falcons, the Clans would have roared through the Lyran Alliance. Your nation would have been destroyed and you would have been made a bondswoman of the Clans. Ask Phelan—being a bondsman is not a pleasant thing."

Phelan looked at Katrina over the lip of his glass. "I doubt you would like it very much at all, Katrina. You have no warrior or scientific training, so, at best, you would be relegated to the merchant caste."

Katrina toyed with the gold bracelet on her right wrist and shuddered. "I have no doubt it would be horrible. You were right to refuse to support me, Morgan, and you were right to draw everyone's attention back to the Clans. Until yesterday, however, I did not see this, which was why I did not invite you to this conference. I am pleased that Victor, for once, displayed some foresight and corrected what would have been a grave error."

"What is important, Katrina, is that Phelan and I are here."

"Yes, Morgan, that is what is supremely important." Katrina sat back and shifted around so she could see Morgan and Phelan both. "And that is why I've called you here. I have some matters of great concern on my mind and wanted to take advantage of your counsel."

Phelan snorted a laugh. "I thought Tormano Liao and Nondi Steiner were your advisors."

"They do advise me but, between us, they have their blind spots. Tormano sees Sun-Tzu as a greater threat than the Clans. Nondi, dear that she is, harbors a great deal of ill will toward you, Morgan, and I have no doubt she sees you, Phelan, and your people, as a Clan taskforce just waiting to explode out of Arc-Royal and consume us." Katrina smiled carefully. "Because of your comments yesterday I know there are things that must be done to prepare the Lyran Alliance for this war with the Clans and I don't think Nondi and Tormano will see that."

Morgan sat forward, resting his arms on his knees. The black steel of his mechanical right hand gleamed dully in the afternoon light from one of the room's large windows. "I am very interested in knowing your plans, Katrina."

"Good." Katrina sighed and settled back on her couch, drawing her legs up onto the cushions beside her. "I wholly agree with the aims of the taskforce we will send. The idea of taking the war to one Clan and destroying it utterly seems like just the right plan. I will support this effort, but I fear that the Precentor Martial and my brother are missing some important factors in all this. I am uncomfortable bringing this up because I know the importance of maintaining a united front, but the fact is that it is all very well to plan an offensive strategy, but it seems they aren't taking into consideration the domestic front."

Morgan frowned. "I'm not certain I follow you."

"Victor talks about a campaign that will take years to prosecute. It is entirely possible that the Clans—and Phelan, you would know this better than anyone—could fracture and the Crusaders could suddenly renew their effort to conquer the Inner Sphere. While we are trying to push the Smoke Jaguars out of the Inner Sphere, the Jade Falcons and the Wolves could burst forth and ravage the Lyran Alliance."

Phelan nodded. "It it possible. Vlad is in charge of the Wolves and might do anything. Marthe Pryde, the Jade Falcon Khan, would surely love to take Terra. I don't think you'd like being a bondswoman to either of them."

"No, not at all. Nor would any of my people." Katrina glanced down at her hands. "This is why I want you to keep your Arc-Royal Defense Cordon in place. I want the Kell Hounds and the Wolves to remain in the Lyran Alliance while the war against the Smoke Jaguars goes off. I want you here to be able to protect the Lyran Alliance."

Morgan closed his eyes for a moment, then slowly shook his head. "I think you missed the point of what I said yesterday and why I refused to help you before."

"No, I understand you perfectly. I'm *agreeing* with you!" Katrina sat up straight. "You're the only one I can trust to keep my realm safe."

Morgan smiled indulgently. "Ah, but you see, I am disinclined to trust *you*, Katrina."

"What?"

"You heard me."

"Why wouldn't you see me as trustworthy?"

Morgan's voice dropped to a low growl. "I have seldom had reason to find murderers trustworthy."

Outrage and shock rimmed Katrina's eyes with white and dropped her jaw. "Murderer, me? I'm no murderer."

"Your protestations of innocence mean nothing to me, Katrina." Morgan Kell stood abruptly, and Katrina shied back away from him. "I know, I *know*, Victor did not murder your mother. Just before her death Melissa confided to me that she had offered to abdicate in his favor. He refused to let her do so. She was not an impediment to his taking power, but Victor *is* an impediment to *your* taking power. Your mother had to be removed, and shifting blame for her death to him allowed you to usurp his position *here*."

Katrina covered her face with her hands and her shoulders shook with sobs. "How can you say that, Morgan? I loved my mother. I was present when she died. And I saw to it that you had the best care possible here during your recovery. While you lay sick, I visited you every day. How could I have done that, why *would* I do that, if I were the person responsible for your injuries?"

"Guilt?" Morgan looked down at her. "In all the times you visited me you expressed regret at the death of my wife and at the loss of my arm, but never regret about your mother's death. You were more concerned that I couldn't attend the funeral than you were about her being dead."

"No! I was just being strong, trying to comfort you in your tragedy. If you hadn't been so gravely hurt and doped up, you would have seen the pain in my heart. Just because you didn't see it doesn't mean it wasn't there."

"Oh, Katrina, you played the role of grieving daughter very well—too well. You bore up under the pressure like a champion, and you were certain to let all the media in the Inner Sphere know how brave you were." Morgan's flesh and blood hand curled into a fist. "I especially loved how you protested against those who would have blamed your brother, which only seemed to persuade people that he *must* have killed Melissa if you were so bent on defending him."

Morgan reached down and grabbed her jaw, tipping her face up so she could see him. "I did not realize all this at first because, yes, the grief of losing my wife and my arm and your mother blinded me. That blindness was temporary, so now I see things very clearly."

Katrina slapped Morgan's hand away, then stood and backed away from him. "Never lay a hand on me again! Never! *I* am the Archon!"

"The office I can respect, Katrina, but I have long been a man willing to oppose the person in the office. Your namesake knew that. You should as well. And you should fear it."

"Fear? You?" Katrina threw back her head and laughed aloud. "If you had any proof that what you say is true, you'd have used it already. You have nothing and, therefore, cannot threaten me."

Morgan stared at her for a moment, then shook his head. "You're the worst kind of fool, Katrina—one who does not listen. If I used my evidence to depose you right now, I would weaken the Inner Sphere. I won't do that. But after the Clans are defeated, I will not feel so constrained."

"*If* you survive the fight against the Clans."

The cold fury in Katrina's voice jolted adrenaline through Phelan. He hurled his tumbler against the far wall, where it exploded into a wet stain. Before Katrina's gasp had fully escaped her throat, Phelan took a long stride forward and locked his right hand around her neck. He hoisted her up, hearing only the gurgle in her throat and the scrape of her tiptoes against the carpet.

"You murdered my mother and now you threaten my father? You actually dare to threaten my father?" He pressed up with his thumb, hooking it in directly beneath the corner of her jaw. He wanted nothing more than to tighten his grip and crush the life from her, but somehow he resisted that desire. "Understand this: if *he* dies, you die. If *I* die, you die."

A metal hand dropped on Phelan's right shoulder. "Let her go."

Phelan's shrugged his father's hand off. "Listen to me, Katrina, for these are not empty threats. I have a world full of Wolves who will stop at nothing to avenge me and my family." He watched her face slowly turn purple and her eyes begin to bug out. He could feel her pulse pound against his fingers and palm. The image of his mother floated before his mind's eye and he slowly began to constrict his grip.

His father's voice cut through the red rage seeping into his brain. "Phelan, release her."

Phelan dropped Katrina to her feet, but did nothing to help her as she staggered back against her couch.

Katrina rubbed at her throat and said nothing. She gave Phelan a venomous stare, but he looked past it and smiled at the bruises already purpling her pale neck.

Morgan nodded to her. "I believe our audience is concluded. Understand this, Katrina: as long as there exists a greater threat to the Inner Sphere than you, you are safe. Once the Clans are eliminated, justice will be done."

Katrina rubbed at her throat after the door closed behind the Kells. She wanted to scream in rage, but would never give them the satisfaction.

Or, maybe it was fear that stopped her.

Then fury overrode fear. Phelan Kell had touched her and could have killed her in an instant. All her carefully wrought plans would have died with her. Had Morgan not been there, she would no doubt be a corpse right now. And had Phelan known of her alliance with Vlad of the Wolves and the clear danger it presented to his own group of Wolves, she doubted Morgan would have been able to stop Phelan.

*And there is little chance Morgan would have wanted to.*

She was also angry with herself for having doubted her initial read of Morgan Kell and his reasons for forming the Arc-Royal Defense Cordon. Morgan had been insulting her, taunting her. He was in open rebellion, and the only reason he didn't try to topple her was because he wanted to save his shells and 'Mechs for the Clans. He and his son were a long-term threat to her power and survival. Though in the past she had thought it a good thing that Morgan had not died along with Melissa Steiner, the sooner she was rid of the Kells, the safer her world would be.

Fear again edged at the fury, but this time only seemed to feed it. Katrina knew better than to imagine that Morgan Kell would have dared speak to her so without evidence of her complicity in Melissa's assassination, but she also knew he did not have the resources to gather it. Her agent inside the Kell Hounds had reported neither an investigation of the assassination by the Hounds nor any rumors concerning it. But she also knew her source was not privy to confidential messages passing between Victor and Morgan Kell.

*Fool that he is, Morgan has told me that I'm sitting within the jaws of a trap, and has given me time to get myself free. If he and Victor won't strike until after the Clan threat is eliminated, that gives me plenty of time to discover what evidence they have and destroy it. While they're off saving the Inner Sphere, I will save myself.*

Inviting Morgan Kell into his wood-paneled office, Victor Davion did not think he had ever seen the mercenary commander looking so haggard. "Can I get you something to drink, Morgan?"

"Whiskey, if you have it. Straight up."

Victor took a bottle of Irish whiskey from the bottom drawer of his mahogany desk and set two glasses beside it. "Want a double? That's what I always have after speaking with my sister."

Morgan held up a finger. "One finger—just a taste to steady my nerves. Never use the stuff to fix problems because it doesn't." The older man smiled. "And you shouldn't have any since you're wringing wet from fencing. Dehydrated as you are, it'll go straight to your brain."

Victor poured Morgan a single finger of the amber liquid and slid the tumbler across the desk to him. He left his own glass empty.

Morgan smiled. "You can drink if you want to, Victor. You're a grown man."

"Not so grown that I don't respect wisdom when I hear it." Victor watched Morgan drain the glass. "How did it go with Katherine?"

"Better and worse than you predicted." Morgan set the glass back on the desktop. "She wanted to mend fences and ask me to keep the Hounds and Phelan's Wolves in the Lyran Alliance when the campaign began. I refused, told her I didn't trust her and when she asked why, I said I didn't know many murderers who were trustworthy."

Victor's jaw dropped open. "That's pretty direct."

"True. I know you asked me to do no more than hint that I knew she'd killed your mother and my wife, but Katrina wallows in such a sea of lies that I figured she'd miss subtle hints, or twist them until they looked like whatever she wanted them to be. If I'd been subtle she'd have gone right on believing I think you murdered your mother and my wife—and I couldn't stand her playing that line out with me." Morgan shrugged. "I thought the offensive was the stronger play."

"How did she react?"

"Tears, then threats. Impressive display." Morgan's dark eyes smoldered. "Phelan came close to breaking her neck."

"What? How close?"

"High-necked fashions just became the *in* thing here on Tharkad."

Victor nodded slowly. "I see. Thanks."

"Do you see, Victor?" Morgan frowned. "I was willing to let Katrina know we were suspicious of her because that's what you wanted, but are you sure that *is* what you want?"

"I don't think I have any choice, Morgan. Katherine—and I will never call her by my grandmother's name—is certainly self-absorbed, and now I need to make her more so. If this taskforce goes off after the Clans and I go with it, it means I have to leave Yvonne on the throne in New Avalon. I don't want Katherine casting her eyes at reuniting the Federated Commonwealth under her leadership while I'm gone."

Victor tugged at the buttons securing the collar of his fencing jacket. "Besides, she did a good job covering her tracks in the murder of my mother. Only she knows the mistakes she made, the loose ends that still have to be tacked down. If we make her think we already have evidence against her, she's going to have to move to destroy that evidence."

"And by watching her you might be able to snatch it out from beneath her grasp?"

"I have very good people working on doing just that."

"It's a dangerous game, Victor."

"It's not a game."

"But if your people fail, you'll never be able to prove she murdered Melissa."

Victor shrugged. "I can't prove that now. Katherine's ambition is hurting the Inner Sphere's attempt to destroy the Clans. Anything we can do to deflect her from that and set her up for a fall later is to the good. I wish there was another way, but I don't see one."

"Damnable thing is that neither do I." Morgan patted Victor on the shoulder with his organic hand. "The Kells will do all we can to support you. You know that."

"It's one of the reasons I actually believe we have a shot at succeeding." Victor gave Morgan a broad smile. "First we attend to the greatest good for the greatest number, *then,* and only then, will those who deserve special treatment get their due."

# ═ 13 ═

Victor put a smile on his face—one that was inviting but far from jocular—as he welcomed Thomas Marik to the palatial chalet at the edge of the Sigfried Glacier Reserve. "I'm very pleased you were able to visit me here, Captain-General."

Thomas stood in the middle of the oak-floored foyer with his hands clasped at his back and looked around the wood-framed stone building. "You really gave me no choice, did you? Granted the rustic charms of this place are all that Yvonne represented to Sherryl in enticing her to come here for the weekend, but using her to get to me—well, I should expect that from you, shouldn't I?"

*This is going to be tougher than I thought.* Victor nodded and preceded Thomas down the wooden steps into the chalet's great room. The whole south wall had been constructed floor to ceiling of glass, allowing them a full view of the glacier and the ski-slopes on the surrounding mountains. The mounted heads of various game animals hung on the walls, and a lattice-work of thick, rough-hewn wooden beams screened the lower part of the room from the interior of the high-pitched roof. On the east wall a fire roared in a massive fireplace while to the north stairs led up to a walkway and the corridors to the building's northern wings.

Victor waved Thomas to one of the overstuffed couches, then stopped and stood beneath the snarling visage of a dagger-toothed snowtiger. "I know that what I did to you and your family—and I accept full responsibility for my actions— was unthinkable. To you, and to most people, it was abominable. I agree, *now*, but I want to explain to you why I did what I did."

Thomas stood before the couch but did not sit. "You misjudge me mightily if you think explaining anything to me while you lurk beneath that predatory visage will be accepted at face value. Don't think of me as someone who can be stage-managed into believing you."

Victor looked up, frowned, and then moved aside. "Believe me, you're not being stage-managed here, I am. This little retreat was built by and for the favorite of Alessandro Steiner. You may remember him even though I don't—he died when I was but an infant. He was the Archon that my grandmother— the real Katrina Steiner—deposed. My sister Katherine granted me use of this chalet to remind me that, like Alessandro, I have been displaced by a Katrina Steiner."

Thomas's eyes narrowed. "If you knew this, why accept use of this place?"

"Because Katherine doesn't know that during my time at the Nagelring, I used this chalet rather extensively with friends, to study and to relax. For me, it has pleasant memories. The first time I came here, I decided to make the place my own, to redeem it from the treachery Alessandro had practiced. By letting me use it again, she has given me back something I have always seen as mine."

"Much as you anticipate she will one day return to you the Lyran Alliance." The Captain-General nodded slowly. "You're very arrogant or very foolish."

"Perhaps I'm both." Victor shrugged. "Or perhaps I only wish to lead others to think so. Please, sit. I don't expect what I'm going to tell you will redeem me in your eyes, but it may give you a better understanding of who and what I am."

"And what good will that do me?"

"It will let you decide how far you can and want to trust me."

Thomas nodded and sat.

Victor hugged his arms around himself, chilled despite the

thick, cable-knit sweater he was wearing. "The plan to create a double of your son originated with my father for two reasons. The first is something you may or may not know about: over thirty years ago Maximilian Liao almost succeeded in taking over the Federated Suns by creating a double of my father and placing him on my father's throne. My father was kidnapped—the whole affair might as well have been ripped from the pages of Dumas' *The Man in the Iron Mask*. Ironically enough it was an 'iron mask' that saved my father since only he could trigger the ignition sequence on his Battle-Master, using a secret code no impostor could know."

"So this was the inspiration your father had for seeking to substitute someone he controlled for my son."

Victor shook his head. "No, not at all. Liao's trick showed my father what the use of a double might do. I literally owe my life to it because a double for my mother made appearances in the Lyran Commonwealth while the real Melissa was with my father in the Federated Suns. My mother's double even saved the life of the first Katrina Steiner by foiling an assassination attempt against her. If not for that double, I would never have been conceived and the political landscape of the Inner Sphere would be quite different.

"Which brings me to my point about the use of a double to impersonate your son. You saw the move as something evil, but my intention was purely an attempt to buy time—a year, maybe two. I needed time to calm down the rebellion in the Isle of Skye. Your son did die a natural death. If I tried to hide that from you, it didn't change the truth that his life could not be saved."

Thomas nodded slowly. "Are you trying to say there was nothing wrong in what you did?"

"No, Captain-General, but neither did I intend to do harm. You've been sent all the treatment records for your son. Surely your own medical experts have told you we did everything we could."

"I do not think you murdered my son, Prince."

"Good." Victor hesitated for a moment, then sighed. *Here goes nothing.* "I know it was stupid to think anyone would believe that an individual substituted for another during a hospital stay—out of sight while recovering—could take the place of the real person and rise to power in his place. That was not my intention. That could never happen—it just wouldn't work—and you have to believe that I'm smart enough to know that."

The Captain-General was very good and covered his reaction almost perfectly. "I never would have thought you so foolish, Prince Victor." A momentary hitch in his voice and an increase in the number of times he blinked his eyes were the only clues Victor had that his gambit had paid off.

"I appreciate your kindness, Captain-General." Victor kept his voice even, though he wanted to shout to heaven with his joy. The only good thing that had come out of the debacle with Thomas' son Joshua was a series of genetic tests that proved conclusively that Thomas had fathered Joshua, but that the man was in no way related to Isis Marik. Isis had been born out of wedlock to one of Thomas Marik's mistresses during the time when everyone thought he had died in an assassination attempt. Thomas had stunned everyone by reappearing after disappearing for eighteen months. Though hideously scarred, he was otherwise ready to assume his duties as the heir to the Captain-Generalcy of the Free Worlds League.

To the best of Victor's knowledge only he, a handful of his advisors, the double, and personnel in ComStar knew the truth about the current Thomas Marik. Victor assumed the man had been substituted for the real Thomas Marik by ComStar's previous Primus, Myndo Waterly, in her attempt to stage a revolution that would have put the whole of the Inner Sphere under her control. Her plan had died with her, but Thomas' control of the Free Worlds League meant that its resurrection was a distinct possibility. The fact that the Word of Blake—a reactionary ComStar splinter group that still held to the mysticism that was the core of ComStar belief—had taken Terra over meant that Thomas' currently passive attitude might not always remain that way.

It occurred to Victor that one part of his assumptions about Thomas could be wrong. *What if he doesn't know he's not the real Thomas?* In reality it meant little—Victor's ploy of hinting at his knowledge would be for naught, but if Thomas needed such a thing to remind him that Victor could be a nasty foe, the situation was worse than even Victor thought it was. *I'll have to get Jerry Cranston to work out the implications of Thomas being a sleeper agent. If Word of Blake is waiting to activate him, a radical shift in policy could be necessary and we have to plan for that possibility.*

Refocusing his thoughts on his guest, Victor opened his hands. "I hope you understand a little more about why I did what I did. I have been trained as a warrior, and I have been forced to learn more about politics than I ever wanted to, but I realize that's all necessary if I'm to serve my people well. Even though I am a warrior, I want you to know I don't default to war in all situations. I'd rather win by cooperation than by combat."

"That's rather enlightened of you."

"I also have a desire to make certain we're all reading from the same datafile when it comes to the current situation." Victor looked up and studied Thomas' face without flinching. "I know you met with my sister recently."

"You refer to Katrina, yes?"

"Yes."

"Ah, I did meet with her, indeed." Thomas smiled quickly. "I've also met with Yvonne concerning some of the constitutional issues in reestablishing the Star League. You have done well to let her represent you in those sessions. She is very intelligent and keeps us on point with a certain ferocity."

"Yes, she is impressive." Victor smiled more broadly than he wanted to, but then decided it was no sin to show Thomas that he was proud of his sister. *If Thomas respects her, there's less chance he'll try any mischief while the taskforce is off fighting the Clans.* "However, I wished to speak with you about Katherine. I know you are friendly."

"It is an informal alliance of convenience, Prince Victor. She could no more afford going to war with me than I with her."

"I understand that." Victor turned and looked out at the glacier. "There are some things you should know about her, however. First among these is that she is capable of murder."

"You can't mean your mother's assassination. I was under the impression that the late Ryan Steiner's hand was involved there."

"SAFE's sources have gotten very good."

"Much of the information came from Solaris in the aftermath of Ryan's death. Had my intelligence apparatus actually improved much, I would have known earlier about my son."

"True. Concerning my sister, I was not referring to my mother's death, *though her role in it has not been fully determined.*"

"Really?"

"Really." Victor turned to face Thomas. "What I was

referring to was a trap she laid for me on Coventry. She allowed information to leak out that reduced the estimate of Clan troops on Coventry by *half*. Had I arrived with only the troops under my command, plus your Knights of the Inner Sphere, the Harloc Raiders, and the other troops Katherine gave me, I would have been woefully under-strength. Chances are excellent I would have been killed in the fighting."

Thomas remained silent as he considered Victor's words. "You defeated her plan by detouring to pick up two regiments of Kell Hounds."

"Yes, and that was more luck than anything else. Had we not gotten the help of Ragnar and made use of his insights about the ways of the Clans, all the troops on Coventry would have been badly mauled. To get at me she was willing to sacrifice the lives of thousands."

"You believe this, yet you let her govern the Lyran Alliance?"

"Do I have a choice?" Victor lowered his voice. "You and Sun-Tzu are poised to strike against me if I make a move toward reconsolidating my realm. I can't do that now anyway since the Clans still need to be the focus of our attentions. As long as Katherine can supply me with troops and munitions, I can't afford to depose her."

"But she could be a greater danger to the Inner Sphere than the Clans."

Victor pointed a finger at Thomas. "Understand this: she may be a threat to the Inner Sphere, but she is still my blood. Her people are my people. Any external attempt to remove her will meet with swift and terrible retribution."

Thomas frowned. "I was not suggesting military conquest, Victor, though I can see how you might interpret my remark as such. But I'm confused—if you aren't suggesting a joint operation against her, why tell me what you have?"

Victor drew in a deep breath, then let it out slowly. "You understand better than most that stability is vital right now, Thomas. You are an anchor of reason in the maelstrom of trying to remake the Star League and launch an assault on the Clans. You are an honorable man who is willing to believe the best of others until you are shown that your judgment is wrong. I need you to continue to be a stabilizing influence, but I don't want you to fall prey to Katherine. You will deal with her however you choose to deal, but I want you to be aware that beneath that exterior is a woman who is willing to kill to get what she wants."

"I see." Thomas nodded. "This from a man who hid the death of my son from me—a man who put an impostor in the boy's place, a man who probably murdered his own mother and certainly had Ryan Steiner assassinated."

"I won't deny, Thomas, that I have done some things wrong, and that I have blood on my hands. I'm not proud of everything I've done, but I accept responsibility for my actions." Victor folded his arms across his chest. "The trick is to avoid having my blood on someone else's hands. That's a trick you also want to master."

"Why give me lessons, Victor?"

"Because I believe you are someone I can trust. That's not something I can say of Sun-Tzu." Victor smiled grimly. "I expect to go off with the taskforce to take the war to the Clans. When I return home, I want to be able to recognize the Inner Sphere. With you alive I figure my chances of doing that are better than even. If you fall, well, the question is whether or not there will be any reason to return."

# ═══ 14 ═══

**Sigfried Glacier Reserve**
**Environs, Tharkad City**
**Tharkad**
**District of Donegal, Lyran Alliance**
**13 October 3058**

**N**aked save for the thick terry cloth towel draped across his loins, Victor lay back on the sauna's upper tier bench and gathered a folded towel beneath his head as a pillow. Closing his eyes he let the heat begin to sink through his flesh and began to catalog the various aches and pains he felt. *Chronologically I'm only twenty-eight years old, but I feel older than Alessandro ever did, I'll bet.*

The pains came in two varieties. The sharp stabbing pains came from bruises all over his body and two particularly tight hamstring muscles. He thought he'd stretched enough before the morning's fencing clinic with Tancred Sandoval, but his muscles were telling him that he had not. The bruises had come from the various places where points had been scored off him. The proliferation of them should have made Victor angry, but the fact was that most of those points had been won by Tancred. Kai and Hohiro were able to hit him, but not as much as he hit them. *Finally a sport I can win at.*

The overall aches came from the skiing he'd done in the afternoon. Knees, thighs, hips, shoulders, and back all hurt, and a lot more than he ever remembered from the aftermath of skiing trips in his cadet days at the Nagelring. *Sure, I was younger then, but not all that much younger.* He'd attacked the slopes with the same youthful abandon, but conceded that the slopes might have ended up winning the day.

Skiing had been fun, but running the media gauntlet had not been. Victor refused to have his security people clear the lift lines to the top, so he'd had to queue up to wait with everyone else. That gave the reporters time to shout questions at him from all sides. When he failed to respond, the holojournalists only made the questions nastier, hoping to provoke a response.

*In my younger days I would have reacted, too.* It had taken all the composure he could muster to ignore the questions and keep chatting with the other skiers. He realized that privacy was not really an option, but neither was spectacle the only alternative. He kept his temper under control, kept his guard up, and worked out his frustrations on the slopes.

*And even now, when I'm relaxing, I still have my guard up.* He resented having to wear a towel in the sauna, but knew he had to be careful lest some holojournalist manage to sneak in and digitize a picture of him lounging naked. *I don't want to even think about what kind of headline they'd use to cover the picture.*

Victor drew in a deep breath, trapping hot air in his lungs. The heat in the room had risen sufficiently to start him sweating. He could taste salt on his lips and feel the light burn of sweat in his eyes. He shifted the towel around so one end lay between his knees, then used the other end to dab at the sweat in his eyes. He ran it down his chest, soaking off the perspiration there, then flipped the end away, leaving it covering him like the front half of a loincloth.

There had been positive points to the day. He and Omi had managed to share part of a run down the mountain on one of the easier slopes. Though she and her family were staying at one of the chalet's guest houses, Victor had seen very little of her, so the run was welcome time spent together. Strictly a beginner, Omi took to skiing with enthusiasm and a lot of good humor. Victor recalled her going down in thick powder snow, then coming up with her face covered in white. She brushed the snow away with a laugh, and Victor couldn't think when he'd ever seen her look more beautiful.

At another point, when he waited on line for the chair lift, a reporter asked a barbed question about Omi and his relationship with her. Even before Victor had a chance to consider an answer, a man stabbed his skis and poles into the snow, and stalked out toward the reporter.

"Have you no shame?" he asked angrily. "Have you no decency? This man has the toughest job in all of the Inner Sphere and you're asking after his love life? Don't you realize that what he does on his own time is of absolutely no interest to anyone with enough neurons to form a synapse? The measure of a man is not in who he dates or what he says, but what he does. He kicked the Falcons off Coventry and rescued Lady Omi's brother from the Clans at Teniente. The latter's enough to make them friends, and the former means you should have more respect for him."

The man's spirited defense prompted applause and cat-calls from the others in line, bringing a smile to Victor's face. He tried to thank the man, offering to pay for his skiing, offering him dinner, but the man refused. "Look, Highness, if not for you and your father and your mother, we'd all be Clanners now. I appreciate the offer of a free dinner, but the fact is you've made certain I can be free to have dinner. Defending you here was the least I could do for you."

The man's remarks heartened Victor because they confirmed what he'd always hoped deep down. In the Lyran Alliance he did have a core of support that he could call upon in the future. *Katherine might be the media darling here, but the people don't believe everything the holovids tell them. This is good.*

Victor heard the door to the sauna open and felt the breeze as the hot air rushed out. The door closed quickly enough, but the chill sank in through the sheen of sweat on his skin. "You might want to nudge the heat up a bit, just to get rid of the cold."

"*Sumimasen,* Victor-*sama.* I did not mean to make you cold."

At the sound of her voice, Victor rolled up on his left side and, with his right hand, caught his towel and kept it in place. "Omi! What are you . . . ?"

With her black hair worn up and a white towel covering her from armpits to mid-thigh, she seated herself on the lowest bench opposite him. She moved carefully and precisely, yet casually as well. It almost seemed as if, for a moment, she had forgotten he was there and was alone in her own private sanctuary.

She brought her hands up so her slender fingers loosened the knot that held her towel closed. Watching the towel fall away as if in slow motion, Victor drank in every curve and shadow it revealed as it puddled on the bench. The black bathing suit Omi wore hidden beneath it was cut high at the hips and fastened with a red cord embracing her chest several centimeters beneath her collar bones. The thin material hugged her body like flesh, pulling taut over her flat stomach as she lay back.

Victor stared at her with his mouth hanging open. She had always been beautiful in his eyes, sensuous and sensual, but the times they had been together had always been formal and distancing. On the ski slopes, in her parka, hat, mittens, and quilted ski overalls, was the most casually he had seen her dressed. Neither that outfit, nor any of the others he'd seen her wear hinted at such raw, languid sexuality. Her long legs, the gentle swell of her breasts, that perfect face, and the first golden glistening of perspiration on her flesh—Victor could feel desire for her rising in him.

He sat up and rearranged his towel. "Omi, what are you doing here?"

"Enjoying the sauna." She gathered up her towel and wadded it into a pillow. "It was recommended that I might take a sauna bath after skiing—by Duchess Kym Hasek-Davion, I believe. Since my father, brother, and a number of their military advisors are using the one in our building, I came to the main building. If you want me to leave . . ."

"No, no." Victor held his hands up. "No, it's just that, well, I would not think your father . . ."

"My father knows I am meeting with you. There are things we must discuss."

Victor arched an eyebrow at her. "Your father knows you are here, like this, with me?"

"My father is very busy. Details of no importance are of no importance." Omi opened her eyes and looked at him. "Please, Victor, relax."

"You don't make that easy, Omi." Victor rubbed his left hand across his chest, smearing blond chest-hair into bar dexter. "I've, ah, I've never seen you so . . ."

"Nor have I you, except in my dreams." She blushed. "Forgive me, Victor, for indulging myself without considering your feelings. I am being selfish."

"Don't, Omi. You're not doing anything wrong."

"I know that. I believe it." She closed her eyes and crossed her arms behind her head. "In the time since you and I were together, on Arc-Royal, I have traveled much, as befits my position as one of my father's aides. I was on Solaris to watch Kai defend his title. I have traveled throughout the Combine, I have been to Northwind and other worlds. In all these times and places I have watched others and how they deal with the feelings you and I share. Customs differ, methods for displaying affection differ, but no matter where I go, the gulf that separates us is the sort of thing people see as tragic."

Despite the heat in the room, Victor felt a chill run down his spine. What the two of them were doing right then—sharing a sauna—would have been seen as laughably quaint and sedate on the vast majority of worlds of the Inner Sphere. There were also fundamentalist sects who would have seen it as cause for eternal damnation, but most other people would consider such an encounter completely unremarkable. *Except most other people are not the daughter of the Coordinator and the First Prince of the Federated Commonwealth.*

Omi continued. "All the time since we have been apart I have remembered kissing you and how that made me feel inside. I remember dancing with you, feeling your hand against my back. I remember the press of my body against yours, feeling your breath on my neck and inhaling the scent of you. At the time I did not want to part from you, but to stay with you forever, and since then I've often wished to trade a piece of my soul for just a few more seconds with you."

Hearing the melancholy tones in her soft voice, Victor wanted to spring up and cross to her side. He wanted to sit beside her and smother her mouth with kisses. And he would have except he knew it would not stop there. He wanted her fiercely, but to surrender to his desires would alter forever his relationship with Theodore Kurita, Hohiro, and Omi, destroying friendships and perhaps even shattering the foundation of the new Star League.

"Please, Omi, I beg of you, stop." Victor knotted his hands into fists and slammed his left one against the bench. The pain arched up his arm and brought him some clarity of mind. "Believe me when I tell you that I've thought the same thoughts, had the same dreams. I've relived all our time together and woven it into countless fantasies. I want to reach out to you, to touch you, to feel you next to me, but we cannot. Not here, not now."

"I know."

"Then why come here?"

Her blue eyes opened and sparkled. "New memories for new dreams."

Victor sat back against the sauna's wall and laughed. "Yet another reason I love you, Omi Kurita. Some people barely dare to dream, but you dare to plan for your dreams."

"Plan for *our* dreams, Victor. Were this just for me alone, I would not be so bold."

"*Domo arigato,* Omi-*sama.* I am in your debt. Yet again." Victor gave her a broad smile. "It occurs to me that if your father knows we are meeting, what does he think is its purpose?"

The serenity on Omi's face vanished. "You are perhaps aware that there was an attempt on my father's life a few months ago?"

Victor frowned. "My sources indicated that Subhash Indrahar has dropped out of sight, but we'd heard no rumors of an assassination attempt against your father."

Omi was silent for a moment. "Subhash Indrahar gave his life to help save my father."

Victor shifted his shoulders uneasily. "Indrahar's devotion to your family was well known. His sacrifice does not come as a surprise, nor as a total tragedy, from the FedCom point of view. We've known of the existence of reactionary elements opposed to the changes your father is making in the Combine, and Indrahar must have known who they were. They're the only ones with the motive to try to kill your father, and they would have had to be fairly powerful. All in all, the math is pretty simple when you look at it that way."

"Only to a gifted mathematician is it simple." Omi sat up and crossed her ankles. "My father is fairly certain that when what we are deciding here gets announced, the rumors will begin to fly. He suspects that the use of the Combine as a staging area will become translated into an attempt by you to make certain any Clan reprisals come against the Combine instead of your sister's realm."

"That's a novel idea." Victor sighed. "I expect the media here to suggest I'm abandoning the Lyran Alliance and stripping it of troops. Ditto the press in the Federated Commonwealth. They'll castigate me for using our troops to win

Combine worlds back from the Clans or exhort me to take those worlds in the name of the Federated Commonwealth. I'm sure your father would love that idea."

"He trusts you, Victor, to keep your word."

"Just make sure he never asks me to promise never to see you again."

"I do not think that will be a problem." Omi smiled easily. "My father has several plans in mind to fight the reactionary element in the Combine, but they will require your cooperation."

"Details?"

"I have many to share with you, but not here." She stretched and Victor's heart caught in his throat. "Perhaps I could explain his thoughts over dinner?"

"You've read my mind." Victor nodded toward the door. "You can shower and change in any of the northeast wing's guest suites. That will give me enough time to arrange for dinner—a dinner from which we can weave a legion of dreams."

# === 15 ===

Feeling drained and as weak as a puppy, Vladimir Ward of the Wolves pulled himself up into a half-sitting position and tucked a pillow between himself and the bed's headboard. He tugged at the sheet, teasing it up over his right leg so he could soak up the runnels of sweat pouring down his face and chest. His hand fell limply across his chest and his eyes closed. He felt the soporific aftermath of sex start to tug him toward sleep, but he refused to give in to it.

His body, sated and exhausted, allowed his mind to wander, and he found himself thinking about things that had never occurred to him before. Because all breeding within the Clans' warrior caste was conducted artificially, the linkage between coupling and procreation did not exist. Carnal pleasure became a gift shared between friends, a means of celebration, and even a form of competition where no one lost. He knew that between members of the lower castes sexual intercourse was loaded with myriad other meanings and shadings, but he had never thought much about that one way or the other. He lived as a warrior should and that was all that mattered.

Coupling with comrades was one thing, but love was not part of it. Love was something for the lower castes—and the misguided denizens of the Inner Sphere—and Vlad knew they used the word to cover a vast range of affinities. Warriors, on the other hand, valued friendship and camaraderie, but the exclusivity that seemed to accompany *love* would have spawned jealousy and rivalry. Both were destructive to military discipline and order, and those were especially honored by the warriors of the ruling caste.

Vlad recalled a time when one of his former sibmates—a young woman he had known since infancy—had confessed that she had fallen in love with someone. The experience had confused her terribly, a confusion made even worse by the fact that she had fallen in love with the bondsman Phelan Kell. Ranna had come to Vlad seeking guidance, and her need for reassurance had landed them in bed together.

At the time he had not understood what she was going through or why she began to avoid him later. *She came to believe she had betrayed Phelan with me.* That realization had come before Vlad ever met the woman he believed he loved, but until now, until he had coupled with someone other than the woman he loved, he could not fully grasp what Ranna had felt. He had dismissed her feelings as a mental aberration, but now he knew it was something more than that.

In Katrina Steiner he had found a woman for whom he ached. It was so much more than physical attraction and lust, though that component could not be ignored. As he spoke with her, spent time with her, he felt a unity of spirit that he had only previously known with other warriors. He knew he should have reviled her because she was not a warrior in any way, shape, or form, yet her internal strength burned as brightly as his did. It felt as if he had discovered a part of himself that he had not known was missing.

The pang of fear trickling through his guts surprised him. *The pain of betrayal is the fear of losing the one who has been betrayed.* He could intellectualize the emotion, dissect it, and analyze it, but somehow that did not drain it of its power. He was afraid of losing Katrina over an incident that, among the Clans, would pass without comment. *Yet she would see it as betrayal, hence I fear I have betrayed her. Very interesting.*

Vlad glanced over toward the entrance to the bathroom. The sound of water running in the shower cut off, then the shower stall door clicked open. He heard the gentle rasp of a towel being drawn from the rack, then the lights in the bathroom went out.

The woman who emerged into the room's half-light used the towel to dry her hair. Droplets of water still glistened on the flesh of her long legs and pert breasts. Vlad could see the shadowed tracery of her ribs and watched muscles move with fluid power as she approached the bed. His body recalled moving with and against her, prompting a smile to creep across his lips.

Marthe Pryde tossed the towel back over her shoulder, swept black hair out of her face with her right hand, then stretched herself out on the bed beside him. She sighed contentedly, then rested her chin on her arms and looked up at him. "When you invited me to meet with you and discuss our situations, this was not what you expected to happen, *quineg*?"

"Neg. I find no cause to complain, but this was unexpected."

Marthe smiled slyly. "Good. I think it is best if you remember you can be taken by surprise."

"You may have sprung the ambush, Marthe Pryde, but I was under the impression I gave as good as I got." Vlad rolled over onto his right flank and rested his head on his right hand. "Were all surprise attacks resolved to this level of satisfaction, I might willingly seek them out."

"Ah, but the resolution is always part of the surprise." She closed her eyes for a moment. "And this was a very pleasant one. You Wolves can be quite inventive."

"And you Falcons can be quite artful in the use of traditional methods." Vlad allowed himself to laugh lightly. "Of course, news of this alliance would shock our followers."

"Less them, I think, than our colleagues in the Grand Council." Marthe frowned slightly. "I cannot believe none of them had the good grace to die as they tested out to be considered warriors again."

"Agreed. I was particularly impressed at the performance of the two Nova Cat Khans. They are both ancient, yet both won stunning victories over their opponents."

"It was almost as if they knew what the others were going to do before they did it. The Nova Cats have long spouted nonsense about their *visions* of the future. I have never believed any of it, but prescience would explain how well they did."

"Prescience or orchestration." Vlad's brow wrinkled in a

frown. "I suspect that is how the Ice Hellions' Taney won his contest. Either he choreographed the fight or is one of the luckiest men alive."

"I would favor luck over planning because Taney has never displayed much in the way of forethought." Marthe levered herself up on her elbows. "He is trusting in his luck as he campaigns for ilKhan. He does not realize that your comments about needing a leader who was tested on Tukayyid killed his chances of becoming ilKhan. You will easily defeat him when it comes to a vote."

"You think *I* mean to become ilKhan?"

"I believe your election would be premature." Marthe bobbed her head once. "You do not have the seasoning needed to be an effective ilKhan."

"I concur."

"You do?"

"Completely. I am not afraid of shouldering the responsibility that would be thrust upon me, but I do fear failure."

Marthe hesitated for a moment, then nodded. "And you feel you would fail in the conquest of the Inner Sphere?"

"No, there is no spectre of failure there." Vlad smiled easily. "What I fear is a failure when it comes to leading the Clans. Think about how the Clans are aligned right now: We have four divisions: Crusaders and Wardens, then Invading Clans and the Home Clans. Weakest of all are the Home Wardens, followed by the Invading Wardens. The true power struggle is between the Crusader factions, with the Home Crusaders determined to step to the fore. While your assessment of my comments in the Grand Council was pleasant, I think it was less than wholly accurate."

"Perhaps." Marthe shrugged. "I do not see Taney and the Home Crusaders being able to gather much power to oppose any other ilKhan candidate."

"Taney and the Home Crusaders are not wholly stupid. They are agitating among the young warriors in the Home Clans to get them to put pressure on their leadership."

Marthe nodded solemnly. "Ah, this is why there has been so much delay and insistence upon all the testing and Bloodname contests. They want to be able to pack the Clan Councils with young warriors who are looking forward to winning glory in a renewed invasion."

Vlad smiled. "Yes. It is the same technique that Marialle Radick and I used to precipitate the leadership crisis in the

Wolf Clan. We used the spectre of the truce to make people afraid they would never have a chance to prove themselves. The Home Crusaders are using the spectre of being frozen out of the renewed invasion to do much the same thing."

Her eyes narrowed. "This explains a great deal. Like you, I have spent much time here on Strana Mechty overseeing Bloodname contests. From the newly Bloodnamed warriors I have been hearing anti-Smoke Jaguar sentiment by the bucketful. Taney and the others see the Smoke Jaguars as likely leading the new invasion."

"Appropriate, *quiaff,* since Leo Showers of the Smoke Jaguars was the invasion's first ilKhan."

"Aff, especially since your comments in the Grand Council seemed to anoint Lincoln Osis as the next likely ilKhan."

"Noticed that, did you?"

"You could not have been more obvious."

"Thank you." Vlad traced a finger across the sheets, making nonsense symbols out of the wrinkles. "The divisions in the Clans mean that whoever becomes ilKhan—Osis or Taney or anyone else—will be leading a force that is fragmented. The Home Crusaders hate the rest of us for our successes, and they fear us because of them. The Wardens don't like Crusaders and will be very hesitant to do anything that will contribute to our continuing success. The Smoke Jaguars, seeing themselves as the strongest of the Invading Crusaders, will push hard to finish off the Draconis Combine *and* push on to Terra. Even if another Clan takes Terra, having the Combine as a vassal state will make the Smoke Jaguars a force to be reckoned with."

"Your analysis seems flawless." Marthe extended her hands, touching his chest as she stretched. Drawing one arm under her chin again, she asked, "So what do you see as a viable course of action in all this?"

"Several things need to happen." Vlad raised a finger. "First the Smoke Jaguars must be humbled. We accomplish this by engineering Lincoln Osis' election as ilKhan. In that position he will try to push the Jaguars ahead, but he is in a very poor position to do so. The Ghost Bears are Wardens, so they will offer him no quarter if the Inner Sphere fights back. If the Jade Falcons and Wolves do little or nothing on our front, we allow the Inner Sphere to shift troops around to deal with the Jaguars."

"What about the Nova Cats?"

"We have no way of knowing what they will do, but there has been fighting between them and the Smoke Jaguars, so I do not imagine they will support Osis' war. The Inner Sphere *must* react to renewed hostilities, and the Smoke Jaguars are tactically primitive enough that they can be defeated."

Marthe smiled. "If Osis' offensive results in a loss of worlds, he proves he is no leader."

"True. More important, losses will mean that the Home Clans will feel threatened. That should help unify the Clans—a unity that Osis won't have since the Home Clans will be frozen out of his renewed invasion."

"How do you figure that?"

"Where will they come in? You and I will not surrender any of our worlds to them. The Ghost Bears will not allow them in, so the only choice is for Osis to provide them an attacking vector through his occupation zone. He will not do that, nor will he allow them to attack beyond the scope of the original attack vectors because that would allow them to go against areas that have not been built up to repel an attack."

"Though that would be the wisest plan."

"Agreed, but he is viewing the invasion as a contest with a prize at the end, not as a military action with the goal of destroying the Inner Sphere. His lack of foresight means that instead of drawing upon the strength of the Clans united, he looks to win a contest that will give him a unity and loyalty he would be better off earning."

Marthe nodded. "So, by giving Osis what he wants, we allow him to destroy himself and his Clan."

"Correct. And when it comes time to replace him and choose a new leader for the Clans, only two candidates will fulfill the job description."

"You and me."

Vlad nodded. "You and me. I know which of us I would choose, but, ultimately that choice will not matter."

"No?"

"No." Vlad smiled coldly. "When the true conquest of the Inner Sphere is resumed, there will be more than enough glory for both of us and enough power to be won to sate even the most avaricious dreams either of us had ever had."

**Capellan Cultural Center, The Triad**
**Tharkad City, Tharkad**
**District of Donegal, Lyran Alliance**
**5 November 3058**

**K**atrina Steiner found the office Sun-Tzu had appropriated at the Capellan Cultural Center far too dark for her tastes. Dim lighting deepened the hues of the teak and mahogany furnishings. Though pinpoint spots did brightly illuminate many of the wonderful rice-paper paintings hung on the walls or the delightfully delicate jade carvings sitting atop pedestals, their light did not extend much beyond the treasures they showed off.

Katrina knew exactly what sort of emotion the display was designed to inspire. *People feel humbled when surrounded by such antiquity and beauty. The treasures are links back to Terra, the womb of all humanity, and I am meant to be impressed. The link to Terra also suggests a legitimacy of Liao claims concerning leadership and supremacy in what was once the Star League.* She allowed herself to smile. *However, I can render planets uninhabitable with the stroke of a pen. I am not easily impressed.*

Sun-Tzu uncoiled himself from the chair he'd been using. The snarling tigers worked into his gold silk jacket matched the carved tigers forming either edge of the chair's back. The chair next to his, which clearly was meant for her, showed similar fine craftsmanship, though the creatures used to decorate it were peacocks. Katrina wondered if that was some sort of slight or meant to honor her.

Sun-Tzu towered above her and offered her his hand. "I am most honored by your acceptance of my invitation to visit me."

Katrina shook his hand briefly, then clasped her hands at the small of her back. "Is there a reason, Chancellor, that you thought I would not accept?"

He smiled and waved her to the peacock chair. "As I last recall, you were somewhat put out by my conquest of Northwind."

"Conquest?" She forced a smile to cover her quick flash of anger. Sun-Tzu had moved to take worlds that she had declared as part of her Lyran Alliance. That proclamation had been more to annoy her brother than anything else, though Northwind *was* a prize she wished she had kept. The famed mercenaries, the Northwind Highlanders, made their home there and being able to add them to one's army was far from a bad thing.

"As I recall, Chancellor, you gave the world to the Highlanders—a world they would have taken and could have held apart from your Confederation. Your control over them is nominal."

"Ah, yes, much like your control over Colonel Kell and his Kell Hounds."

Katrina seated herself and crossed her legs. Her pale gray skirt rose enough to permit a view of the gray leather boots encasing her legs to the knee. "Were there no disappointments in life, we would all be bored. Your claim on Northwind was not to my liking, but I hardly see it as justifying enmity between us. In fact, I believe I am in your debt."

Sun-Tzu's jade eyes widened. "In my debt? How did I manage that?"

"Your attack on Morgan Kell in the opening session pleased me. Morgan's presence will, in the long term, prove useful, but at the time it was an insult to me, propagated by my brother."

The Chancellor nodded. "Victor is akin to a fish bone in the throat: small but difficult to ignore, and potentially fatal."

"I can see how you formed that opinion of him." Katrina sighed. "He has his uses, however. The trick is making certain that the throat he sticks in is not your own. In this case, I think the Clans will choke on him, and they're welcome to him."

Sun-Tzu frowned. "You really think Victor would consent to lead the taskforce?"

"Consent? He sees it as his destiny. Why else does he have Yvonne here? She's getting on-the-job training so she can take his place running the Federated Commonwealth while he's gone." She laughed lightly. "The difficult job would be in keeping Victor here. And, face it, no one else is better suited to leading the taskforce."

"No?"

"Who would do it? You?" Her laughter came a bit more quickly. "The Precentor Martial is too old, Hohiro Kurita is valiant, but his record against the Clans is not very good. Kai doesn't have the political standing either, while the rest of the leaders are too old or not suited to waging warfare. No, Victor will be the leader. Nothing you or I could do would change that."

"Good." Sun-Tzu nodded solemnly. "I will find it easier to rest if your brother is off fighting the Clans and Kai is with him."

Katrina sat back and watched Sun-Tzu through half-closed eyes. The Sun-Tzu she had met or communicated with previously had always seemed a bit more off balance than the man seated across from her. His hatred for Kai and Victor was legendary and had prompted occasional tirades that could carry on for tens of minutes in the middle of an otherwise mundane message. *Irrationality was his shield. Why is he letting it slip now, with me?*

"Chancellor, you surprise me. Usually the mention of my brother or Kai seems to inspire you to apoplexy."

"A tiger's stripes, Archon. Protective coloration. My realm is tiny, and many dismiss it because they believe I have inherited my family's madness." Sun-Tzu shrugged. "If I am underestimated because of this, then I have an advantage over others."

"Why let me know you've been playing us all for fools?"

"It is a calculated risk. Many take you to be a social butterfly who is ruling by force of personality alone, but I do not believe that."

"No?"

"No. If that were true, my uncle never would have deigned to come and work for you. And, since you have not launched a major effort to destabilize my realm, I know that he does not have undue influence over you, suggesting there is more steel to your spine than I have previously imagined." Sun-Tzu opened his hands. "The both of us wear masks and that makes us allies of sorts."

"Allies? Why would I consider you an ally?"

"We share enemies, Archon. Your brother, for one, would love to wipe out both of our realms. Thomas Marik is also an enemy to each of us, and he uses us against each other. You have to worry about his realm falling to Isis and me. I have to worry that he will wed you and produce an heir to both of your realms."

"Thomas marry me?" Katrina barked out a laugh. "Never happen, I am afraid. Your worry is not for my child, but for the child of his consort. Sooner or later you know he will have one by her."

"Yes, that will be a problem." Sun-Tzu looked over at her. "Of course, I could marry you and Thomas would find himself trapped between us."

Sun-Tzu's comment caught Katrina by surprise. Part of her rebelled instantly, but she smothered the cutting snicker with which she wanted to answer that suggestion. She knew Sun-Tzu's lack of appeal to her came because of years of conditioning. Since childhood, the spawn of Maximilian Liao—with the exception of Candace—were usually demented monsters. Maximilian had tried to take the Federated Suns away from her father and that was justification enough to hate him and all of his progeny. There had even been hints that Candace might have been born of Maximilian's wife, but that any connection to Max himself ended there—all in an attempt to justify why she was suitable to maintain as an ally.

An alliance between Katrina and Sun-Tzu would create a significant power block within the Inner Sphere. It would allow for the immediate pacification of the Chaos March and strengthen the Lyran Alliance by bringing back into it more worlds than were lost to the Clans. Thomas Marik would be put in a difficult position by the marriage, but unable to conquer his enemies, he would reach an accommodation with them. Three realms would become, in effect, one, allowing battle lines between her and her brother to be cleanly drawn.

"You and I marrying, Sun-Tzu, would produce some advantages, but I am unconvinced that now is the time to consider such a thing." Katrina smiled. "You are, after all, engaged to Isis Marik."

"Indeed, I am, and have been for over six years." Sun-Tzu hissed out the time span as if it were a bitter poison. "Thomas has reneged on his word for setting a date, so the engagement is a sham. He holds his realm out like a carrot, but keeps hitting me with the stick. Granted, his support of my strike into the Sarna March was a taste of the carrot, but the fact of the matter is that he never intends me to have it."

"Ah, and what does the carrot think about this?"

"Isis?" Sun-Tzu's eyes narrowed. "I suspect she is another who hides behind a mask. I know she has ambitions, but I don't know what they are. I don't think she is working fist in glove with her father to engineer the absorption of my realm. If that were true we'd already be married *and* I'd have suffered an accident by now."

Katrina made no effort to hide her surprise. "You think she would have you murdered?"

"Remember, Thomas ascended to the throne of the Free Worlds League because of the assassination of his father. Victor came into his birthright the same way. Even you owe that assassin a debt of gratitude for your position. With Isis in place, my days could be numbered. Fortunately I have insurance: Kali."

"Ah, she would unleash a reign of terror to avenge you?"

"The trouble with her and her Thugee cultists is the difficulty of controlling them. When you let them loose, they are damnably effective and annoying." Sun-Tzu gave her a brief smile. "Not that you should consider yourself threatened."

"Of course not." Katrina returned the smile. "I'll just remember that if I want to kill you, what I must do is have you destroyed and evidence planted that points to another of my enemies."

"Crude but effective. Perhaps I'll have to fake my own death and employ that methodology."

"Feel free, as long as I am not implicated." Katrina flicked her thumbnail against the index finger nail. "What is it you would have of me, Sun-Tzu?"

"If not your hand in marriage, then your support in the political councils." Sun-Tzu pulled himself up to his full height. "I wish to be First Lord of the Star League."

Katrina kept her face an impassive mask. "As I recall from the discussions we've been having, we already have an agreement for a rotating leadership position. The terms will be for three years. Your turn will come quickly enough."

"I wish to be the initial First Lord." Sun-Tzu frowned. "I know the position is largely ceremonial as we have defined it, but the prestige is what I seek. It will be a tonic to my people—what I need to make the Capellan Confederation strong again. You don't know what it did for my nation to conquer worlds in the Chaos March. My people again feel strong and capable, not the defeated wretches that your father broke and my mother punished for breaking."

"When you say this will make your nation strong again, how do you envision projecting this strength?" Katrina's blue eyes became slits. "The Federated Commonwealth is *mine,* Sun-Tzu. If you were to even think of expanding across the 3025 border, I would have to destroy you."

"The 3025 border?" Sun-Tzu hesitated, then nodded. "This would seem to leave the St. Ives Compact outside your protective umbrella."

"I do not care about the Confederation's internal political problems. If you can subdue a rebellious part of your realm, so be it. I don't care."

"Then I can count on your support?"

Katrina thought for a moment. *If I support Sun-Tzu, I know Victor will oppose the suggestion with every fiber of his being. Theodore and Thomas will likely back Victor, meaning Sun-Tzu loses. I can make a speech about how their action is hardly appropriate, given the spirit of unity that recreating the Star League is supposed to engender. All of them will feel ashamed, leaving me as the only logical choice for First Lord.*

"I definitely could vote for you, Sun-Tzu. I would even be glad to nominate you."

"You are most kind."

"I am, Sun-Tzu. Do not forget that." Katrina smiled. "There will come a time when I ask for this kindness to be returned, or you will find yourself with your mask torn off, your eyes torn out, and your nation nothing but a memory."

# SMOKE JAGUAR

**SMOKE JAGUAR**

Richmond

Idlewind
Rockland
Schwartz
Tamby

Turtle Bay
Virentola
Bjarred

Brocchi's Cluster
Almunge
Sawyer

Nykvarn
40
Stapelfeld
Chupadero

Garstedt
Coudux
Kabah

Schuyler
Hanover

Savinsville
Jeanette
Lonaconing

Courchevel
Alberio
Bangor

Luzerne
Jeronimo
Matamoras

Byesville
Wolcott
McAlister

Labrea
Marshdale

Outer Volta
Hyner
Cheriton

Itabaiana
Maldonado
Tuscarawas

Juazerio
Teniente
Peshi
Ebensburg

Caripare
Irece
Meiacos
Unity

Yamarkov
Cyrenacia

Asgard
Kilmarnock

Kiamba
Mualang
Port Arthur
Kagoshima

Kanowit
Tarazed
Avon
Shimonoseki

Baruun Url
Luthien
Chatham

Tahn Lihn
Braunton
Leiston

Odabasi
Xingyang
Bicester
Corsica Nueva

**DRACONIS COMBINE**

Darius
Ogano
Yumesta

Arkab
Sakai

Paracale
Dover

Baldur
Dyfed

Otho
Tok Do
Shibukawa
Peaceck

○ SMOKE JAGUAR WORLD
● NOVA CAT WORLD
◍ SMOKE JAGUAR/NOVA CAT WORLD

# DRACONIS COMBINE BORDER

**Royal Court, The Triad**
**Tharkad City, Tharkad**
**District of Donegal, Lyran Alliance**
**14 November 3058**

**V**ictor Davion found it slightly disturbing that the Precentor Martial had yet to arrive for the afternoon review session of the planned assault on the Smoke Jaguars. Every member of the strategic planning committee had, at various times, been called away on official business, but Victor would have thought that finalizing the plan for the assault would have ranked as a number one priority. *I have a hard time imagining what he could find more important than this.*

Victor stood as a map of the Combine/Smoke Jaguar border glowed to life in the center of the room. "This is our last chance to review the plan and make certain it's airtight before it goes to the political session for ratification. If anyone has any objections at all, make them here and now because we won't have another chance for correction. You have to understand that."

Around the room the various other military leaders nodded their heads.

"Good. I also want to thank all of you and your staffs for working so hard and well on all this. The Inner Sphere hasn't seen an assault requiring this level of cooperation since Aleksandr Kerensky led the Star League Defense Force in overthrowing Stefan Amaris on Terra. This operation has to work, and it will work, but only because of the effort we've all put into it—and the effort our people will put into it in the field."

He moved from behind his desk and approached the floating hologram. "As we discussed, our operation is set up for five phases of attacks. The first wave rolls out with all the units bearing SLDF and Combine markings. The initial targets are five Jaguar worlds: Hyner, Port Arthur, Asgard, Tazared, and Kiamba. Additional units will move into Nova Cat worlds and take them, staging for the second wave. Yes, Senior-Colonel Wu, your question?"

Wu Kang Kuo pointed toward the map. "What assurances have we that the troops we move onto Nova Cat worlds will not be challenged and destroyed?"

Hohiro stood. "Our people are still in discussion with the Nova Cats, but they have issued preemptive batchalls that give us a clear picture of the number and quality of defenders they will use to keep us off those worlds. For all intents and purposes we will not be opposed."

Wu frowned. "But we still will be fighting?"

Phelan leaned forward over his desk. "After a manner of speaking, yes. In the past, when a deal for the exchange of technology or worlds has been negotiated between Khans, a preemptive batchall is issued. It results in a largely ceremonial fight—not that one is rigged, but one in which the outcome is fairly predictable. It is considered a way of preserving honor and respecting tradition while avoiding combat over things that really matter little."

Marshal Byran shook her head. "And what if they decide to betray us?"

"We'll know before planetfall whether or not they will be honoring their batchall." Phelan smiled. "We can decide to engage at that point or bring in reinforcements."

"What if they decide to ambush us?" Morgan Hasek-Davion's quick question preempted Marshal Byran's riposte to Phelan's remark. "What if they suck us in and take us down?"

Phelan greeted the question with a nod. "You realize that I cannot guarantee the Nova Cats will *not* betray us. The fact is, however, that for them to engage in such treachery they would have to act absolutely and completely against type. I'd sooner believe we might designate hospitals, churches, schools, and orphanages as military targets than that the Nova Cats will strike from hiding against us.

"The reasons go specifically to their very essence as Clan units. For them to strike from ambush that way, to deploy more troops than they offer in their batchall, would make them *dezgra*—disgraced. Treachery on the scale we're talking would result in sanctions against them and the possibility of absorption by another Clan. The Nova Cats are not strong enough to fend off a take-over, so this would be counterproductive for them."

Wu sat back. "Won't entering an alliance with the Inner Sphere also make them *dezgra*?"

"They won't really be entering into an alliance because we'll be taking control of their worlds through conquest. They will not lose honor in that sense, so they will not be *dezgra*. This is a very good thing because the possibility of disgrace is one of the things that will set off a negative reaction by them. Whatever we are asked to do to take these worlds, we must do it sincerely, or we could turn the Nova Cats against us." Phelan opened his hands. "Regardless of how we take these planets, the Nova Cats won't be loved by the rest of the Clans for how the campaign against them will go. It can only be that someone highly respected among them has had visions that are pushing them to do this—it's really the only logical explanation for their actions."

Morgan nodded. "You trust them?"

The Wolf Clan Khan nodded. "You're welcome to run my troops in on their worlds, if you want, though we'd prefer tangling with the Jaguars."

Victor looked around. "Other questions?" When he saw none he gave Doc Trevena a nod and the image shifted. "Our second phase has a wave jumping way out, leapfrogging the next logical line of worlds to hit those worlds further from our front. We should be pouncing on worlds the Jaguars leave either undefended or garrisoned only with second-line troops, while their first-line Clusters are digging in on our next logical targets. We'll be staging from some Nova Cat worlds, as well as Wolcott and Brocchi's Cluster, so we'll have support and strike deeper than they could have expected us to strike."

The image shifted in response to another nod from Victor. "The third phase will strike deeper into the occupation zone *and* bring up our reserves to pound the worlds we've bypassed. Sir Paul Masters, you have a question?"

The commander of the Knights of the Inner Sphere pointed at the map. "I understand how, within this entropy-based warfare doctrine, our plan forces the Clans to move around, and I certainly applaud it. I am, as yet, uncertain how we will get them to move where we want them to move. Were I a Smoke Jaguar commander, I would look to the strategy Scipio Africanus used against Hannibal and would strike deeper into the Inner Sphere. That would force us to react and blunt our advance."

"Agreed, which is why our strategic reserve will be in place to land where they land and attack them. We will be severing their supply lines, and the Combine has stepped up efforts to modernize defenses and make the worlds they might take very dangerous to hold. Recall that the Clans won't have ComStar to administer their worlds, so they'll have trouble holding what they take."

Hohiro nodded. "The Combine is well aware of the burden that might be thrust upon our people given that this strategy might be employed against us. We hope it will not be, of course, but it will be the duty of every citizen to resist and endure. They know this and will accept it, for the good of the Combine and the Inner Sphere."

"They may well have to endure more than we expected." The Precentor Martial's voice came low and solemn as he entered the chamber. "Forgive me for being late, but I was delayed by a matter of great importance." He adjusted the eye patch over his right eye as he came around toward the Federated Commonwealth's table. He handed Doc Trevena a holodisk.

"Please call up file XR1."

Victor turned to face the Precentor Martial. "What is it?"

"Our salvation or damnation, depending upon what we choose to believe about it." The Precentor Martial gestured at the new map burning in the center of the hall. "Ladies and Lords, I offer you the Exodus Road."

Victor looked at the map and at the bottom recognized the edge of the Inner Sphere where the Clans had conquered a wedge of worlds. A chain of golden stars rose from it like a lightning bolt, arcing toward the ceiling. It led off to a far distant star that coruscated brightly.

The Prince of the Federated Commonwealth blinked. *They*

*come from so far away, and are so different from us in their*
*mannerisms and culture. To save themselves from destruction*
*they fashioned their own traditions and mythology, drawing*
*their names from animals on the worlds they conquered and*
*their symbolism from the stars they relied on for life. They*
*remade themselves into the ultimate warriors and now we*
*have a route to one of the worlds that has given them life.*

With his hands clasped at the small of his back, Anastasius
Focht looked up at the star map. "I have people working to
match these stars to actual stars noted by astronomers so we
can determine the true locations of the way stations and final
destination, but this is a rough map of the route to the Smoke
Jaguar homeworld of Huntress. This is the wellspring of the
Smoke Jaguars' power. It is our ultimate goal."

"Good." Sharon Byran pounded a fist on her table. "Let's
forget all this piecemeal stuff and go straight for this
Huntress."

"Impossible." Victor shook his head. "There's too much
here we don't know about. We don't know how reliable this
information is."

Focht nodded. "I consider it ninety-nine percent reliable.
Any errors I would expect to be unintentional and easily cor-
rectable. As you may or may not know, ComStar began an
infiltration process of the Clans sometime back, and it
resulted in this information being delivered to us. In addition
to the Exodus Road, I also have updated files on the disposi-
tion of Smoke Jaguar troops in the Inner Sphere, including
tables of organization and equipment, supply inventories,
and the like. We have been handed the Smoke Jaguars on a
silver platter."

Victor folded his arms across his chest. "Is it one of your
people who is bringing us this information, or someone else?"

"It is a Clansman, one turned by my agent, who is the
source of this data."

"Why would he betray his Clan?"

"It is trite to suggest that everyone has his price, but the
fact is that our warrior had progressed within his Clan as far
as he could go. He was thirty and soon to be on the downhill
side of Clan life." Focht sighed. "He determined that the
leadership of the Smoke Jaguars was wrong about many
things and had betrayed the true intent of Nicholas
Kerensky, the founder of the Clans. He believes the evil represented by the Smoke Jaguars must be destroyed."

Victor winced. "He is to the Smoke Jaguars what the Word of Blake is to ComStar."

"An unfortunate analogy, but one that is apt."

Wu Kang Kuo looked up at the Precentor Martial. "What was the traitor's price?"

"He asked to be given a command so he could lead people into battle. I have offered him the command of my body-guard unit."

"That's not possible." Marshal Byran shook her head with disgust. "If we're going to run up that chain and destroy the Smoke Jaguars, we can't have someone with us who might change his mind and betray us. That strike has to come as a total surprise."

"I did not ask for your counsel before I made Trent the offer," the Precentor Martial said coldly, "nor do I regret that decision. The offer has been made and accepted. It was the condition of obtaining this information."

Victor scowled at Byran. "And don't be getting it into your head that we're going to launch some long-range knock-out punch on the Smoke Jaguars. We have our strategy and we'll stick to it. Knowing where they lair is useful and provides us with a goal, but hitting Huntress isn't going to do the job we need to do. No raid."

Morgan Hasek-Davion stood. "You're wrong, Victor."

"What?"

"You're wrong about the raid." Morgan gestured toward the hologram. "All of our planning doesn't change because we now have this, and the missions we've laid out should go forward, but there has always been one aspect of this whole thing that's bothered me. It goes back to entropy-based war-fare and the presentation Dr. Pondsmith gave on that first day. He noted that we have to 'shock' the other side before they will collapse."

"We *will* shock them. We're going to hit them hard, with full Regimental Combat Teams." Victor tried to keep the feeling of betrayal out of his voice, but did not wholly suc-ceed. "We're going to hit them very hard."

"But will it be hard enough?" Morgan leaned forward, posting his arms on the table. "When you analyze Clan war-fare at its most basic level, the underlying doctrine is always one of minimizing damage."

Sharon Byran laughed aloud. "You've lost it, Morgan. How can you say that?"

"I can say that because I've looked at what we're dealing with, thank you. Through the bidding process the Clans limit damage. They commit only the troops they want to commit. They play by rules that work fine when others play by them too, but those rules insulate the Clans from the true horror of war. This is not to say they aren't vicious and ruthless in war, but that they have found a way to compartmentalize the tragedy of it."

"Yes, exactly." Victor clapped his hands. "That's why we're taking the war to them and putting them on the defensive."

"Agreed, Victor, but if we play by their rules, all we do is *legitimize* their rules. We encourage them to see warfare as a game or contest. We may win a round, but they will always be there for the next round."

Focht narrowed his eye. "I thought, Marshal Hasek-Davion, that this was the reason we were planning to eliminate one whole Clan."

"True, Precentor Martial, but I don't think we've given adequate thought to what eliminate means. Paul Masters' allusion to Hannibal and the Punic Wars brought this fully to my mind. What I think we need is a strike at Huntress that is designed to raze it, much as Scipio Africanus razed Carthage. We would remind the Clans of the savagery of war and let them know we don't consider it a game."

Morgan bowed his head wearily for a moment, then looked up again. "I'll admit that, over the last thirty years, I've seen a lot of warfare, and I've hated every minute of it, but there are times when unleashing the full maelstrom is the only way to convince a foe that you aren't going to lie down and die. I think the Clans need that sort of lesson, and a strike at Huntress is the perfect opportunity to teach it to them."

Phelan Kell nodded in agreement. "Until you phrased it that way, Morgan, I had not really taken to heart the safety-zone aspects of the Clan doctrine of warfare. Even when a Clan is absorbed, its identity is preserved because of the breeding program. Natasha Kerensky carried in her a strain of Widowmaker blood—a Clan the Wolves had long ago absorbed."

"Fine, Phelan, but what about Morgan's other point?" Victor scowled heavily. "Is it going to take the razing of Huntress to shock the Smoke Jaguars?"

Phelan shrugged uneasily. "I think it is true that our assault could shock them and precipitate a collapse, but that will be on a world-by-world basis, not a Clan-wide basis. I do know that the one time a Clan was wiped out, as I mentioned before, the Clans still refuse to speak its name. I know that is supposed to be because of the offense that started the campaign against them. I also believe it is because of the sheer savagery of that pursuit. The unnamed Clan was slaughtered, man, woman, and child. I do not think anyone has pleasant memories of that war."

"Nor should they." Paul Masters shot to his feet. "I cannot believe you're even contemplating the slaughter of innocents."

Morgan straightened up. "I do not think that is necessary, Sir Paul. What I do believe we must do is raze the martial aspects of Huntress. We can turn it into an agrarian world that will support the people, but all traces of the warrior caste will be effaced. We will destroy their bases—replacing them with great smoking craters on the face of the planet. The only reminders of war will be the blackened ruins of anything military."

"And military prisoners? The wounded?"

Morgan's expression became impassive. "If they renounce their adherence to the warrior caste, they can live. If not, we try them for crimes against humanity and have them executed."

Color drained from Masters' face. "How can you say that?"

"I can say that because it is what *must* be done." Morgan opened his arms. "What did all of you expect we would have to do when we agreed and had our leaders agree that a Clan had to die? Did you expect some bit of Clan legislation that would change the name of the Smoke Jaguars to something else, thereby absolving them of any responsibility for what they have done? Have you forgotten what they did to Edo on Turtle Bay? Have you forgotten the fight for Luthien? Have you forgotten all the men and women who have died throughout the Inner Sphere because of the Clans?"

Masters shook his head. "Blood for blood is evil."

"This isn't about retribution, it's about deterrence." Morgan raked his fingers back through his long hair. "We want the invasion to end. We have to show the Clans that we can fight more efficiently and better than they can. We have to stun them, which is why we will wipe out a Clan. We now have the means to do that, through our assault here and an attack on Huntress. Between the two actions we will destroy a Clan *and* make our point with the others."

Victor held up a hand to forestall Paul Masters' follow-up

comment. "Even if we acknowledge that what you say is true, where do we get the troops to send?"

Morgan smiled. "You've got me in command of a strategic reserve of troops that includes some of the most elite units in the Inner Sphere. I propose we take half those units and head out for Huntress. We can't follow this route exactly, but I'm sure the Precentor Martial's people can use the information the Explorer Corps and other scouting missions have gathered to find us another path to Huntress. Because our reserve units will be staging within the Combine, we can use their monopoly on the media to continue to produce disinformation that will convince the Clans we're still there waiting to get into action while we make our way to Huntress."

Focht regarded Morgan carefully. "Which units would you take?"

"My First Kathil Uhlans, the Eridani Light Horse, the Northwind Highlanders, some of your Com Guards if you have them to spare—preferably your Invader unit—Marshal Byran's Eleventh Lyran Guards, the Second Sword of Light, one of the regiments from McCarron's Armored Cavalry, the Second St. Ives Lancers." Morgan smiled at Kai Allard-Liao. "I'd love to have you with me, Kai, but the First Lancers will have to be very visible to hold the Jaguars' interest."

Kai nodded. "I understand. If I weren't with Victor, the Clans might sense deception."

Morgan looked over at Paul Masters. "I'd also like to have your Knights of the Inner Sphere."

"Why? We're not the sort given to wholesale slaughter."

"Perhaps the taskforce will need a conscience. There's a line I don't want to cross and having you there to point it out will be very helpful."

"I could consent to filling that role."

"I would appreciate it." Morgan glanced past Victor toward Phelan. "I'd ask you to send people along, but I think this has to be an Inner Sphere taskforce. I don't fear betrayal by you, but . . ."

"I understand," Phelan smiled grimly. "We will also serve as a lightning rod for the Smoke Jaguars, so our staying here will keep them focused on the Inner Sphere."

Haakon Magnusson slowly stood. "You may have whichever of my units you require, Marshal Hasek-Davion."

"Thank you, Prince Haakon, but I would prefer it if your

troops were available to liberate your worlds. Pushing the Clans back in the area of the truce line is important enough a job that I dare not take away your strength. If you can spare advisors to liaise with my staff, that contribution I would welcome."

Victor scrubbed his hands over his face, not believing what he was hearing. *All of our careful planning has been overthrown by information from a Clan traitor. Some of the best units in the Inner Sphere will be sent out and away on a wild strike that may or may not succeed. If it does, it could cut our campaign in half. If it does not, much of the cream of Inner Sphere military might well be devoured hundreds of light years away from their homes. We will never know what happened to them, never have any record of what they did or how they died.*

He looked over at his cousin. "Morgan, you know this idea of a long strike is harebrained."

"No more so than the plan you advanced for attacking the Clans on Twycross eight years ago."

Victor felt a chill ripple down his spine. *If not for Kai's heroics, Twycross would have seen a lot of us killed.* "You're not going to have Kai with you if things go sour."

"Then if things go sour, I had best hope you and Kai arrive from this end of the Exodus Road." Morgan's expression softened, but a touch of fatigue tightened the flesh around his eyes. "This is a mission we have the means to accomplish, and the gain outweighs the risk. We *need* to do this, so we will."

Victor looked around and saw respectful nods of assent. His eyes narrowed, but he nodded along with the rest of them. "Then if we have to do it, let's make sure we do it right." He rolled up his sleeves. "We've got twenty-four hours to dot every i and cross every t before we can present this at the political session. Let's hope it surprises the Clans as much as it surprises the rest of us."

He took a deep breath and continued in a more sober tone. "We've got to do everything we can to make certain the Exodus Road doesn't turn out to be a one-way path to hell."

# ≡ 18 ≡

**Grand Ballroom, Royal Court**
**The Triad**
**Tharkad City, Tharkad**
**District of Donegal, Lyran Alliance**
**15 November 3058**

**K**atrina Steiner sat back in her chair as the Precentor Martial finished his briefing on the campaign against the Clans. The addition of the long strike against Huntress provided a hammer to pound the Smoke Jaguars against the anvil of the slow assault. *If it is successful, it could cut the campaign down, accomplishing in two or three years what could take seven or ten or more.*

Her eyes traced across the words scrolling up on her note-puter's screen, but she didn't really read Nondi Steiner's questions and protests about the operation. *I see Victor's hand in all this, so I know, for better or worse, that the operation will be viable. Victor is nothing if not an efficient little warrior.* The operation, as outlined, would be very effective in achieving its objectives: the destruction of the Smoke Jaguars and the cessation of the Clan War. *Any quibbles with it are going to be minor and largely confined to unit assignments and tactical objectives.*

Katrina found the proposed operation both exhilarating and bone-chilling. In it lay the seeds of salvation for her Lyran Alliance. Once the Smoke Jaguars had been driven from the Inner Sphere, the next phase would be to drive the rest of the Clans from worlds they had conquered. The taskforce would fall on the Ghost Bears, and she could unite with the Wolves to crush the Jade Falcons and Steel Vipers between them. Such an alliance would cost the Free Rasalhague Republic some worlds, but it would make her stronger than before, making having to listen to Magnusson's whining a fair price to pay for her gain.

What chilled her about the operation was the fact that she could not warn Vlad about its launching or objectives. Without knowing his location there was no way she could engineer for a message to be sent to him outlining the plan. She suspected he was on Strana Mechty, the Clan homeworld, but without coordinates for it, she could not have a message hyperpulsed to him. *And that assumes I could somehow get ComStar to send such a message blind and then forget they had done so.*

Her concern for him made her cautious, but she realized that the operation really was not much of a threat to the Wolves. Its objective—the destruction of the Smoke Jaguars—would actually benefit Vlad. *Did we not meet because I showed up at a Smoke Jaguar world that he had just finished raiding? My enemy is his enemy, which is why we are friends.* Eliminating the Smoke Jaguars as a power block would allow more power to flow to Vlad, which made the success of her long-range plans a lot more likely.

*Vlad can take care of himself. If he cannot see what's coming over the next several years, he's too stupid to be my partner in what is to follow.* Katrina closed her eyes for a moment and scratched at her forehead. *I have my own, more immediate threats to deal with here.*

She raised her hand and smiled when the Precentor Martial acknowledged her. "Thank you for the thorough briefing, Precentor Martial. All seems to be in order, though you do not mention any recommendations for who would lead the two phases of the assault. I assume you will lead the main assault, but who would you have commanding the long strike?"

"I assume that question is one that will have to be answered by this body." Focht pressed his hands to the top of the podium. "It would be my recommendation that Marshal Morgan Hasek-Davion be given command of the long strike. He has had plenty of experience fighting the Clans and organizing large operations like this. His first campaign, for those of us who were alive then, involved a long-range strike at a world well beyond the lines. He carried it off admirably well, with less planning and training than he will have for this operation."

Katrina slowly nodded as Focht listed out Morgan's qualifications, and in the back of her mind she supplemented them. *If Morgan is off leading this taskforce, he won't be around to support Victor. One more of Victor's backers will be gone. And the chances are very good that Morgan could be killed during the Huntress operation, permanently removing him from Victor's team. The losses of our father, mother, Galen Cox, and the retirement of Alex Mallory have all eroded Victor's support network. Only Hohiro, Omi, and Kai remain, yet none of them are as close to him as Morgan. Remove him from the picture and Victor will be dancing on a highwire without a net.*

"Is Marshal Hasek-Davion willing to undertake this task?"

Morgan rose from a seat beside Victor. "I am, Archon, provided no better candidate comes forward."

Theodore Kurita smiled across the room at Morgan. "Short of Hanse Davion or my father rising from the grave, I can think of no one who would be more suitable."

Victor nodded. "If the job is going to be done right, Morgan is the man to do it."

Paul Masters leaned over and made a comment to Thomas Marik, who then nodded and spoke. "I believe this choice is acceptable."

Sun-Tzu Liao gestured broadly. "Far be it from me to protest the absence of the leader of the Capellan March. Having that dagger removed from my throat is a welcome thing."

Candace Liao and Prince Haakon Magnusson likewise agreed to Marshal Hasek-Davion as leader of the taskforce, leaving Katrina last to vote. "Any protest or dissent I would offer would mean nothing. I wonder, though, if his absence won't be noted by the Clans and I wonder if his expertise might not be better used in the grand assault."

Focht smiled. "We have ways of making it seem as if Marshal Hasek-Davion is still very much present in the Inner Sphere, so that should not concern you. As for the loss of his experience and judgment, this I regret as well. Still, I think it is better we have a man of his vision in a position where that vision is required than to have him here where he will be underutilized."

"Good points, Precentor. I agree to his selection." Katrina smiled graciously. "And I take it that you will be leading the major assault force?"

Focht clasped his hands at the small of his back. "That, too, is a decision to be made by this body. I would willingly accept that duty, but you must remember that I am an old man. While I would like to think I am weathering the aging process well, the truth is that I am slowing down. I will rely heavily upon my subordinate officers, as I already have." He glanced over at Victor Davion. "You should know that I will appoint as my deputy Prince Victor Ian Steiner-Davion."

Thomas Marik sat forward. "Will Prince Davion be able to acquit his duties? He is the leader of the Federated Commonwealth. Surely he cannot abandon his realm during the time it will take to prosecute this campaign."

Victor cleared his voice. "I have already begun to make provisions for the running of my state in my absence. My sister Yvonne will serve as Regent. She has my full confidence, as do her advisors. If there is a true emergency, I can be recalled, of course, but I do not think anyone would see wisdom in taking advantage of my realm while we're off destroying the Clans."

Sun-Tzu flicked a hand against the screen of his noteputer. "Given the equipment and personnel you've requisitioned from all of us for your war, none of us would have the means to attack you while you fight the Clans."

"Nice of you to say, Chancellor, but I think you're ingenious enough to find a way to cause me trouble, if that is your desire." Victor looked around. "I am more than willing to serve as the Precentor Martial's deputy. In many ways I feel as if I have trained all my life for this task and if the one thing I do is to successfully acquit it, I can die a happy man."

Katrina glanced at her icy white fingernails, then looked up. "I must echo the words my brother has spoken. Though we have had our differences in the past, in this we are united: he is the person best suited to aid the Precentor Martial in taking the war to the Clans. He has my full support in this."

She ignored both the astonished look on Victor's face and the hisses from Nondi. Her reasoning had been simple and certain: the more Victor fought, the better his chances of dying. She half expected a pang of guilt there, but was not surprised when she felt none. *Victor believes he is playing the long game—looking toward the future and taking actions to make that future the best it could possibly be. His problem is that he's only looking at the death of the Smoke Jaguars. I am looking beyond.*

Sun-Tzu Liao wore the happy expression of the dog who'd just been slipped off lead. "Godspeed you, Victor. I choose the Precentor Martial and his aide to lead the taskforce."

Theodore Kurita nodded. "The Precentor Martial and Prince Victor have our full confidence."

Candace Liao smiled. "I am willing to put the lives of my warriors in their hands."

Thomas Marik and Haakon Magnusson also agreed to let the Precentor Martial lead the assault force against the Clans.

Focht bowed his head. "I thank you for your vote of confidence in us. This war will be savage and brutal and long, but I believe we have the means to win it. Now, the next step is to ratify the plan."

Katrina stood. "Given that we have agreed to the choices of leadership, I would suggest we adopt the plan presented by acclamation."

"I second the motion," said Haakon Magnusson.

The Precentor Martial nodded. "Seeing no opposition, the operational plan for the Clan War is adopted. I believe, since we have agreed to the draft of the Star League Constitution, what remains is for the final copies of that Constitution to be drawn up and signed."

Katrina frowned. "I believe we have to select a First Lord for the Star League, do we not?"

Prince Haakon Magnusson stood. "The constitution calls for each member of the First Council to serve a three-year term as the First Lord, with the succession being determined by lot."

"I know that. I've read the document." Katrina smiled. "The constitution also provides that with a two-thirds vote of the First Council, the lot choice can be voided and another candidate can be installed as First Lord. It seems to me that if we are reforming the Star League specifically to give us a foundation for taking the war to the Clans, then we ought to exercise due consideration in choosing a leader. Selecting our leader by lot would no doubt seem rather careless and cavalier to the Clans."

"Archon Katrina has an excellent point." Thomas Marik

tapped his tabletop with a finger. "While I would hope the Star League will prove to be more than a sham or a means for facilitating a military operation, the fact is that appearances must be maintained. We agreed to reform the Star League to provide our troops a legitimate reason for going to war against the Clans."

Katrina returned to her chair and tried to suppress her smile. *We've agreed to let my brother go with the taskforce, now I need to guarantee everyone else sees why it is a good thing he is gone. I need to let Victor paint himself as disruptive and divisive, and this should do it.* "Perhaps, Precentor Martial, since ComStar is not a voting member of the First Council, you would act to chair the election of our First Lord."

"Very well. Are there any nominations?"

Katrina nodded. "I place into nomination the name of Sun-Tzu Liao."

"What?" Victor's jaw nearly hit the floor. "You're nominating Sun-Tzu?"

"I am, brother dear." Katrina gave him an icy glare calculated to infuriate Victor. "He is capable and intelligent, the ruler of a realm just like the rest of us. Because his realm is small it will not have as active a role in the assault as yours or mine or the Combine's, hence having him represented in the leadership of the Star League would emphasize his participation in this effort. His engagement to Isis and his ties to the Free Worlds League also bring another connection into his regime."

Thomas Marik nodded slowly. "I second that nomination. In the time I have known Sun-Tzu I have become convinced he has the qualifications and capabilities to deal with the demands of the office."

*Especially since those demands are largely ceremonial.* Katrina kept her face impassive. *What little power there is in the office can be multiplied by the prestige of it, so it can become an effective position from which to influence the course of the Inner Sphere, but only in the hands of the right person.*

Looking around the circle, she knew Sun-Tzu's nomination was doomed. It required a two-thirds majority, which was effectively five votes out of seven. Victor, Theodore, and Candace would never vote for Sun-Tzu, guaranteeing failure. She, Thomas, and Sun-Tzu would never vote for

Victor, so he couldn't win either. *Of all of us here, there is only one candidate who can possibly win. Me.*

She glanced over at Victor and saw his hands knotted into fists and his knuckles white with rage.

Sun-Tzu smiled. "I have to say I think I am an excellent candidate and will do my utmost to rule with wisdom and justice."

Candace's eyes narrowed. "Your mother once made that pledge. She failed to keep it."

"I am not my mother."

"Pity. She is dead."

"Wait." Victor stood at his place and held his hands up. "This is pointless."

Katrina smiled, waiting for Victor launch into a tirade. *He does have a gift for character assassination when he gets going. This should be good.*

Victor's hands slowly unclenched. "As far as I'm concerned, if Sun-Tzu is good enough for my sister, he's good enough for me. He will have my vote."

Katrina felt the blood drain from her face. *What? How is this possible?*

Victor continued. "Sun-Tzu Liao, I don't really trust you further than I can throw a 'Mech, but I'm really given no real choice in the matter. Either you will accept the responsibilities of this office and see to its duties for the good of the Inner Sphere, or you'll leave it in such a shambles that the Clans will walk all over us. I grew up hating you and it hasn't done me any good. I don't suppose your being hated did you any good, either. Maybe giving you this responsibility will. All I know is that those of us who are going to be shedding blood for the Inner Sphere will be counting on you to get us the weapons and supplies we need to do our jobs. If you fail, we'll be the first to die, and far from the last."

The sense of horror threatening to choke Katrina spiked as Victor sat down and winked at her. *He winked at me! He had the gall to wink at me.* Her hands tightened and she felt her fingernails stab into her palms. *He couldn't have anticipated this move on my part. Now I have to support Sun-Tzu, which means he'll be selected First Lord. While Victor's off fighting the Clans, I'll have to put up with Sun-Tzu!*

She wanted to scream, but instead politely nodded her head in response to the Precentor Martial's call for the vote. Sun-Tzu beamed with his selection. He rose from his place, clasping both hands triumphantly over his head. Before he sat down again he looked in her direction and bowed his head respectfully, then flashed her a prideful smile.

*As if this victory means anything at all!* Katrina's eyes narrowed. *You did not get what you wanted, so now you must take what you've been given and find another way to reach your goal. Is there a way I can turn Sun-Tzu's election into something that will hurt Victor?*

Katrina directed a smile at her brother. *First blood is yours, brother mine, but the winner in our fight will be the last one standing, and I have no intention of letting that be you.*

**Sigfried Glacier Reserve**
**Environs, Tharkad City**
**Tharkad**
**District of Donegal, Lyran Alliance**
**16 November 3058**

As Victor Steiner-Davion turned around, the snowball caught him square in the forehead. It exploded down over his face, the snow's cold caress feeling like fire on his flesh. He reflexively jerked his head back away from the blow, then found himself overbalanced to the right. He tried to steady himself, but the knee-high crusted snow trapped his legs.

He went down hard on his side, crackling through the crust and launching a cloud of powdery snow into the air. He heard the fragments of crust pitter-pat over his parka, then felt the lighter snow drift down over him. As the sound of a child's happy laughter reached his ears, the haunting, uncomfortable sensation of snow working its way down the collar of his shirt made itself felt.

Heavy footsteps crunched their way to his side. "Are you all right, Victor?"

The Prince flicked snow out of his right eye and looked up at Kai Allard-Liao and the little boy peering from around Kai's leg. "Can't you tell your son to pick on someone his own size?"

"He was."

"Thanks."

Kai reached down and hauled Victor to his feet. "He was throwing the snowball at Morgan's grandson when you got in the way."

Victor glanced over to where Morgan Hasek-Davion was playing with his grandson, George Hasek, Junior. Morgan's father, Michael, had changed the family name to Hasek-Davion after he wed Victor's aunt Marie. After Michael turned out to be a traitor and was killed by Kai's father, Morgan announced that the Hasek-Davion line stopped with him. Now his son had a son and the Hasek line had an heir to continue its rule over the Capellan March of the Federated Commonwealth.

Kai's son, David Lear, held up a snowball. "Here you go, sir. You can throw it at me." He waited until Victor had plucked the snowball from his mittened hands, then went running off across the top of the snow crust. The navy blue snowsuit so insulated him that the boy could barely move, but the happy laughter trailing in his wake gave no sign he noticed or cared about his restrictions.

Victor lofted the snowball over David's head. The little boy watched it fly, spinning around to do so. He immediately lost his balance and crashed down, giggling madly as he went.

The Prince looked up at Kai. "Were we ever that carefree?"

"Probably, back when dust clouds were congealing into planets around stars." Kai winced as David tried to stand up and failed spectacularly. "And just as graceful."

Victor smiled. "He's how old?"

"Five and a half, same as George Junior."

"Does it bother you that when we head out you won't see him? When you come back he'll be twice his age." Victor sighed and let the breeze carry his vaporous breath away. "I mean it's easy for me to go because I don't have the same responsibilities you do."

Kai shook his head. "No. No, you don't. I have to look after my family, and you're responsible for billions of people, but I know that's not what you meant, is it?"

"Isn't it?"

"Nope." Kai pointed toward the chateau and the various people standing behind the great room's glass wall. "Yvonne will take good care of your people and govern wisely in your stead. You're worried about other things."

Victor nodded. "Yeah, like Katherine."

Kai laughed. "Seeing her reaction when you agreed to support Sun-Tzu was wonderful. She never saw it coming."

The Prince smiled. "True, that was something she didn't expect. It was strange, Kai, because when she nominated Sun-Tzu I immediately saw red. I knew she was using him to provoke a reaction out of me, and she started to get it. Then I began to wonder what she would get out of having Sun-Tzu made First Lord."

"Nothing, as nearly as I can tell."

"Right, which is why I decided her motive must have been to draw a bad reaction out of me." Victor reached back and pulled a clump of snow from inside his collar. "All of a sudden things started to click into place in my mind. The only person who could be hurt by my angry reaction to the nomination was me. I realized that Katrina wanted me to start a fight, then she'd withdraw her nomination and, because she was a peacemaker, would be the logical candidate for the post. Only by agreeing to Sun-Tzu's election could I thwart her."

"You could have blocked her election—the Coordinator and my mother would have voted with you—and suggested a return to drawing lots."

"Sure, but then I might have won."

Kai gave him a hard stare. "Are you telling me you don't want to be First Lord of the Star League?"

Victor hesitated. "I know that was my father's goal, and the goal of every Inner Sphere leader since the dissolution of the Star League, but I guess I never got infected with that bug. I always assumed my father would win the post. Then the Clans arrived and priorities shifted. Given a choice between being known as the First Lord of the Star League and the man who conquered the Clans, I'd take the latter spot in history in a second. The First Lord's position is largely ceremonial anyway, and you know I don't like much in the way of ceremony."

"I know. I also don't buy that as your reason for refusing to go into Tharkad City tonight to attend Katherine's birthday gala."

"I sent a present." Victor shrugged. "Some planet or other."

"That's all well and good, but this party is going to be a celebration of all that's been accomplished here. In another five days the constitution gets signed and the Star League is reborn." Kai rested a hand on Victor's shoulder. "You've earned the right to celebrate."

"Have I? Inside six months, if all goes as planned, we'll initiate an assault that will kill hundreds of thousands, even millions of people. It will be slaughter on a scale undreamt of by anyone within hailing distance of sanity." Victor snorted steam from his nostrils. "How can I dress up and celebrate before we go off to do that?"

"You can and you will because by your presence at the celebration you will strengthen ties that will make the operation go more easily and smoothly. Comments you make there, positive comments, will be circulated. They will trickle down so every soldier being sent into that battle will know you're so confident of victory you dared take time to enjoy yourself. Your attendance may not boost *your* morale, but it will boost the morale of others."

"I don't want to go, Kai." Victor frowned. "Don't people with children have trouble finding baby-sitters? That's what I'll do—watch over David and George and your Melissa while you all go off and have fun."

Kai coughed lightly. "Ah, Victor, I hate to break this to you, but all the children have nannies and there are enough security personnel in this chateau of yours that nothing's going to happen to them. I'd also point out that I don't think you've ever changed a diaper. Talk about something that requires courage."

"Right. I forgot the biohazard part of the job." Victor gave Kai a sidelong glance. "You don't really believe that morale-boosting pap, do you?"

"It'll boost my morale to have you there."

"How so?"

"My wife indicated to me that a certain lady would be disappointed if you weren't there."

"And your job was to make sure I would be?"

Kai nodded.

"Damn, you always take on the dangerous missions." Victor smiled. "Far be it from me to let you disappoint Dr. Lear."

"Thanks." Kai smiled. "So what kind of planet did you give Katherine? A gas giant?"

"Would have been a nice choice. Maybe next year." Victor shook his head. "Nope, it was a lifeless little ball; cold, hard, and ugly to the core. Reminded me of her. Hope she likes it."

\* \* \*

Victor was so engrossed in watching Omi join her father on the dance floor for a waltz, that he didn't notice the woman's approach until he felt her hand on his shoulder. He turned toward her and gave her a pleasant smile. "Duchess Marik. I hope you are enjoying yourself this evening."

"Isis, please." She smiled warmly at him. "May I call you Victor?"

"Please."

"I didn't mean to surprise you." She stood before him with her chestnut hair gathered on top of her head and a shimmery, sleeveless silver gown sheathing her slender figure. "I suppose I could be put out that you did not notice my approach, but that sort of pettiness is the domain of your sister, Katherine, isn't it?"

Victor coughed into his hand to hide his surprise. "Forgive me. I did notice your approach, but I did not think you would be coming to speak with me. I haven't earned much favor with your family."

She nodded sympathetically. "Joshua's death was a blow, but I very much appreciated what you did to keep him alive. I know your father started his treatments, but you could have terminated them after the Clan truce. Joshua was no longer needed as a hostage then."

"But that would have been inhuman, which could sound funny coming from me, given what happened." Victor frowned. "I bore him no ill will, and the same goes for you and your father—for your nation, too."

"I never really knew Joshua, so I did not have an emotional bond with him. I think I saw him as the wall between me and all manner of insanity."

"Excuse me?"

A certain sadness dragged at her face. "You know I was born out of wedlock while Thomas—I hardly think of him as my father—was missing. My mother and I were well taken care of, but we were kept out of the way. I only became legitimized after Joshua was diagnosed with leukemia, thrusting me into a position I never wanted to be in. Think of it: I was made next in line for the throne of a realm where assassination is seen as just an alternate manner of shifting the power structure. Then I was tossed like a bone to Sun-Tzu to tantalize him with dreams of power that will never come true."

Victor scratched at his throat and tugged on his collar to

loosen it. "You surprise me, Isis. The impression I had of you . . ."

"The one I made on Outreach when I started flirting with Kai and Sun-Tzu and caused that argument." She blushed. "I was young then, very young, and very taken with all the uniforms and celebrity. All of you, the young royals, you were all there together and you knew each other. I felt I had to make an impression. I did, but not the one I wanted to make."

She reached out and clutched Victor's left forearm. "And I don't want you to think I'm here, now, making a play for you. It's rather obvious who you're waiting for. She's gorgeous and very nice."

Victor glanced over to where Omi danced with her father. The gown she wore was cut along the same lines as the one Isis had on, including the plunging backline and teardrop neckline, but it was black, with red trim at the hem, waist, neckline, and back. *Just like that bathing suit she wore.*

"Omi is wonderful."

"And I think you two deserve all the happiness you can find together." Isis smiled. "What I wanted to do was to thank you for supporting Sun-Tzu and making him First Lord of the Star League."

Victor nodded. "I would be less than honest if I didn't tell you I voted for him to frustrate my sister."

"I know that. She's not easy to read, but not impossible, either." Isis let go of Victor's arm. "What you said to him, though, about responsibility and hatred, I think that got through to him. I think—I know—he's spent most of his life waiting for someone to come destroy him. He thought it would be Kai or you or Thomas and he went out of his way to provoke you just so he could survive your attack and thwart you. He never felt you respected him and I think he resented the fact that the Clans captured more of your attention than he did."

Victor's eyes narrowed. "You're really in love with him, aren't you?"

She stopped, clasped her arms around her middle, and looked down. "I hope that doesn't make you think less of me."

"Not at all. In fact, I envy you."

Her chin came up. "You what?"

"I envy you." Victor patted her on the arm. "At least you

have a chance to be with the one you love someday. That's more than I'll have."

She shook her head. "You have as much chance at happiness as I do."

"Then we're both doomed, because I have no chance of ever being with Omi and marrying her."

"How can you say that?"

Victor shrugged. "It's unfortunately easy for me, I fear. Were I to marry Omi, the people of the Draconis March would assume I had betrayed them. My judgment would be called into question and open revolts would result. Katherine would certainly do all she could stir up trouble. She'll point out that the Lyons thumb—which the Combine occupied at the request of ComStar and with my permission—stands as proof of how I will merge the Combine and the Federated Commonwealth. I'll be painted as the junior partner in that union. It would be utter ruin if I married her."

"Utter ruin for whom, Victor?" Her brown eyes narrowed slightly as she pointed to the people on the dance floor. "When you look at them, do you see what I do? Look at Kai and his wife, or your Morgan Hasek-Davion and his wife, even Thomas and Sherryl. All of them are happy because they have found someone with whom to share their lives. No one questions their judgment and no one has a *right* to question their judgment. The only sign of insanity you could possibly suffer would be to let Omi go."

Victor heard her words and felt them resonating in his soul. *How is it that billions of people will march with me into war, yet will rebel if I choose to marry someone I love? If they cannot count on me to make the right decision concerning my personal life, if they cannot trust me to pursue my own dreams, how can they trust me to govern them?*

He looked up at her and smiled. "Thank you."

"For what?"

"For pointing out the border between sanity and insanity."

"Victor, I saw my mother spend the rest of her life being profoundly unhappy because she could never again be with the man she loved. I live in dread of Thomas or Sun-Tzu deciding to separate me from Sun-Tzu. What I want for myself I can't but want for you and everyone else." She smiled carefully. "The heartache you know is the same heartache all humans go through. It is what makes all of us equal. Don't let the expectations of others strip you of humanity."

"You're right. I won't do that." Victor smiled as the music ended and Omi came walking over with her father. "You know Isis, of course."

"Good to see you again, Duchess."

Isis smiled broadly. "You were magnificent out there, so graceful. I would love to dance, but Sun-Tzu doesn't like to dance."

Omi frowned at Victor. "You should have invited her to dance."

Victor blinked. "I would have but . . ."

". . . But he would be thinking of you while dancing with me, Omi." Isis shook her head. "He was too polite to say so, but I could read it in his eyes. The two of you should just go out and dance. I'll live vicariously through you."

Victor offered Omi his hand. "If you would do me the pleasure."

Omi looked at Isis. "It would not be polite to abandon you."

"No, it is impolite for me to stand in the way of your joy. Please, put your concerns for me aside."

Omi nodded and followed Victor onto the dance floor.

"A wise woman, that Isis." Victor looked up into Omi's eyes. "She's grown up quite a bit since Outreach."

"So she has." Omi smiled down at him. "What did you talk about?"

"This and that." Victor nodded slowly. "She gave me a lot to think about—a lot for *us* to think about."

# ═ **20** ═

In the rear of the Grand Council chamber, Vlad Ward of the Wolves sat back and steepled his fingers. He dared risk the hint of a smile, primarily because he knew it would infuriate Khan Asa Taney of the Ice Hellions. Vlad had even placed his helmet on the desk in front of him in such a position that Taney would have no trouble seeing him at all. *He knows who has driven the knife into his back, now I want him to know who is twisting it.*

In the weeks leading up to the vote for the new ilKhan, Taney had worked hard to fashion a coalition of the Home Clans. He had continued to push new and younger warriors to pressure their leadership to back him. Vlad had let this effort continue until it began to gain momentum, then he had stepped in to gut it.

It had been readily apparent to everyone, because of Taney's argument, that the Home Clans and their warriors would not be able to join the fight against the Inner Sphere without a Taney victory. Vlad, who still needed seasoned warriors to rebuild the Wolves, let slip his intention to engage in a series of "harvest wars" in which he would challenge various Clan units to battle, demanding as his prize the possession of that unit if his forces won. Most warriors realized that the way to war with the Inner Sphere would be more open if they were part of the Wolves. Even if Taney won, the Clans that supported him would still have to battle for the right to participate in a renewed invasion, so the chances of any particular warrior actually getting to fight against the Inner Sphere diminished appreciably.

Once the rumor of the "harvest wars" began to spread through the Home Clans, preemptive batchalls flooded into the Wolf command center. Vlad had replied to them that he could do nothing until the new ilKhan was selected, and he hinted strongly that a change in the status quo would cast into doubt the Wolves' participation in a renewed invasion. Very quickly the ardor of Taney's movement drained away.

Vlad glanced to his left and gave his saKhan, Marialle Radick a quick nod. *Time to twist it even deeper.*

Vlad's small, honey-blond compatriot stood and doffed her helmet. "Loremaster, I wish to place a name in nomination for ilKhan."

Kael Pershaw looked up from his position at the front of the room. "This is your right, Khan Radick."

"To spare Khan Taney the embarrassment of defeat, I nominate Lincoln Osis to be ilKhan." Marialle thrust a hand toward the dark-skinned Elemental. "He has been in the forefront of the invasion, and has risen to the rank of Khan among the Smoke Jaguars through his valiant and tenacious efforts on their behalf in the fighting. We count it remarkable for an Elemental to win a Bloodname, and here Lincoln Osis has become a Khan. If there is a greater accomplishment among the invading Clans, I cannot think of it."

Severen Leroux of the Nova Cats rose and seconded the nomination, sending a curious chill through Vlad. *Leroux also seconded the nomination of Elias Crichell for the office of ilKhan. No doubt they view his election as an important building block of the future they see for the Clans. I have no use for their visions, but if what they foresee works in my favor, I have no reason to oppose them.*

The Loremaster nodded toward Lincoln Osis. "Khan Osis, you have been nominated for the position of ilKhan. Do you know of any reason why you should not be allowed to be elected to this position?"

Vlad's smile broadened. *Someone doesn't want a repeat of Elias Crichell's early removal from office to repeat itself, hence the addition of this line to the voting procedure.*

Lincoln Osis stood slowly. "I know of no reason why I should not be allowed to serve if elected." He balled his big hands into fists, then turned to fix Vlad with an icy stare. "If there are any who would oppose me, I would ask them to make their objections known now."

Vlad said nothing.

The half-man, half-machine Loremaster hit several keys on his noteputer. "The name of Lincoln Osis has been placed into nomination. All of you will vote aye or nay in this matter. If Khan Osis receives fifty percent plus one of the votes cast, he will win. I will poll you individually."

Pershaw began at the front of the room and worked his way back. Osis required just over half of the votes cast by the Khans. With two Khans from each of seventeen Clans voting, he would become ilKhan with eighteen votes—fewer if any Khans chose to abstain. With the Smoke Jaguars, Jade Falcons, Nova Cats, Steel Vipers, and Ghost Bears backing him, he started better than halfway to his goal—according to Vlad's estimates. An even split of the remaining votes would put him over the top, and from the beginning it became apparent that Taney's coalition had collapsed.

Marialle Radick voted for Osis, but Vlad and Marthe Pryde both voted against him. They exchanged brief smiles, then stood to applaud as the result was announced. Osis won twenty-two to twelve, a resounding victory.

*Osis seems even taller as he marches to the fore.*

The Elemental reached the Loremaster's side, shook his hand, then turned to face the assembled Khans. "In choosing me you have chosen wisely. I am a warrior who knows victory and has not forgotten what is required to win it. I will lead us to victory over the barbarians of the Inner Sphere."

Asa Taney stood. "When you say you will lead *us* to victory, do you mean you will order a reshuffling of the invading Clans to allow the rest of us to participate?"

Osis' expression darkened. "What have you done to earn that right?"

Taney sniffed. "In your eyes the answer is, apparently, nothing, *quiaff*?"

"Then why do you ask for something you have not earned?"

Vlad raised a hand. "I believe, ilKhan, that Khan Taney is really asking if there will be time for his Ice Hellions to chal-

lenge one of the invading Clans to win the right to participate in the renewed invasion."

"Perhaps. If they work fast." Osis' dark eyes glittered. "It
is my intention to begin offensive operations immediately."

Marthe Pryde rose to her feet. "I believe, ilKhan, it is your
right to propose to this body that we begin operations immediately, but it is not your prerogative to order a resumption
of the war."

"Are the Jade Falcons tired of war, Marthe Pryde?"

"Ha!" Marthe's white teeth flashed dangerously with her
laugh. "We have fought the Inner Sphere so long we weary
of fighting inferior troops. I would not be averse to sharp-
ening our talons on any Clan that wanted to wrest away some
of our occupied worlds. I can see no reason why you would
not provide the others this sort of opportunity, unless you
fear the Smoke Jaguars would be left without staging areas
for the resumption of the invasion."

*Well played, Marthe.* Vlad nodded. "I, too, would welcome testing my Clan against those who have remained
behind." *The more fighting we encourage among the Clans,
the more difficult will be Osis' job, and the more time the
Inner Sphere will have to prepare to defend themselves
against the Smoke Jaguar onslaught.*

Bitterness and anger curled the ilKhan's lip and tightened
the flesh around his eyes. "And how long would you like to
be able to play at war. Six months? A year?"

Marthe pointed toward Taney. "This is a question that
should be answered by the challengers, of course, but no
Clan worthy of the honor would require more than nine
months to resolve this issue."

Taney nodded. "Nine months will be more than enough
time to prove our worthiness to join the invading Clans."

Vlad smiled. "Perhaps, ilKhan, you would like to come up
with the wording of such a rede, so you do not feel this has
been forced upon you."

Osis massaged his left fist with his right hand. "It is my
recommendation as ilKhan that each Clan take the next six
months to plan and prepare for the resumption of the campaign against the Inner Sphere. All challenges against
invading Clans, all Trials of Possession for invasion-corridor
worlds, should be made within three months of today and
completed within ninety days from that date. All remaining
disputes will be adjudicated by the Grand Council, and the

Clans will have three months to prepare for the resumption of the invasion."

Osis' words came in frosty, low tones, full of frustration and anger. "Is that acceptable?"

Vlad nodded. "Seyla."

The other Khans echoed the ancient oath, adopting the proposal unanimously.

Osis bowed his head in their direction. "So shall it be until we all shall fall."

*Indeed.* Vlad lowered himself into his chair and caught a nod from Marthe Pryde. *The fall of Lincoln Osis begins now.*

# ═══ 21 ═══

**Grand Ballroom, Royal Court**
**The Triad**
**Tharkad City, Tharkad**
**District of Donegal, Lyran Alliance**
**21 November 3058**

**T**hough he normally detested the pomp and circumstance that accompanied affairs of state, Victor found the ceremony surrounding the signing of the Star League Constitution appropriate and even enjoyable. It seemed to him somehow correct that the occasion of reestablishing the Star League three centuries after its collapse would be marked with vari-colored banners and brassy renditions of the Star League anthem. The honor guard presenting the flags of the constituent nations was even clad in archaic but regal uniforms from the bygone era.

Victor watched as his sister approached the tall glass table where the eight copies of the Constitution awaited her signature. She wore a bolero jacket over a long gown, both in glittering white brocade. The tiara holding her hair back sparkled brilliantly, casting a rainbow of light around her head. *Add wings and she'd look every bit an angel.* Victor shook his head. *The Angel of Death.*

Katherine signed her name on the documents in pieces, changing pens between them. Each used pen was set aside and a new one picked up. The pens would later be handed out to aides and supporters, giving them a piece of history to treasure forever. Victor normally balked at such gestures, but on this occasion would have been willing to use a different pen for every letter of his name. *I wish there were enough mementos that I could hand one to every warrior we're asking to fight for us.*

As she finished signing, Katherine walked over to the crystalline podium to the right and smiled despite the blinding sea of light before her. "We have come, this day, and joined together to facilitate the rebirth of the greatest and most noble height to which mankind has ever risen: the Star League. For centuries wars have been waged to accomplish this end; yet the Star League was reborn in peace, not in strife. No matter how long I live, or whatever else I do, providing the venue and framework that accomplished this great work will be the pinnacle of my career. The rebirth of the Star League will stand as a monument to those here who sign their names in ratification, and to those for whom it was signed. This day there is once again a united Inner Sphere and that should strike fear into the hearts of our enemies everywhere."

She left the podium and moved further right, to stand with the other leaders who had already signed the Constitution. One by one she shook hands with them: the Precentor Martial, Thomas Marik, Candace Liao, Theodore Kurita, and Prince Magnusson. Beaming from ear to ear, she took her place at the end of the line and appeared to luxuriate in the applause echoing from throughout the Grand Ballroom.

Sun-Tzu Liao next approached to sign his copy of the document. The order of signing had been decided by lot, and Victor felt fortunate he would go last. *That means I can say anything I want in my concluding remarks and we don't have to worry that someone will take offense and refuse to sign.* So far the comments made by the signers had all been positive and encouraging, though decidedly banal, to Victor's mind. Only the Precentor Martial had commented about this being the first step in the future of the Inner Sphere—but he could afford to gamble since he was the victor of Tukayyid and his signature was vital on the Constitution if the Clans were to take it seriously. Victor meant for his own remarks to drive home the seriousness even if it might take the edge off the festive mood.

*Then again, my little bombshell announcement should make for good copy.* Victor reined in his smile as he caught

Katherine looking at him. *Sun-Tzu's election and Morgan Kell's threat have Katherine uncertain about what is going on. Good. I hope dealing with Sun-Tzu for the next three years will continue that trend.*

Sun-Tzu took his place at the podium. "It is with the greatest of pleasure, and the deepest sense of humility, that I have signed the Star League Constitution. Before this compact was broken it showed us how to be truly civilized and humane. Since the Star League's destruction we have lost that and have become something less than we were meant to be. Its destruction was our destruction, and its rebirth is *our* rebirth.

"There are no words to describe the deep sense of gratitude toward my fellow leaders of the Inner Sphere and the pride I feel in being chosen First Lord of the Star League. My term will last for three years, and it is my intent, in that time, to establish a very high benchmark of service for my successors to follow. This office is not, to me, a ceremonial one. It represents a sacred trust—one I will guard to the best of my abilities. The Star League will be even finer at the end of my reign than it is now and so, I hope, will be all of humanity."

Victor had been waiting for deception in Sun-Tzu's words, or traces of gloating. He heard none of that, but that did not surprise him. *Sun-Tzu learned at his mother's breast to hide his intentions and feelings. There is certainly more there than I ever imagined before. Perhaps Isis is right: perhaps having this sort of responsibility thrust upon him will give him a focus. I don't know. I can only hope he doesn't make our campaign harder by obstructing it.*

Victor waited for Sun-Tzu to take his place in the line next to Katherine, then he stepped forward and crisply walked over to the table where the treaties waited for him. The top of the table came up to about ten centimeters above his navel, but Victor didn't care that its height emphasized his lack of same. *If any of us signing this document are judged by our physical size, the person making the judgment is a fool.*

He uncapped the first pen and scratched out his title. He loved the rasp of the nib over the parchment and watched the blue ink lighten as it sank into the paper and dried. Another pen inscribed his first name, and another his middle name.

Two more pens worked to add his surname to the treaty, then he moved on to the next copy.

He noted that both Sun-Tzu and Theodore had used kanji to sign their names, and that Katherine's signature was little more than a bumpy snake track with breaks every place she switched pens. Though Victor's penmanship had never been a thing of beauty, he took great care to inscribe his name so it would be legible, and even added a grand flourish by underlining his name with a stroke at the end.

Once finished with the final treaty, he recapped the last pen and carried it with him to the podium. A flood of light washed over him—it was bright enough that he could feel waves of heat pulsing from all the lights. He reached up and adjusted the microphones lower, both so he could speak into them and, more important, see over them. He gave himself a second to collect his thoughts, then swallowed hard and began.

"The remarks you have heard so far are a fair tribute to the need for the Star League and a monument to the hard work we've accomplished here in just over six weeks. Our work is, of course, built upon the foundation laid down by the framers of the first Star League Constitution, but adapting that document to make it work in these turbulent times has been difficult. All of us, our aides, advisors, and staffs have worked tirelessly to make this Constitution suit our own times. The signing you have just witnessed is a victory for every man, woman, and child in the Inner Sphere, and beyond."

Victor did his best to peer past the lights and pick out faces in the crowd behind the media galleries. "Just as we have built on the foundation laid down by others, now we must continue building a sound structure to carry us into the future. It should surprise none of you when I point out that the Inner Sphere has been beset by enemies from without and rivalries from within. The recreation of the Star League puts an end to the internecine fighting that has plagued us for centuries. Now, united, of like mind and spirit, we will turn our attention to the Clans and ending the threat they pose to us all.

"Let there be no mistake about it, opposing the Clans will not be simple. It will require the supreme effort from our people in the field and all those who support them. This must be a concerted effort by all of us because if we do not succeed in throwing the invaders back, we can never be free of the fear that pervades everything we now do."

Victor smiled. "I know the thoughts going through your minds. Many of you think it is well and good that we can all reach an agreement here, but that it won't really change things. You think we might even be able to coordinate joint operations to go after the Clans, but that there will be no real unity beyond that. I understand those doubts—we've all seen hypocrisy on multiple levels and are rightfully cynical. Were I in your position, these would be my thoughts, too.

"I am not in your position, and this is due to more than an accident of birth. I have been here, at the Whitting Conference. I have witnessed the changing of minds and the melding of spirits. We *are* united and committed to a bright new future. We *will* make it happen."

Victor paused for a moment, then let his smile tighten down into a smirk. "You rightfully ask for proof of these changes—signs that they are in the works. You will see them, I promise you, and this is not an idle, empty promise. As proof I offer one thing—the first of many you will see. From here, from Tharkad, I will be traveling, at the invitation of the Coordinator of the Draconis Combine, to Luthien. There I will greet the new year, with my friends and allies, and welcome a new era for humanity."

The murmurs of shock and outrage melted into an ocean of applause. Victor held his head up, keeping his expression pleasant without allowing it to become triumphant. *There, Katherine, you've claimed credit for building the launching pad. Now I'll just use it to take flight.*

He raised his hands and waved the din back down to silence. "There are those of you who'd have thought a Davion setting foot on Luthien was a sign of the apocalypse—a harbinger of the end of the universe as we know it. Let me assure you that the latter is true. The old universe, the one that was the womb of the Succession Wars, is no more. We are choosing to make a new universe for ourselves and for you. With your support and consent, we will destroy the barriers that divided us and surge through into brightest future mankind can possibly know."

# ≡ 22 ≡

**Sigfried Glacier Reserve
Environs, Tharkad City
Tharkad
District of Donegal, Lyran Alliance
22 November 3058**

Victor Steiner-Davion seated himself on the edge of the heavy oaken desk behind which Alessandro Steiner had plotted all manner of treason and smiled at Morgan Hasek-Davion. "Go ahead, open the present now. It's nominally for Christmas—mostly it's to speed you along on your adventure."

Morgan sat back on the brown leather couch and popped the ribbon off the rectangular box. He started peeling the paper back, then smiled when he read the label. "Glengarry Black Label, Special Reserve! Victor, you know your scotch."

Victor smiled sheepishly. "No, actually, Cranston's security people know *your* scotch. Their datafile on you is fairly complete and they noted you've developed a habit of indulging in a nightcap. They also tell me this is your favorite poison."

Morgan laughed lightly. "You don't know this stuff if you can think of it as poison. And, yes, I have developed a taste for it, but only one drink before going to sleep."

"Good. I've got a case of it going out with you. I don't expect that will be enough, but if I load you up . . ."

"Folks could wonder where I'm going that I can't get it. I'll ration it carefully." Morgan glanced at the box, then back up at Victor. "I'm surprised you were able to get a case off Glengarry."

"I didn't." The Prince smiled. "Jerry said some of his special operatives were getting rusty, so they pulled a black-bag job on Katherine's liquor cellar during her birthday party. His people do good work."

"I bet." Morgan set the box on the couch beside him. "So, what else do they have in my datafile?"

"Nothing out of the ordinary—just service records and medical reports. Congratulations, by the way, on checking out on your physical. As far as the doctors were concerned you'd be in great shape even for someone twenty years your junior." Victor nodded solemnly. "This campaign's not going to be easy on you, but the doctors say you're more than up to it."

"I hope they're right."

"What do you mean?" Victor frowned. "You're the only real choice for this operation. You've got the experience, the reputation, and the intelligence needed to carry it off."

"I'd like to think you're right about that, but what does concern me is the nature of the coalition force. While *we've* all agreed to cooperate, I'm not certain all the disparate parts of the force have worked that out yet."

"That's what the training period is for, Morgan, to get used to each other." Victor eased himself off the desk and walked over to the wet bar built into the corner of the room. "Want something?"

"Water, please." Morgan sat forward, stretching the scarlet ribbon wrapped around the package between his hands. "The training period will help, certainly, but our journey to Huntress is going to take a long time. There'll be plenty of opportunity for friction to stir up trouble."

Victor returned and handed him a glass of water. "As long as the leadership presents a united front, it should be easy to tamp that sort of thing down."

"True, but there's a potential for the leadership to fragment if we don't deal with some issues right from the start."

"Such as."

"Operational security." Morgan grimaced. "We won't have the resources necessary to let us keep Clan prisoners, and we won't be able to free them lest the enemy find them and learn that a big force is moving through their occupation zones previously undetected."

Victor sipped a bit of his own glass of mineral water as he thought. The necessity of secrecy meant Morgan's taskforce would be operating under a communications blackout. They could neither send messages out, nor could messages be broadcast to them. The Clans might intercept those messages, and even if they couldn't break the codes used, they would have to start searching for whoever was meant to get the message. Premature discovery of the taskforce would lead to a battle on the way in to Huntress or, worse yet, Morgan and his people would arrive there to find the world fortified and reinforced.

Because they could not keep prisoners, they had to get rid of them. Marooning them on a world without communications devices was one solution, but unless they were lucky and found a habitable world that had not previously been colonized, chances were that most planets Morgan's force ran across would be lifeless and inhospitable. Sending prisoners back on a ship risked discovery by any number of means *and* would significantly reduce the taskforce's resources.

The other alternative was to kill the prisoners. *Except in cases where the enemy's conduct allows for a court martial and summary execution, it's hard to justify killing them. While the death of one man might guarantee the safety of a taskforce that would win the freedom of the Inner Sphere, using those ends to justify murder is indefensible.*

Victor met Morgan's green-eyed stare. "How do you feel about having to order the deaths of prisoners?"

"I don't want to do it, of course, but if it's the only choice I'll have, I guess . . . well, I don't know. Able-bodied individuals who've been fighting against us would be easier to kill than invalids and children, but I just don't know. I'm figuring I'll take things on a case-by-case basis and hope there's a way to avoid having to kill noncombatants." Morgan shook his head. "Does that make sense?"

"It's about the only thing that does in all this." Victor sighed. "That's going to be a hard decision, but I know you'll make the best choice if you're confronted with it. The issue comes down to judging how much risk you want to put your people in. If your operation gets blown, the Inner Sphere will shed a lot of blood to accomplish what you will do with, hopefully, a lot less in the way of casualties and deaths."

"Oh, I understand the stakes, I'm just not certain I like the game at which we're wagering." Morgan drained his glass, then balanced it on the arm of the couch. "I'm sure I'll have a lot of help in making the decision, too."

Victor smiled. "Yeah, I'm looking forward to coordinating a coalition force as much as I would to herding wet cats. From here I head to Tukayyid, where we've scheduled some planning meetings, then it's on to Luthien to finalize things. In many ways I envy you the time you'll spend cut off from all the Inner Sphere chaos."

"At least I'll be around to see the reaction to your arrival at Luthien." Morgan shook his head. "A Davion an honored guest on Black Luthien. Never thought I'd see the day."

"Nor I." Victor barked a little nervous laugh. "Facing the Clans will be easier than setting foot there."

"I don't think so," Yvonne offered from the doorway. "Forgive the interruption, but I heard Morgan was going to be leaving and I wanted to say goodbye."

She crossed to where Morgan now stood and gave him a hug. "Be safe, Morgan, and repay them in full for all the misery they've caused."

Victor couldn't hear what Morgan said in return to her, but Yvonne relinquished her hold on him and wiped a tear from her face. "I wish you weren't going—either one of you."

The fear in her voice surprised Victor. "We have to do this, Yvonne, just as you have to take my place on New Avalon. You have my complete confidence."

Morgan smiled. "And mine. Us red-haired people are naturally smarter and able to handle more pressure, you know."

"Great, then I'll get gray just like you too, I suppose." Yvonne did her best to put a brave expression on her face, but Victor was painfully reminded of how young she really was. "I'm not ready for this, Victor."

Before Victor could reply, Morgan rested his hands on her shoulders and turned her to face him. "None of us are ready for what we're going to have to do, Yvonne, and do you know why? Because the only way we become capable of handling these sorts of situations is through experience. That experience is what we get by doing our best to meet the challenges thrust at us. We do what we can, see what mistakes we made, and then learn from those mistakes. You're smart enough to know that and smart enough to avoid making the little mistakes that anyone else in your position might make."

Yvonne glanced at her brother. "What if Victor's little mistake is trusting me?"

Morgan smiled. "Victor's one of the people who makes very few mistakes—which makes me think he's really a red-head and just dyes his hair to confuse us."

Victor reached out and stroked Yvonne's arm. "You can do this, Yvonne. I wasn't ready to take on this responsibility when I was your age either, but that's because I thought being a warrior was all the training I needed. I've learned, to my regret, that I was wrong in believing that. You've got the intelligence and the education and the advisors to help you through this. Listen to Tancred, listen to Morgan's wife Kym. They will help you keep the state running smoothly."

She shook her head. "I don't know about this."

Victor smiled. "Hey, think about how good running the Federated Commonwealth will look on your resume! You ought to be able to get in to any law school you want. I'll give you a good recommendation."

"So will I."

Her gray eyes narrowed. "What if I decide I don't want to give up the throne when you come back?"

The image of Omi flashed through Victor's brain. "If that happens, I might be able to come up with another arrangement that will make both of us happy."

"Your swift and safe return is what will make me happy, Victor. You, too, Morgan."

The Marshal of the Armed Forces of the Federated Commonwealth took a step back, then bowed low toward her. "Your wish is my command."

Yvonne's mouth slackened. "Victor, how will I handle Katherine?"

Ice formed in Victor's guts and drove sharp spikes out in all directions. "I think Katherine will have enough on her plate to keep her occupied for a long time. If not, contact Agent Curaitis through the Intelligence Secretariat. He'll know what to do."

Morgan smiled confidently. "Don't worry about your sister. She's going to be spending her time scheming up ways to take credit for your brother's victories. It'll be a full time job."

Victor slapped them both on their shoulders. "That it will be. After all, once I've conquered Luthien, the Clans will be no challenge at all."

# $=$ 23 $=$

*Royal Palace, The Triad*
*Tharkad City, Tharkad*
*District of Donegal, Lyran Alliance*
*23 November 3058*

As much as it pained her to do so, Katrina decided she owed her brother a little more respect than she had paid him in the past. *The time was once when Victor didn't know politics from a hole in the ground. He's learning—his ability to learn has always been his greatest asset. With the military campaign, he's directed back toward being a soldier, which should keep him away from learning about politics for awhile. This is not the moment for him to have a chance to resume those studies.*

Katrina did her best to analyze Victor's performance at the Whitting Conference, and she had to conclude that she had constantly underestimated him. From the moment he set foot on Tharkad he'd directed himself toward obtaining the goal he wanted—taking the war to the Clans—and he let nothing deflect him from that course.

His single-mindedness was no surprise to Katrina—she'd lived with it all her life. It had allowed her to work around Victor and manipulate him into situations where the resolution he desired came through her intervention. Victor's putting her on the throne of the Lyran Alliance after their mother's death was just such an event. As it was, the realm later seceded, but bloodlessly, leaving the Lyran Alliance intact and under her control.

Two things Victor did had completely surprised her. The first was his approval of Sun-Tzu's election to the position of First Lord. That move legitimized Sun-Tzu and elevated him to the level of the other major players in the Inner Sphere. It enhanced his position, which could easily affect the balance of power in the Chaos March, where Sun-Tzu was jockeying to get back more of the worlds that had once belonged to the Capellans. Katrina found it inconceivable that Victor would sanction something that would cost him planets that had been conquered by their father. *Victor has always been the first acolyte in the Cult of Hanse Davion. That he would allow some of Hanse's victories to become defeats while he is in control just makes no sense.*

*Unless, of course, one chooses to believe Victor's nattering about choosing to do his duty for the Inner Sphere over worrying about the concerns of his realm.*

Katrina knew that was a lie the second she heard it. Victor's drive to join the campaign to destroy the Clans was as bald a grab for power as she'd ever seen. The Precentor Martial had said he was old and would be relying on Victor, in essence ceding to him credit for any victories. Her brother clearly intended, by defeating the Clans, to return to the Inner Sphere like the reincarnation of Aleksandr Kerensky so he could assume a position at the head of the Star League worthy of a returning hero.

In that light, his support of Sun-Tzu made perfect sense. Sun-Tzu was as likely as not to falter in his role. Being who he was, he would over-reach himself and fail—much as his uncle Tormano had done. In comparison to Sun-Tzu, Victor would appear to be the best and brightest possible leader the Star League could have, hence the mantle would fall to him next.

*And he will never relinquish it.* Grateful commanders and troops could guarantee his position and prevent any attempts to oust him. Dissent against him would become treason and the Star League would become more than just a union of equal states. Victor's grasp on power would tighten and the ruin toward which he had been guiding the Federated Commonwealth would become the destination for the whole of the Inner Sphere.

The second surprise Victor had presented Katrina was his

choice of Yvonne as Regent. In his place, she would have chosen their brother Peter—but he had vanished since his adventure on Solaris. She doubted Victor had ordered him killed—assassination was something to which he resorted only when pushed. *He'd never have killed Ryan Steiner had I not insisted the man must die for killing Galen Cox.*

Their other brother, Arthur, was still at the Battle Academy on Robinson and was not really a suitable choice for Regent. Arthur wore his emotions and loyalties on his sleeve, but tended to move in the direction of the prevailing wind. His presence on Robinson meant he would be steeped in anti-Kurita sentiment, which made him the last person Victor wanted ruling in his stead, especially while he was on Luthien. *And Arthur has always been more heart than head—fine for someone who performs ceremonial duties, but not for the one who has to wield actual power.*

Yvonne was an interesting choice—and the only logical alternative because of Morgan Hasek-Davion's assuming leadership of the long-strike taskforce. She had changed in the years since Katrina had last seen her, but she still seemed to default to the big sister-little sister mode of behavior when they spoke. *She is uncertain enough about herself to be vulnerable to manipulation. Having her on New Avalon does more for me than Victor knows. It gives me the time I need to deal with the Kells before I have to deal with her.*

Katrina's slow spiral up toward anger was interrupted by a quick knock on her door followed by its opening before she could grant permission to enter. Anger spiked immediately, and she would have given vent to it instantly had Tormano Liao been alone. "What is it, Mandrinn?"

"Please forgive me, Archon, but I knew you would not wish this woman to be forced to deal with bureaucracy. Only you can help her, and time is paramount, hence my haste." Tormano stepped aside to let Katrina see the petite, dark-haired woman who blushed fiercely and refused to look her in the eye. "This is Frances Jeschke."

Tormano's voice made it sound as if he were introducing Jeschke as the next incarnation of the Dalai Lama. Katrina smiled graciously and extended her hand to the woman. "Welcome to my office, Miss Jeschke. How may I help you?"

The woman's hand trembled as she shook Katrina's. "It's Mrs. Jeschke, Highness." A horrified expression spread over her not-unpretty face. "I didn't mean to be critical—I might as well be a Miss, as he's gone."

"You're a widow?"

"I hope so." Jeschke's lower lip quivered. "I don't know—he was working on Coventry and I haven't heard from him. Doesn't matter because he'd left me and our child. Can't blame him."

Tormano draped an arm around Jeschke's shoulders and guided her to a chair. "Frances here comes to you for two reasons, Highness. The first is that she is aware of your concern for children who have serious illnesses. Her son Tommy has non-Hodgkin's lymphoma, undifferentiated."

"He needs a marrow transplant or he'll die." Frances wrung her hands. "His dad is gone and I'm not a candidate to donate."

Katrina sat beside her on the couch and stroked her hair. "We'll do everything we can to help." Looking up beyond her at Tormano, Katrina gave him a glare that could have melted a 'Mech's ferro-ceramic armor. "Is there something specific, Mandrinn, that requires my attention?"

"Indeed there is, Archon." Tormano's smile was oily and confident enough that Katrina was determined to hurt him if his estimation of Jeschke's value to her was wrong. "Mrs. Jeschke here has done some detective work of her own and has found a suitable donor of marrow: Jerrard Cranston, your brother's aide."

Katrina frowned. What little she knew of juvenile disease and marrow transplants was that finding a match from outside the family was decidedly rare. "Cranston was typed and had the data logged in his files?"

"Yes." Frances looked up at her. "I was hoping you might be able to ask him to donate. I was hopeful because, well . . ."

Tormano smiled. "In her search for a donor she discovered she was adopted. When she traced her parents she discovered her father was Anderson Cox. He had an affair with her mother and she was the result."

Katrina felt a chill run down her spine. "I know that name."

Frances nodded. "Anderson Cox was Galen Cox's father." The woman reached out and clutched Katrina's hand. "I don't know if what the holovids and all said was true, but I was hoping you had fond enough memories of my half-brother to try to see to it that his nephew had a chance at life."

Katrina gave the woman's hand a squeeze, then looked up at Tormano. "I was unaware Galen had a half-sister."

"Apparently Anderson's philandering was unknown to Galen. I checked Galen's records and, it turns out that, had he not been slain, he would have been a perfect match for Tommy. *As good as Jerrard Cranston, in fact.*"

A jolt shot through Katrina. *If Galen Cox did not die on Solaris, if he is Jerrard Cranston . . .* Her mind raced. Victor was not so cruel that he would have kept word of Galen's survival from her while she mourned his death. *The only reason Victor would have had for doing that was if he knew the bomb that killed Galen had been a present from Ryan Steiner. Ryan had been trying to send me a message about my vulnerability. Victor must think he knows about the conspiracy to kill our mother, yet if he had proof of my complicity, why wouldn't he have revealed it by now?*

She shivered. *He clearly does* not *have proof. Between what he thinks he knows and Morgan Kell's insistence that I killed Melissa, Victor must be thinking it's only a matter of time before he uncovers the proof he needs to expose me. Had this woman not come forward, I would not have seen Victor's position in this, only Morgan Kell's. I've just gotten a warning that Victor does not want me to have.*

Katrina tried to mentally superimpose Galen's face over Jerrard Cranston's, but she realized she had seen little of Cranston during the conference. *Victor no doubt figured I might recognize him, yet he is so dependent on him that he couldn't bear to leave him behind on New Avalon I should have seen it sooner, much sooner.*

Katrina covered her shock with smile. She tipped Jeschke's chin up so the woman would look her in the eyes. "It will be my pleasure to do everything I can to see your son gets as much of Jerrard Cranston's marrow as he needs. Nothing will stop me, for your child represents the gateway to the new future for this realm. Making sure he and the Lyran Alliance thrive is a sacred trust, and one I will accomplish no matter the cost."

As Frances Jeschke settled into the back of the hover-taxi, she let the worried-mother-of-a-sick-child personality melt away. She glanced up at the reflection of the driver's icy eyes in the mirror. "Mission accomplished. If you'd wanted both Katherine and Tormano Liao dead, they would have been. Tormano was so taken with my story that he ushered me into Katherine's office without so much as even a cursory search of my person."

Agent Curaitis snorted from behind the wheel. "Since the conference is over and came off without a hitch, everyone is relaxing. It's unfortunate we had to pass on this opportunity, but that's the way the Prince wants it."

Francesca Jenkins pulled her jacket tight around herself. "I know you can't comment, but I need to work this out. It seems, from the Archon's reaction to my story, that Jerry Cranston and Galen Cox are one in the same—or that's what you want her to think. Cox was killed on Solaris in a bomb blast meant for her. Ryan Steiner's assassination after that would lead one to believe that he died in retribution for Cox's death. Since Ryan's grab for power in the Isle of Skye had been blunted repeatedly by Katherine and, before her, Melissa, and bombs were meant to kill both of them, the obvious implication is that Ryan had Melissa killed."

"It would seem obvious, wouldn't it?"

"Sure. So Katherine is left thinking that Cox is alive, which means she had to figure out why her brother wouldn't have told her he survived the bombing. The logical conclusion is that Victor didn't trust her for some reason. Her taking the Lyran Alliance out of the Federated Commonwealth certainly shows she's not to be trusted, but that's proof that follows the event we're looking at. Even so, Katherine's secession couldn't have been accomplished if Melissa still lived, so the clear implication is that Victor believes Katherine was involved in killing their mother."

Cold eyes watched her in the mirror.

Francesca's jaw dropped. "The Archon murdered her own mother?"

"Your security clearance was just upgraded to Alpha One. The only way it could be any higher is if you could read the Prince's mind."

Francesca suddenly felt very cold. "There's more to this mission than gaslighting Katherine, right?"

Curaitis nodded. "The fact that you will disappear after dropping the little bombshell you did means that Katherine will have to figure out how and why Victor would want her to know that he knew what she had done. We assume this will make her move to cover her tracks . . ."

"Letting her expose areas of vulnerability we didn't know

existed. She'll point us toward the evidence that will prove her complicity in Melissa Steiner's death."

"So we hope. We've got some basic leads and will be checking on them, but we will be looking to Katherine to guide us along here." Curaitis slowed the taxi for a stoplight, then turned and looked back at Francesca. "The Prince is setting out to save the Inner Sphere from the Clans. He's charged us with the duty of saving the Lyran Alliance from his sister."

She felt the weight of responsibility crush her down into the seat. "And we've got until he returns to do what needs to be done?"

"If we're lucky." Curaitis' arctic eyes narrowed. "Katherine is not stupid. Our window of opportunity may close abruptly if we can't reach her targets before she does. If we fail, a murderer will continue to rule the Lyran Alliance, and chances are excellent that her thirst for power will not be slaked until she rules everything."

# BOOK 2

# Bleak Crusade

# 24

***Tukayyid***
***ComStar Garrison District, Free Rasalhague***
***Republic***
***15 December 3058***

Victor saw Kai's hands lower, and he ducked under the crescent kick aimed at his head even before Kai's right foot was halfway there. The Prince crouched on his right leg as the kick passed over him, then shot his own left foot out. Sweeping it forward, he caught Kai's left leg behind the knee, buckling it and dropping Kai flat on his back against the olive-green practice mat.

Kai hit with a solid thump, but Victor didn't see him go down. He'd already spun away and taken up a fighting stance a good three meters away. Over the tops of his gloved hands, Victor saw Kai lying there, his bare chest heaving and covered with sweat. Then Kai lifted his head, smiled, and slapped the mat twice to indicate surrender.

Victor slowly lowered his hands and, for the first time, acknowledged how leaden his arms felt. He had aches and pains all over, starting with mat-burns, passing up through multiple bruises, and culminating in the throbbing pain of the little toe on his left foot. Despite taping it to the next toe over, he'd aggravated it. It wasn't broken yesterday, but it probably was today.

Kai spit out his mouth guard and began working on the chin-strap to his padded headgear. "Either I'm getting slower or you're getting faster. I should have dropped you with that kick."

Victor smiled and, just for a second, considered not revealing to Kai his weakness. "When you get tired, you drop your hands to balance yourself before making a high kick."

"Bad habits return." Kai winced. "My father noticed the same thing a long time ago and pretty much cured me of it."

"Yeah, well, I don't think anyone you're really fighting will be around long enough to see you get that tired." Victor dropped to the mat and pulled his gloves off, then removed his mouth guard. "If you'd been going all out, I'd be as purple as the Marik crest."

"That might have been true a few months ago, but not any longer." Kai levered himself up into a sitting position, then leaned back on his elbows. "You're not the greatest fighter in the world, but you're smart and quick, which means you anticipate and avoid damage. It actually isn't that easy for me to tag you."

Victor removed his headgear, then shook his head, spraying sweat from his hair. "Realistically, I'll never be able to beat you, right?"

Kai shrugged. "Me? Probably not, but that's because I know how dangerous you can be. My size gives me an advantage over you that I'm not going to surrender. Other people, bigger people, might underestimate you and give you a chance to surprise them."

"The biggest surprise being my security people descending upon them."

"That works, sure." Kai smiled. "Just remember this: if *you* ever find yourself in a fight, it'll be for keeps. Hit the other guy as hard as possible with the largest object you can find, and keep hitting him until he doesn't get back up."

"I think that's a strategy that will work against the Clans, too." Victor glanced over and nodded to the Precentor Martial, who'd just appeared at the training room doorway. "We'd offer to stand, but we've just beaten the stuffing out of each other."

Focht smiled as he hooked his thumbs into the belt of his khaki jumpsuit. "I envy you your youth and energy. I don't mean to interrupt, but there are a couple of matters I thought you should know about. Morgan Hasek-Davion has agreed to use the world of Defiance as his staging and training area.

His units are en route. He reports that April is the soonest they can possibly head out, with June or July being more realistic."

The Prince of the Federated Commonwealth narrowed his eyes. "Morgan tends to be conservative in his estimates. Barring any serious problems, I'd bet he'll have his forces ready to roll out in May or early June. If we focus on that time frame, we can be in position to occupy the Jags while Morgan starts on his hook."

The Precentor Martial nodded. "I agree with your assessment. There will undoubtedly be friction between the various groups, but I'm hoping we can keep them to a minimum. At any rate, I think the chances of the Clans discovering what we're doing will be minimal. Billing Morgan's units as our reserve explains why they're off training, and as they begin their move toward the Combine, they will naturally seem to be moving into position to attack."

Kai smiled. "Morgan and his people will be minor news. Victor's trip to Luthien will capture everyone's attention."

Victor felt a knot begin to tighten in his stomach. "It should be very interesting."

The Precentor Martial and Kai shared smiles that made Victor feel as if he were stepping into a trap. Victor forced himself to his feet. "All right, out with it."

Focht frowned. "Out with what, Victor?"

"Whatever you're thinking."

Kai lazily crossed his legs. "Well, what I'm thinking is that you sound less enthused than I'd have expected for someone who was going to have Omi Kurita showing him her world. I thought you loved her."

"I do."

Kai leaned his head forward. "And?"

Victor started to say something, then stopped. *Too many thoughts all tangled up here.* "Anything I say is going to sound stupid."

Focht smiled. "Spoken like a man in love."

"What would you . . ." Victor stopped and folded his arms across his chest. "Sorry. We've spent enough time together dealing with serious problems that I feel I know you, but then I realize I don't. I was going to ask what you know about being in love, but I know next to nothing about you. For all I know . . ."

The Precentor Martial rested his hands on Victor's

shoulders. "For all you know I may have had many woman, done all manner of things, and could deny any and all of it. I apologize if this seems a sign of a lack of trust, but I assure you it is not. Of my life before becoming Anastasius Focht, I think very little was of value. I wasted much of my previous existence because I did not focus on the important things. Case in point, I did love a woman very fiercely, but I put her second to my ambition. I lost her and lost much more."

"I didn't meant to pry."

"I know." Focht smiled benignly. "As I said before, I envy you your youth. Had I to do it all over again, I would avoid some of my mistakes. Because that is not possible, perhaps telling you of my experiences might help prevent you from traveling the same path."

Victor nodded, then looked up into Focht's one good eye. "So, tell me, how would you feel about going to Luthien if you were me?"

"That is not for me to say." Focht took a step back and clasped his hands at the small of his back. "I do think I would sort out my priorities first. For example, how do you know you love Lady Omi?"

The question surprised Victor. "I know because, well, I know. She's everything I'm not and yet she knows me. She can anticipate me and I can do the same with her. And not only is she beautiful, she's smart, too."

Kai laughed. "Sounds like love to me."

Focht nodded, then gave a small smile. "That it does. You've already met her family, so there should not be much concern there."

"No, not really." Victor frowned. "Initially there was hostility—her father forbade her to correspond with me back during the Clan War, but her grandfather overruled Theodore. Hohiro was also very wary of our relationship at first, but he has warmed to it. Theodore isn't exactly warm, but he's not hostile, either. Her mother and her younger brother Minoru I've not met yet."

As Victor thought about the Combine's royal family, the source of his trepidation became clearer. "I think what I'm afraid of, my friends, is how the people of Luthien will react to me. I fear embarrassing Omi and her father. Their culture is full of hundreds of strictures, any one of which I can violate by looking or not looking, misinflecting words, doing all sorts of things that I take for granted here."

Kai raised an eyebrow. "If you're more afraid for her than you are for yourself, then you're going to be fine. If you're afraid for yourself, you'll compound one error on another and make a dreadful mess of the whole thing."

"Thanks for the vote of confidence."

The Precentor Martial raised his right hand. "What Kai is saying is very important, Victor, and you need to listen to him. You have two things to think about here. First, what is the purpose of your visit to Luthien?"

"There are multiple purposes. One is to deflect attention away from Morgan and the long strike. Another is to show the people of the Inner Sphere that we truly are united as a new Star League. Yet a third is to show the people of the Combine that we are in fact committed to winning back from the Clans a portion of their nation."

"Very good." Focht nodded solemnly. "Your very presence on Luthien will accomplish those goals. There will be no doubt in the mind of anyone who sees you on Luthien that the old ways have been set aside, if not buried outright. A new era will begin with your arrival on Luthien."

That made sense to Victor, though only in an abstract way. "Fine. What was the second thing I needed to think about?"

"How the people of the Combine are feeling about this visit. As keyed up as you are about it, Victor, they must be even more so. You're coming to them, to visit them and see them. You—the leader of a realm that has not suffered as greatly from Clan predation as they have. Theodore's son would be dead if not for your efforts. You will be like a god to them, coming down to see if they are worthy of your help in the future."

Victor frowned. "I think you're getting a bit ahead of yourself there, with all due respect, Precentor Martial."

Kai disagreed. "The Precentor Martial is more right than you know. Until recently the Combine has kept its people innocent of many things. Their control of the media has resulted in a populace that knows less about the Inner Sphere than in your realm, yet on New Avalon or Tharkad you are viewed with great respect despite scandalvids doing their best to tear you down. The power of celebrity is much greater in the Combine. Theodore knows that, which is undoubtedly why he asked you to visit."

The Prince thought for a moment. *Omi told me of a recent attempt on Theodore's life, which suggests some internal troubles in the Combine. Perhaps showing his people that there is a greater cause will heal those rifts. The Precentor Martial may not be that far off the mark.* "So you think the people of Luthien and the Combine are going to be more concerned that they don't offend me than they will be that I make mistakes?"

"I wouldn't bank too heavily on that point—you will be praised for your efforts to conform and some errors can be overlooked, provided you don't show yourself to be a total barbarian." Focht nodded toward Kai. "Fortunately you'll have Kai with you to translate and steer you out of trouble. The fact is, however, that they *will* want to make a good impression on you."

Victor nodded, then unfolded his arms. "So, what are the chances that I'm going to be in danger?"

"Danger? How do you mean that?" Kai rolled forward onto his knees, then stood. "If you're ever alone with Omi, well, you could be lost."

"Brother, you don't know the half of it." Victor sighed, recalling the sauna. "I mean physical danger. There are reactionary elements on Luthien."

Focht's face became a very serious mask. "There was an incident fairly recently that resulted in the neutralization of the hard-liners. That faction should be no problem. Whether or not your connection with Lady Omi will spur protest is hard to say. Your relationship with her is all but unknown in the Combine."

"What's the reaction of those who do know?"

"Mixed and guarded. Some think giving her to you is an excellent way to get you to support the Combine and fight against the Clans." Focht adjusted his eye patch. "Others think that is shameful and would be ready to believe that you are pressuring Theodore to give his daughter to you in return for your support. There is a small but influential group of women who find the story of your romance very exciting and wish Lady Omi all happiness."

Victor sighed. "You know, Kai, I think you did it right. You found the right woman and let nothing stand between you and winning her."

Kai gave Victor a strange look. "Ah, that's revisionist history there, Victor. She hated my guts and it was only during months of being hunted by Jade Falcons on Alyina that she came to see the true me. And even then she rejected me. It wasn't until my uncle tried to have her killed that we got back together again."

"Yeah, whatever, the details don't matter." Victor covered his face with his hands and rubbed his eyes. "The point is that you were able to focus on what truly mattered despite all that. You loved her, she loved you, and now you're together."

"But I'm not the head of a government."

"You're next in line for the throne of the St. Ives Compact."

"Not really the same thing, Victor." Kai shook his head. "Besides, I'm ready to abdicate to my sister, Kuan Yin. She's got the temperament and wisdom to handle the job. You can't do what I did."

"Why not?"

The question brought shocked expressions to the other two men's faces. Kai blinked away his surprise. "Are you serious?"

"I *am* Prince of the Federated Commonwealth—who could stop me?" Victor shrugged. "I won't die if I'm not the Prince, you know."

Focht stared down at Victor. "The person who will stop you, Victor, is *you*. You are the Fox's son, and you are the man who will destroy the Clans. You have it in your power to not only guarantee the future of the Inner Sphere, but to shape it as well. The Prince is who you *are*, but the Prince is also what you must be. You have a great responsibility and duty to the Inner Sphere. To abdicate that duty when only you can perform it is an evil of a magnitude equal to that of Stefan Amaris destroying the original Star League."

The vehemence in Focht's voice shocked Victor.

Kai stared at the Precentor Martial. "Don't you think that's laying it on a bit thick?"

"Not at all." Focht looked from one young man to the other. "For you the great evil has always been the Clans. Yes, you can remember the War of 3039, but you were children then and not capable of understanding the horror of one nation setting upon another. I do remember and I know that without someone as strong as you, Victor, at the helm of the Federated Commonwealth, the Inner Sphere will fall apart again. Can you imagine that your sister Katherine does not hunger to be First Lord of the Star League herself? Do you think Sun-Tzu will be happy while a single world that ever belonged to the Capellan Confederation has a FedCom flag flying over it? Kai, do you think Sun-Tzu does not mean to take back the St. Ives Compact into the Capellan Confederation? And Thomas Marik, will he be pulled apart by forces from without or within his realm, or will he be forced to go after Sun-Tzu or your sister?

"I am an old man who has watched nearly a century of conflict because of leaders who lacked the moral courage and internal fortitude to resist temptation and greed. Our history, the history of humanity, is full of such weaklings and, in the fortunate cases, they are kept out of power. Those who keep them out are the strong and forward-looking leaders, much as the two of you are—and much as you will have to be. Your happiness, Victor, is something I wish for you, but you cannot let it come with an abdication of your duty. That would destroy you and Omi."

Victor looked down at the floor for a moment, then brought his head up. "But there is no way for me, the Prince of the Federated Commonwealth, to be allowed to take Lady Omi for my wife. The people of our realms would revolt."

"Perhaps that is true, Victor. Perhaps the Prince of the Federated Commonwealth cannot marry Lady Omi." Focht's good eye narrowed. "On the other hand, I do not think he who is the savior of the Inner Sphere could ever be denied what makes him and his love happy. By winning a future for the Inner Sphere, you win a future for yourself. And the first step toward that victory will be your first footfall on Black Luthien."

# ═══ 25 ═══

**Zetsuentai Terminal, Takashi Kurita Memorial Spaceport**
**Imperial City, Luthien**
**Pesht Military District, Draconis Combine**
**29 December 3058**

His heart firmly lodged in his throat, Prince Victor Ian Steiner-Davion waited at the doorway of the *Leopard* Class DropShip for the signal to proceed down the tunnel to the reception area of the Imperial City spaceport. Though Kurita officials had shuttled up to the incoming DropShip and spent two days briefing Victor and Kai on all that would be going on, Victor still felt ill-prepared for his arrival. *Even encased in a 'Mech I don't think I could be ready for this.*

Everything had been orchestrated for their arrival to have the maximum impact. They had been tutored in proper conduct, provided with a suitable wardrobe, and even given aid dressing properly. *Which was a good thing, actually.*

Victor looked over to where Kai stood in the mouth of the gantry-tunnel. Kai wore his kimono, the pleated, oversized trousers called *hakama* and the *haori* jacket with large sleeves, long tails, and extended shoulders as if born to them. Kai's clothes had been fashioned of black silk and trimmed with gold at hem, cuff, and sash, using the colors of the stable for which Kai fought on Solaris. The kimono and *haori* had been emblazoned with crests at the back, the breasts, and on the sleeves. In Kai's case the crest was a black mechanical fist grasping a supernova. The disk of the star had been replaced by a red and blue yin and yang symbol—the crest of Cenotaph Stables. That crest was famous as that of the former champion of Solaris, and often appeared on hats and shirts and jackets throughout the Inner Sphere.

Victor's clothing had been cut from dark green silk and trimmed with black, making it a match for the uniforms of the Dragon's Claws, the Coordinator's personal bodyguard unit. The crests he wore were not those of the Dragon's Claws, however, nor were they the armored fist and sunburst symbol of the Federated Commonwealth. Instead Victor wore a crest consisting of a ghostly figure in white, ringed by red serpentine dragons chasing each other in a circle. *This is the crest of the Revenants, the unit I formed to oppose the Clans and to rescue Hohiro Kurita from the Clans back on Teniente.* The dragons were the Combine's addition to the crest, marking the important role the Revenants had played in Combine history.

Further up the tunnel someone signaled, and their procession began to move in toward the spaceport. Victor was looking forward to seeing what it looked like, for it would be his first actual glimpse of ground details. The DropShip's descent into atmosphere had been delayed until night was falling on Imperial City. When he'd asked about this, he was told it was for the purpose of security, but Victor was sure that was not the main reason for a night landing. In a private moment Kai had speculated that the scars of the Clan assault on Luthien might still not have healed even after seven years and that the Kuritas did not want to be embarrassed by the condition of their world.

Victor was certain Kai was closer to the mark, but his experience with Katherine made him believe there was yet another layer over everything. *The darkness, this tunnel into the light, it's as if we're being reborn into Luthien. Our initial experiences will be exactly what Theodore Kurita wants them to be. We will see what he wants seen, hear what he wants heard, and feel what he wants us to feel. Centuries of mistrust on both sides must be laid to rest here, and a stunning spectacle might be enough to do it.*

And stunning the spectacle was. The red carpet leading from the DropShip along the gantry gave way to a mottle-gray pattern easily identifiable as that painted on Smoke

Jaguar 'Mechs and Elemental armor suits. Woven into the carpeting were little birds, all fanciful and of differing sizes and shapes, but united by the fact that they were all canary yellow. Victor thought that a rather whimsical element for the design of the carpet, then he recalled some of the Kurita mythology he'd been taught. *The yellow bird is the only dangerous enemy the Dragon has. By linking the image with the Smoke Jaguars, then having Kai and I walk over it, crushing it down, everyone will know we come to destroy the threat to the Dragon.*

Victor found it both thrilling and daunting to imagine that such symbolism would impress a people. Part of him saw the whole thing as the manipulation of a superstitious populace, but he knew his own people were equally vulnerable to manipulation. *There will be plenty of fear-mongers who will try to make my trip here into the surrender of my realm to Theodore, and some people will let the image of this visit influence them when it's the substance of it that should be important.*

Out past Kai and their escorts, Victor caught glimpses of the reception area. It rose three stories in height, with the ceiling held aloft by teak pillars. Huge silken banners hung down from the rafters, alternating green, gold, and black. A very slight breeze ruffled them, adding life and movement to what would have otherwise been a static and dead display. Moreover, the lack of symbolism on the banners meant that emphasis was placed on the people present in the waiting area.

Stepping out of the tunnel, Victor dropped into line beside Kai and bowed to their waiting hosts. They both made their bows deep and respectful, and held them a heartbeat or two longer than instructed. Opposite them, Theodore Kurita, Hohiro, Omi, and two other individuals waited and then returned the bows. Theodore's did not plunge as deeply as Victor's, nor was it maintained as long, but the Prince took no offense. *Theodore's world, Theodore's rules.*

Victor quickly recognized the other two members of the Kurita family. The woman back with Omi clearly was her mother. Of Tomoe Kurita, Victor knew little—the file his Intelligence Secretariat had gathered was obviously full of errors and relied heavily on gossip. What he did know was that Theodore had met and married Tomoe almost ten years before their union was made public knowledge and that all three of their children had been born prior to that revelation. Takashi Kurita, the previous Coordinator, had not been pleased with his son's choice of a mate, but had warmed to her in his later years as her children proved to be loyal and intelligent.

*The other one, that has to be Minoru.* Again the IS file on him was annoyingly incomplete. Slight of build and wearing glasses that seemed far too large for his face, Minoru looked much younger than his twenty-eight years, though he was only two years younger than Omi. The datafile suggested that Minoru had become something of a mystic, steeping himself in occult rituals designed to strengthen his spirit. Victor's intelligence analysts had opined that these pursuits neutralized the young man as a player in Combine politics, but Victor knew that was largely based on their disbelief that such studies could produce results. Though Victor would have welcomed empirical studies to prove the existence of *chi,* his experiences with martial arts and kenjitsu had suggested to him that there might be more to human beings than could be conveniently measured by science. *And until a Nobel Prize is awarded for the formula that describes creativity, I'll continue to have my reservations.*

Flanked by their guides, Victor and Kai took ten steps forward, then knelt in the center of the reception area. Both of them ended up with their knees crushing the head of a yellow bird. Victor sat back on his heels and rested his hands, palm upward, on his thighs. He resisted the temptation to wipe his hands off and followed Kai's example of concentrating on his breathing.

Theodore Kurita first approached Kai. Hohiro trailed in his father's wake, then knelt at his father's feet. In his hands he held up two swords. The longer one was a katana in a black lacquered scabbard, with a gold crossguard and pommel-cap. The hilt had been wrapped with black cords that dangled from a loop on the pommel-cap. The wakazashi ran to a length of close to fifty centimeters, making it about two-thirds as long as the katana.

Theodore took the katana from his son and presented it to Kai. Without saying a word, and keeping his eyes focused on the floor, Kai slid the sword home through the obi-sash over his left hip. The wakazashi followed, then Kai bowed deeply to Theodore. The Coordinator, still standing, returned the bow respectfully, then moved one step to his left as Kai straightened up.

Omi shuffled forward to her father's side, her orange and brown kimono rustling like autumn leaves in a breeze. She knelt and lifted another two-sword set to her father. Lacquered green scabbards encased these blades. The hilts had been wrapped with green cord, and the crossguard and pommel-cap were both fashioned from fire-blackened steel. They appeared to be the same size as the weapons given to Kai, though Victor thought his katana might be a centimeter or two longer than the one Kai had received.

Victor accepted the katana from Theodore's hands and felt time melting away. The weapon, by its weight, the smooth texture of the scabbard, and even the hypnotic swaying of the twin tassels at the end of the hilt took Victor back to a more primitive time. Duels fought with a weapon like the one in his hands did not have the distance and detachment of an engagement in the thirty-first century. *We may style ourselves as knights in shining armor or samurai warriors fighting for our lords, but our forebears knew a conflict that was more savage and primal. The fact that BattleMechs are often humanoid makes us believe in the illusion of combat being equivalent to the warfare known by the ancients on Terra, but it is not. With this blade I'd engage an enemy whose eyes looked into mine, whose breath fell upon my face, and whose blood would drench me.*

Victor had heard much from Hohiro about the warrior and his weapon becoming one, and even Tancred Sandoval had spoken about a sword becoming an extension of the fighter's arm, but for the first time he had an inkling of what that union really meant. *A warrior and his weapon cannot succeed if they are separate. The weapon becomes the instrument of the warrior's will, and the warrior becomes the engine that allows the weapon to fulfill the purpose for which it was created. With these weapons I can see that union taking place, I can understand it and respect it. The whole is greater than the sum of the parts.*

By the same token, Victor sensed danger in extending that philosophical point to warriors and 'Mechs. *Because we are detached from what we are doing, because we are removed from those we kill, the union does not make us better. To become united with his machine, the warrior must surrender some of his humanity. He pays with a piece of his soul for being able to visit so much destruction on his enemies.* It seemed clear to him that such a loss had been part of what had warped the Clans. *We have to be careful not to let ourselves be caught in that trap even as we defeat the Clans because, from that trap, there is no redemption.*

Victor slid the katana home through his obi and paired it with the wakazashi. He bowed deeply, pressing his nose to the carpet, then straightened up. His gaze flicked toward Omi, but she kept her eyes downcast. Without looking at him, she rose and shuffled back to her position beside her mother.

The Coordinator turned from them and walked over to where a rug with a snarling, coiled dragon had been laid out. He pressed his hands together for a moment, then looked up and out toward a gap between two of the cloth banners defining the reception area. Until the moment he did that, Victor had not noticed the lack of holovid cameras.

*All of this has been recorded and broadcast, but the cameras are hidden so as not to not spoil the ceremony.* Victor cringed inwardly, imagining the vulgar display his nation's media would have made out of the ceremony. While he fully supported the idea of a free and unencumbered media, he did admit to himself that there were times when a little control would go a long way.

Theodore opened his hands toward the gap like a father welcoming home a brood of children. "*Komban-wa,* citizens of the Draconis Combine. You have my sincere apologies for being compelled to watch this ceremony unfold, but this was important enough that I wished all of you to share in it. Today a Davion has come to Luthien, without arms and barefoot, crushing beneath his feet our enemies. As you have just seen, he has been given a *daisho.* Those twin swords define him as a warrior of the greatest repute and skill; and he shall be treated as such by all of us, for the duration of his service here, for the duration of his life, and the duration of his memory."

Theodore paused for a moment, which allowed Kai to finish his whispered translation.

"Is that really what he said?"

Kai nodded almost imperceptibly. "Some honorifics do not translate directly—if anything he was more appreciative than I made it sound."

The Coordinator resumed speaking. "He has brought with

him a companion of great skill and greater courage. Kai Allard-Liao is the son of warriors and the progeny of noble houses. He destroyed the Jade Falcons at Twycross, saved Victor Davion's life at Alyina, and then proceeded to harass Jade Falcons to the point where they allied themselves with him and vanquished a dishonorable foe they had both come to hate. After that, to honor the memory of his father, Kai traveled to Solaris, and again an Allard was champion of the game world. This warrior has earned his *daisho,* and shall be revered among us until time itself is no more.

"These two men are a vanguard of forces that are coming here to the Combine. You will see more of them welcomed here in the coming days. You will see their units on your worlds, training with our troops, working on exercises together. And you will see them all gathered beneath the banner of the Star League. We are united with them in spirit and purpose."

The Coordinator bowed his head toward the holocams for a moment, then looked up. "Seven years ago the Smoke Jaguars came to Luthien and tried to crush the Dragon's heart. They failed because the fathers of the two men kneeling behind me had the courage to send their own troops here to help us. The warriors who fought on their behalf will be here again, as will many more. Their purpose, *our* purpose, is to attend to the next part of the cycle of life. Seven years ago the Smoke Jaguars came to Luthien and now, almost seven years to the day later, we are going to take the war back to the Clans.

"Among you there may be those who see this acceptance of help as dishonor, but I tell you it is not. A warrior who does not accept help when it is freely offered and he is in need is a fool. In wars, fools die and their nations die with them. The Draconis Combine is not a nation of fools. We are a nation of warriors, and a nation of victors. It is time we remind ourselves of those facts and teach them to our enemies."

# = 26 =

*Royal Palace, The Triad*
*Tharkad City, Tharkad*
*District of Donegal, Lyran Alliance*
*3 January 3059*

**W**atching the holovids of her brother's reception at Luthien, Katrina Steiner decided to remain disappointed in Victor even though she knew her expectations concerning his conduct were unrealistic. As Theodore Kurita handed Victor the sword, she was hoping her brother would show some skill with a draw-cut and drop the Coordinator where he stood. She knew it wouldn't happen, but just for an instant she thought Victor might have remembered his roots and eliminated the Combine threat to the Federated Commonwealth and the Lyran Alliance.

The rest of the transmissions concerning his first two days on Luthien were equally filled with disappointment after disappointment for her. Victor seemed to be on his best behavior. He stoically endured traditional Japanese theatre and concerts of music written on a scale she found only suitable for transcribing the howls of cats in heat. Victor had been shown sampling all sorts of delicacies, including *fugu*, but the chef had prepared it well and saved her brother an agonizing death.

All of that could have been endured, but Victor actually looked as if he was enjoying himself. He smiled a lot, even when absent from Omi's side, and Katrina knew it wasn't his

I'm-so-bored-I'm-going-to-die smile. She supposed it was actually possible he was developing a rapport with the people of the Combine—and their respect and reverence for warriors could easily have laid the foundation for such a thing. Thrust into a deadly trap, Victor not only survived but thrived.

Katrina waved a hand at Tormano Liao, who she'd called to her office to join her for the viewing. "Please, Mandrinn, shut it off. Any more of this and my blood will crystallize. The Combine's editors must have worked for hours to put that shameful display together."

Tormano pointed the remote at the holovid viewer and punched a button. The picture went black, then he turned back to her. "At the risk of ruining your day, our people believe all that was raw footage and of genuine events, not staged events."

"I find that hard to believe. Victor couldn't be so spontaneous without a lot of practice," Katrina sniffed. She paced around behind her desk and sat down, forcing Tormano to twist uncomfortably on the sofa so he could still see her. "This is footage fed to our media by the Combine's state media organization?"

"Some of it. They've actually given the rest of the Inner Sphere's media unprecedented access to their holovideo content. Aside from meetings and functions from which even we would ban recording devices, we're getting everything." Tormano shrugged. "There's enough of it that we can account for the vast majority of Victor's time. If there are rehearsals for some of these events, he's only sleeping two hours a night."

"I don't care how much sleep he gets." Her blue eyes narrowed. "Any word on who he might be sleeping with?"

Tormano shook his head. "No, but I doubt there's any deception on that score. The Combine's Dictum Honorium stresses the values of purity and harmony above all others. Omi Kurita has taken over as the Keeper of the House Honor, and her elevation to this position is seen as a very positive omen in the Combine. Back in 2333, the first Keeper of the House Honor was also named Omi Kurita."

"I'm certain the Dracs all find this fascinating."

"Indulge me, Archon, because this next bit is on point concerning your brother's sex life." Tormano interlaced his fingers and rested his hands on the top of the couch-back.

"The first Omi Kurita began codifying matters of honor after her younger sister was executed by their father for violating the dictums of Purity and Harmony. It seems that young Shada Kurita had taken a commoner as a lover and became pregnant, violating the ideal of Purity. Her father ordered her to get rid of the fetus, but she refused, violating the ideal of Harmony. For that she paid with her life."

"No indication what happened to Shada's lover?"

"No, but I do not imagine he outlived the Coordinator's daughter."

"Ah, then there is hope after all, if my brother gets frisky." Katrina rolled her eyes to heaven. "How widespread are these images?"

The Capellan smiled. "Some of it has been used in news broadcasts, but only little snippets. I've issued a call for all the footage to be sent here first, with the promise of using it to produce a documentary. We have a preliminary script to work from, and are preparing edited versions of it for various portions of your realm. Tailoring sentences to remind the viewers of past Combine atrocities is a subtle way to reinforce the idea that Victor is really treating with the enemy."

"Excellent." Katrina smiled slyly. "You will be preparing versions suitable for distribution in the Draconis March of the Federated Commonwealth, yes?"

Tormano hesitated, and she read the confusion on his face rather easily. "I had not included your brother's realm in our planning, Archon."

"I can understand the oversight, Mandrinn Liao, but I do not expect such mistakes in the future." Katrina gestured toward the holovid player. "My brother is off winning the hearts of allies so he can lead them against the Clans. He has placed my little sister on the throne in New Avalon, but you and I know she doesn't have the experience to be able to safeguard that whole nation. Just as my brother still feels proprietary about my realm, so I have concerns about his. Preparing documentaries like this for his realm will keep his people informed. An informed populace can make the right decisions concerning its future."

"And you don't think he will see this is meddling?"

"Of course he would, *if* he could pinpoint my fine hand in it. I was thinking, Mandrinn, that sales of a holovid documentary about my brother might produce handsome profits.

Since any direct funding of your Free Capella movement would be seen as divisive war-mongering by me, I was thinking your people might undertake the production and distribution of such a product, using the profits to our mutual benefit."

A smile slowly blossomed on Tormano's face as he took the bait. "As you probably know, Archon, my people have already undertaken a similar scheme concerning the publication of a holovid that presents Sun-Tzu as even more of a danger to the Chaos March."

"It was your success with that project, Mandrinn, that gave me the idea for this one. I also think a streamlined version of your holovid about Sun-Tzu, with emphasis on Victor's collusion with his elevation, would have interesting effects in the Capellan March of the Federated Commonwealth."

"When?"

"We have six months. By then Victor will be embroiled in a war. If we do things correctly, we can destabilize the Federated Commonwealth. Because it's needed to fund and supply the war against the Clans, I want it still functional. When Victor comes home, however, he should find his hands full of unrest." Katrina sat back in her chair and propped her feet on the desk. "Besides, after driving off the Clans for good, he's likely to find the Inner Sphere boring. We wouldn't want him to come home and find he had nothing to do, now, would we?"

## JumpShip *King of Monkeys*
## *Zenith Recharge Station, Marik*
## *Marik Commonwealth, Free Worlds League*

Sun-Tzu contemplated what he had seen in the holovids from the Draconis Combine. He noted, first and foremost, that the arrival ceremony had been orchestrated perfectly, with a great deal of attention paid to details. He knew that to individuals who had grown up within a culture whose origins went back to Asia and relied on a written language using symbols that represented whole words instead of just sounds, the symbolic content was as important as real content. Omens and auguries had more influence, and form could color the perception of anything. Had Kai or Victor so much as sneezed while being greeted, had the illusion Theodore sought to create been compromised in some way, that disaster would have shaded every following event with meaning.

The fact that the greeting had been wildly successful had certainly done the same thing. Wherever they went, both Victor and Kai were received with enthusiasm—the generation of which was remarkable given the squalid and stultifying conditions of most of the people on Luthien. *Prior to this I would have thought the denizens of Luthien's factories didn't even know the Federated Commonwealth existed—in most Combine school texts the union of the Lyran Commonwealth and the Federated Suns was never even acknowledged.*

Victor's acceptance didn't bother Sun-Tzu, primarily because Victor needed to excite people if he was going to lead them into battle against the Clans. While the Precentor Martial would have overall command of the operations, Victor would be his primary fighting general. Troops would rally around Victor and pound the enemy just to earn his praise. That Victor actually knew what he was doing and always did his best to keep his troops alive certainly did not hurt force morale.

Kai's reception on Luthien did concern Sun-Tzu, specifically because it called into question an underlying assumption he realized he'd harbored for as long as he could remember. Back at the time Hanse Davion and the other Katrina Steiner had agreed to an alliance, Maximilian Liao—Sun-Tzu's grandfather—had entered into an accord with Janos Marik and Takashi Kurita, leaders of the Free Worlds League and Draconis Combine, respectively. The Concord of Kapteyn was a mutual-defense pact and was still in force. Sun-Tzu had always expected that if he made a move against the St. Ives Compact that the Combine would threaten the Federated Commonwealth enough that his effort would meet with no interference.

The holovids cast this eventuality into severe doubt. While Sun-Tzu had been aware that Kai had developed a following in the Combine because of his stint as Solaris' Champion, he had not given the true meaning of that development sufficient thought. If Kai was actually that popular, then any move against his homeland might meet with a negative response in the Combine. *Moreover, if Kai is seen as a key person in the defeating of the Clans and the saving of the*

*Combine, the Dracs could be openly hostile to my takeover attempt.*

Isis Marik appeared in the hatchway of his cabin. "May I come in?"

"Of course, beloved." Sun-Tzu punched a button on a remote and the holovid died. "What is it?"

"I see you have been watching the holovid of the Luthien visit."

"I have."

"And you have seen the potential problem there?"

Sun-Tzu nodded, then caught himself. Isis was not a stupid woman—not by a long shot—yet her sensibilities were attuned to things other than those that concerned him. "I have seen problems of various sorts. What did you see?"

Isis hooked a hank of chestnut hair behind one ear. "Prince Victor appears to be a glowing success there. The people seem to love him."

"As would be expected when Theodore dresses him up in the uniform of the Dragon's Claws, makes him a samurai, then all but attributes the salvation of Luthien to him and Kai." Sun-Tzu shrugged. "Of course, this is all to the good because Victor will be in the forefront of the fight against the Clans. Theodore engineered all this to guarantee Victor massive acceptance by his troops."

"Exactly." Isis nodded solemnly. "Which is the key to the problem."

"What problem?"

Isis frowned at him. "You know as well as I do that twenty-five to thirty percent of Victor's worlds lie in the Draconis March region. The Sandoval family has long been wary of the Combine and has agitated against any alliance with the Combine because they believe the Combine cannot be trusted. Victor has appointed Tancred Sandoval as one of Yvonne Davion's advisors, in effect placing someone who will view Victor's actions dimly in a position of extreme power within Victor's government."

"That was rather silly of Victor, wasn't it?"

"Especially in light of what Katherine will undoubtedly do with the holovid gigabytes you've just viewed."

"Indeed." Sun-Tzu looked around the sparsely furnished cabin and smiled as he imagined Katrina's reaction to Victor's reception. "She'll attempt to use his every success to poison the Draconis March against him. If successful, she could heighten tensions on the border with the Combine." *The Draconis March would become an effective barrier against Combine action in St. Ives and might even demand enough attention that the Federated Commonwealth will be forced to withdraw from the St. Ives Compact and leave it to me.*

Isis nodded. "So what are you going to do about it?"

Sun-Tzu shrugged. "If Katrina destabilizes the Federated Commonwealth, I imagine we can use the situation to our benefit."

"What?"

He looked at her in confusion. "I don't understand your question."

"Clearly." She put her hands on his shoulders and gave him just the slightest angry shake. "You are the First Lord of the Star League. You have been given an opportunity to guarantee your place in the future and your place in history. You can't be thinking of minor conquests and mischiefs that will bring misery to millions of people. Your responsibilities are greater now than they have ever been before. What you do in the next three years will determine the course of the Star League's future and whether or not you ever get a chance to be First Lord again."

Sun-Tzu frowned. "Are you suggesting I ignore a chance to benefit from the downfall of a Davion? After all they have done to my realm?"

"I suggest nothing of the sort." She dropped her hands, but her tone still had its sharp edge. "I suggest you look at reality. The Capellan Confederation is the weakest of the five major Inner Sphere houses, yet you are accorded a political parity with the leaders of much larger nations. Why? Because the Capellan Confederation could severely hurt another Great House. Granted your realm would be no more, but the damage done would weaken the other House to the point where it would be unable to fight off opposition."

He slowly nodded. "I see this."

"Look further ahead, my dear. If or when Victor returns from the war with the Clans, he will return at the head of an army the like of which the Inner Sphere has never seen before. His people will be highly trained, highly skilled, and unbelievably proud of what they have accomplished. They will believe they are returning to an Inner Sphere that has not changed—at least not for the worse—while they have been gone. Anyone practicing adventurism while they are away will immediately become a focus for punishment, and I don't think you want to be in that position, do you?"

"There is a certain wisdom to what you are saying."

"Think about this, too, then. Katherine Steiner has risen, in three and three-quarters years, from a social butterfly to the throne of one of the five Great Houses of the Inner Sphere. She clearly meant for you to lose the election to the position of First Lord, and probably thought she could get herself elected First Lord by quelling the acrimony surrounding your nomination. It was only Victor's choosing to frustrate her that won it for you."

"You're trying to tell me she's not to be trusted."

"Right."

Sun-Tzu reached out and stroked Isis' cheek. "This I already know, beloved. She relies upon my uncle, which makes her foolish as well as untrustworthy. That said, I will take to heart your words. As First Lord, I need to use power to build toward the future, not reap short-term gains for myself."

She smiled at him then, her expression both proud and tender. "Exactly. The Star League really is the best situation for the Inner Sphere." Isis kissed his palm. "Channel your energies into it, improve and strengthen it, and you will find your rewards greater than even you could imagine."

# 27

**V**ictor knew he should have been exhausted after all his many activities in this week on Luthien so far, but he was excited enough to be running on nervous energy. In between the planning and strategy sessions, he had been run all over Imperial City, among others. He had toured factories and battlefields, visited graves and said prayers at temples. Every experience seemed crafted to give him an insight into the ways of the Combine and its people, and to let them get to know him as well.

Before the coming of the Clans, the tours he was getting would have been out of the question. At the Luthien Armor Works not only had he been given unprecedented access to the factory producing BattleMechs, but he'd actually been given a chance to pilot a *Grand Dragon* on their proving grounds. The *Grand Dragon* had always been a bogeyman of a 'Mech for Federated Commonwealth troops, and seated in the cockpit Victor could see why. The long-range missile rack and extended-range particle projection cannon gave the 'Mech superior long-range support capability, while the trio of medium lasers and heavily armored hide meant it could stand up to and deliver punishment in a close-up brawl.

Victor had also been toured over the battlefields surrounding Imperial City by Shin Yodama and Hohiro Kurita. They had pointed out where the Clans had come in across the Tairakana Plains, and where they had died in the hills of the Kado-guchi Valley. In the inflections of their words Victor caught much of the tension that had reigned that day seven years ago. The Combine and FedCom mercenaries had broken the back of a joint Smoke Jaguar and Nova Cat assault. Though a few Nova Cats actually reached Imperial City, they only managed minor damage before a Wolf Dragoons air strike put them down. One of the Nova Cats 'Mechs remained frozen in place, its blasted and ruined condition speaking of one of the few times the Inner Sphere had handed the Clans a shocking defeat.

Oddest of all the trips he had taken was a visit to the grave of Takashi Kurita. While he found the display to be in keeping with Kurita ideas about simplicity and circumspection, it didn't seem right to Victor. Centered in the gray granite slab was a meter-long coral panel that had been carved to show Takashi in traditional samurai armor. Coiled about his feet was a dragon, and one of Luthien's moons hung over his head like a halo. To Victor he appeared very much like a saint.

Looking down at the modest stone memorial, Victor found himself full of mixed emotions. Takashi Kurita had always been the devil incarnate to the Davions. Hanse Davion had blamed Takashi for the death of his older brother Ian. Takashi had embodied the threat the Combine presented to the Federated Commonwealth. He had been unrepentant and unreasonable even while his son, Theodore, had been willing to make changes to allow for the defeat of the Clans.

As much as Victor knew he should have been put off by being asked to visit Takashi's grave, he did feel he owed a debt to the man buried there. Theodore Kurita had been against Victor and Omi forming any sort of friendship. When Omi had asked Victor to take the Revenants and rescue her brother from Teniente, the price of her getting permission to stage such an operation was agreeing to sever all communication with Victor. She had agreed to this condition to save her brother.

Victor had been prepared never to see or hear from her again, but Takashi Kurita had intervened. While Omi was bound by tradition to obey her father's prohibition on communication for the sake of harmony, so Theodore was bound to obey his father when Takashi lifted that prohibition. As much as Victor knew he should hate Takashi, the man who had been a lifelong enemy of the Davions had, toward the end, rewarded a Davion by rewarding his own granddaughter for her sacrifice.

He offered a quick prayer of thanks over Takashi's grave, then let himself be led away and brought to the Palace of Serene Sanctuary. The Palace was yet another of the contrasts on Luthien. Huge factory complexes covered the planet, with sprawling metropolises in place to house all the workers needed to make the factories function. The pollution had once been so bad that the world had earned the nickname of Black Luthien. Despite efforts to reverse the ecological damage, the epithet stuck—though among the Combine's enemies the adjective black came to apply to the soul of the rulers as much as the world.

Imperial City looked little like the rest of the planet. All the architecture hearkened back to earlier, more feudal times on Terra. Several structures had been broken down and transported to Luthien stone by stone, but around them had grown up many more, like mushrooms surrounding a parent plant. The Palace of Unity had been fashioned entirely of teakwood, making it as much a work of art as a building.

The Palace of Serene Sanctuary, located a half-dozen kilometers from the Palace of Unity, was no less magnificent. Stone, wood, and tile combined to create a building that looked lifted straight out of the thirteenth century on Terra. A tall wall surrounded it, holding the rest of the city at bay, as if it were a preserve for a more gentle, less hectic era. Passing through the outer gates, Victor felt as if he were walking back in time.

Omi met him inside the foyer. She wore a white kimono decorated with embroidered pink cherry blossoms. It reminded him of the dress she had worn on Arc-Royal almost four years earlier. He remembered their walk in the garden that night and kissing her. *I wanted very much to sweep her off her feet, to carry her away so we could share our love, but we both knew that could not be.*

She bowed to him. "*Komban-wa*, Davion Victor-*sama*."

He returned the bow. "*Komban-wa*, Kurita Omi-*sama*." Straightening up, he smiled at her. "You remind me of a night on Arc-Royal."

"As do you." She smiled at him. "Your kimono is the

same one you wore that night. The swords are an addition, but a good one."

Victor started to slip the katana and wakazashi free of his obi, but she pressed her hands to his. "Those swords are a symbol of your rank here, Victor. For you to abandon them would be disharmonious, and on a night like this, that would be a bad thing."

He caught her hands in his and nodded. "Whatever you wish of me, Omi, it will be done."

"You honor me with your trust, Victor." She freed her left hand from his right and swept it out to direct his attention to the rest of the palace. "I would show you my home."

Victor finally looked beyond her and suddenly felt overwhelmed. The palace interior had been constructed completely of oak left in its natural color. Strips of oaken planking had been precisely fitted together for the flooring while pillars and beams seamlessly hooked into each other, making it very difficult to pick out the lines where they had been joined. Moreover, the artisans who had shaped and fitted the wood had taken exquisite care to see that the wood's natural grain patterns flowed together and eddied apart, giving the stationary wood a sense of motion and life. The interior felt vital and peaceful.

Omi began to lead him through the building. "Seven years ago today the Clans attacked Luthien. The fifth of January was a day marked by a battle that ran from dawn to well after evening had fallen. The fighting was terrible and ferocious and lives in the memories of all who were here. On this day, on the fifth of January, people throughout Luthien return to the place where they were when the Clans attacked, using that time to remind them of the things that truly matter in life. We mourn those who died and offer thanks for those who survived."

Victor felt a cold chill cut at his spine. "Seven years ago I was on Alyina. I was fighting the Jade Falcons. They knew I was there, and they came after me specifically. They had me trapped, then Kai appeared out of nowhere. He crushed part of their force and, I believed at the time, died doing so."

He reached up and slipped a jade monkey pendant from beneath the cloth of his kimono. "Kai had given this to me at Christmas. It's Sun Hou-tzu, the King of the Monkeys. He said it was meant to give me luck, and to remind me to forever be myself. As I evacuated Alyina I thought it was all

I had left of Kai, all I had to remember him by; so I understand the mourning and sacrifice you commemorate here on
this day."

"I know where you were, Victor." Omi led him through a
pair of doors and into a garden thick with dark plants, mani-
cured shrubs, and trees covered in fragrant blooms. "You
were also here, with me, through that day and into that
night."

"Here?" Victor frowned. "With the Clans coming for
Imperial City, you couldn't have been here. Your father must
have evacuated you to some place safe."

"He tried, but I remained here." She glanced down at the
crushed stone ocean defining a semi-circle near the doorway.
"My brother told me that you understand the principles of
*giri* and *ninjo,* duty and compassion. While my father would
have wanted me to leave Imperial City, he did not order me
to evacuate. I knew, just as he and my brother and my grandfather would be out there on the plains defending Imperial
City, I had a duty to be *here.* The men and women out there
fighting against the Clans knew they were fighting for our
nation and our future, but my being here gave them a focus.
Dying to preserve a nation is an abstraction that does not
provide comfort."

Victor nodded slowly. "Galen Cox told me much the same
thing as we left Alyina. He said Kai had sacrificed himself to
save me. He said I had a duty to Kai to make certain his sacrifice had not been wasted."

"Much as I have a duty to my people to see to it that their
sacrifices were not in vain." Omi stepped away from him,
raised her arms and spun around. "So I was here while the
fighting raged out there. I could hear the sounds of explosions growing louder as the Clans forced our troops back."
She traced a finger through the night sky. "I watched fighters
spiral and die. I saw errant bolts of laser light burn through
the air, all the while waiting for one to find me."

She hugged her arms around herself. "I have never been so
terrified in my whole entire life. In my fear I sought refuge
in my memories of you, Victor. I recalled our kiss on Outreach and how safe I felt in your arms. I remembered our
time together, the laughter and the sorrow and the sharing. I
resolved that terror was not an appropriate reaction if I was to
be worthy of you and your love."

Victor reached a hand out toward her, then drew her close

and enfolded her in his arms. "I wish I had been here to calm your fears."

"But you were." She reached up and stroked his cheek with her right hand. "And had you been here on Luthien, you would have been in your 'Mech, driving the Clans away. As much as you would have liked to give me succor, your sense of duty would have overridden it. Hush, no, do not deny it, for it is not a fault or flaw. I understand these conflicts."

Omi kissed him lightly on the lips, then slipped from his grasp and retreated into the shadows of a cherry tree. "You are aware that I am the Keeper of the House Honor?"

Victor nodded. "You are the arbiter of what is correct behavior and incorrect behavior." He drew his arms to his chest to preserve the warmth of her on his flesh.

"And you are aware of the two ideals that govern everything here in the Combine?" Her blue eyes glittered in motes of light that threaded their way through the tree's foliage, making her appear more spirit than woman. "Harmony and Purity govern everything. It is to these ideals that we aspire."

"This I understand."

"Do you?" She watched him carefully. "Today is a day for remembrance and mourning, but tomorrow, the day after the great victory, will be one of celebration; yet that celebration will encompass Harmony and Purity. Families will begin tomorrow as they did seven years ago. They will go out into their neighborhoods and work with others to pick up litter, to repair broken fences, to prune shrubs, and pull weeds. They will do what they can to make the world more beautiful, to destroy the scars of disharmony and the impurity wrought by the Clans and by the inconsiderate and unthinking among us. Only after that they will rejoice."

Victor shivered. While the knew there were plenty of people who used holidays as a day to perform housework or to beautify their own gardens, he couldn't image the sort of compulsive community action Omi described taking place in his realm. *While I have no doubt our people love the Commonwealth every bit as much as the people here love the Combine, we see ourselves as a nation of individuals, not as one massive society bound by grand philosophies.*

"Though my nation does not operate the same way yours does, I think, after being here, that I grasp much of what you are saying. It seems that substance is more important here than form."

"It is, but we are not without our ways of turning form into substance or vice versa. My love, the Dictum Honorium is full of anecdotes, rules, and aphorisms that indicate there are many shades to these things. For example, when your father sent the Kell Hounds and Wolf's Dragoons here to oppose the Clans, that action had the appearance of disharmony. Your father and my father had an agreement concerning the respect for each other's borders. Your father knew we needed help, but he had said he would not permit Federated Commonwealth troops to cross the border until the Clans were defeated."

Omi smiled slowly and stepped back into the light spilling into the garden from the palace doors. "Your father's solution was to order mercenaries to come to Luthien to help us. They were not Federated Commonwealth troops per se, so he preserved Harmony while allowing his goals to be serviced.

"Similarly it is often thought that the ideal of Purity is served by virginity or sexual abstinence, but this is not true." Omi opened her hands and approached him. "Were it true, there would be no children in the Combine. Purity in this sense is bound up with fidelity and discretion, choosing the appropriate partner and keeping what passes between them between them alone."

Omi pressed herself against him and settled her arms around his shoulders. "Victor, I would have you with me this night as I imagined you were seven years ago. I will give you the comfort I wish I could have given you then, and you shall comfort me as I would have had you comfort me."

Victor wrapped his arms around her waist and held her tight against his him. "I want this more than you can know, Omi, but I would not cause disharmony by having you disobey your father."

"Quiet, love." She cupped his face in her hands. "I cannot disobey him by doing something that has not been forbidden."

*Not forbidden? But the Coordinator must have known this might happen.* "Your father knows . . . ?"

"He knows what he wants to know." She kissed Victor on the forehead and then his lips. "This place is my world, *our* world. We would cause disharmony if we denied the purity of the feelings we share for one another. Tonight my sanctuary becomes our sanctuary."

Victor leaned his head forward to kiss her throat. He drank in the scent of her body, which mingled with the cherry blossoms perfume to become an intoxicating fragrance. Beneath the silk of her kimono she felt warm and soft, slender and strong. He felt her long black hair tickle the back of his hands as she unbound it.

Bringing his head up, he kissed the point of her chin. "Omi, I love you."

"And I, you, Victor."

*"Iie!"*

The snarled denial of their love lashed at them and spun them apart. Victor came around to see three figures clad from head to toe in black. Light reflected back from the night-vision goggles riding where their eyes should have been. All three wore katanas strapped across their backs, and the foremost among them drew his with practiced fluidity. Light gleamed along its razored edge, and Victor's mouth went dry.

Omi's voice took on an edge he had never heard in it before. "What is the meaning of this intrusion?"

"We have come to save you from being soiled by this barbarian." The speaker leveled his sword at Victor's chest. Though four meters separated them, Victor knew his life was the man's to take. "We will not have you become a Davion whore."

Victor stabbed a finger at the speaker. "How dare you dishonor her!"

"Ha! I cannot—she has already been dishonored by her conduct with you." The man shook his head. "I will slay you, then we shall oversee Lady Omi's suicide. Only by killing herself can she redeem her honor."

"No." Victor shook his head adamantly. "She has done nothing wrong. I swear it, on my honor, as a samurai."

"What do you know of a samurai's honor?"

"I know Harmony and I know Purity." Victor looked back over his shoulder at Omi. "I know she is pure and has not been soiled. And I know her death would disrupt the harmony of the Combine. And what I know of honor is that a samurai would do his duty as best he could so others could show compassion."

Victor hit duty and compassion with emphasis, then tugged at the neck of his kimono with his left hand. "It's me you really want, not her. I will do my duty, I will die as a samurai would die, provided you do yours and make it a clean cut. Say you answered her cries for help as I attempted to ravish her. Make yourselves into heroes, but leave her alive."

"No, Victor, no." Omi clutched at his left arm. "I will not let you do this."

"*Iie*, Omiko-*sama*, this is what I must do." Victor tipped his chin up to stretch his throat. "Have we a deal?"

"*Hai!*" The leader looked back at his men, exchanged nods with them, then stalked forward. "I will give you the honorable death you do not deserve."

"I'll earn it." Victor pulled his arm from Omi's grasp, took a step forward, and dropped to his left knee. He brought his left hand across his chest to grab his right tricep and bowed his head forward. *This better work.*

The crushed stones crunched as the assassin came to a stop in front of Victor. As the man raised his sword, Victor dropped his right hand to the hilt of his katana and drew the blade as he started to come up. The draw cut was weak, but slashed at the assassin's face, knocking the goggles askew. The man began to spin away from the attack as Victor flicked his wrist and arced the tip of his sword around one hundred and twenty degrees. With two hands now on the hilt, he chopped the katana down and to the left, slicing cleanly through the assassin's spine.

The blade came free and splashed a black line of blood across the white stones.

"Run, Omi, run!" Victor brandished the katana and interposed himself between her and the other two assassins. "Run, Omi."

"*Iie*, Victor, I will not run."

He heard fear and resignation in her voice, but the next assassin leaped at him and gave him no time to convince Omi to leave. The assassin's attacks came fast and furious, causing Victor to retreat quickly. He dodged right and left as he went, trying to make the assassin repeat the mistake made by his compatriot. *Night-vision goggles severely limit the user's field of vision. When I dropped to one knee, I literally dropped from the man's sight for a few seconds. This one seems smarter than his dead companion.*

Beyond the assassin Victor saw Omi sink to her knees beside the first man's body. The third assassin knelt on one knee beside it and reached a hand out toward the first assassin's throat, ostensibly to feel for a pulse. Victor saw no more as his foe forced him back to the palace doorway, then engaged him in the high-ceilinged oak room.

Victor parried an overhand head-cut, then tried to disengage his blade and slash at the assassin's belly, but his opponent leaped back from the attack. Worse yet, the assassin reached up with his left hand and tore the goggles from his face. He tossed them at Victor, and when the Prince ducked to avoid them, the assassin closed.

Victor blocked a transverse cut, then ducked below a head-cut and backed away. Their blades rang as they met, sending shivers up the Prince's arms. He twisted aside from one lunge, felt the burning sting of a slice over his ribs, then tumbled over an oaken banister and into a narrow corridor. The assassin's slash at him planed a curly wisp of oak from the railing, then the killer vaulted the banister and came at Victor even harder.

Panic threatened to overwhelm him, but Victor forced it away. He focused on the center of his foe, not watching arms or legs, but watching his heart and his belly. Everything else he could see at the periphery, but by watching the man's core, he could see the attacks coming and read the feints. Victor narrowed the cone of his own responses to attacks, blocking them before they could do damage, but not letting his blade get drawn too wide by a feint.

Victor parried a cut at his left shoulder, then quickly brought his blade over and around in the sort of circular fencing parry Tancred Sandoval had shown him. As the katana's point swung back into line with the assassin's chest, Victor lunged. The blade pierced the man's shirt on the left and a hissed breath told Victor he'd hurt him, though he guessed the blade had scored only a flesh wound over a rib.

Without warning the assassin's left fist crashed in and snapped Victor's head around to the left. The Prince saw stars explode and began to stumble back. His world went black for a moment, just a heartbeat, but as his vision cleared he discovered he was off balance and falling. He heard his left elbow crack against the hardwood floor a second before he felt pain shooting up through the limb. A half-second later he landed hard on his back. Somehow he managed to keep his head from hitting, but the jarring impact freed his sword from his grip.

His katana clattered against the floor as the assassin loomed over him like the shadow of Death. The assassin raised the katana like a sacrificial dagger and plunged it downward as Victor leaned to the left and whipped his right foot up into the assassin's groin.

In the half-second before silvery bolts of agony shook him, Victor felt the pressure of the katana punching through a rib on the right side of his chest. It stabbed clean through him and drove on into the oaken floor. A scream ripped through his throat, and for a heartbeat the sound overrode the pain coursing through him. In its wake the pain receded for a moment, leaving Victor an instant of clarity in which he realized he was more seriously wounded than he had ever been before.

Anger exploded in him and he commanded himself to stop whimpering. *I will not go to my death mewling like a whipped kitten!* He clenched his teeth against the sound and only then realized he was not producing it. Raising his head, he looked past the shaft of steel sticking up from his right side and saw the crumpled, simpering figure of a man clutching at crushed testicles.

*I will not die like this.* Keeping his teeth clamped together, he reached up and grasped the hilt of the katana pinning him to the floor. He tugged it to the left using all the strength he could muser, but it barely budged. He realized then that he could feel very little with his left arm and that the elbow didn't seem inclined to work very well. *No matter. I will succeed. I am not a bug to be stuck this way in someone's collection!*

He pulled on the sword again, then hit the crossguard with the heel of his right hand. The sword popped free of the floor, then slid partway from his chest. He could feel the blade grating against the bone it had shattered. Each crackle, each little vibration set off torturous tremors. He wanted to stop, wanted to give himself a second to recover, but he knew his downed enemy would never grant him that chance, so he kept pushing.

The blade came free accompanied by a bubbling hiss. *Lung hit. This is very bad.* Despair crested over him in a black wave and pounded at him. He started to draw his knees up toward his chest, to curl up into a little ball and wait for the pain to stop.

*No! Only death will free me, and I cannot die here, now. She needs me still.* Victor rolled to his right and levered himself up so he could gather his knees beneath himself. He tossed aside the assassin's sword and snatched up the one he had dropped. He inched his way forward, dragging his knees beneath him, then laid the blade across the assassin's throat.

"You. Stupid. Shit." Victor desperately wished he knew enough Japanese to curse properly. "Davions take a lot of killing."

He wanted to raise the sword and behead the man with one stroke, but he knew he did not have the strength to do it. Placing his left hand on the back of the blade near the tip, he leaned forward and used his weight to saw the blade through the man's throat. The first stroke severed the carotid artery, spraying blood up over Victor's face and chest. The second ended the man's muted screams and the third cut through the spine. The assassin gurgled to death in a pool of his own blood.

*And not a little of my own is mixed in there.* Victor used his sword to get himself to his feet, then he slipped in the blood and sprawled forward over his victim. He broke his fall with his left hand, but it collapsed as pain arced through his arm. His right shoulder hit the floor, but not that hard, so he maintained his grip on his katana.

*Have to keep going. Omi is still in danger.* He slid off the dead man's body and slowly crawled forward. He made his way toward a wall. *Get up, Victor. You need more mobility.*

Again he got himself to his feet and managed a weak smile despite the agony wracking him. He staggered forward a step or two, with each step bringing a shallow breath that prompted a wet cough. His head began to spin, so he leaned heavily against the wall to steady himself. *Keep going.*

The hissing sound from his chest and the burning pain in his lungs reminded him how badly he'd been hurt. *I'm bleeding too much.* He clamped his arm down over the wound, but he could feel bloody bubbles bursting at the exit site on his back. *Not much time. I must save Omi. Not much time. Keep going.*

Another step, then he crashed to the floor. He didn't remember falling, but could feel the burn of his face sliding along the floor's oak planking. He could see a ghostly reflection of himself in the wood's glossy surface and tried to smile in response to it. *Always wanted to leave a beautiful corpse.*

Darkness began to nibble at the edges of his sight, but he heard something and forced himself to look in that direction.

In the dimming distance he saw a figure, a woman, walking toward him through a golden tunnel of light. He recognized the white kimono she wore and the cherry blossoms decorating it, but he could not understand, at first, why the sleeves were different. He could plainly see that they were stained a deep, deep red from wrist to elbow, but he could not determine why.

Then it hit him with a certainty that rocked him like a physical blow. *He made her slit her wrists. She is dead, too.*

He did all he could to smile at her. *Don't be afraid, Omi. We will be together, finally. In death we will find our Harmony.*

He looked to her for understanding and a knowing smile, but blackness stole over him before he ever read her response.

# 28

*Palace of Serene Sanctuary, Imperial City*
*Luthien*
*Pesht Military District, Draconis Combine*
*5 January 3059*

The evening had started out as an exercise in surreality for Kai Allard-Liao, and events quickly escalated beyond anything he could have imagined. He and the Precentor Martial, who had arrived two days after Kai and Victor, had been invited to share a traditional Combine meal with Theodore and Hohiro Kurita. Things had begun very normally, but Kai quickly realized he was kneeling at a table with the Coordinator of the Draconis Combine and Anastasius Focht, the man who had defeated the Clans at Tukayyid.

*At some point they'll take notice of me and send me packing.* The special nature of the meeting was not lost upon Kai. He could easily imagine generations of historians arguing over the content and import of this gathering. Indeed it seemed to him that Theodore and Focht had layers to their relationship that he knew nothing about, and he had no doubt that things were happening on multiple levels—including levels he couldn't even dream existed.

Theodore Kurita inclined his head toward the Precentor Martial. "It appears there has been a breakthrough in the discussions with the Nova Cats. Our liaison officers made them a gift of the holovid of the Star League Constitution's signing, as well as a facsimile copy of the document itself.

The holovid disk also contained images from Victor's arrival here."

Focht smiled. "And the Nova Cats were impressed?"

"As nearly as we can determine, images in both presentations matched up with elements in visions the Nova Cat Khans have apparently been experiencing. We first began speaking with the Nova Cats about two years ago and have seen the greatest movement toward a solution to our problem when and if one of their Khans or prominent warriors has a vision that applies to our situation." Theodore's face brightened. "Apparently the image of Victor Davion as a samurai indicated how sincere we are in making the Star League work. As predicted, this is causing something of a crisis of conscience for them. By the time the counter-invasion goes off, I would expect we will have won them over enough to guarantee neutrality."

Hohiro smiled. "Imagine if they were to come over and join us."

Kai nodded. "Phelan's Wolves will be nasty enough, but another Clan joining our fight will mean serious trouble for the Smoke Jaguars."

Before the Coordinator could comment, a stricken servant whispered a message into Theodore Kurita's ear. The Coordinator's eyes grew wide, then he snapped a command to the servant and another to Hohiro, both of which came so fast Kai could not understand either. Theodore rose immediately and sped from the room.

"What's happening?" Kai frowned. *Have the Clans returned to Luthien on this anniversary of their defeat?*

Hohiro stood. "Something has happened. My father asks me to take you to my sister's palace."

*Victor was supposed to be spending the evening with Omi.* "Hohiro, what is it?"

"Details are sketchy. We will know better when we get there."

Kai and Focht followed Hohiro and got into a hovercar that whisked them off through darkened streets toward the palace Omi called home. As they drew close, Kai saw an ambulance racing in the opposite direction, lights blazing and siren wailing. A cold lump of ice congealed in his stomach. *Something must have happened to Victor. This is not good, not good at all.*

Luthien Constabulary officers surrounded the Palace of

Serene Sanctuary and tried to wave the hovercar off, but the driver snarled a command at them, and the officers allowed the car to pass. It slid to a halt behind a line of police vehicles. The doors opened, and the trio of men leaped out to run to the palace entrance.

One step into the palace Kai felt an icy hand clutch at his heart. He saw blood and plenty of it, not in little droplets, but tiny ribbons that ran back and forth, as if dribbled off a finger on a limp arm. Further in he caught the bright glare of holocameras being used to record the scene. Following Hohiro, he passed through the building and into the garden, then saw Theodore having a conversation with someone Kai took to be a police inspector.

They stood over two bodies, and Kai noticed that the head of one corpse was no longer connected to his body.

Theodore looked up, then nodded to the inspector and approached Kai. "You have my deepest apologies for this incident. I do not have the complete story, and will not have it until I have spoken to my daughter. From what I have been told, she is shaken but physically unharmed. She is on her way to Jihen Military Hospital, with Victor."

"Is Victor okay?"

"Our people are doing all they can for him." Theodore's hands clenched into fists. "What happened, as nearly as can be made out, is that three men came over the wall into this garden and accosted my daughter and Victor. They threatened to kill both of them, and Victor offered his life for that of my daughter. As the first assailant approached him with sword drawn, Victor dropped to one knee, then used an *iai* draw-cut to kill the first man. The assassin has a slash on his face and his spine is severed."

The Coordinator pointed at the other body. "While a second assassin attacked Victor, this third man stopped to check on the condition of his compatriot. My daughter used the first man's katana to behead his friend."

Kai shivered. He knew Omi well enough to know she had the strength of spirit and even body to do almost anything she needed to do. Even so, cleanly decapitating an enemy was a task from which even the strongest person might shrink. Kai knew people often did extraordinary things when their lives were threatened, but killing another person was seldom what they had to do. *Then again, if she felt the threat was to both her and Victor, she wouldn't have hesitated a second.*

The Precentor Martial looked back toward the palace doorway. "The second assassin pursued Victor into the palace itself?"

*"Hai."* Theodore hesitated. "What you will see is not pretty. Victor battled the second man through the palace until they got into a corridor."

Kai followed silently in Theodore's wake, then stopped at the mouth of the corridor. Beyond the Coordinator and around the forensic techs working down there, he saw blood everywhere. One body lay like an island in an ocean of it. Bloody footprints led away from it, and bloody hand prints decorated one wall. Finely spattered droplets even dotted the ceiling as if someone diving into that ocean had splashed blood all about.

"Again, we do not know exactly what happened here, but Victor was knocked down and stabbed through the chest there at the far end. There is actually a hole in the floor where the sword transfixed him and stuck him there. At the same time his assailant wounded him, Victor seems to have disabled the assailant. Victor freed himself, killed the assassin, and tried to get back to the garden." Theodore pointed to the bloody smear closest to them. "He made it this far when Omi found him."

As the Coordinator spoke, Kai could see the fight in his mind's eye. He saw Victor go down and get stabbed. He watched his friend trapped on his back, tugging at the sword, centimeter by centimeter working it free, and then killing his would-be murderer. He could hear Victor's ragged breath as he slipped and stumbled and dragged himself to his feet again. The fire burning in Victor's gray eyes stared out at him from a mask of blood, then he saw his friend go down again, for the final time.

Kai sank to his knees as a lump rose to his throat and choked him. Victor had always been the one who believed in him, who had pushed him and promoted him. Victor had always been a friend who demanded the most from others, but never stinted in rewarding them for their efforts. *If not for Victor and his encouragement, I would not be what I am today. He is the best friend a person could ever have, and yet when he needed me, I wasn't here for him.*

Kai felt hands on his shoulders. He looked up and saw the

Precentor Martial standing above them. "There was nothing you could have done, no way you could have been here."

"You're right, Precentor Martial, but I still don't feel absolved of my guilt."

"The guilt here is mine to bear." Theodore's voice came heavy and thick with emotion. "It was inconceivable to my daughter that anyone would have wanted to do her or Victor harm. She was right, for she is beloved by the people, but *my* enemies would use her and Victor against me. When she asked to spend the evening alone here with Victor, much as she spent it during the fight for Luthien, I chose to indulge her."

Focht frowned. "There was *no security* here tonight?"

Theodore's head came up. "I did not leave her unprotected. I respected her privacy, but there were patrols in the area. Apparently they were *compromised*."

*He allowed Victor and Omi to be here alone tonight?* Kai rose to his feet again. "You trusted Victor to see to your daughter's safe-keeping."

Theodore nodded. "I am sorry to have discovered in this manner that my trust was well placed, but of it I had no doubt."

Kai and Focht exchanged knowing glances, then turned back to Theodore as the police inspector approached them. The man whispered in the Coordinator's ear, and Theodore went white. He nodded to the man, who immediately headed toward the front door, shouting orders to uniformed constabulary.

Theodore waved the others after him. "Come, we go to the hospital."

Cold dread clutched at Kai's throat. "It's Victor, isn't it?"

*"Hai."* The Coordinator's voice sank to a whisper. "There have been . . . complications."

Victor found himself in a *place,* and his inability to identify it as anything more than that scared him. He appeared to be in a sphere of clarity surrounded by a white fog that glowed without giving off any warmth. Up, off in the distance, he saw a bright disk, a light, that looked to him like a sun seen through clouds.

He noticed it was very quiet and nothing seemed to move in the fog.

He looked down at his chest and saw a ragged little wound about three centimeters beneath his right nipple. In many ways it looked far too small to have caused him so much pain. He remembered that the sword actually hurt more coming out than it had going in. The lack of a hiss from air escaping his punctured lung surprised him more than his nakedness. *Something is definitely not right here.*

"That is hardly accurate."

Without doing anything conscious to move, Victor spun around and found himself facing a man in a white robe. He recognized the face, but only because he'd seen it on coins and in old holovids. "You look like my father."

"I *am* your father." Hanse Davion smiled. "In the hereafter you lose a little gray from your hair, a little weight from around your waist—you become what you were at your peak."

"The hereafter?"

Hanse frowned slightly. "You're dead, son. I've come to take you with me."

*"Iie!"* Another voice, more gruff and insistent, burst into the sphere. Another man materialized, wearing a samurai's armor that was completely red. Slightly shorter than Victor's father, but bearing himself equally regally, the man bowed his head toward Victor. "He is meant to come with me."

"What are you talking about?" Hanse scoffed at the interloper. "This is my son, of whom I am most proud. He belongs with me, Takashi. No surprise your wanting him, though, because you have always wanted what was mine."

"Ha! I only wished to save what was yours from your incompetence." Omi's grandfather smiled slyly. "Your son died to protect my granddaughter's life. He fought for her honor like a samurai, met his death like a samurai. He is meant to be with samurai for the rest of eternity."

Hanse's blue eyes narrowed. "I was going to ignore the *how* of his death, which would never have happened if your people weren't so oppressed that assassination is the only form of expression open to them."

Victor's jaw hung agape. He refused to believe he was dead. He knew he was having what some called a "near-death-experience," but he also knew that scientists had theorized that such things were flights of imagination. The light within the void was a reflection of his body's sensory apparatus shutting down, providing him only a pinpoint of a window on the world. *This is all in my head.*

Takashi looked sternly at him. "This is happening to you,

Victor. If it were not, if you were not dead, we would not know what you were thinking."

Victor frowned. "If this is just my imagination, of course you can know what I'm thinking, since I'm just imagining you with the ability to read my mind."

Hanse smiled. "I've always told you he was a smart boy."

"And that is exactly the reason he will choose to go with me." Takashi extended his hand toward Victor. "You have proven yourself a consummate warrior. You have known great victories and great defeats, yet you always push yourself on to new heights, past new challenges. This is what makes you samurai."

"Nonsense, Takashi—that's what makes him a *Davion*." Hanse extended his hand toward Victor. "Come with me, son. Trust me. I know what's best for you. Follow me, you'll see."

"No."

Hanse looked surprised. "No?"

Takashi beamed. "He comes with me."

"No!" Victor shook his head. "I'm going with neither of you."

Hanse folded his arms across his chest. "You can't make your own way over here."

Takashi nodded in agreement. "Not allowed, not allowed at all."

"Then I'll go back to where I *can* make my own way."

Both men laughed at him. Hanse gave him a kindly smile. "Son, there are limited paths for you to tread. You've walked the Davion path all your life, and now you've flirted with the Kurita path. For you there are no other choices."

"That can't be right."

Takashi smiled. "*Hai,* it is so."

Victor's right hand rose to his throat in his surprise at their agreement. Despite being naked, he felt the cold stone smoothness of the jade pendant Kai had given him. *Sun Hou-Tzu. Kai gave it to me to remind me to always be myself.* Victor began to smile as he saw the expression on his father's face sour. *I must always be myself.*

Victor threw back his head and laughed. "All my life I've held myself to the standard you set, Father. Many is the time I've told others that I would surpass you if they would only let me do that, but they weren't holding me back. *You* were."

Anger arced through Hanse's eyes. "I *never* held you back."

"No, not you, but your image." Victor opened his hands in a plea to his father. "You were a good father, as good a father as I could ever have wanted, but you were also a daunting presence, and impressive, too, very impressive. I am nothing in comparison to you, but that's because mine is a different time and the challenges are different. Yet every time I get set to do something that will surpass what you have done, will eclipse what you have done, I hesitate because surpassing you will result in a diminution of your image. As I grow up, as I move away from you in time and experience, you become less and less a part of my life, and I never wanted to lose you."

Victor turned and pointed at Takashi Kurita. "And you, you're just the same. You were an implacable foe, an unbeatable foe. You were my father's bane, yet before I could test myself against you, you died! Your death robbed me of the chance to prove I was as good as you or better. And now, knowing your son and grandson and granddaughter, in learning about your realm and your ways, I become stronger and better, but you're always there, a spectre lurking in the background. There's always a question as to whether or not you would approve of what I have done, what your child and grandchildren have done; and we can never have an answer for that."

Takashi waved the words away contemptuously. "Your fear of losing something, your desire to know what we might have thought, this is what holds you back. The problem lies with you, not with us."

"Oh, I agree because I know why I see you the way I do here." Victor pointed at his father. "You're the Hanse Davion of legend, the man who snapped up half the Capellan Confederation as a wedding present for your bride. And you, Takashi Kurita, you're the image on your gravestone. You're of the age you were when you took over for your assassinated father and initiated reforms to alleviate the suffering he had imposed on your people. The both of you are here as the legends you have become. And I'm on that path, too.

"This is what I understand now, it isn't about *me* and who I am. I am who I am and I will remain that way until I die. Five or ten or fifteen or fifty years from now no one will really know the true me or you or you. *Who* we were will be lost. What we *did* is what will be remembered and judged, revered, or corrected down through the years. Will the Inner Sphere be better or worse for my having lived? I would like to think it will be better, but there is more I must do to guarantee it."

Victor balled his fists. "That's why I won't be going with either of you. I'm going back. I'm not going to die."

Hanse chuckled. "That's fine for you to say, but you don't know the way back."

Victor touched the pendant again. "I don't, but he does."

Takashi laughed. "That thing won't help you."

"Sure it will." Victor rubbed it and felt the stone warm. The jade monkey grew in size, then loosened its grip on the leather thong around Victor's neck. "You see, if this is all in my imagination, then I can imagine Sun Hou-Tzu to be my guide out of here. And if this is the realm of the supernatural and really the gateway to death, well, he tricked Yen-lo-wang and freed his people from the King of the Dead, so I win on those grounds, too."

Takashi begrudgingly nodded toward Hanse. "He *is* a clever boy."

"He'll need to be."

Victor smiled and took the jade monkey's hand. "I cannot and will not worry about what you might have thought, or what others think about what I do. I must remain true to myself and true to what I know is right. To do anything less would be to fail myself, and that is something I absolutely refuse to do."

Kai Allard-Liao looked up from his place at Victor's beside. His neck felt stiff from having fallen asleep in the chair, but he'd refused more comfortable accommodations when they were offered. He didn't want to leave Victor.

From the other side of the bed Omi looked over at him and smiled. "You heard him?"

Kai nodded and stood. Looking down, he saw Victor's eyelids flicker, then open. "Easy, Victor, you've had quite a time."

Omi took hold of Victor's right hand and gave it a squeeze. Tears rolled down her face, and Kai felt a lump rising in his own throat.

Victor coughed lightly and winced, then forced a smile onto his face. His chest worked up and down two or three times, with his flesh tugging at the tape securing his bandage, then the Prince tried to speak past his oxygen mask.

"What?" Kai shook his head and leaned closer.

"Love. Hurts."

Kai began to laugh. "Don't do that, Victor. You've been at death's door."

"Beyond." Victor slowly licked cracked lips. "Back."

"Damn right you're back." Kai looked over at Omi. "He's going to be fine."

*"Hai,"* she whispered softly. Reaching out with her left hand, she caressed the side of Victor's face. "The doctors have said that it won't be long before you are up and around."

"Good." Victor's voice gained slightly in volume. "Beat death." His eyes sharpened. "Smoke Jaguars . . . are next."

# === 29 ===

**Palace of Serene Sanctuary, Imperial City
Luthien
Pesht Military District, Draconis Combine
7 January 3059**

*Dear God, grant me the strength to get through this.* Victor
Davion closed his eyes, then opened them and consciously
corrected the swaying of his body. Forty-eight hours after his
battle, he found himself again in the garden, wearing the
same clothes he'd worn then, bearing the same sword. It
didn't feel like *déjà vu* to him, primarily because the fluids
and painkillers they'd packed into him gave him a certain
sense of detachment, but instead he felt like a criminal
returning to the scene of a crime.

Kai's voice echoed in his right ear, courtesy of a small ear
piece and microphone. "Victor, are you with us?"

The Prince opened his jaw slightly to allow him to subvocalize
his reply. The microphone would pick up the sound of his voice
through his own ears and the Eustachian tube, which was just as
well as far as Victor was concerned because he really didn't think
he could muster enough of a breath to speak above a whisper
anyway. "I'm here, Kai."

"Are you all right? Are you cold?"

Victor couldn't answer the questions immediately. His
bloodstained kimono had been draped over him so that his
right arm and the right side of his chest were bared. The
smallest of bandages covered his wounds, and both had been

painted white so any blood would not show. The kimono hid his left elbow, which had swollen up. Magres scans had indicated a hairline fracture of his ulna. Somewhere back in the palace was the sling he was supposed to wear, but it had no part in the drama that would unfold in the garden.

"I'm doing okay, Kai. How much longer?"

"Sixty seconds and counting."

"And we're still on an 'outside the Combine blackout'?"

"The Precentor Martial is standing right here. Nothing will go out through ComStar unless you give it a green light." Kai's voice lightened slightly. "He says that by the time Word of Blake manages any covert distribution, we'll have enough holovids of you in action to label anything they come up with as a complete fraud."

"Good." Victor coughed slightly and felt a tiny jolt of pain shoot through his body. One of his major concerns was word of his wounding getting out to the Federated Commonwealth. The Draconis March would go insane and might even begin military operations against the Combine to avenge him. *A few short-sighted hotheads could destroy the best chance we have to destroy the Clans.*

He also feared what Katherine would do with the news. Any weakness on his part would provide her with an opportunity to cause trouble. He was not certain how she might capitalize on his misfortune, but it would be just one more problem for him to deal with. *One more distraction to divert me from my true goal.* He could not allow that, so a holovid blackout beyond the Combine's borders was the only real solution to the situation. As much as he loved a free and open press, there were times when the autocratic nature of the Combine had its uses.

Victor swallowed hard as Omi walked into the garden. To Victor's left the various lights from the holocams came on to capture her entrance. The bright lights transformed her white silk kimono from a garment into a glaring aura. They made her beauty transcendent, and Victor found himself uncomfortably reminded of the place where he had spoken with his father and her grandfather. *It's as if she hovers in the doorway between this world and the hereafter.*

Omi walked past him without acknowledging his presence. Her steps failed to coax sound from the crushed stone walkway, and her kimono barely whispered as she knelt on the tatami mat at Victor's feet. On the mat in front of her sat a low lacquered table—little more than a tray really—with a sake bottle, a cup, a piece of white rice paper, and a razor-sharp tanto. The knife's hilt had been wrapped with white cord, and the pommel-cap and cross-guard were cast platinum.

With her left hand Omi reached out and took up the sake bottle. She filled her cup with two pours, then set the bottle back down. Victor saw a single droplet of sake roll down the bottle's side like a tear and felt his guts knot up. He wanted to stop her, he wanted to kick the tray and the knife away, but he knew that was not the part he was to play.

Omi raised the cup to her lips and drank. In two gulps she drained it, then set it back down. She rested her hands on her thighs, then looked up at the holocameras. "*Komban-wa.* I am Kurita Omi." She paused for a moment, drew in a deep breath, then continued. "I am speaking to you from the Palace of Serene Sanctuary. It was here, seven years ago, that I waited as my brother and my father and my grandfather battled the Smoke Jaguars, thwarting the Clan attempt to take Luthien from us."

Kai's simultaneous translation of Omi's words provided Victor with content, but the calm urgency in her voice imparted to him the full depth of meaning. Emphasizing where she'd been when the Clans attacked was clearly a move to establish a rapport with her audience and remind them that she shared that experience with them. The tone of her voice told them that she, too, had been afraid and uncertain, yet she had conquered her fears and abided, with them, by whatever outcome fate had in store for the warriors defending the world.

"It was here, two nights ago, as I shared the most solemn of occasions with my friend, Prince Victor Davion, that three men accomplished what the Clans could not. They stole through the silent streets of Luthien and came over the wall into my sanctuary. They came into this very garden." Omi pointed toward the holocameras, yet raised her hand so the audience would not think she was pointing at them. "They came here to murder me."

Omi's voice dropped to a hushed whisper. "These men claimed that I had violated the precepts of Purity and Harmony. They said I was a Davion whore. They had come to kill me and they would have, for here, on that night, I was defenseless. I would have died had not Victor been here.

Despite being grievously wounded in the fight, he slew the assassins, using the katana my father presented to him on his arrival here on Luthien."

Victor kept his face impassive as the translation of Omi's lie reached him. He knew he had killed only two of the three assassins. Omi herself had taken up the first assassin's katana and beheaded the third man as he bent over his fallen comrade. Though the samurai tradition was full of stories about women warriors, and Omi was as skilled as any of them, her image in the Combine as Keeper of the House Honor was more genteel and refined. No one would have doubted her ability to kill one of her assailants, but that reality did not fit in with fiction being presented to her nation. *For her sake and mine, this lie must become the truth.*

"As Victor was my protector that night, now he stands as my *kaishaku*. With the sword he used to save me from the assassins, he will now save me from dishonor." She reached down and grasped the piece of rice paper. "He will see to it that the only pain I know will be of the heart and not the body."

Omi stared directly into the holocams. "The assassins claimed I had violated the precepts of Purity and Harmony; and this is the perception I must assume that you, also, hold in your minds. I cannot bear the dishonor of that judgment because it is not true. It hurts me more than you could know to have *you* believe that I think so little of you, of our nation, and our traditions, to violate them for personal reasons. My life has been lived for the Combine, and would have continued to be lived for it. I am nothing if I am not your servant.

"I will not deny that I love Victor Davion. He has been a friend to me for years. He risked the ire of his nation to rescue, at my request, my brother Hohiro from the Clans at Teniente. At all times Victor has ever been a man honorable. What we share in our hearts and minds, we have not allowed ourselves to share with our bodies. Our love has not violated Purity, it defines Purity."

She raised her chin to stretch her throat and let the audience see the pale flesh she would slash open with the tanto. "Neither has our love been disharmonious. I have obeyed my father's directives concerning us absolutely and completely. The price my father demanded to let me ask Victor to rescue my brother was that I cease all correspondence and contact with Victor. This I did, though with each day of the prohibition I felt another piece of my spirit die. I was willing to endure this so that the Combine would have my brother back, so the Combine would have an heir to the Dragon. This was my place and my plight and I complied.

"It was my grandfather, Takashi-*sama,* who lifted this prohibition. By his action he condoned and encouraged what I felt for Victor. There is no one who can even entertain the idea that my grandfather would permit his granddaughter to dishonor herself or his nation. He knew me. He knew what I would do. He knew he could trust me never to commit any act that would bring shame upon my house. My father saw the wisdom of his father's judgment and did not reinstate the prohibition after he inherited the Dragon's Throne."

Reaching her right hand down, Omi grasped the blade of the tanto with the rice paper. Three centimeters of the blade remained bare. Slowly, as she spoke, she raised the sharpened steel to her throat.

"The shame I feel, the dishonor with which I cannot live, is that I somehow led you to believe I would put myself before the nation. That you can think this directly points out a flaw in my character. I cannot correct it, clearly, for why else would assassins have been sent to slay me if I could? While I have tried to always be strong and represent your hopes, dreams, desires, and honor, I failed. For this failure there is only one way to atone."

Victor caught the faintest of tremors in Omi's hand as the blade reached her throat. As she held it poised, he slid his katana from its scabbard. He closed his left hand around the hilt and used his right arm to raise the blade over his head. His job was to strike fast, beheading her with one stroke before the pain of her slashed throat could register on her face.

Millimeter by millimeter the tanto's point approached her flesh. Victor waited, his left arm leaden, the pain in his chest beginning to spread like cancer. The tremble in her hand as the steel pressed against her skin, indenting it slightly, mirrored itself in the palsy causing his blade to quiver.

In an instant he saw her hand stop shaking, and he knew she was resolved to go through with her *seppuku.* While part of him screamed that this was madness, he, too, stilled his blade and prepared to do his duty. *My duty is to show her compassion.* Despite his injuries and weakness, he knew he would strike clean, fast, and strong. It would tear his heart out, but he would not fail her.

"*Iie!*"

Theodore's shout from the palace doorway brought Victor's head around. Though the Coordinator's intervention had been expected, had been scripted in, Victor had thought it would come sooner. Only as Theodore strode through the garden, his firm step crunching along the walkway with a martial cadence, did Victor realize that both he and Omi had become caught up in the drama. They had been ready to play their parts to the fullest. *We went from acting out our roles to actually living them. Theodore could have interrupted us at any point, but he waited until even we could not doubt our sincerity and resolution.*

Theodore raised his left hand and lowered Victor's sword. He turned and slipped the tanto from Omi's hand, leaving her clutching the pure, white rice paper. The Coordinator examined the small knife's blade, then threw it down with disgust. The tanto stuck into the lacquered table. Its impact toppled the sake bottle and sent the cup spinning to the ground.

"I am the Dragon and I forbid you to commit *seppuku* for twenty-four hours." He waved Omi to silence with his right hand. "The shame you say you bear is not yours. That shame, that willingness to think the worst of you and of *Victor-sama,* is a shame that must be borne only by small-minded individuals who have married themselves to a past that cannot be recaptured."

Theodore opened his arms. "Proof of their foolishness comes with the day they chose to attack you. Who among us could have forgotten the presence of the Clans on that day? It is the day when Luthien ran with the blood of loyal sons and daughters of the Combine. It is the day that mercenaries, sent by Hanse Davion, also shed their blood to help us preserve Luthien. It is the day that marks the crest of the Clan invasion. It is the day we proved the Clans can be defeated decisively; but to mistake that for the Clans' total defeat is to live in a world of fantasy.

"Those people would claim that I and my father and sons and daughter live in such a fantasy world, for we are placing our trust in the Davions. Let us examine this idea. Hanse Davion and I agreed that no Davion troops would enter the Combine while the Clans were a threat. Hanse Davion abided by this agreement and sent mercenaries—the only troops at his disposal that could reach Luthien without violating our agreement—to fight with us against the Clans. After that, FedCom troops *did* enter the Combine, but at the request of my daughter, with my permission, to save her brother from the Clans. *We* had no troops to devote to that effort, but, beset as his own realm was, Hanse Davion pledged his son, put *his* son at *risk,* to save *my* son.

"And now, a Davion, here on Luthien, here in this refuge that kept my daughter safe while the Clans ravaged this world, here in this garden, here on this spot, a *Davion* slew three assassins sent by *my own people* to murder my daughter. A *Davion* put his life at risk, he bled to save her, and all but died in doing so. To the assassin who drove a katana through his chest, Victor said, 'Davions take a lot of killing.' A true warrior who did not shirk from duty that imperiled his life, Victor Davion did more to keep my daughter safe than any of the rest of us."

Theodore's open hands became fists. "So there is no evidence of Davion perfidy. Since the coming of the Clans they have ever been the shield for the Kurita family. They saved Hohiro, they saved Luthien, and now they have saved my daughter. In doing all of these things, they have preserved the Combine and have worked with us to oppose the enemy we share.

"These people would also say that I have somehow shamed my daughter and my family and the Draconis Combine by allowing her to associate with Victor Davion. You have heard from her lips what is the nature of their love. If her declaration is not proof enough of its strength and purity, then look behind me. Look at the wounds on Victor Davion's chest and the blood on his kimono. Among his people it is said there is no greater love than the willingness of one man to lay down his life for another. With us, the proof of love is acquitting one's duty no matter the cost to the individual. In what he has done, Victor has shown on both scales that he loves my daughter. He has shown Omiko honor, and she has done the same for him; yet their sense of duty, their respect for Purity and Harmony, has led them to deny themselves the unity their hearts and minds cry out for."

Theodore reached down and stroked Omi's left cheek. "The pain in their hearts comes from us. They do their duty and keep themselves apart, yet we show them no compassion. Would it be easier if they did not love each other? Certainly, for us, for the rest of us, it would be easier because it would not force us to think beyond the nature of the world in which we grew up. What they share would have been unthinkable just a dozen years ago, but now it is the harbinger of the future and a reflection of the past when we were all united, as we are now, in the Star League.

"I said before that the past cannot be recaptured; but it can be recreated. The traditions that make us strong will continue to provide us strength. They will give others strength, as they gave Victor the strength to overcome the assassins. These traditions give us a foundation on which can be built our future."

The Coordinator clasped his hands at the small of his back. "Those who struck at my daughter were striking at that foundation. Those who thought to preserve our traditions were destroying them. If they truly have any respect for our ways, our history, our *honor,* they should shoulder their own burden, not leave it as a load to be borne by a woman, no matter how strong she may be.

"Let there be no question: the only disharmony associated with Victor and Omi is the disharmony resulting from their being kept apart. The only lack of purity is the deception we foster upon our selves to deny the depth and beauty of their ties. In ways more numerous than the drops of blood he shed here, Victor has proven himself worthy of my daughter. In everything she has ever done, Omiko has proved herself worthy of such a match as Victor. Those who would deny the veracity of my statement are refugees from a time that is no more. Their choice is to adapt and work toward a new future or else consign themselves to history and the dead era that spawned them."

Theodore bent and helped Omi to her feet. He brushed away tears from her face and began to guide her back toward the palace as the holocamera lights died. They walked past Victor and did not look in his direction. He understood their introspection and did not wish to intrude. He homed his blade and watched them walk away.

It wasn't until Kai touched him gently on the shoulder and handed him his sling that Victor realized he was no longer alone. "Thank you, Kai. And thank you for the translation."

"It could have been better. Theodore alternated between

very polite terms on down to some vulgar ones. Shifting between them was tough."

"Still, you did a good job." Victor glanced down at the white stones, searching in vain for any sign of blood from the fight. "I think, though, there were nuances I missed."

"Doped to the gills, I don't doubt it. I'm not certain I caught everything either, but there were some fairly strong undercurrents in Theodore's talk." Kai scratched at the palm of his left hand. "He essentially called for a new nationalism within the Combine. He held you and Omi up as icons of that nationalism—one that is proud and proper, while accepting of change and help and allies. He didn't ask his people to abandon their sense of superiority, but he suggested that using it as a justification for rampant xenophobia and paranoia was wrong."

"He made us into 'icons'?"

"In essence he used you and your feelings for each other as an example of what the best things about this new future will be. Your happiness will be the happiness of a nation, and your commitment to bringing about this future will be the commitment of the people to bringing it about as well." Kai hesitated. "He's leveraging your future with Omi to unite his nation for the future."

Victor blinked, both at the implications and the risks inherent in what Theodore had done. "Will it work, do you think?"

"Time alone will tell."

Victor nodded. "And Theodore allowed only twenty-four hours for some indications."

Within twelve hours, the heads of three conservative politicians appeared on the steps of Theodore Kurita's Palace of Unity. No one knew how they got there, but everyone knew *why* they got there, and that was more than enough.

## 30

*Palace of Unity*
*Imperial City, Luthien*
*Pesht Military District, Draconis Combine*
*13 May 3059*

Victor Ian Steiner-Davion looked at the holographic display slowly rotating above the center of the briefing table. "That would appear to be it, then. We're good to go." He looked around at his advisors. "Any last-minute things to cover?"

Down at the far end of the table, Colonel Daniel Allard of the Kell Hounds raised his hand. "I just want to double-check the priorities for units being held in reserve for the second wave or as reinforcements if a first-wave attack runs into stiffer opposition than expected. With Operation Bird-dog you've got fairly small units hitting worlds to harass the Smoke Jaguars prior to our getting there. Most are on first-wave worlds, but you've got Raymond's Company from Cogdell going in on Yamarovka, and we won't get there for, at best, six weeks after their insertion. What happens if we get a report that they're getting slaughtered? Are we going to save them or not?"

Victor narrowed his eyes. "I'm not going to let them die if there's any chance we can support them or rescue them, but I'm not going to feed troops into a meat-grinder just so they can get banged up either. The Hounds and other reserve units in the first wave are being held back in case the Nova Cats have a change of heart and we have to guard against their activities. We should know fairly quickly whether or not they're going to move against us. If they don't, then we'll have resources to devote to Yamarovka or similar targets.

"Let there be no question about it, people, we will lose warriors. My goal is to minimize those losses, and our bird-dogging the Jags will mean they pin some troops in place. Those troops won't be shooting at us on other worlds, which means we accomplish our objectives and move on. We need to hit hard, hit fast, and keep moving, just as the Clans did when they attacked us. We want them reacting to us, not making us react to them. We've already lost that kind of war and we don't need a repeat now."

The Precentor Martial got up from the seat Victor had been occupying during the earlier part of the briefing and replaced him at the head of the table. The older man smiled at Victor, giving the Prince a sense of accomplishment he really hadn't felt since the death of his father. *I was born to this job, and now I have dedicated myself to it.*

"Thank you, Victor, for the assignment and doctrine review. I cannot emphasize enough that the key to our success is a unity of purpose and drive. All of our operations are multi-national, yet all of our troops will be going in under the Star League banner." The Precentor Martial smiled. "Marshal Hasek-Davion's force has already started out on its long journey to Huntress, so in many ways we're bird-dogging for them. Coordinator Kurita, you have something you would like to say?"

Theodore Kurita rose from his place near the center of the table. "The Draconis Combine is a nation that has labored hard to pay homage to a code of conduct and honor we call *bushido,* or the Way of the Warrior. To many of you who have fought against us, *bushido* is the thing that made our warriors into implacable foes. No quarter would be asked or given, but acts of heroism, valor, self-sacrifice, and courage would be revered perhaps out of all proportion with what you would consider normal."

The Coordinator glanced at Dan Allard. "Colonel Allard and the Kell Hounds have a long history of conflict with the Combine, yet they were also part of a force that helped us hold off the Clan invasion of Luthien. This repayment of enmity with kindness is alien enough to us that even now my people are having trouble understanding it, but the coming together of this great taskforce to drive the Clans from Combine worlds is something for which they are very thankful. In short, they may not comprehend why you are here, but they respect, appreciate, and will support your efforts.

"For myself, I understand the sacrifice all of you are making. I know this sacrifice is being made for mankind as a whole, but the Combine will be the immediate beneficiary. Though it is insufficient, I offer you and your people my thanks and pledge that, from this point forward, the effort made on the Combine's behalf will never be forgotten."

Led by the Precentor Martial, the dozen other leaders present stood and applauded the Coordinator's message. Victor joined them and applauded heartily, both for what had been said and because he had already seen how the Combine had begun to change. *My father never would have believed it possible.*

In the four and a half months since his wounding, Victor had become immersed in Combine culture. His immersion began because, at first, he had no alternative. His convalescence had been a matter of honor for the Combine. He had been given a suite of rooms in the Palace of Serene Sanctuary with round-the-clock care and rehabilitation. His Japanese improved greatly because most of the servants attending him spoke neither German or English. He was given clothing appropriate to a Combine warrior and his meals were Combine cuisine, with foods chosen to restore harmony to his system and to help repair the damage done by the assassins.

Even his physical therapy had followed accepted Combine practices. Hohiro's own swordmaster had tutored Victor. DEST commando instructors paced him through conditioning exercises, and even Omi's younger brother, Minoru, had guided him through exercises that combined *t'ai chi chuan* moves with chants and complex finger formations meant to strengthen his spirit. Victor would have rejected Minoru's contribution to his recovery if not for the intensity in the young man's eyes and Minoru's mentioning that he knew Victor had spoken with Takashi Kurita even though Victor had told no one of his experience.

After a month of intensive therapy Victor had resumed normal duties. These consisted largely of traveling from Luthien to the various staging worlds for the offensive. Combine units formed the spearhead of each assault, with

FedCom, ComStar, or other Inner Sphere units added to strengthen the forces and lend credence to the operation being a Star League operation. Units like Phelan's Wolves and the various mercenaries involved in the assault had all been relegated to reserve roles for the initial wave. Their chance to shine would come in the second wave.

Victor found that the various unit leaders—who rightly enough pointed out that they had come to fight and wanted to get to it—understood the necessity for the Combine to lead the way when this need was explained in terms of the Combine's complex social structure.

Victor's growing understanding of the Combine made interfacing with Combine commanders much easier. Where previously he would have issued orders and expected them to be obeyed no matter what the local commander desired, now he anticipated concerns and was able to calm them before they became problems. He was able to point out to leaders that assigning objectives to the non-Combine units in each strike force was important, for the other leaders had their own concerns about honor. More than one Combine commander saw the wisdom of assigning objectives early on, as opposed to getting his force into a situation where it had to be rescued later. "It is easier to share the glory of war than to live with the shame of defeat," Victor had learned to say, to great effect.

Victor's transformation could not have come about without Omi's help. She had overseen every detail of his recovery, quietly insisting on how things would be. If not for her, Minoru wouldn't have had anything to do with Victor, and FedCom medical personnel would have taken over his care instead of just consulting on it. Victor likely would have even had bilingual servants or, rather, servants who were willing to speak to him in a language other than Japanese.

He realized that his becoming inculcated into Combine culture was as much a matter of her survival as it was his. Theodore had told his people that Victor was worthy of his daughter, but the proof of that would be in how Victor came across to the people of the Combine. If he failed to pass muster with them, they would reject him and Omi would truly be seen as soiled and shamed. To prevent that from happening, and to increase the chances for the operation's success, Victor had immersed himself in the ways of the Combine.

While he was still physically weak, Omi saw to it that his physical needs were met. She helped change his bandages and made certain he took his medicines at prescribed times. She also made sure he never missed a therapy session, selected the clothes he would wear, and oversaw preparations for his travels. It often seemed to Victor that she found the solution to a problem before he even realized a problem existed.

After he had recovered, after bones had knitted and flesh had healed, the barriers his convalescence had placed between them fell away. He could still vividly recall the first night she came to him, slipping into his bed in the dark. It felt as if her body were on fire, and as she pressed against him, her warmth flowed into him. He recalled stroking her body, the flesh so flawlessly smooth that he felt self-conscious about the puckered scars on his chest and back. With a kiss and a caress she showed him they meant nothing, that what mattered to her was the man inside the skin, not the skin itself.

Urgency had marked their lovemaking that night, as if each of them feared the return of the assassins who had almost destroyed their happiness. Little mistakes—the click of teeth, a misplaced elbow, or an obtrusive knee—prompted giggles and whispered apologies. The small mishaps kept the experience from being perfect, but they somehow made it more intimate. Perfection would have been for the mating of a Prince of the Federated Commonwealth and the Keeper of House Kurita's Honor. Clumsy, playful, and passionate was how love was meant to be shared between two people, and there, in the dark, that is what they aspired to be. Titles couldn't enhance the experience, so they were forgotten like bed clothes in the heat of the moment.

After that first time they spent the night together whenever they were in the same solar system. While they thoroughly enjoyed each other's company, their yearning to be together grew out of more than a desire to explore the physical dimensions of love. Simple touches, midnight kisses, whispered dreams, and even tussles for possession of the covers provided each of them glimpses of the true people they were. The time they spent together outside the bedchamber further expanded on this.

More than once Victor found himself saying something or doing something he had seen shared between his parents in a semi-private moment. It surprised him how much of his mother and father lived on in him, and yet he also saw how much he had become his own person. He identified behaviors he wanted to modify and took steps to change himself for the better—for Omi and for the mission.

Victor's blinked as someone slapped him on the back and out of his reverie. "I'm sorry, Kai, did you say something?"

His friend smiled. "I should have known better. I recognize that glazed look in your eyes."

The Prince blushed, thankful the briefing room had emptied of everyone save himself and Kai. "Am I that bad?"

"Not the worst I've ever seen."

Victor narrowed his eyes. "Don't I recall you mooncalfing over some woman at the New Avalon Military Academy during the one year I transferred there?"

"Right. Wendy Sylvester." Kai nodded slowly. "She's in the Davion Heavy Guards now."

Victor thought for a second, then nodded once. "Kommandant Wendy Karner. She got married a few years back."

Kai smiled. "Yeah, to a poet, of all things."

"You think that's funny?"

"Nope, I think it reflects a shift in her thinking. It breaks with a family tradition, just as your choice of lovers does." Kai shrugged, but kept the smile on his face. "I'm as happy for her as I am for you."

"Good." Victor frowned and looked down at his boots. "Then perhaps you could do me a favor."

"Name it."

Victor chewed on his lower lip as he brought his head back up. "You and Morgan and pretty much everyone else in this taskforce have taken leave of a loved one. I've never done that. I've never had anyone I really loved before and I don't know what to say."

"I understand. The clichés about 'tomorrow I may die' are accurate, but lack sincerity. Anything else seems to downplay the danger and that's disingenuous and trivializes the fear the person left behind is going to feel."

"You've given this some thought."

"Deirdre is pretty much a realist, so facing the truth is the way to go with her." Kai rested his hands on Victor's shoulders and looked him straight in the eyes. "What's important is that you share with her what's in your heart. Remember that you might never get a chance to tell her how you feel, and that what you say may be the last thing she gets to remember about you. More important, what you say is going to have to be what sustains her through those nights when she wonders if you're dead or dying on some airless planetoid."

"You're a wise man, Kai Allard-Liao."

"Not really, Victor, not really." Kai smiled. "If I was really that wise, I'd have long ago figured out a way to settle the Clan question so we'd never have to leave our lovers at all."

That night Victor found Omi waiting for him in the garden of her palace, the whole scene alive with the light of hundreds of candles. It surprised him to find her there since the garden was a place of painful memories. *The happiness we've known has grown in other places in this building.*

She turned to face him when she heard his first crunching footfall and so casually brushed away a tear that he almost did not notice the motion. *"Komban-wa,* Victor-*sama."*

He bowed his head toward her and extended to her the one perfect blue rose he'd found in Imperial City. "It should be this rose that cries, for its beauty pales in comparison to yours."

Omi smiled and graciously accepted the flower. "You are most kind."

"You put me to shame on that score." Victor held up a hand to forestall her reply. "I have something to tell you and I don't think I'll ever get through it unless you just let me talk so, please, hear what I have to say."

She nodded and seated herself on a whitewashed stone bench.

Victor started to pace, but stopped when the sounds the stones made beneath his feet reminded him of the crackle of shattered 'Mech armor being marched over by troops. "Omi Kurita, I love you more than I thought it was possible to love someone. I wish I was a poet so I could write you sonnets or an artist so I could paint pictures for you. I am a warrior, and proud of it, but offering to slay enemies for you seems wrong as a sign of love; but that's exactly what I will be going off to do. I will fight the Clans because they seek to destroy you and everything you hold dear. I will not let that happen.

"Here, in this garden, on that night months ago, I was ready to die to save you. When I lay on the floor inside and I saw you in a bloody kimono, I thought you had been slain and I was happy that we would be together in death. What I know now is that you mean more to me than life itself, and that I never want to be separated from you. It's not as if you and I are each halves of a whole, because I think we're each more than that, and what we become together is nothing short of incredible. With you I can imagine no more perfect a life."

Victor swallowed hard to force the lump back down out of his throat. "As much as I don't want to go away from you, I must. I will make this sacrifice because it's the only way I know to guarantee that we never need be parted again. Forgive me. Don't forget me and have no fear, I will return."

Omi nodded again slowly, then looked up from the tear-anointed rose and gave him a smile. "I believe you, Victor, because I know you would not lie to me. I can only let you go because I know you will come back to me."

She pointed the rose toward the palace. "When I saw you there, lying in your own blood, I felt my life draining from me. I had only one reason to live—to see you live. Had you died there, I would have joined you, so we would have been united in death."

Omi stood and spread her arms. "That night I invited you into this garden because it was my sanctuary. Here you had kept me safe and sane during the Clan invasion of Luthien. Then, that night, you again kept me safe from forces that would destroy me. Since then we have both avoided this place because of the evil taint it had acquired. Tonight, on the eve of your departure to wage the greatest war humanity has ever known, I would ask of you a small favor."

"Whatever you ask will be done."

Omi worked slowly at the knotted sash holding her kimono closed. "Before you retake worlds from the Clans, help me retake this garden from any foul memories that still cling to it. When you are gone and I come here, I wish to remember this as a place of love and life, not hatred and death. Love me here, Victor Davion, be my sanctuary again in this place, and thus I will be sustained until your return."

## 31

*Ragnarok Plains, Asgard*
*Smoke Jaguar Occupation Zone*
*27 May 3059*

Though encased in the *Devastator*'s armored bulk, Kommandant Wendy Karner felt very vulnerable. Curiously enough it wasn't because of her battalion's exposed position in the hills that eased the transition from the mountains of Odin's Retreat down into the Ragnarok Plains. The Davion Heavy Guards RCT First 'Mech Battalion had taken its position for very specific reasons and, as night fell, she knew that the wisdom or folly of their deployment would be proven before the dawn.

Her vulnerability, she realized, came from the fact that the *Devastator* smelled *new*. She couldn't remember ever being in a 'Mech that smelled *new*. Her initial training had been in the family AgroMech, and from there, through the New Avalon Military Academy and even the Clan War, she'd always fought from the cockpit of a 'Mech far older than she was and, in the case of the 'Mech she'd piloted just before being assigned the *Devastator,* she fought in a 'Mech that her mother and even grandfather had used in the Heavy Guards. She knew that *new* wasn't *bad,* and that the 'Mech's design was good, but the *Devastator* still felt weird.

Despite her misgivings, she did like the ten-meter-tall, broad-shouldered BattleMech. Its lack of hands did bother her a bit, but since both arms ended in the muzzles of Gauss rifles, she overlooked that defect. Particle projection cannons were mounted on both sides of its chest, right below medium lasers. The 'Mech's other two medium lasers were mounted in the head and right over the 'Mech's spine—allowing her to shoot easily at targets to her rear. The humanoid 'Mech also packed a lot of armor, so not only could it hit hard at long range, but it could survive an extended firefight.

She felt pretty certain that the firefight that was coming wouldn't be very long in duration. *But it will make up in savagery what it lacks in length.*

The assault on Asgard had been accomplished with surprising ease. The Fourth Jaguar Dragoons constituted a single cluster of front-line Clan BattleMechs. That put their strength at approximately sixty 'Mechs, which was roughly half the 'Mechs in the Heavy Guards RCT. By all conventional reckoning that made the Jags and the RCT an even-up match for strength.

Conventional military wisdom also dictated that an attacking force required at least a three-to-one advantage over their foe to be able to win with acceptable casualties. For this reason, the Star League force deployed on Asgard included both a Combine and ComStar regimental-sized unit. The Third Proserpina Hussars spearheaded the Combine regiment, and two battalions of the Third Benjamin Regulars brought it up to reinforced regimental strength. The Regulars had been included because they had originally lost the world to the Jaguars and desperately wanted to win it back and regain their honor. ComStar's contribution to the fight was the 278th Division, an elite unit that hailed from Rasalhague.

When the Star League force arrived in the Asgard system, the Fourth Jaguar Hussars was stationed in Vernan, the largest city on Asgard's southern continent. *Tai-sa* Angus McTeague wanted to engage them there because the Regulars had been pushed from Vernan to Odin's Retreat and eventually onto the plains back in 3052. The Jaguars anticipated him by pulling back into the rocky mountains of the Retreat. McTeague then deployed the Com Guard unit to the south of the mountainous formation and let the Davion Heavy Guards slip behind them to set up on the eastern retreat route from the mountains, while the Combine force drove it at the Jags through the western approaches the Jags had used themselves to dislodge the Regulars seven years earlier.

"Hammer One, this is Daniel Seven."

Wendy keyed her radio microphone. "Go ahead, Daniel Seven."

"Passive motion detectors are picking up movement on the way down." The forward infantry-spotter hesitated for a moment. "They're popping down into Grid Sector Twenty-three thirty-six."

"Twenty-three thirty-six copy, Daniel Seven. You've done your job. Pull yourself and your people out of the Jaguar's den."

"Roger, Kommandant." The relief in the man's voice was palpable. "We'll be out in two."

"Roger, Seven. Haul it because we're going to make it hot." Wendy switched her radio over to the battalion's tactical frequency. "Hammer One to battalion. We have incoming. We don't know the number or size, but they'll be coming at us through Grid Two-three-three-six. Hold your fire until you are cleared to fire."

Punching another sequence of buttons on her communications console, she brought up the regiment's artillery frequency. "This is Hammer One. I need a barrage on Grid Sector Twenty-three thirty-six—two-three-three-six—in one minute. Repeat, one minute. Follow with a second shot in thirty seconds."

"Roger, Hammer One. You're first on the board."

Finally she switched back to her battalion tactical frequency. "Okay, Hammers, let's light them up." She looked up at the holographic sensor display hanging in the air in front of her. It compressed a full three-sixty degree view of her surrounding environs into a one-hundred sixty-degree arc. Gold bars on either side of the display marked the firing arc for her forward weapons. She quickly punched up some magnification and shifted the scan over to starlight mode to make the most of the sun's dying light.

In the distance, well outside her 'Mech's maximum range, she saw a group of eighteen BattleMechs. They bore the mottled paint scheme favored by the Smoke Jaguars, but most of it had been obliterated from the 'Mechs' armor. They gave every indication of having been in a hellacious series of fights, and if the flashes near the top of Odin's Retreat were any indication, the fight was still raging furiously.

Though First Battalion made no attempt to hide their presence, and had even courted danger by daring to skyline themselves on the hills, powering up their sensors should have alerted the Jaguars that the Guards weren't hanging around just to watch. Flicking their sensors on was the equivalent of an old Terran knight lashing another knight with a gauntlet in challenge.

The only real problem with challenging the Clans that way was that Clan BattleMechs could actually hit at that range. The strikes wouldn't be hard, but they would do some damage and would come with impunity since the Guards couldn't shoot back. To some that would hardly seem sporting, but Wendy had learned that the only people who worried about fairness in war were writers who'd never seen combat and the poor slobs getting pounded without being able to strike back.

She keyed her mike. "Steady now, people. They've got us where we want them."

Taking advantage of their weapons' superior range, the Jags spread out and fired at the Guards. Green bars of coherent light from large lasers stabbed through the darkness and hit Guard 'Mechs. Long-range missiles jetted forward from the launchers mounted in the Clan 'Mechs, filling the air with smoke and fire. Two missile groups hit Wendy's *Devastator,* grinding away at the armor over her 'Mech's heart and on its left ankle. A tremor rippled through the BattleMech, but the damage itself was insignificant.

Reports of battle damage filtered in through the radio, but no one had been hit terribly hard. The Davion Heavy Guards used some of the largest BattleMechs available, which meant it would take more than one scattering of shots to bring any of them down. *Looks like the Smoke Jaguars are sticking with their traditions of honor and picking out single targets instead of combining their firepower to take any one of us down.* She could almost see that action as noble, but it came all wrapped up in stupidity, moving her more toward pity than admiration.

She dropped her cross hairs onto one of the heavy-set 'Mechs featuring metal talons built right into the massive hands. Her targeting computer wouldn't give her a lock, but it did report the 'Mech to be a *Kodiak.* Wendy smiled. *So the Jags are using Kodiaks. Good, we'll get experience with them before we go hunting Ghost Bears.*

The first artillery barrage hit the Jaguars just as they were preparing for another long-range assault on the Guards. A couple of small explosions presaged the attack, then fire washed the sector with gold and red sheets. It seemed for a second as if the very air had detonated. An instant later the strike's rumbling roar reached the Guards, and Wendy frowned. *No one should be subjected to that kind of pounding, but I'd rather have them die there than be here killing my people. Somehow, though, I don't think that's an option.*

Boiling out of the smoke came the surviving Clanners. The artillery strike had cut their number by a third, taking down most of the smaller, weaker 'Mechs and leaving the heavy ones to lumber on into combat. On they came, up the slight incline toward where the Guards waited for them. Their weapons blazed in the dusk, flashes of light freezing them into nightmare images for an instant, then cloaking them with darkness in the next.

"Guards, you are clear to fire." Wendy dropped her cross hairs onto the outline of a *Kodiak*. She had no idea if it was the one she'd seen before and, she realized, she didn't care if it was or not. The second a gold dot pulsed at the center of her cross hairs, she tightened up on her triggers, firing the *Devastator*'s twin Gauss rifles.

Two silvery balls shot from the rifle muzzles and nailed the *Kodiak*. Each supersonic slug hit on the left side of the Clan 'Mech. One shivered a ton of armor from the left arm while the other reduced the armor over its shin to crumbling flakes. The twin impact twisted the 'Mech to the left and, for a moment, Wendy thought it might go down, but the pilot proved skillful enough to keep the machine upright.

The *Kodiak* fired back at her with the large laser mounted in its chest. The verdant beam sizzled in at the *Devastator*'s right leg. Kilojoules of energy boiled armor away in a molten furrow across the 'Mech's thigh. Despite the loss of armor, the leg had more than enough protection to survive several more attacks like that. *And you're not going to get that many shots at me.*

Ted Mooraine's *Falconer* swung its weapons in line with the *Kodiak*. The *Falconer* always seemed to be broken, primarily because its body thrust forward from the hips as opposed to standing tall like the *Kodiak* or the *Devastator*. Mooraine had always maintained that that made him a smaller target for the enemy to hit. Wendy knew it was more his ability to hit with his weapons that guaranteed his survival than his 'Mech's low profile.

The particle projection cannon built into the 'Mech's left arm spat a jagged line of azure energy at the *Kodiak*. The PPC's energy whip flayed armor from the *Kodiak*'s left arm. Half-melted ferro-fibrous armor plates dropped from the 'Mech's arm and ignited small grass fires. The Gauss rifle in the *Falconer*'s right arm launched a ball straight into the *Kodiak*'s chest. It skipped off what would have been the sternum in a human, reducing armor to scree that poured in a landslide to the ground.

The *Kodiak*, having closed enough to reach a range where the rest of its weapons became effective, shifted the focus of its attack to the *Falconer*. The change made no sense to Wendy, since the *Falconer* had taken no damage *and* could deal less damage to the *Kodiak* at that range. *It's as if the pilot is incensed that Ted would interfere with our battle. If so, what comes next will really torque him off.*

The *Kodiak* opened up on the *Falconer* with everything available to hit at that range, which made for a very impressive display of firepower. The 'Mech thrust both fists forward, bringing the hand-mounted medium lasers to bear. Of the quartet mounted in the right arm, three hit. The trio of beams slashed armor from all across the *Falconer*'s torso, from right to left. The left-arm beams also achieved seventy-five percent accuracy and vaporized armor on the *Falconer*'s left breast, arm, and leg. While none of the shots got through the armor to do serious damage to the targeted BattleMech, the loss of so much armor threw the 'Mech seriously out of balance. The *Falconer* wavered slightly, then went down on its left side.

"Ted, get up and out of there. Guards, fall back after this exchange!" Wendy started her *Devastator* backing up, but still trained her cross hairs on the *Kodiak*. The silver ball from the right-hand Gauss rifle careened off the *Kodiak*'s chest, compounding the damage done by the *Falconer*. The other argent projectile spanged off the ursine 'Mech's right arm, blasting fragments of armor away in a blizzard of ceramic slivers. Despite the devastation, the Clan pilot kept his 'Mech upright and right on coming.

Wendy's battalion retreated in good order. Ted's *Falconer* sprinted past while her *Devastator* backed its way down the

hill's reverse slope. In her display she saw the *Falconer*
come back around and aim its weapons upslope, taking
advantage of the cover offered by the crest of the hill.
*They've got to know we're lying in wait for them here, but do
they have any choice except to attack?*

At a full charge the Clanners came up and over the hilltop.
Their momentum was such that even if they'd chosen to
stop, it probably would have been too late for them. If they'd
intended to stop, they showed no signs of it and instead
bravely came on despite what awaited them below.

Unlike the Combine units the Smoke Jaguars had faced at
Odin's Retreat, the forces of the Federated Commonwealth
fought by a doctrine of war built on a combined-arms
approach. A Regimental Combat Team was not just a regiment of 'Mechs and support services, but a unit that worked
in conjunction with armor, infantry, air, and artillery elements. The artillery had already devastated the Clan 'Mechs,
and the air units had swept the Clan fighters from the sky.
Now the retreating 'Mechs lured the Clanners into a valley
where FedCom armor was deployed to turn it into the Valley
of Death.

Though it was true that BattleMechs were the most powerful
weapon system ever devised, armor was not without its uses.
The heavy armor regiment of the Guards RCT had dug into the
reverse slope of the hill and waited with their vehicles hull-
down and ready to fire. Once their own BattleMechs had
retreated past them, they were clear to fire as their Clan foes
appeared at point-blank range.

A half-dozen Alacorn Mk VII heavy tanks opened up first.
Each one sported a trio of Gauss rifles mounted in the turret,
and two targeted the *Kodiak*. The first hit with a pair of
shots. One shattered armor on the 'Mech's right breast, and
the other pulverized armor on the *Kodiak*'s right leg. The
second Alacorn's attack proved more critical as the two of
its projectiles that hit did so on the right side of the *Kodiak*'s
torso. The last of the 'Mech's armor disintegrated under the
assault, and the second slug careened through its chest.
Splintered metal shards spilled from the 'Mech's side, and a
secondary explosion shot smoke from the muzzle of the
autocannon built into the *Kodiak*'s chest.

Still the *Kodiak* remained upright and dangerous.

Wendy swung her Gauss rifles into line with it and let fly
again. Only one of the Gauss rifle projectiles hit the *Kodiak*.

The silver ball shredded all but the last of the armor on the Clan 'Mech's right arm. The trio of medium lasers lanced out and stabbed into the *Kodiak*. One melted armor on the left side of its torso, the second burned more armor from its left arm, and the final one cored in through the crater in the middle of the 'Mech's chest. A gout of superhot steam shot back out through a hole over the 'Mech's heart, and the *Kodiak* shuddered.

*Gyro hit!* Wendy watched as the huge 'Mech struggled to remain upright. As good as the Clan pilot was, Wendy's last shot had damaged the gyroscope that helped keep the 'Mechs upright and working. The *Kodiak* tottered, limbs flailing, and went over. In an effort to remain upright, the pilot posted off the right arm, but the stresses snapped the support structures, shearing the arm off at the shoulder. The severed limb rolled down the hill toward the waiting Guards while the *Kodiak* crashed down into a cloud of dust and greasy black smoke.

Elsewhere along the hill crest the other Clanners fared even less well. Two Brutus assault tanks used their pair of large lasers to fill a tiny *Hankyu* 'Mech's chest with fire. It was inconceivable that the light little BattleMech should have survived as long as it did. When the green beams transfixed it and melted their way through its armor, green energy poured from all the joints. Smoke quickly followed and the 'Mech stopped, frozen, at the top of the hill with smoke wreathing its upper body.

Another *Kodiak* ran afoul of two blocky *Penetrators*. The Inner Sphere 'Mechs sported a half-dozen medium pulse lasers, each of which stitched lethal laser darts all over the giant 'Mech. They savaged its armor, reducing much of it to molten slag, with one laser coring through to the center of the 'Mech. Black smoke geysered up out of the whole as the Clan 'Mech pitched over backward.

Wendy moved her *Devastator* forward and surveyed the battlefield. The Clan 'Mechs were down, some smoking, some burning, others crippled and some unrecognizable as what they had been just minutes before. Heading upslope, she trained her cross hairs on the *Kodiak* she'd helped to bring down, and pumped one round through its left elbow. The shot shattered the joint and severed the forearm, ending the *Kodiak* pilot's futile attempt to get his 'Mech back on its feet.

"Lances, report."

Reports came back indicating that no Clan 'Mechs were operational. The damage her unit had taken wasn't bad. Most 'Mechs had lost armor only, though three had lost limbs and one pilot had died when her cockpit was crushed by a Clan Gauss rifle slug. The armor commander reported his unit operational, with the loss of only two tanks, both of which had been crushed by falling 'Mechs.

Wendy shifted over to the regimental frequency. "Hammer One to Home Base."

The cool voice of Marshal Anne Adelmara came back over the radio. "Report, Hammer One."

"Enemy engaged and stopped. We had eighteen, that is one-eight, come out of the Retreat. They are all down. Casualties are minimal for us."

"Very good, Karner, excellent. You're certainly in keeping with your family's tradition of service. The Dracs are mopping up in the Retreat, so you might still find stragglers. Remain where you are. I'll have Two Battalion head in to backtrack your friends. We'll have salvage crews coming out soon, too."

"Understood, sir. Hammer One out." Wendy found herself smiling uncontrollably. She shifted the radio to the battalion's tactical frequency. "Listen up. Secure the area. Friendlies will be moving through to backtrack the Clanners. Be careful, but also be proud. For the first time since Tukayyid, an Inner Sphere force has showed the Clans that while they might be good at warfare, that isn't the same as being the best at it."

# === 32 ===

**Wolcott, Draconis Combine Free Zone**
**Smoke Jaguar Occupation Zone**
**30 May 3059**

**V**ictor rubbed his burning eyes, then looked again at the holographic data display hovering over the center of the darkened briefing room's black table. The red and green icons and alphanumerics there splashed Christmassy colors over the Precentor Martial's khaki jumpsuit, and for a second Victor thought that for the Inner Sphere Christmas had indeed come early. *Granted we're concentrating a lot of force on only five worlds, but this outcome is all but unbelievable.*

Victor leaned forward on the table, supporting his upper body on his hands. "If we'd gotten these results in simulations, we'd probably think we were working with faulty data."

Phelan Kell, the room's other occupant, nodded. "Your father proved that overwhelming force can make short work of the enemy. What we didn't factor in was the Dracs' desire to kick the Jaguars in the teeth." He pointed toward an icon representing the world of Kiamba. "Hohiro used the First Kestrel Grenadiers and Third Drakøns to hold Collins Ridge, then his First Genyosha and the Com Guards Eleventh Division herded the 362nd Assault Cluster into Hecate's Swamp. The Jags remembered only too well the trick the Dracs had tried when they first took the world away from the Combine. They didn't want to get trapped, so they moved out of there faster than they should have, and in bad order. They couldn't dislodge the Grenadiers or Drakøns from the Ridge, so they were stuck in the open, and the Genyosha ripped them apart."

The Precentor Martial nodded in agreement. "On Tarazed, the Seventh Jaguar Dragoons made a move toward the Mosaikan Canyon Preserve, hoping to use the network of canyons to string our forces out. The Second Genyosha moved in far more quickly than the Dragoons thought possible and hit their supply convoy hard. The Third Donegal Guards RCT deployed to cut the Dragoons off from the Preserve, then Kai and his First St. Ives Lancers joined the Genyosha and ate the Dragoons up."

Victor smiled. "Kai apparently won the surrender of a Star of OmniMechs by challenging the Star Captain commanding it, then defeating her in single combat. He seems to have developed an affection for that *Penetrator* he first piloted back on Solaris, and it's done quite well for him."

"No surprise Kai won," Phelan said. "And no surprise a Jag would be willing to bid a Star away for the right to distinguish herself in combat."

The Precentor Martial frowned. "I'm not certain I follow your reasoning, Khan Kell."

"It's simple. On Asgard we pounded the Fourth Jaguar Dragoons flat after forcing them to retreat along the same path the Benjamin Regulars had taken seven years ago. On Hyner the Second Sword of Light tore through the Third Jaguar Cavaliers, leaving the First Regulan Hussars and your Ninth Division to mop up." Phelan pointed toward the icon representing Port Arthur. "The Combine units going into Port Arthur didn't expect opposition, but then ran into the 168th Garrison Cluster, which was last reported on Labrea. Even though the Fifth Sword of Light is considered green, it held its own at Zouave Vale while the Seventeenth Benjamin Regulars and Second Legion of Vega came in from Disher and knocked the snot out of the Jags."

Victor arched an eyebrow through the display at his cousin. "And your point is?"

"My point is that we caught the Smoke Jaguars utterly and completely asleep. The preliminary information we've got coming back indicates to me that they weren't thinking in terms of defense or being hit at all. Weapon selection on OmniMechs has far too many missile launchers and auto cannons in it for a defensive array. If I had to guess, I think they were gearing up for an expansion—possibly even a renewal of the invasion."

Victor straightened up and folded his arms across his chest. "They'd need a new ilKhan for that."

"Like as not." Phelan smiled capriciously. "I think they've elected one, and I think he's a Smoke Jaguar."

Focht narrowed his good gray eye. "Are you speculating, or do you have information from within the Clans?"

"You mean to ask if I'm holding out on you?"

Victor sliced his hands through the air. "That wasn't the question, Phelan. The Precentor Martial and I know you too well to think you'd withhold information from us. We're also aware that you've got spies back with the Wolves, and if this information has come from them, well, that's a bit higher level of veracity than your handicapping the candidates for us. Not that we wouldn't respect your insight into that matter, too."

The Wolf Khan nodded as if mollified, but Victor sensed there would be a price to pay for such easy acceptance of his remarks. "What I do know is that there was a return of the Khans to Strana Mechty to elect a new ilKhan. At that time there really were only three possible candidates for election, and the fact that none of the non-invading Clans have started to filter into the Inner Sphere suggests there were no surprises in the election.

"The three candidates were Marthe Pryde of the Jade Falcons, Vlad Ward of the Wolves, and Lincoln Osis of the Smoke Jaguars. I believe Osis was chosen."

Victor thought for a second. "You think the Wolves and the Falcons are still too weak for their Khans to be elevated to the office of ilKhan?"

"That's part of it. The invasion started under a Smoke Jaguar, Leo Showers. After him Ulric was named ilKhan, but he agreed to the Truce of Tukayyid and made the Clans abide by it. Because of that, the Clans will be reluctant to elect a Wolf as ilKhan, and Vlad still does not have enough of a track record to be trusted. The fact that he killed the interim Jade Falcon ilKhan also makes him too volatile for the other Clans to feel safe with him in charge."

"He murdered an ilKhan?" Victor was impressed. "I wonder if I could introduce him to my sister."

Phelan shook his head and smiled. "I don't know which one I'd pity in that match. But, yes, Vlad killed Elias

Crichell, but only after previously killing the other Jade Falcon Khan, Vandervahn Chistu. Marthe Pryde is now the senior Jade Falcon Khan. She has an excellent reputation, but she would have been hurt by the compromise at Coventry. She is also quite wary and intelligent, so she would want more time for the Falcons to recover from their war with the Wolves before she goes off into battle."

The Precentor Martial ran a hand over his chin. "That leaves Lincoln Osis. I don't believe I met him."

"No, I don't think you did. He wasn't part of Leo Showers' entourage. Osis is an Elemental who was made a *true* Khan after Tukayyid, though he was called Khan even before then."

Focht frowned. "What do you mean by that?"

Phelan scratched at the back of his neck. "The Smoke Jaguars throw around the term *Khan* a lot more loosely than most other Clans. Warriors who prove themselves exceptional leaders in battle situations are often called 'Khan' for the purposes of an operation. Osis probably deserved the honorific and his election, however. His rise to that position was the result of a lot of hard work and some rather audacious tactics." The Wolf Khan shrugged. "He is, in my estimation, something of a tactical genius."

"That's not good." Victor looked at the icons again. "Our plans have been based on the idea that the Smoke Jaguars are more traditional than, say, the Wolves, which means we can use flexibility against them. If Osis is in charge, that could seriously compromise the situation."

"Victor, next time try actually hearing what I'm saying." The Prince frowned. "Bring it again, a bit more slowly."

"I said Osis was a *tactical* genius. That's not going to be very useful against us." Phelan pointed to Victor. "You're here working on strategic and operational details, but you're leaving the tactical decisions to the people on the ground. Why is that?"

"Because trying to micromanage every assault is a quick way to guarantee failure." Victor winced. "Okay, I get your point. He's not going to be functioning at all well in this situation."

The Precentor Martial smiled. "I would imagine his difficulties will only compound when we launch our second wave."

Phelan nodded. "I agree. Seeing how well all our attacks

have gone off so far, are you going to crank the timetable forward?"

Victor slowly shook his head. "I'd love to, but I can't at this point. Our staging and supply operations are hitting their deadlines, but we didn't expect things to go this fast. Since we're talking about moving men and machines tens of light years—hundreds, in some cases—speeding things up isn't that easy."

"But I thought . . . the initial salvage and recovery numbers indicate we're picking up a lot of Jaguar hardware and munitions." Phelan frowned as he studied the floating numbers. "We can put that to good use."

"Agreed, and we are. Our front-line units will be one hundred percent operational when they hit their next assignments, and the garrison units left behind will be reinforced by whatever salvage remains. That means I can begin to assign supply shipments for the third wave early, so perhaps we can bring it off sooner and be ready to follow it up, but that will only happen if the second wave achieves the same level of success as this one."

Victor heard doubt in his own voice and he regretted it, but he knew he had to temper his elation at the first wave's success or he'd be anticipating utterly unrealistic results for the future. His job was to account for the worst-case scenario and hope for the best case. He had done that with the first wave of attacks and would continue to do so with each of the other four waves.

Phelan's eyes hardened. "I understand what you're saying, but you can't become too hidebound here. This first wave hit five worlds, the next one will nail eight—though I would add in Nykvarn, Turtle Bay, and Labrea. The results are going to vary, but you have to look at momentum. You talked about administering shock to the Clan troops on a tactical level, well, this will be a shock that will travel straight to Osis' brain. If we push on and take twice as many worlds in this wave as we did in the last, we'll have him in complete disarray."

The Prince drew in a hissed breath. "Nykvarn only has a Provisional Garrison Cluster available."

"The Ryuken-go regiment is ready to go." Phelan hooked a thumb toward the door. "They're aching for a shot at the Jags. The Sixth An Ting Legion isn't going to get any experience here on Wolcott, and Sun-Tzu's Red Lancers

Regiment will backstop LRMs as well as any other target. I know they're all part of your reserves, but they will take Nykvarn and, better yet, can hold it against a counterattack."

"I can buy that." Victor's eyes narrowed. "Your analysis sounds as good as Doc Trevena's."

"So Doc, Ragnar, and I kicked some ideas around." The Wolf Khan shrugged. "If I want you to buy an idea, I know I have to package it nicely."

"Okay, who takes Turtle Bay?"

"All three Legions of Vega—the Second, Eleventh, and Sixteenth."

Victor frowned. "The Legions of Vega?"

"Interesting." The Precentor Martial nodded enthusiastically. "The Smoke Jaguars destroyed the Fourteenth Legion of Vega on Turtle Bay—Hohiro Kurita and Shin Yodama are two of only a handful of survivors. They escaped after breaking out of a prison and staging an uprising. The Smoke Jaguars retaliated by using a planetary bombardment to raze the capital, Edo. By using the Legions to retake Turtle Bay, they would win back the honor they lost. Their success would also raise the Coordinator's stock, since he once commanded the Eleventh Legion of Vega."

Victor punched a data request into the computer keypad at his end of the table. A representation of Turtle Bay started rotating in the air, but nothing in the data scrolling up beside it indicated the presence of any Clan troops. "Looks like it is clear, though that's what we thought about Port Arthur."

"Port Arthur had troops on it for other reasons," Phelan said. "I suspect the Jags leave Turtle Bay ungarrisoned because the world can't be pacified. The people there know about Edo. They know they'll be dead if a Jaguar decides they should be dead, so they have nothing to lose in opposing their conquerors. Short of depopulating the planet, the Smoke Jaguars can't make it secure, so they've declared it pacified and moved on." He scratched at his throat. "We'll get it without a fight, and I can't imagine the Jaguars ever trying to take it back from us."

Victor nodded. "I can see including it on our list of targets. Since it was one of the first worlds to fall to the Clans, taking it back this quickly should amplify the shock. Why Labrea? You think it's undefended because the 168th Garrison Cluster that showed up on Port Arthur was stationed on Labrea?"

Phelan shook his head. "There are troops on Labrea. Very good troops."

"Do you *know* this, or are you speculating?" The Precentor Martial raised his hands. "No disrespect intended, of course."

"Call it an educated guess." Phelan folded his arms across his chest. "A web of relationships binds the Smoke Jaguar units together. It's vaguely similar to the way sports franchises maintain farm teams to feed them new recruits, though in the case of the Jaguars, the reverse is true. The 168th Garrison Cluster is a tributary unit of the Sixth Jaguar Dragoons. The Sixth sends them broken-down warriors, hand-me-down equipment, and the like. The Dragoons also use the 168th as a valet service: the 168th cleans up after them or prepares for their arrival. The 168th arrived on Port Arthur to prepare a staging area for the Sixth Jag Dragoons to launch into the Combine."

"So you're supposing that the Sixth Jaguar Dragoons are on Labrea?" Victor brought the image of Labrea up and opened a data window. "What do you know about them?"

"They're a storied unit that has often ended up in conflict with the Wolves—but that was well before my time." Phelan smiled wistfully. "During the invasion they participated in the conquest of Tarnby, Byesville, and Yamarovka. They won their battles in a walkover—too fast for them to win any sort of glory. In October, 3050, an Elemental Binary—that's fifty Elementals—took the world of Byesville away from the militia with less than a half-dozen shots being fired."

Victor smiled slowly. "And the leader of that Elemental action was Lincoln Osis?"

"Right. The Sixth Jaguar Dragoons also fought on Tukayyid, in the Dinju Mountains. ComStar's 299th and 323rd Divisions hit them pretty hard, but those who did get out managed to do so because Osis organized their retreat. Being beaten was a bitter pill for them to swallow, but they did, and Osis' actions were rewarded with his election to the post of Khan. Since then he's devoted a significant amount of resources to rebuilding the unit. I'm sure he sees it as his showpiece—the best the Jaguars have to offer. More important than taking Labrea will be killing that unit."

"Good point." Victor glanced over at the Precentor Martial. "If we roll the First Genyosha, First St. Ives Lancers, my Tenth Lyran Guards, and your 79th Division together, we should be able to crush them."

"No, Victor, that won't work."

Victor frowned at Phelan. "What do you mean? Hohiro, Kai, and I have trained together for just this sort of operation, and the 79th Division is one of ComStar's best. We're talking a dream-team of units."

"Yes, but we don't need a dream here—it's got to be a nightmare." An edge crept into Phelan's voice. "We want it to be Lincoln Osis' nightmare."

The Precentor Martial brought his head up. "What do you propose, Khan Kell?"

"Give Labrea to me."

"What?" Victor stared at his cousin. "All of our assaults are combined-unit operations. They all go off under the Star League flag. That's part of proving our legitimacy and our right to exist."

"I know that, and we will go in under a Star League banner, but hear me out." Phelan leaned heavily on the table. "First, Osis' esteem is tied up with the Sixth Dragoons. If Inner Sphere units pound it, he'll feel honor-bound to pull out the stops to avenge them and regain his honor. If I smash them—and I will—he'll be angry with me, angry with Ulric, angry with Vlad, and anyone else he can conceivably blame for my having hit his unit. Second, our going in under a Star League banner will really muddy the waters. If we hit hard enough, I'm sure we can capture the survivors. Then we release them and send them off to other garrison worlds, or at least let them communicate with other worlds. That way we get everyone questioning the legitimacy of their occupation."

"Good reasons, but none that will not be served by your units going in combined with other units."

"Then let me drop the final reason on you." Phelan's face became a mask of anger. "The Sixth Jaguar Dragoons will be one of the toughest units we face this side of Huntress. I can't defeat them without shedding blood. My people will die. I need that to prove to everyone that my warriors are truly part of the Inner Sphere. If any other unit is present and takes damage, it'll be said we used them as armor. And if the other unit stays completely out of the fight, the Wolves will be seen as selfish for wanting all the glory or stupid for not taking help in a tough fight. I won't have that. This is my chance to go nose up with a Clanner and deliver the message to him that we're here and they aren't going to be. I don't want anyone else in the way when I do that. We'll win this one for you, then we'll fight alongside you because, in the future, we'll have earned trust with our blood."

Victor regarded his cousin dispassionately. "What will you take against them?"

"Three Clusters: Fourth Wolf Guards Assault Cluster, First Wolf Legion Cluster, and First Wolf Strike Grenadiers. Only the first has the designation it had when we left—the others were created when we reorganized my forces on Arc-Royal. You will still have Second Legion and Second Strike Grenadiers available as reserve forces—right now they're attached to the Kell Hounds."

"Those are good troops." Victor nodded. "Okay, Labrea is yours."

"Really?"

The surprise in Phelan's voice brought a smile to Victor's face. "You thought I would refuse?"

"Well, ah, yes." Phelan straightened up. "When you started to put yourself into the mix for the assault, I assumed . . ."

"You assumed I wanted all the glory."

"You're too much a leopard to change your spots now, Victor."

"I think you'll find, Phelan, that I've got my head screwed on a bit tighter." Victor rubbed at the scar on his chest. "My job is to do the most with the least number of casualties. You're right about the trust factor concerning your troops and I was blind to it. No more. Go to Labrea. Take the Sixth Jaguar Dragoons apart, then get back here. There will be plenty of work for you and your troops in the future."

# 33

**Colodney River Valley**
**Colodney, Labrea**
**Smoke Jaguar Occupation Zone**
**29 June 3059**

*They come not like Smoke Jaguars to fight a war, but like lambs to a slaughter.* From the Highland Rim Phelan could see the whole of the Colodney River Valley, even on down to where the river joined the Boreal Sea and the city of Colodney had sprouted. During the invasion the Fifth Jaguar Regulars had chosen the gently rolling plains as the place to destroy the Third Royal Labrean Defense Regiment—two armored battalions desperately interposing themselves between a Clan Trinary and the city that was their home. The planet's verdant undergrowth had completely erased the scars from that earlier battle, though his sensors proved that vine-covered hillocks were actually twisted metal hulks that had once been tanks.

*And so the Jags return here to die.* The whole of the Sixth Jaguar Dragoons Cluster had moved into the valley. They had arrayed themselves in Trinaries—three stars of five 'Mechs each—as if Phelan would devote one of his Clusters to destroying each one. Such an expenditure of personnel and firepower would have been justified if the Dragoons had remained in defensive positions, dug in, but they had ventured forth from the valley's gently rolling hills, splashing through the river that ran through the center, taking up positions suited to bravado, not any sort of military savvy.

Phelan keyed his radio to the challenge frequency established earlier when his troops had burned into the system. "This is Khan Phelan Kell, commander of this Star League expeditionary force. Star Colonel Logan Moon, your deployment makes no sense whatsoever. Why are you making this so easy for us?"

Static crackled through the reply. "I have been chosen by ilKhan Lincoln Osis to lead this unit." Logan Moon's voice came through strong, but Phelan sensed that his words were spoken with a false confidence. "This unit was hand-picked to continue the glorious history of the Sixth Jaguar Dragoons."

"And you will do this. The carnage here will repeat the folly of the Dinju Mountains."

"So you say, false-Khan, but we have exchanged no shots, so this claim is hollow."

"I cannot believe you so willingly embrace death, Moon."

"I cannot believe you can conceive of a way that I can survive this encounter, Kell."

Phelan felt a chill run down his spine. "Is there something you wish of me, Logan Moon? Do you want *zellbringen*? If we fight a duel, I will take your Dragoons as my *isorla*. You will become my chattel."

"I can only speak for my Alpha Trinary, but this is acceptable."

"And your other Trinary leaders are prepared to make the same agreement if they are defeated, *quiaff*?"

"Aff."

"And you know you will get no concessions from us if you win, *quiaff*?"

Surprise shot through the Smoke Jaguar's voice. "You will not allow us to withdraw from this world?"

"The only way you will leave this world is as victors, Wolves, or corpses; but this should be no surprise to you. As I burned insystem, I pledged everything I had to taking this world, and you pledged all to defending it. Has the Jaguar developed cold feet?"

Resignation hung heavily on Moon's reply. "It was merely my wish to be able to return to Huntress to report your death."

"If that is your goal, your wait could be very long." Phelan started his humanoid *Gladiator Alpha* working its way down toward the valley floor. "Unless you can shorten it."

"I will do my best."

Phelan switched over to his command frequency. "Ranna Kerensky, you will engage the leader of Bravo Trinary. You fight for possession of that Trinary." Glancing at his sensor data Phelan realized that the Jaguar third Trinary was made up of medium-sized 'Mechs. "Ragnar, you will fight for the Charlie Trinary."

The three match-ups were close to even, with an advantage in armor going to the Jaguars in each case. Phelan faced a *Daishi,* which would eat him alive if he allowed Moon to outmaneuver him. Ranna, winner of Natasha Kerensky's Bloodright, pitted her bird-legged *Masakari Charlie* variant against a *Turkina Bravo.* If those two 'Mechs closed range, Ranna would be getting the worst of things. Ragnar matched up against the Jaguar *Shadow Cat Alpha* fairly well, and would be at his best if he closed quickly with his foe.

The trio of Wolves came down the rim in line, but fanned out as they reached the valley floor. The Jaguar commanders brought their 'Mechs forward while the rest of their commands retreated. Though the six 'Mechs would be fighting one another, the potential for damage being taken by other 'Mechs in the area was pretty high. Just because a laser missed its intended target did not lessen its ability to melt armor or kill pilots.

Phelan brought the challenge frequency on-line with his radio. "In the name of the Star League, I fight you, Star Colonel Logan Moon, for possession of your Trinary and this world of Labrea."

"I, Star Colonel Logan Moon of the Smoke Jaguars, accept this challenge. Let all who witness this duel abide by its outcome until the stars have all burned away to nothing and mankind is but a memory."

Phelan, bound into the command couch of his BattleMech by restraining straps, nodded. *You have the soul of a poet, Logan Moon. I will kill you only if you force me to.* It struck Phelan as odd, as he targeted the *Daishi*'s low, bird-legged silhouette, that millennia before there had been entertainment holovids pitting human gladiators against low-slung velociraptors. *As a fantasy, such a pairing of opposites would be diverting, but now it is very dangerous. His is the advantage, but that does not guarantee victory.* His targeting dot pulsed and Phelan hit his triggers.

The trio of large pulse lasers in the *Gladiator*'s left arm filled the air with a blizzard of green energy darts. They blistered the armor over the *Daishi*'s heart and bubbled it off both the 'Mech's left arm and left leg. The *Daishi* staggered a bit, but Moon kept the 'Mech on its feet and moving forward to close with Phelan.

Moon fired back with everything he had that could hit at that range. One of the *Daishi*'s large pulse lasers scattered green energy needles over the *Gladiator*'s right flank, carving away half the armor. Another large pulse laser did similar damage to the armor over the *Gladiator*'s midline. The third pulse laser and the left-arm Gauss rifle both missed their targets, saving Phelan's 'Mech from the *Daishi*'s full fury.

Phelan immediately started his 'Mech moving away to his right, which protected his flank and gave him a slightly better chance to hit the left side of Moon's *Daishi*. His maneuvering gave him an excellent view of the aftermath of Ranna's first exchange with the *Turkina*. The squat, bird-legged Smoke Jaguar 'Mech had gone down hard on its right side, though black smoke rose from a hole in the center of its torso. Phelan couldn't see any damage to Ranna's *Masakari*, which meant either that the *Turkina* pilot had missed her or that she'd taken everything on the left side of the 'Mech.

Beyond her, Ragnar had closed to middling range with his foe. That left him vulnerable to the *Shadow Cat*'s extended-range large lasers—a fact proved by both weapons slicing deeply into the armor on the *Fenris'* right arm and leg. That damage hardly slowed Ragnar down because his quartet of return shots all hit. The medium pulse lasers flayed the armor from both of the *Shadow Cat*'s arms and started to pick away at the naked limbs' internal structures. One heat sink exploded in a cloud of yellow-green vapor. Despite the damage done to each of the smaller 'Mechs, their pilots managed to keep them upright and functional.

With his maneuvering Phelan managed to keep his distance from the *Daishi,* but he knew that wouldn't last long. If he continued on his circular path, he'd run up onto some steep terrain that would slow him down and allow the *Daishi* to close. *Once he gets close enough to use his short-range missiles, I'll be lost.* Swiveling his 'Mech's torso to the right, Phelan targeted the *Daishi* and cut loose with everything.

Two of the large pulse lasers peppered the *Daishi*'s chest with fire, vaporizing yet more armor over its heart. The other green flight of darts chewed away at the armor on the 'Mech's right leg. The quartet of extended range medium lasers in the *Gladiator*'s right arm flashed their ruby beams at the *Daishi*. Three of them liquefied all but the last of the armor on the 'Mech's left arm, while the last beam ate into the armor remaining on the *Daishi*'s chest.

"Stravag!" Phelan swore as a wave of heat roared into his cockpit. Firing all of his weapons had overwhelmed his 'Mech's heat-exchanger system, spiking the monitor up into the red zone. The 'Mech began to respond only sluggishly, which would allow the *Daishi* to make up some of the distance that separated them. *I knew this was what would happen when I fired everything. Why couldn't he be fighting in something easier to kill, like a* Kodiak? *Why doesn't Moon have the good grace to go down?*

*Because he's a warrior, that's why.* Phelan braced himself for the *Daishi*'s return strike. Again the Gauss rifle's projectile whizzed past without doing damage, for which Phelan found himself profoundly thankful. As if to make up for that error, and with a precision that struck Phelan as being preternatural, one of Moon's large pulse lasers again hit the *Gladiator*'s right flank. The beam burned away the last of the armor over that location. *If he hits me there again, I'll be down. Hard.*

The other two pulse lasers hit and though they did not exploit the damage to the right flank, they still hurt the *Gladiator*. The second flight of energy darts scoured armor from the 'Mech's right arm. More significantly, the last one bored through the 'Mech's center torso armor and skewered the engine. More heat immediately flooded into Phelan's cockpit, and a gout of black smoke cut off his view of the battlefield for a moment.

Phelan wrestled against gravity and managed to keep his 'Mech upright. He felt the behemoth slowly return to his control and continued to extend the range between it and the *Daishi*. Phelan began to grin, then that grin turned into a full-fledged smile. The smoke cleared in front of him and he saw that the *Daishi* had gone down. As he watched, Moon struggled to bring the big war machine back to its feet, but failed in his first attempt. The 'Mech crashed down to the ground again, chipping armor from the cockpit and chest. On the second attempt the 'Mech came all the way up, but the damage had clearly rattled the pilot.

Even better, beyond the *Daishi,* Phelan saw his compatriots had fared well in their fights. The *Turkina* Ranna faced had regained its feet, but her attack drove it again to the greensward. The *Turkina*'s fire eroded some of the armor on the *Masakari*'s right arm, but in no way impaired its ability to wage war.

The *Shadow Cat* shot two green beams at Ragnar's *Fenris,* but one missed high. The emerald beam that hit melted the last of the armor on the *Fenris*'s right leg, leaving it unprotected, and worked a bit on the structural members and myomers it had exposed. Ragnar returned fire with four pulse lasers. The trio that hit did significant damage. One vaporized most the armor over the *Shadow Cat*'s forward-jutting cockpit. The second burned the 'Mech's right arm completely away, exploding another heat sink and slagging the large laser built into the limb. The last scarlet storm of energy darts scorched the armor on the right side of the 'Mech's torso, leaving that half of its chest a blackened ruin.

*Time to put Moon and his 'Mech down.* Because of his own problem with overheating, Phelan could only fire two of his pulse lasers. In a pitched battle that would have been disastrous, but in a duel it could be deadly if he made those two shots count. He took a moment more than he might have to make sure his cross hairs spitted the ragged gashes over the *Daishi*'s heart, then thumbed the trigger.

Both flights of verdant energy needles pulsed through the Jaguar 'Mech's torso armor, filling its chest with green fire. Smoke began to pour from the *Daishi*'s chest. The big 'Mech wavered slightly, and Phelan guessed that his shots had damaged the gyro helping Moon keep the *Daishi* up and running. The BattleMech teetered and was obviously going down, but that did not stop Moon from firing back with his Gauss rifle.

This time the Jaguar's Gauss rifle was right on target. The silver ball slammed into the *Gladiator*'s left arm, shattering the armor into delicate ceramic fragments. The damage pared close to two-thirds of the armor from that limb, but it didn't concern Phelan overmuch as he watched the *Daishi* fall yet again. The fall flaked the last bit of armor from the 'Mech's left arm, which was good, but hardly a fatal wound. *He's down, but that 'Mech's dangerous no matter how wounded it is.*

The *Turkina* fighting with Ranna got up from the ground again, but Ranna did not give it much of a chance to get back into the fight. Her pulse laser missed wide, but the twin lightning bolts from her particle projection cannons drilled through the armor over the 'Mech's heart and exploded like a supernova. Structural members glowing white-hot rode vapor jets out of the blast and started little fires wherever they landed. A billowing black cloud with little tongues of fire licking at it began to billow out of the *Turkina*'s chest. Another explosion splashed silver through the cloud for a second, marking the death of a jump jet.

The *Turkina*'s return strike came from the pair of large pulse lasers mounted in the 'Mech's left arm. Their spray of green bolts tore into the armor on the *Masakari*'s torso center and right, but came nowhere near penetrating the virgin armor or stopping the OmniMech.

The *Shadow Cat* fired the laser in its left arm at Ragnar's *Fenris,* but missed low. The undergrowth immediately caught fire, raising a curtain of smoke between the two battling 'Mech's, but the red darts from Ragnar's pulse lasers pierced it and effortlessly carved armor from both legs and the center torso area of the *Shadow Cat.* The Smoke Jaguar 'Mech remained up and circled to the right, doing its best to present Ragnar with undamaged armor to shoot at.

*For someone who is convinced he's going to die here, Moon has a lot of fight left in him.* Phelan marveled as the Jaguar wrenched his dying *Daishi* back up onto its feet and sent it lumbering after him. Fortunately for Phelan, the hill that had slowed his maneuver now stopped Moon's pursuit for a second. The *Daishi*'s large pulse lasers swiveled up and spat green energy at the *Gladiator.*

Molten armor smoldered around his tracks as one storm of energy bolts scorched armor off the *Gladiator.* The other laser that hit similarly stripped armor from the 'Mech's right arm. The Gauss rifle's argent projectile pounded into the *Gladiator*'s left leg, shivering armor plates from it.

Phelan kept the *Gladiator* moving and managed to keep it upright despite the pounding it had taken. Heat still swirled through the cockpit, but he brought the 'Mech's left arm around to point at the *Daishi* anyway. *Only can fire two. This better do it.*

The paired bursts of laser fire again raked their way across the *Daishi*'s chest. One savaged the unblemished armor on its right breast, but the other ripped through the gaping hole in the middle. Green flashes sped through smoke as glowing metal rods and globules poured out like vomit. The *Daishi*'s head dipped lower as the whole center torso-support evaporated, leaving the pilot staring down at the ground while the glowing maelstrom that had once been the engine, gyro, and central skeleton of his 'Mech silhouetted the cockpit. Unbalanced, the 'Mech sagged to the right, then collapsed in a tangle of angular limbs.

Ragnar's *Fenris* again fired all four of its pulse lasers at the *Shadow Cat*. The streaming scarlet energy bolts gobbled up the whole of the 'Mech's left arm, disintegrating the 'Mech's other large laser. More laser fire melted armor on the 'Mech's left breast and leg, then the final laser's fury spent itself denuding the *Shadow Cat*'s right flank of armor.

Yet even as Ragnar's assault thoroughly ravaged the *Shadow Cat,* the Smoke Jaguar shot back with the large laser. The green beam lashed armor from the *Fenris*'s left leg. The shot would have hit higher, but the melting arm had begun to droop, lowering the aim point to where weapon proved relatively harmless. As if ashamed of itself, that arm vanished in a cloud of molten rain spattering the ground.

Limbless and unable to strike at the *Fenris*, the *Shadow Cat* started to rush straight at its tormentor. The damage resulting from the collision could have hurt the *Fenris,* though Phelan thought it unlikely it would have crippled Ragnar's 'Mech. Avoiding even the remotest possibility of that happening, Ragnar cut his 'Mech to the left and fired back through the gaping hole that had once been the armor on the right side of the 'Mech's chest. A typhoon of red energy darts swept through, devouring internal structures. They boiled on through the right side of the chest, then vaporized the gyro keeping the 'Mech erect.

The *Shadow Cat* sprawled forward, gouging a brown scar through the valley's vegetation. Smoke rose from its arm holes and mingled with the smoke from the *Turkina*'s snuffed engine to darken the sky.

Phelan marched his *Gladiator* down to where the *Daishi* lay. He flicked on his external speakers, unable to determine if Moon lived or had radio communications in his cockpit. He patched the radio into the speaker line. "It is over, Logan Moon. Your Cluster and your world are mine. You have been defeated in the name of the Star League, but you fought well and I would honor you in the way of the Clans. I make you all bondsmen, and will allow you to resume your roles as warriors at the earliest convenience."

Weary and clearly in pain, Logan Moon replied through the radio. "Explain to me one thing, Kell."

"If I am able."

"Why the fiction of the Star League?"

"What fiction?" Phelan waited a second, knowing the other Jaguars would be paying close attention to his reply. "The invasion of the Inner Sphere was launched by Leo Showers to reestablish the Star League. The invasion accomplished this end—not in the way any of us expected, for no Clan conquered Terra and won the right to rule the Inner Sphere. Despite that, the Star League has been reformed, under a charter which is virtually the same as the original charter, and the signatories to it are many of the same states."

"But this Star League, this newly formed Star League is a charade."

"Is it? If the Star League had reformed five years after the Amaris Usurpation, could ilKhan Leo Showers have justified his invasion, *quineg*?"

Moon hesitated. "Neg."

"So we agree that the reestablishment of the Star League is enough to obviate the invasion, but we argue over the number of years. I maintain the number does not matter, just the act of its reestablishment." Phelan shrugged. "You can argue a number, but you can no more justify one than another, so I can argue you into accepting five minutes or five centuries. You have lost. The invasion is wrong, and continuing it is not only a crime, but a violation of all the Clans hold sacred."

More pain underscored Moon's reply. "I do not know what to say."

"Admit you were wrong, and embrace the chance to make things right." Phelan kept his voice cold and razor sharp. "You and your people will be allowed to communicate with your sibkin to advise them of your change in status. After that we will leave this place and you will put your skills to use doing what Nicholas Kerensky intended when he created the Clans. You will defend the Inner Sphere from predacious enemies and you will find it the grandest duty you have ever known."

## 34

**Bjarred**
**Nova Cat Occupation Zone**
**1 July 3059**

The pale gray silk of *Tai-sa* Katherine Oltion's kimono allowed some of Bjarred's cool evening air to reach her flesh, though she knew it only *found* goose bumps there, it did not *create* them. Though she had complete trust in her superiors—and even respected the Precentor Martial and Victor Davion—she had serious doubts about the bid she had been ordered to give when the Nova Cats had inquired about the forces she intended to use to take Bjarred. *If my suicide was desired, the Coordinator should have just invited me onward, not ordered me to bid myself alone to take this world. Why make the Nova Cats complicit in my death?*

The leader of First Battalion of the Combine's Sixth Ghost Regiment descended the gangway from the *Leopard* Class DropShip and slowly walked toward the waiting knot of Nova Cats. The DropShip was the smallest available to her unit, and had enough firepower to wipe out the reception committee in and of itself. What made Katherine feel particularly vulnerable was that she'd not even been allowed to put her BattleMech aboard the DropShip. While orders had not forbidden her to carry her swords—the very mark of her being a warrior—any weapon of more recent heritage had not been allowed.

The Nova Cats appeared to be representatives from the

various parts of the warrior caste. Huge, hulking Elementals towered over the tiny, macrocephalic pilots. More normal in size and appearance was the MechWarrior who, by dint of her position at the head of the group, appeared to be its leader. The streak of white amid her long black tresses would have struck Katherine as a sign of the woman's age, but given the agist leanings of the Clans, she doubted that was the case. Instead she saw the white forelock as a genetic trait that was prized among the Nova Cats, since it made her hair match the Clanner's black leathers and the white, supernova-like blaze over the left shoulder and breast.

Katherine stopped a short distance from the Clan warriors and bowed. Straightening up, she introduced herself, following the precise formula given in her orders. "I am *Tai-sa* Katherine Oltion of the Sixth Ghost Regiment, currently attached to and in service of the Star League Expeditionary Force. I have come to contest the possession of this world."

The Nova Cat MechWarrior returned her bow. As she straightened up, the woman's eyes gave no evidence of amusement, anger, or fear—all of which Katherine would have expected to see. Instead the other warrior seemed reverent as if the proceedings were all but sacred to her.

"I am Star Colonel Olivia Drummond of the 189th Striker Cluster of the Nova Cats. Your arrival has been foreseen. I am here to answer your challenge. Your bid of one person to take this world is impressive."

"In ordering me to make that bid, my superiors wished me to assure you that no disrespect was intended."

"None was taken." Drummond gave her an open, brown-eyed stare that felt almost electric in its intensity. "It was assumed with this bid that you are a skilled warrior. I offer myself as your opponent and trust that you will find me your equal."

*She's following the formula as scripted. Unfortunately, the script runs out soon.* "I have no doubt you are my equal and probably my superior. Between us, however, we shall stipulate equality, *quiaff?*"

"Aff."

Katherine's mouth began to dry out. "A warrior like you knows that in combat there are only two elements: skill and chance, *quiaff?*"

"Aff." The woman's voice did not waver, nor did her eyes betray reluctance to play her part.

*Here we go into the unknown.* "Since we have eliminated skill, all that is left is chance." Katherine freed a large gold coin from a small pocket sewn into the hem of her kimono. On the face it had the profile of Sun-Tzu Liao, current First Lord of the Star League, and on the back was the Star League Defense Force crest. The date of the Whitting Conference was rendered in Roman numerals around the edge. She held it up and rotated it slowly so the Nova Cats could see that the front and back were different. "I propose we flip this coin to decide who wins the world. I will flip it and you will call it in the air. Chance will decide who wins."

She had tried to keep a tremolo from her voice, but she failed. *I have been assured I need fear for nothing, but standing alone on a Clan-conquered world makes believing that difficult.*

If Star Colonel Drummond noticed the wavering of her voice, she gave no indication of it. "This is acceptable. Proceed."

Katherine hooked her thumb beneath the edge of the coin, dropped her hand a bit, then brought it back up quickly and flicked her thumb hard. The coin rose quickly in the evening air, lights from the spaceport flashing from its sides. The coin rang with a pure tone that faded slightly as the coin reached the apex of its arc and built as it began to descend again.

The Nova Cat warrior smiled. "Edge."

Katherine's jaw dropped as the coin hit the ground. It bounced up off the ferrocrete, rotating faster, then landed again. It flipped back and forth a few times, then spun rapidly around the coin's edge and eventually came to rest with the Star League Defense Force crest uppermost.

Katherine closed her mouth and nodded. "It has been decided."

Drummond nodded and extended her right hand toward Katherine. "We have been defeated and are yours to command. We hope you will accept us as your bondspeople and allow us to prove ourselves worthy of becoming warriors again."

Katherine unknotted her kimono's *obi* and looped the gray sash around the Nova Cat's right wrist. She then drew her *wakazashi* and sliced the improvised bondcord in half. The gray silk pieces fell to the ferrocrete and slowly twisted up as a slight breeze began to rise.

"You are warriors again, all of you, with the full rights, privileges, and responsibilities of the warrior class." Katherine gave each one of those assembled a nod and smile. "As it is, I cannot afford to devote troops to garrisoning this world. You are charged with the duty of keeping it safe, in the name of the Star League. As you may know, other Nova Cat worlds have been lost to the Star League. You are free to communicate with those worlds and their personnel to make decisions about your future. It is my duty and pleasure to welcome you to the Star League."

"Thank you very much, *Tai-sa* Oltion." Star Colonel Olivia Drummond smiled broadly. "It feels very good to be home again."

"So the question really is, ilKhan Osis, how long had you intended to keep this Inner Sphere offensive secret from us?" Vlad, standing in the rear of the Hall of the Khans, opened his arms wide to take in the rest of the Khans gathered in Grand Council. "According to the rather sketchy information I have been able to accumulate, there were multiple strikes against targets in your occupation zone and your forces have been roundly defeated in a series of pitched battles. There is even evidence of a second round of attacks."

Osis' face contorted itself into a mask of fury. "I did not withhold information from this body for the purposes of deceiving it."

"Then what was your purpose, ilKhan?" Vlad kept his voice light, but fed into it enough of a mocking tone that the worlds still skewered Osis. Vlad's information had come purely from intelligence missions into the Inner Sphere. Small DropShips were sent through the Jade Falcon Occupation Zone to inhabited systems in the Lyran Alliance. The ships popped in, soaked up as much as they could of popular news-media broadcasts from the world, and jumped out again before the planet's garrison forces could attack. In some cases that meant they pulled in a dozen or more hours of news, including interesting holographic footage of the battles against the Smoke Jaguars.

"I believed it was necessary to determine the full extent and nature of this action against us before doing something that might have raised alarm needlessly." Had Osis' eyes been lasers, Vlad knew he'd have been flash-fried in a second. "This is a complex situation which, among other things, points to treason by members of this body."

A hushed rumbling of voices began to fill the chamber, but Khan Marthe Pryde stood and her clear voice cut through it. "Perhaps, ilKhan, you would tell us what is going on."

The anger on the ilKhan's face slackened for a second into pain. "At the end of May and beginning of June, Inner Sphere forces—largely from the Combine, but with elements from throughout the Inner Sphere—hit five worlds we had occupied. On Kiamba, Asgard, Port Arthur, Tarazed, and Hyner, our Clusters were pitted against six times their number of 'Mechs and were forced to surrender possession of the worlds. Reports have come back piecemeal, but we were facing some of the elite units of the Inner Sphere, many of whom were using technology salvaged from our units or newly developed in the last seven years."

Vlad smiled. "Forgive me for interrupting you, ilKhan, but your description of the reports you have gotten begs a question: were your people able to withdraw or were they wiped out?"

Osis began to quiver and his voice tightened. "There were considerable losses. I will admit that preparedness was not as high as it should have been, but these were troops in garrison."

"Again, forgive me, ilKhan, but four of those worlds were garrisoned by frontline units, including your Fourth and Seventh Jaguar Hussars." Vlad knitted his brows with concern. "If they were wiped out, this is a serious threat indeed."

"If you would refrain from interrupting me, Khan Ward, I could provide you with more details on the assaults." Osis wiped spittle from the corners of his mouth. "In addition to these attacks, the Inner Sphere inserted guerrilla units onto other worlds to distract and harry our troops, giving us a false picture of the nature of the assaults. A second wave of attacks began within the week, and we are still sorting out details from them, but one thing is very clear: these attacks are being accomplished with the help of the Nova Cats!"

Severen Leroux rose at his place as the other Khans turned to look at him and his fellow Khan, Lucien Carns. Leroux calmly removed his enameled helmet and placed it on the table in front of him. "I anticipated that you would attempt to foist blame for your disaster on me, Lincoln Osis. This accusation is false, of course." He turned and looked up at

Marthe Pryde. "Tell me, Khan Jade Falcon, did the ilKhan inquire of you whether or not your garrison forces had been attacked, *quineg*?"

"Neg."

Leroux shifted his gaze to Perigard Zalman. "And, Khan Steel Viper, did he ask you if your worlds had been attacked, *quineg*?"

"Neg."

Leroux nodded. "Nor did he ask the Nova Cats if we had been attacked. Had he inquired—conducting an investigation into the matter as he should have as ilKhan—he would have learned that while he lost five worlds, we lost all or part of *nine* worlds to Inner Sphere assaults. When this happened and no inquiry came from the ilKhan, I was forced to draw one of the following conclusions: either the ilKhan was unaware of the attacks *or* he had chosen to treat them as an internal problem that my Clan was to deal with on its own.

"Since two of the worlds we lost were Avon and Caripare— worlds we garrison in unison with the Smoke Jaguars—I knew my first conclusion was in error. There could be no way the Smoke Jaguars on those worlds did not report to him that we had been attacked. I had to assume, then, that we were to deal with these attacks by ourselves."

Leroux's eyes sharpened. "That being said, the ilKhan will acknowledge that I provided him with a report on our losses, but he chose not to reply to it."

"That report was inaccurate."

"Was it?" Leroux's voice crackled gruffly, betraying his advanced age. "Did you ask for clarification of it, *quineg*? Did you expect me to have more details on the worlds I lost than you did on yours, *quineg*?"

"Your report suggested things that were wrong." Osis' eyes narrowed until Vlad was certain the man could see only silhouettes before him. "On Avon and Caripare your troops joined with those of the Inner Sphere to attack and destroy Smoke Jaguar troops."

Leroux shook his head. "I believe, ilKhan, that even the fragmentary reports you have gotten about those actions will indicate that the First Nova Cat Guards and our First and Third Garrison Clusters are now designated the First *Star League* Nova Cat Guards and First and Third *Star League* Garrison Clusters. They were won by the Star League when our portions of those worlds were taken."

As Leroux's mention of the Star League started new chatter among the Khans, Vlad's smile slowly grew. The news reports he had gotten from the Inner Sphere talked about a reestablishment of the Star League, but he had considered it merely another Inner Sphere trick to try and hold off the Clans politically. After all, the Clans saw themselves as destined to restore the Star League. Perhaps the leaders of the Inner Sphere were foolish enough to think this ploy would be enough to tame the Clans. Vlad knew that none of the Khans would acknowledge the Inner Sphere leadership—especially that of a non-warrior like Sun-Tzu Liao—but the ploy did reveal how much the Inner Sphere had learned about the Clans.

The defection of the Nova Cats could have been anticipated, but only after attacks had begun. They were the least warrior-like of the Clans because of their mystical beliefs about the nature of man and the universe. While Vlad could respect their embracing ancient warrior traditions and their reverence for courage and valor, the whole spiritual overlay bothered him. *It gives them a belief in a higher authority to which they must answer, when the truth is that* we *judge the Clans, not some unseen spirits or silent deity.* Perhaps their spirits or ghosts or whatever they were had told them to embrace the Star League fiction.

From the reaction by the other Khans, this Star League ploy, when coupled with a strong assault, seemed to carry some weight. That struck Vlad as odd for a second or two, then he noticed the thoughtful expression on Marthe Pryde's face as she stared distantly past him. That she might have to think a moment before dismissing the charade surprised Vlad, so he forced himself to reason his way through the implications of the Star League being reformed and dealing the Clans a series of defeats.

*Of course, I should have seen it before.* The Crusader faction of the Clans was the group that had initiated the assault on the Inner Sphere. They were the ones who had declared the realms of the Inner Sphere to be illegitimate and barbaric. Their mission was to conquer Terra and reestablish the Star League themselves. Proof of the fact that they were right, that their motives were right and that their cause was just, was the ease with which their forces overcame the Inner Sphere troops they faced.

That conviction, based on the results of battles waged with

inferior troops, carried with it the seeds of deception and self-doubt. It had almost been easy to rationalize defeat on Tukayyid because ComStar was an organization that held itself apart from the realms of the Inner Sphere—in fact, because of the way it had influence throughout the Inner Sphere, it was closer to the old Star League than anything else. The warriors of ComStar could almost be seen as pure and free of the taint of the older, more corrupt realms. *And, after all, some of the Clans did win their engagements on Tukayyid, so our defeat was not complete.*

Defeats on other worlds, like Twycross and Wolcott, could be put down to deception or luck. The defeat of the Smoke Jaguars and Nova Cats at Luthien could be explained away simply because of the presence of Wolf's Dragoons—a renegade Clan unit—and the fact that Luthien had never been an easy world to take. The Jaguars had overreached themselves there and gone after it primarily because the Wolves had taken Rasalhague, the capital of the Free Rasalhague Republic. Defeats such as those were really of little consequence—exceptions they proved that either the Inner Sphere troops were devoid of honor or that they could get lucky once in a while.

The problem with the Star League assault in the Smoke Jaguar and Nova Cat occupation zones was that it was clearly an operation planned and pursued with the same sort of precision the Clans themselves reveled in. It was nothing less than an invasion of Clan territory by the Inner Sphere, and Vlad could almost share the shock and sense of doom the citizens of the Inner Sphere had felt.

Since the ease of their earlier victories had confirmed the virtue of the Crusader mission, their losses now cast it into doubt. Vlad could almost feel Katrina's fine hand in both this presentation and the choice of targets. *They are going after the Smoke Jaguars, my enemy.* This invasion helped Vlad much more than it hurt him.

He glanced over at Marthe Pryde. "Hurt, are you, Marthe, that they did not choose to attack you, *quiaff?*"

A quick flash of fire in her eyes told him he'd hit very close to the mark, but she covered it with a shake of her head. "What could have happened at Coventry was enough to put them off the Jade Falcons, I think."

"No doubt."

Marthe snarled silently at him, then stared down at Lincoln

Osis. "Is this true, ilKhan? Are the troops of the Inner Sphere claiming to be of the Star League?"

"Yes, but it is a tissue of lies." Osis leaned forward at his place, holding his body up on his fists. "I already have a plan to deal with this assault. While the Inner Sphere has learned much tactically, their operational and strategic planning leaves much to be desired. Their strikes are aimed at worlds where they will be uncontested or will face garrison Clusters. They have not come at my best troops, and I do not plan to give them that opportunity. We will be blasting into the Combine, expanding our invasion corridor."

Osis lifted his arms and opened them. "This is the opportunity you have all be waiting for. I am prepared to accept bids on assignments for your troops so you can join me in destroying this threat to the Clans."

Vlad laughed aloud. "You are generous now with opportunities whereas you have been stingy with information up to this point. You waited a whole six weeks, until a second wave of attacks began *and* you were questioned here, by this body, about the attacks to tell us what has happened. *And* you still have not told us the whole of what you face."

Osis shrugged. "I had not thought you would send troops to help anyway, Khan Ward, so your protests neither surprise nor influence me."

"They are not meant to influence you, ilKhan. The Star League has given you all the surprise you can handle right now." Vlad looked around at the other Khans. "Lincoln Osis, our ilKhan, chose to keep these attacks a secret and treat them as an internal Smoke Jaguar matter. He even refrained from bringing them to our attention when he had word from the Nova Cats that they, too, had been attacked. And now he has a plan and is inviting all of us to participate in it."

Vlad contorted his face into a mask of disgust and let his voice slip into a growl. "I am not a mercenary who can be bought. What does the ilKhan offer us? He offers us the chance to let our troops shed blood to win worlds for the Smoke Jaguars. It is clear why he thinks such an offer is more than generous."

Asa Taney of the Ice Hellions turned to point a finger at Vlad. "That is simple enough for you to say, Khan Ward, but your forces are already in the Inner Sphere. This is our opportunity to join the invasion."

"No, this is your opportunity to prostitute your troops for

scraps from the Smoke Jaguar table. The assignments he gives you will spread you out around the Periphery, hitting the Combine from a dozen places so they will pull troops off Jaguar worlds. What he has missed in this planning is that more than just Combine troops have been attacking his worlds. This is a coalition, and they are using their best troops. You would be foolish to become involved in this operation."

Marthe Pryde nodded solemnly. "The Wolf Khan has the right of it. The ilKhan has addressed this as a Smoke Jaguar problem, but when things go against him, he seeks to expand it into a Clan problem. This is wrong. It is so wrong, in fact, that I will pledge troops of my own to oppose those bids to aid the Smoke Jaguars. I move that any troops not already part of the invasion must win the right to participate by defeating Jade Falcon troops."

"And I pledge Wolf Clan troops to oppose those who make it past the Jade Falcons." Vlad bowed his head to Marthe. "And I would be most willing to alternate challenges with the Jade Falcons, if Khan Marthe would share this mission with me and my troops."

"The Jade Falcons would be pleased to allow the Wolves to deal with some of these challengers." Marthe Pryde smiled. "There you have it, my Khans. If you wish your troops to prove themselves worthy of joining the invasion, let them prove themselves combat-ready against those who have already defeated the Inner Sphere's troops."

"No!" Lincoln Osis hammered his table with his fist. "What are you doing? Do you not see the threat here?"

"I see it, ilKhan, more clearly than you." Vlad pressed his hands together, fingertip to fingertip. "You are the ilKhan, but you still act like a Smoke Jaguar Khan. This threat is one you should have brought to us immediately. You did not. I have to assume then, that you believed you could handle it. Therefore, I must conclude that, as ilKhan, either you are capable of dealing with it on your own, or you are not. In this latter case, then, I believe you must acknowledge yourself incapable of serving as ilKhan. You should resign and another ilKhan should be elected to replace you; elected to deal with this crisis. Any other conclusion is inescapable."

Osis' face became ashen. "You make light of this threat, Vlad."

"I do not, ilKhan, but I do not see the Smoke Jaguars as

being the soul of the Clans." Vlad's voice became icy. "The Inner Sphere may destroy the Smoke Jaguars, but the Clans are eternal. We shall survive your misjudgment and malfeasance whether or not you do. Your only hope of survival is if your plan to repel this attack works. If it does not, a new ilKhan will go back into your invasion corridor and do things right this time."

# 35

**DropShip Barbarossa**
**Nadir Recharging Station, Wolcott**
**Pesht Military District, Draconis Combine**
**27 July 3059**

Victor Ian Steiner-Davion again scanned the data floating above the projector in the middle of the wardroom. "This was not quite what we expected."

The Precentor Martial calmly shook his head. "Neither was it unanticipated." He adjusted his eye patch slightly. "The Smoke Jaguar commander has mistaken me for Hannibal, so he is playing Scipio Africanus. By attacking five Combine worlds, he hopes we will withdraw our troops and fight to preserve the Combine. We knew this was a possibility."

"Agreed, which is why our second wave extended out beyond the worlds from which the Jags could easily launch assaults on Combine worlds. By getting behind the lines and making supplies more dear, we hoped to lure the bypassed forces outward. We expected this strike at the Combine to come in reaction to our first wave, not in anticipation of our third. This is a problem."

Focht arched an eyebrow at him. "Is it?"

Victor frowned. "Well, it is, but perhaps not an insurmountable one. We had three regiments garrisoning those front-line worlds when we launched our second wave. We've moved some of those forces forward for a third wave here—which will actually be hitting some of the worlds we'd reserved for our fourth wave—and we can shift forces around from the front-line worlds that haven't been hit."

The Precentor Martial nodded. "And don't forget that these worlds have been anticipating a Clan invasion for the past eight years. The Combine has built up defenses and trained their citizenry to repel attacks. With reinforcements coming in, the Clans are going to find these very tough worlds to take. They're expecting to have the easy sort of battle they had in the initial invasion, and that's not what they're going to get. They're going to be tied up for a long time, which means we can respond with as much power as we need to destroy them."

The Prince considered Focht's words. In his inspections of the Combine's frontier worlds he'd found their state of readiness very high. The garrison units drilled constantly and, over the years, had been staffed with veterans who'd seen action against the Clans as well as with new recruits whose youthful enthusiasm provided the fuel to implement strategies. Fortifications had been raised to withstand Clan sieges, and the general population had been trained in anti-Clan tactics. While their survival rate was likely to be minimal, the fact was that the training had turned entire worlds into armed camps, which meant the Clan would find no peace on Combine worlds.

"I would have preferred hammering those units on the worlds they held, but having them disappear into the Combine works, too. I know I wouldn't like dropping onto any of those planets." Victor smiled slowly. "I hope the Clans will hate it."

"They will." The Precentor Martial clasped his hands behind his back. "In reviewing the unit rosters for the attack on Schuyler, I notice you are in command of the Tenth Lyran Guards' First Battalion."

"Those are my Revenants. Of course, I'll be leading them."

"And if I choose to prohibit your entering combat?"

Victor's stomach folded in on itself. "I thought it was understood when we made the Tenth Lyran Guards part of this assault force that I'd be there. Kai will be leading the Lancers, Hohiro will command the First Genyosha, and Phelan will be bringing in his Fourth Wolf Guards. I have to lead the Revenants."

Focht shook his head. "No, you don't. Wait—before you protest, answer me this question: Why must you lead them?"

"They're my people. I picked them. I trained with them. We rescued Hohiro from Teniente. I won't let them go into combat without me because I'm not going to ask them to face danger and risks unless they're risks and dangers I'm willing to face myself."

"Victor, you've taken those risks before—your courage is not in question." Focht frowned. "It's not an easy thing to step back and command without being in the thick of combat. On Tukayyid I wanted very much to climb into the cockpit of a 'Mech and go after the Clans myself. Every death on my side became one I could have prevented had I been there. I felt I'd abandoned my people by letting them race into combat without me being there."

"Right. Exactly. So you know why I need to be there."

"No, I know why you *think* you have to be there." Focht nodded slowly. "My guess is that you also believe your direct intervention in an operation is demanded because of politics. You fear that your sister will make much of the fact that you didn't fight, didn't risk your life to oppose the Clans."

A shiver worked its way up Victor's spine. "I won't deny that is a consideration, but only a minor one." His hands tightened slowly into fists. "You've been around long enough to see the political machinations in the Inner Sphere. You remember my grandmother deposing her uncle Alessandro and taking over as Archon. You certainly recall Ryan Steiner's antics and probably even remember Frederick Steiner's ham-handed attempts at politics. He commanded the Tenth Lyran Guards and should have stuck to the military side of things because, as a politician, he was useless."

"So I recall." Focht's good eye narrowed. "I fail to see how this lesson in history makes your point."

"My point is this . . ." Victor sighed and collected his thoughts. "When I got run through I, ah, I died, or I thought I did. I know I coded and they had to bring me back, but while that was happening, I discovered some things about myself. I am, first and foremost, by heritage, inclination, and training, a warrior. That is what I do, what I am, and what I'm good at. I'm a thoroughbred that needs to run—if I can't, I'll die. And that's not to say I'm going to be a sociopath who goes out and starts wars just so I can mount up in a 'Mech and kill things. I'm someone who feels the need to do and accepts the responsibility for doing what has to be done to preserve the freedom of my people.

"Look, you're right in that I know that planning and evaluating are a vital part of this whole operation. I'm enjoying it, thriving on it, and I think I'm doing a good job."

"You are."

"But the problem is that it's all theoretical. I need to be down on a world, marching my 'Mech around, grounding myself in the reality of war. Without that I'll let myself make mistakes I can't afford to make." Victor looked up at Focht. "You've had enough experience in your life that you may not need any more fighting. You've got the tempering and seasoning I do not."

"And if getting that tempering and seasoning gets you killed?"

"Then I wasn't good enough to be leading in the first place." Victor opened his hands and pressed them to the table top. "I also need to fight to maintain the respect of the troops. Face it, my record isn't that good. My first command got wiped out on Trellwan. At Twycross we'd have been killed except for Kai saving the day. On Alyina I'd have died again, but Kai saved me once more. And, sure, on Teniente the Revenants rescued Hohiro, but his command's intervention pulled me out of a sticky situation. And, finally, on Coventry, we had a non-battle, which was just as well because even if we had won there, we'd have lost in terms of personnel killed and materiel destroyed."

"Kai, Hohiro, Phelan, and the others respect you, and the troops pick up on that," Focht said.

"But that can erode." Victor shrugged. "Maybe it's just me, but I feel like an impostor. I've got a lot of responsibility and yet I have a lot of doubts. I keep waiting for someone to call my bluff and prove I'm not worthy of the position I hold. Going into combat will let me prove my worth. Does that make sense?"

"Of course." The Precentor Martial smiled. "Do you think you're the first leader to have such doubts? All the good ones do. I suspect your father agonized over decisions he made and I know your grandmother did. They knew when to fight and when to lead."

Victor nodded slowly. "So you're telling me it's time for me to lead and not fight?"

"Not quite yet." The Precentor Martial gave Victor a

warm smile. "I just wanted to make sure you wanted to *fight* as opposed to *having fought*. If you were going to drop onto Schuyler just to walk your 'Mech to the Jaguar headquarters and proclaim victory, I wouldn't let you go."

"You think I'm capable of doing that?"

"Not until you're more politician than you are warrior." Focht folded his arms across his chest. "Go, see to it that your unit is ready to roll. I'll issue the orders moving our reserve around to deal with the Jaguar offensive. By the time we're done, the Jags will know we're serious and start sending more troops down here, leaving Huntress open. They'll learn that we've studied Scipio Africanus, too, and that they've got a lot more in common with the Carthaginians than they ever wanted to imagine."

*I am Smoke Jaguar. I am a hunter, not a beast to be hunted!* Elemental Star Captain Vulcan Bowen wanted to scream that declaration over his radio as he stalked through Fuun Township. In his time with the 19th Striker Cluster, he had seen a fair number of Inner Sphere worlds, but the Combine planet of Matamoros was the worst. *They must have to sentence people to live here, it is so colorless.* The garrison unit, the Second Night Stalkers, were famed for their night operations, and Bowen knew it must be because they couldn't bear the sight of the place during daylight hours.

The night was not being his friend. Fuun Township sat fifty kilometers to the east of Wazukana Fortress. The First Free Worlds Guards Regiment had taken up residence there, and the 19th Striker Cluster was having trouble dislodging them. Insurgent action staged by a citizen militia group from Fuun Township had harassed the Smoke Jaguars' siege efforts, so dealing with the problem had been put up for bid. Bowen had not won the initial bidding—instead Star Captain Jeremiah Furey had won by bidding himself down to less than a Point's worth of strength. Furey and his two companions had vanished into Fuun Township without even a distress call.

Bowen and the quartet of Elementals who had accompanied him to Fuun Township had found their compatriots dead, bound to crude X-crosses on the hill at the center of town. What had struck Bowen as odd, and had even unnerved him a bit, was that in their patrol of Fuun Township they had seen no sign of habitation until they reached the center of town. Even the bare dirt around the crosses showed no footprints. It was as if Furey and the other Elementals had been shucked of their armor and killed by phantoms.

Then, without warning, a hail of fire erupted from the surrounding buildings. Heavy machine gun fire and an Inferno rocket had taken Carson down. Bowen immediately ordered his people forward, spraying the building to the north side of the square with his machine gun. The others followed suit and raced toward the blocky brick structure. Once inside, the walls would shield them, then they could clear the building and move through the town mopping up resistance.

On the way to the building, Trevor hit a land mine. It exploded under his right foot with a thunderclap and pitched him high into the air. Trevor spun through a cartwheel and came down on his head and shoulders. Bowen knew that the other warrior was probably no more than dazed, but as Trevor got to his feet again, Bowen could see that he was disoriented. Trevor began to run toward the building to the *west* of the square.

The crossfire from the south and the second story of the western building ripped Trevor to pieces. Chunks of his armored suit flew through the air as the bullets spun him around. Black fluid oozed through the rents in the armor, attempting to seal the wounds, but it sprayed away as bullets punched through it and through the man inside it. Trevor flopped to the ground and twitched as bullets continued to pick at him.

Bowen forced his way into the northern building first, cutting a man in half with a burst of machine-gun fire from the weapon that underslung the armor on his left forearm. Turning to his right he then used the small laser in the right arm to turn another man into a torch. The two of them dropped behind the sandbag-shielded machine gun they had crewed. Grace and Adrienne crowded through the doorway after Bowen and immediately raced to the right and left to secure the rooms off the main chamber. Bowen heard noise from above, so he spun and raked a line of fire with his machine gun across the ceiling. He was rewarded with a scream.

He happened to turn to the right in time to see the floor in the other room collapse beneath Adrienne's feet. Bowen realized they'd been lured into a deathtrap as she dropped from sight. Something fell from above into the hole that had taken her—he couldn't identify it, but it had been metal, at least a meter and a half on a side, and seemed fairly heavy. He felt a tremor run through the foundation as the object hit, and he knew Adrienne hadn't slowed it down even a bit.

He snapped an order to Grace that sent the both of them out the back of the building. To get out Bowen leaped over the sandbag-fortified machine gun nest and planned to follow that with a hop through a window, but his left foot landed in the viscera of the man he'd shot, causing making him skid. As a result his leap came late and his right foot clipped the window sill. Involuntarily up-ended, Bowen somersaulted through the window and landed hard on his back.

Luckily for him, his unceremonious exit saved his life.

Grace landed as effortlessly as her name implied she might, and immediately scanned the alley for any signs of hostility. She started looking left, just beyond him, and came around to the right. About the same time she began to turn toward the junky hovercar plugging the alley to her right, the vehicle exploded.

An orange nimbus surrounded her, then brightened to yellow and on to white, reducing her to a black silhouette. It struck Bowen that she had some how metamorphosed into a Nova Cat, for her armor was black except for the white blaze eating into her left shoulder. It wasn't until her left arm came spinning out over his head that Bowen realized what was happening, and by then her silhouette had evaporated from the knees up.

The force of the explosion lifted him up and sent him tumbling after Grace's arm. His head slammed into a wall, then he felt himself rotating through the air. He slammed down again, hitting on one shoulder. His body whirled and he felt an ankle snap as his foot pulverized brick. He braced himself for the pain, but his power armor had already begun to pump drugs into his system, numbing the injury and boosting his stamina.

He rolled out into a street and scrambled to his feet as best he could. He heard the pinging of rifle bullets bouncing off his armor. An occasional laser bolt stabbed out at him, but those weapons were strictly anti-personnel and were of as much concern to him as rain. The locals had clearly used their best and heaviest weapons on the ambush—the people backing them up were reduced to using lighter weapons. Though they could not kill him outright, they could report his position and delay him enough for another ambush to be set up.

*If I don't move, I'll die.* He looked around for a way out, but couldn't see a clear path to freedom. The roadway was devoid of traffic north and south, but the vehicles parked along it could all have held the sort of bomb that killed Grace. He had to assume, in fact, that they did. *My best bet is to move through buildings and get away from this area.*

He limped his way across the street and into what had been a hole in the wall restaurant. As he moved through it, pitching over tables and lasing the stove into scrap, he tried to open a radio channel to the 19th Striker headquarters. A loud, undulating tone pierced waves of static regardless of which frequency he tried. *Jammed. No wonder we did not hear from Furey.*

Bowen burst from the building and into a narrow north-south alley. He turned to the south and saw a balding, sallow-fleshed old man move into the alley mouth and raise an ancient arquebus to his shoulder. The pure audacity of the skeletal old man surprised Bowen. He knew the muzzle-loader couldn't hurt him, so he tossed a quick salute even as the man was pulling the trigger. The hammer fell, spraying sparks into the pan, then the gun went off with a huge gout of white smoke.

The heavy ball hit Bowen square in the chest and actually knocked him back a couple of steps. A quick glance at the diagnostic display showed that his armor had not been breached, but the shot reminded Bowen that the armor was not proof against the forces of physics. *Accelerate any object of sufficient mass and it will go through this armor.*

The smoke cleared, allowing Bowen to see the old man running for his life toward a building out away from the alley. Bowen gave chase, snapping off a few quick shots at the fleeing insurgent. They missed, and in a flash of red kimono, the man scampered through a doorway. Bowen considered, just for a second, rewarding the man's courage by allowing him to live, but just as quickly dismissed the idea.

*Must be the painkillers. He tried to kill me. To let him live would encourage others. He must die.* Bowen sprayed two bursts of fire across the face of the building, then twisted slightly to the right and ducked his head so he could make it through the doorway with minimal loss of momentum. *A moving target is harder to hit.*

As he entered the doorway, Bowen saw his quarry directly ahead of him, hunkered down behind a breastwork of sandbags. The old man wore a broad, nearly toothless grin matched by the one on the face of the little girl sitting beside him. Their obvious pleasure at seeing him surprised Bowen, but that was because he didn't immediately recognize the device at which they sat as a weapon.

The leaf-spring of a ground vehicle had been mounted on a two-meter-long piece of ceiling joist. A twisted metal cable—a piece of high-tension wire—spanned the curve of the springs and had been drawn back into a V-shape and fastened in position by a simple latching device. Placed along the joist was a meter and a half long piece of iron rebar that had been sharpened at one end and notched at the other, so it fit the cable perfectly. The latch had a long lever connected to it and, as Bowen realized what he was looking at, the old man drove the lever down with his foot.

Though not intended to be part of a makeshift crossbow, the leaf-spring served admirably. It cast the rebar forward with great force, enabling the metal needle to pierce Bowen's Elemental suit over the right flank. He could feel the rebar rip through him and stab out the left side of his armor, but it was the wet, meaty tearing sound that told him how gravely he had been hurt.

He tried to fall back out into the street, but the projecting ends of the rebar caught on the door jamb and frustrated him. He stumbled forward and lased the crossbow, starting it to burn, but the people who had shot him were no longer behind it. He started to turn to find them, but his broken ankle gave way and sent him falling to the floor. He hit on his right side, driving the rebar yet further through him, then flopped onto his back.

He coughed once, hard, and tasted blood in his mouth. When he looked up, he saw blood splashed over his viewport. He felt his armor pumping more drugs into him and saw a little indicator light beginning to blink, signifying that his homing beacon had been activated. *But it will be jammed.*

He wanted to panic, to fight against the drugs and struggle his way out of Fuun Township, but he did not have the strength. He wanted to get up and kill all the people in the town, but he knew that would not save his life. It struck him that the people he had faced and slain in the invasion never would have dared attack him. *But we have given them years to overcome their fear of us. And now we pay the price.*

Bowen glanced up and saw the old man approaching him, with a sledge-hammer raised high. The Elemental ordered his right arm to come up and incinerate the ancient one, and he was pretty certain it had, but could not be absolutely sure as his viewport shattered into shadowed fragments that smothered his consciousness forever.

## 36

*Mitsuhama Ridge, Schuyler*
*Smoke Jaguar Occupation Zone*
*13 August 3059*

As the aerospace fighters completed the second and final strafing run, Victor throttled up his bird-legged *Daishi* Omni-Mech and started into the shadowy switchback defile leading to the top of Mitsuhama Ridge. Though not the swiftest of the Tenth Lyran Guard 'Mechs, the lumbering behemoth he had named Prometheus packed a hefty punch and could take a lot of damage. It was equipped with Clan technology and had been a gift to him a long time ago so he could meet Clan foes on even footing.

*At Alyina and Teniente it kept me safe while allowing me to kill Clanners.* Though he knew that being the first one up the defile would make him a target, Victor was curiously without fear. The Clan line had to be breached and the Fourth Jaguar Regulars had devoted a Trinary to defending this weak point on the ridge. To the east and west the Heavy Guards RCT and First Genyosha threatened the Fourth's flanks, pinning them in place, so it was up to the Tenth to break the Clan center and send them scurrying away.

The other unit on Schuyler, the Twelfth Jaguar Regulars, had broken at Olasin Fjord under relentless pressure from the Fourth Wolf Guards, First St. Ives Lancers, and the Com Guard 91st Division. Though the Clan units were both mere garrison Clusters, and therefore supplied with a mix of first- and second-line 'Mechs, the Twelfth had fought well and the Fourth had stiffened its resistance when they reached the ridge.

The *Daishi* came around the switchback and saw a humanoid 'Mech rise from cover to shoot at him. His computer tagged it a *Grendel,* a medium-sized 'Mech that packed some firepower but was hardly the sort of opponent that could stop the *Daishi. Unless he gets very lucky.*

The *Grendel* brought its left arm up and fired the medium lasers built on the back of the forearm. One of the ruby beams flashed wide to the left, but the other hit the *Daishi* over the left arm, frying armor. The *Grendel*'s right arm came around, with a large laser's green beam flashing out. It caught Victor's 'Mech over the left breast. Withered armor dropped in steaming puddles to the ground. The medium laser built into the crest of the *Grendel*'s head also stabbed toward the *Daishi.* Its fury evaporated armor on the Omni-Mech's right arm, giving it a molten scar that matched the one on the left arm.

Without conscious thought, Victor dropped his 'Mech's cross hairs on the *Grendel*'s outline, simultaneously bringing the trio of large pulse lasers in the right arm and the Gauss rifle mounted in the left to bear. The pulse lasers all hit, picking apart armor on the *Grendel*'s left arm, right leg, and right flank. Through the melted armor vapor shot the silvery slug from the Gauss rifle. It hit the *Grendel* in the right arm, shivering off all the armor on that limb and denting its ferro-titanium bones.

Somehow the Clan pilot kept his 'Mech standing despite the pounding it had taken. The *Grendel* again brought its weapons around to fire at the *Daishi.* Two of the medium lasers ablated armor from the left flank of Victor's Omni-Mech. The ruby beam from the *Grendel*'s head burned armor from his left arm, while the large laser's emerald beam carved armor from the *Daishi*'s right leg.

Renny Sanderlin's *Penetrator* came up behind Victor's *Daishi* and used the pulse lasers mounted in the 'Mech's torso to savage the *Grendel.* One of the beams missed, but the rest all scored on the medium 'Mech. The first ate away the *Grendel*'s right arm, destroying the large and small lasers built into it. Two others boiled armor off the 'Mech's flanks. The one that cored into the right flank finished the last of the armor on that side and liquefied the short-range missile launcher housed there. The last two melted armor over the *Grendel*'s heart and even drilled through to damage it internally. The black smoke pouring from the center and right side of its chest suggested hits to the engine.

Victor ignored the *Grendel* as it crashed to the ground and instead targeted the *Shadow Cat* that fired at him from further up the defile. Its armor already showed scarring from the strafing runs, making it even more vulnerable to the *Daishi* than it might have been otherwise. The *Shadow Cat* matched the *Grendel* in size and rough armor protection, though it was not as heavily armed. With the damage the *Daishi* had already taken, it was possible the smaller 'Mech could hurt him, but unlikely that it could put him out of the battle.

Victor tightened his fingers on the triggers of his cockpit joysticks. Even as the *Shadow Cat*'s arm-mounted large lasers hit the *Daishi*, Victor's laser assault withered the left arm away to a vapor cloud. The Gauss rifle shattered the armor on the right arm and crushed the shoulder joint. The other two pulse lasers scattered a hail of energy darts over the *Shadow Cat*'s left leg and right flank, burning away enough armor that the pilot could not accommodate the sudden shifting of the 'Mech's weight. The *Shadow Cat* whirled to the ground, jamming itself between the defile's wall and a large dolmen.

The *Shadow Cat*'s attack on the *Daishi* had been effective. Both large lasers played their green beams across the 'Mech's chest. One scored the armor over the big 'Mech's heart, while the other sliced through the rest of the armor on the left side of its chest. That latter beam even fried some internal support structures, threatening the SRM launcher, but did nothing to stop the *Daishi* from functioning fully.

A brilliant silver light filled the defile as Renny jumped his *Penetrator* ahead of Victor's *Daishi*. "Let me run interference for you, Victor. We're almost at the top."

Victor bit back a curse. *Renny's right, I'm hurt.* Renny Sanderlin had been Victor's roommate in his last year at the Nagelring, and a good friend from before that. The big man had always been ready to back Victor up or shield him from danger. "Roger, Renny, I've got your back."

At the crest of the ridge a huge OmniMech with scarred armor stepped forward to bar their passage. The heavily built, humanoid *Man o' War* stood only ten meters tall, but there in the pass, skylined as it was, it looked to Victor the way Goliath must have to David. The Smoke Jaguar 'Mech's handless arms came up, with the barrels of two particle projection cannons forming the right forearm and a quartet of laser muzzles blossoming at the wrist of the left arm. The OmniMech was a formidable foe, but Victor knew it would fall precisely because it *had* to fall.

The *Man o' War* fired first. The artificial lightning of the first PPC beam devoured armor on the right side of the *Penetrator*'s chest, and the second coruscating blue beam dissolved armor in the middle of its chest. The scarlet needles of the medium laser in the left arm nibbled away at the armor on the FedCom 'Mech's left leg, leaving armor damaged but no breaches opened in it.

Renny fired back, again hitting with five of the six pulse lasers mounted in his 'Mech's torso. Two boiled armor off the 'Mech's left arm. A hail of ruby needles from one peppered the armor on the Clan 'Mech's left leg. Another strobing beam blistered armor on the Omni's right arm, while the final one misted armor over the middle of the 'Mech's broad chest.

Victor swung his cross hairs over and centered the *Man o' War* on them. A shower of green energy darts splashed armor from the Clan 'Mech's left arm and torso, but the third large pulse laser and the Gauss rifle caused the most trouble when they hit the 'Mech's already wounded right arm. The Gauss rifle's projectile pulverized all but the last of the armor on that arm and the pulse laser evaporated what was left. The unspent energy bolts skewered the shoulder, freezing the arm in place, then exploded one of the two PPCs mounted in the forearm.

Despite the battering the *Man o' War* was taking, the Smoke Jaguar pilot kept his machine up and firing. The two medium lasers mounted in the left arm incinerated armor on the *Penetrator*'s right arm and left flank. The PPC's azure beam missed because the frozen shoulder joint limited its ability to track Renny's 'Mech. The large pulse laser drilled into the 'Mech's right flank, vaporizing the last of the armor and disintegrating one of the pulse lasers housed therein, even as it flashed back in defiance.

Renny's pulse lasers all hit. The trio firing low flensed armor from the OmniMech's legs, while another pair lit up the center of the 'Mech's chest. The last one did the most damage, though, as it burned away the rest of the *Man o' War*'s right arm, eliminating the last PPC, and sending the fire-blackened ruins of the limb crashing to the ground.

Victor's attack continued the Smoke Jaguar's demise. One pulse laser roasted the armor on the 'Mech's chest while a second vaporized the last of the armor on the left arm and began to cook the myomer fibers and ferro-titanium bones. The third pulse laser denuded the right leg of armor and snapped the leg's upper actuator, leaving the broken ends of the manmade muscle twitching. Through the gap opened by the loss of that muscle sped the Gauss rifle ball. It caught the *Man o' War*'s femur in the middle and blasted through it.

The titanic 'Mech came crashing down hard on its right side, then flopped over backward to lay staring up at the dusky sky.

Renny slowed his *Penetrator* a bit so he and Victor could crest the ridge at the same time. Victor came up on Renny's right, using the bulk of his OmniMech to shield the hole in the *Penetrator*'s right flank and likewise using Renny's 'Mech to cover his holed left flank armor. Twin giants with backward-bending legs and forward-thrusting bodies, they looked odd and deadly—machines built for only one lethal purpose.

A small *Hankyu* popped up on the left and opened fire on the *Penetrator*. Of the small humanoid 'Mech's six medium lasers, the ones mounted in the right and left arms dissolved armor from the *Penetrator*'s left arm and left leg. The chest-mounted pulse lasers stippled the armor on the 'Mech's right arm and left breast. The *Penetrator* shed smoking scales of armor, but none of the shots got through to damage the 'Mech's working parts.

The *Penetrator*'s return fire devastated the *Hankyu*. Two pulse lasers scoured armor off each breast, while another picked away at the armor over the 'Mech's right arm. The last two produced a flight of energy darts that burned through the armor on the 'Mech's right leg and bit into the muscles and synthetic bones beneath. The *Hankyu* still managed to remain upright—a tribute to the pilot's skill and misplaced sense of courage.

On Victor's right a *Peregrine* began to fire at him. The humanoid 'Mech had gently rounded armor, including the pods on each forearm that housed a medium pulse laser. They spat out coruscating ruby daggers that stabbed into the armor on the 'Mech's right flank and arm. The 'Mech's larger pulse laser added its verdant fire to the assault on the OmniMech's right arm, but all the attacks failed to do more than pare off armor.

The Prince flicked the *Daishi*'s right arm to the right almost casually and hit his trigger. The green beams skittered over the 'Mech, with two of them carving all but the last bit of armor from the *Peregrine*'s legs. That hardly mattered because the third beam slagged most of the armor over the *Peregrine*'s chest, then the silver ball from the Gauss rifle streaked in and blasted through the final thin veneer. It carried on and crumpled the 'Mech's internal support structure. The *Peregrine* folded in around the shot and flew back, crashing down through an awkward somersault that flicked broken armored sheets in every direction.

The *Penetrator* and the *Hankyu* repeated their exchange of fire. The smaller 'Mech again hit with every shot it took. Molten armor poured in rivulets off the *Penetrator*'s midchest and right arm, leaving it without protection. Two of the lasers boiled off the remaining sheets of armor on the 'Mech's left leg and began scorching the internal structures. Worse yet, the last two lasers bored into the *Penetrator*'s right chest, destroying the last two lasers there and reducing most of the internal structures to scrap.

Renny's shots ripped the *Hankyu* to pieces. While two of the pulse lasers impotently blew armor from the 'Mech's left arm and leg, the other three created a firestorm that consumed the 'Mech's right arm, leg, and all the armor over its right breast. The fury of the assault spun the small 'Mech around, smashed it into a small hummock, and left it lying in a small rain-eroded gully.

"Renny, are you all right?"

"Mech's in need of repair. Jammer's going to have my head, but techs were born to suffer. I'm fine, though."

"I've got the same to report." Victor sighed and realized the sweat pouring off him came from more than the heat that had built up in his cockpit. "Keep your eyes open."

"No need, I think, Victor."

"What do you mean?"

The *Penetrator* pointed an arm toward the horizon. "Those look like DropShips to me, and 'Mechs running toward them is what has raised that cloud of dust."

Victor punched an order to increase the magnification on

his holographic display into his computer. What Renny had reported was accurate, but Victor still couldn't believe it. "But these are Smoke Jaguars—Clanners. They don't run."

A hint of amusement played through his friend's voice. "They didn't run, Victor, not till today."

Victor shook his head and looked at the two smoking 'Mechs lying on either side of them. "Then these were just an Omega Star, left here to delay us enough for the others to get away?"

"That would appear to be the case." The *Penetrator*'s arm came up in a salute as other members of the Guards reached the top of the ridge and began to spread out in a perimeter. "You should be smiling, Victor, smiling real wide. We broke them. We won."

Victor looked from Precentor Martial Anastasius Focht to Phelan Kell and back again as the last of the reports relayed through ComStar scrolled up through the air in the middle of the briefing room. Many hours had passed since the battle on Mitsuhama Ridge, and they had taken over the Fourth Jaguar Regulars HQ in Tsurara City as their own. He felt cold and giddy—either of which, he knew could be the aftereffects of the day's combat and victory—but he blamed his feelings entirely on information he'd just read. "Precentor Martial, how much trust do you put into these reports?"

Focht turned away from the table for a moment, then rubbed a hand over his mouth. "The agents reporting in have always been reliable in the past. Over half the reports are coming from ComStar units that participated in attacks, so I assume their data is as good as ours. Just like here on Schuyler, it appears the Smoke Jaguars on Schwartz, Rockland, Coudoux, and Garstedt put up only token resistance, then fled. The reports about the Smoke Jaguars leaving Idlewind and Richmond seem accurate, and the fact that they destroyed their headquarters buildings and the major industries on those worlds suggest that they mean to deny them to us. I also take that as a sign that they're not returning."

Victor nodded slowly. "That's what it seems like to me. Phelan, what do you make of it."

For the first time ever, Victor saw his cousin appear to be flummoxed. "This is utterly and completely without precedent in my experience. When you forced Marthe Pryde to withdraw her troops from Coventry, it was through an offer of *hegira*. That only applies to enemies that you have engaged and defeated. Letting the DropShips leave the system unmolested was de facto *hegira*. Withdrawal before a challenge or attack is, ah, is something I've never heard of."

"Any idea why they would do it?"

Phelan shrugged, clearly uncomfortable with the question. "I have to imagine that the Smoke Jaguars see a greater threat somewhere else. It could be that they have started fighting with the Nova Cats back on the homeworlds, or that another Clan is threatening them with Absorption. That could make the Jags pull their troops back to Huntress to regroup, retool, and come out fighting. And let there be no doubt about it: we may have hurt them and cost them some good units, but we've not destroyed everything they have or could have."

Victor knew Phelan was right. "What you're saying is that our taskforce could arrive at Huntress and instead of finding a thinly defended world because the Jags are here attacking us, Morgan could run into everything the Jags have left."

"That is about the size of it." Phelan frowned. "We also have to consider the possibility that the retreat is faked."

The Precentor Martial nodded in Phelan's direction. "That's a good point. They could be pulling back to concentrate their strength on a limited number of worlds and hope to engage us there. That would let them choose their battlegrounds—and choose them to their own advantage."

"But is that likely?" Victor got up from his chair and began to pace at the narrow end of the briefing room. "For them to use that tactic would mean they anticipated our assault and had willingly sacrificed dozens of units to lull us into a false sense of superiority. Since we were conducting warfare their way, issuing batchalls and announcing what we were bringing in, they could have retreated in the face of our assaults and accomplished the same thing without the loss of equipment or personnel. Moreover, if they were that organized I think they'd have done on more worlds what they did on Richmond and Idlewind—they'd have destroyed the industry that can give us vital supplies for continuing our campaign.

"After all, in salvage alone we've been able to add three regiments of Clan 'Mechs—not counting the Jaguar Cluster you've made into your Third Wolf Legion, Phelan."

Phelan nodded in agreement. "I had to offer the possibility, no matter how slender I think the chances are of its being true."

"Which leaves us contemplating the unthinkable—the premature collapse of the Smoke Jaguars." Victor shook his head. "We've done in four months what we thought would take four years, and we've done it with a fraction of the projected casualties. This is, of course, wonderful, except it saddles us with another problem."

The Precentor Martial looked over at him. "And that is?"

"Staging an expedition to Huntress."

Focht arched an eyebrow. "One is already on the way."

"I know." Victor knitted his fingers together, then pointed with both hands toward the Precentor Martial. "If this *is* a total retreat, then all of these Jaguar troops are heading to Huntress. They'll surely get there before Morgan, which means he and his people will be slaughtered. We can't broadcast a warning to them because we won't know whether or not they get it, and the Jags might intercept it, which would just compound the difficulties."

Victor freed his hands from one another and knotted them into fists. "We can say we're extending our operations into the Periphery to continue the action against the Jaguars. The Combine can control the distribution of information, and that will be vital because we can't afford for public information to flow into Clan channels and make it back to the Clan homeworlds before we reach Huntress."

The Precentor Martial frowned. "You realize you're proposing to absent yourself and this force from the Inner Sphere for a minimum of a year and a half?"

Victor nodded. "Do I have a choice?"

"I think you do." The Precentor Martial opened his hands. "You have a responsibility to your people. With you gone, there's no predicting what your sister will do in your absence. Going to Huntress was never part of our plan for dealing with the Clans and to do so now will seriously upset the balance of power in the Inner Sphere."

"But if we don't go, Morgan and the other others will die."

"You don't know that, Victor."

"But I have to assume it, Precentor."

Focht shook his head adamantly. "Morgan Hasek-Davion is a smart man. If he comes in and sees the odds are against him, he will do the prudent thing."

"I'd like to think that, but Morgan's also just as capable of whipping his people into a frenzy that will make them believe they can accomplish the impossible. If he were to attack anyway and die in the attempt, I'd . . ." Victor's hands snapped open and closed. "I don't want him to die out there, not if I can prevent it."

The Precentor Martial's voice dropped to a cold whisper. "There are some things you can do nothing to prevent, Victor. You're heading down a dangerous path, making decisions you may have cause to regret. Do not make them lightly."

"I'm not."

"I think you are. I hear in your words echoes of choices I made myself, a long time ago." Focht glanced at the room's closed door, then raised his chin. "The Steiner line seems to breed two types of individual. One is a warrior without equal. You represent that aspect of the family. The other is a political operator, and that is your sister Katherine. In some the traits mix, and both were strong in your grandmother, but rare is that individual. What I am trying to tell you, Victor, is that you are making a military decision while minimizing the political consequences of it."

"That's all well and good, Precentor. Your insight into my family is fascinating, but it isn't germane to this discussion."

"But it is, Victor. You know the famous Santayana quote?"

"Those who cannot remember the past are condemned to fulfill it."

"Exactly." Focht nodded solemnly. "I *am* that past, Victor. I cannot, the Inner Sphere cannot, afford to let you repeat the folly I committed three decades ago."

"I don't understand."

"No, I suppose you don't." Focht smiled carefully, then extended his hand toward Victor. "I am pleased to make your acquaintance, Prince Victor Steiner-Davion. I am your cousin, two generations removed. I am Frederick Steiner."

Victor's mouth shot open as he fell back and leaned heavily against the wall. "That's—that's impossible. You died in the Draconis Combine on Dromini VI. You were a hero, even though you were sent with the Tenth Lyran Guards on a suicide mission because of your plotting treason with Aldo Lestrade. You had left the Commonwealth open to attack from the Combine. You can't be Frederick."

"I assure you that I am, Victor, and a DNA test would

prove that very quickly. The blood that links us is purely matrilineal, from our great-great grandmother down to you, so our mitochondrial DNA would be identical. You can draw the blood yourself and oversee the tests if you want to prove it."

Victor shook his head, already too well acquainted with the accuracy of DNA evidence. *It was DNA comparisons that told us that Thomas Marik is an impostor.* He looked over at Phelan. "You don't seem surprised by this admission."

The Wolf shook his head. "One of the missions I performed for the ilKhan was to crack the secret of the Precentor Martial's identity. I wish it had been as easy as drawing blood."

"Who else knows?"

Focht shrugged his shoulders. "Theodore Kurita, Primus Mori of ComStar, and perhaps a few others. I no longer consider who I once was to be a part of me anymore. I chose my new name because it translates roughly into 'warrior reborn,' and that is precisely how I see myself. I have used my gifts to make the Inner Sphere safe. Dabbling in politics is what brought me to where I am now—out of power, cut off from my family and my traditions. I learned to adapt to this life, Victor, but I do not think you could."

Victor remembered thinking that he could have abandoned everything in exchange for a life of freedom with Omi, so he shook his head. "You're wrong, just like I think you're wrong about the traits we Steiners inherit."

"Oh?"

Phelan smiled and sat back in his chair. "This should be good."

Victor pushed himself away from the wall and came back to standing straight and as tall as he could. "You were no more disposed to being a good warrior at birth than my sister was to being a murderous bitch. Those aren't inherited traits, they're learned behaviors. Now, learning, there's something we inherit. Your skill as a warrior, your ability to adapt to your new life in ComStar, your ability to figure out how to defeat the Clans; that's all learning, and learning is the one thing I do well.

"One thing I've learned well is this: I cannot betray the trust of those who depend on me. And Morgan and his people will be depending on me. Katherine will have plenty to do with Thomas Marik and Sun-Tzu Liao around, so her antics be damned. We've accomplished our half of the anti-Clan operation and now we have a chance to help our friends finish their half. That's what we're going to do."

Focht nodded. "Spoken like a warrior."

Victor smiled slowly. "Katherine, I think, will be inclined to cause trouble if left idle. On the slim chance that Thomas and Sun-Tzu don't keep her occupied, I have set some other little things in motion that ought to give her plenty to think about. I might be out of her sight, but I certainly won't be out of mind."

The Precentor Martial hazarded a smile. "Spoken like a Davion."

"It has to be because the Steiner half of me needs to learn all it can in the next nine months about training a coalition force to pound a Clan into submission." Victor's eyes narrowed. "We have to organize training, supplies, repairs, shipping schedules, security, media relations . . ."

Phelan laughed lightly. "I'll let you take care of those things yourself, Victor. Just let me know when we're leaving."

Victor glanced down at his boots, then back up into Phelan's green eyes. "You and your people can't go, Phelan."

"What?" Phelan uncoiled himself from the chair. "I said before that we would not lead you back to Huntress or Strana Mechty, but I never said we wouldn't accompany you there."

"I know, and I wish I could let you come with us. I can't. We can't." Victor frowned heavily. "The focus of this operation has been to show the Clans that the Inner Sphere will kick them out. Your participation in that effort has been vital because you're part of the Inner Sphere now. The Nova Cats who have come over to the SLDF are also part of the Inner Sphere, but I won't be taking any of them either. Nor will we take Smoke Jaguar bondsmen. What we do in Clan space has to be done by Inner Sphere troops. We may fight with their equipment, but we'll fight without their breeding. It's the only way we can prove that their superiority is an illusion, and that a future plotted together is going to be better than one fashioned by conflict."

Victor softened his voice. "There's another reason, a more important reason, I need you to remain behind. Despite what I've just said to the Precentor Martial, I know Katherine won't be able to resist the temptation to cause trouble while we're gone. With you here, using the troops we leave behind to mop up the last of the Smoke Jaguars, a force will be in place to prevent her from becoming too adventurous. I need to know there's someone Yvonne can turn to if things get out of hand. I can't think of anyone I can count on to protect her more than you."

"Damn you, Victor Davion." Phelan slammed his fist against his open palm. "I was prepared to argue past any of your reasons to prevent me from going, then you ask me to take care of Yvonne. Dammit. You know, I think, she was my favorite among your brood."

"Yeah, well, I always liked your sister Caitlin better, too." Victor met Phelan's stern stare, then the both of them began to laugh. "You're the anchor here, Phelan. Keep the peace until we return."

"Just make sure you return quickly, Victor." Phelan waggled a finger at the Prince and the Precentor Martial. "If the two of you decide to head off like Kerensky and never come back, you won't get away with it. I'll hunt you down and drag you back to this asylum so you can deal with the inmates you're leaving behind."

# Epilogue

*Royal Palace, The Triad*
*Tharkad City, Tharkad*
*District of Donegal, Draconis Combine*
*1 September 3059*

**K**atrina Steiner was limitlessly impressed by her own restraint, which is much akin to erecting a billboard to praise one's own humility. She could have very easily let slip the leash on her emotions and have trashed her office. She was also very tempted to order an air strike to destroy the chateau Victor had used during the Whitting Conference. *It would serve him right.*

Two pieces of news had reached her that filled her with a torrent of conflicting emotions. The first was a hint of Victor's injuries at Luthien. It infuriated her that her brother had not had the decency to die. His death would have eliminated whole levels of complication in the Inner Sphere. She also found it frustrating in the extreme that the report was nothing more than hearsay, and that no solid evidence of his wounding could be obtained. And the most recent report from the fighting in the Combine indicated that Victor had acquitted himself valiantly on the battlefield, but had suffered a slight injury that would leave him some scars—*neatly explaining away the scars resulting from having a katana shoved through his chest!*

She sat down at her desk and leaned back against the

white leather chair. *Clearly, if I want him dead, I'll have to order the job done myself.*

Her experience in that realm formed the foundation for worry over the second item that had been brought to her attention. Frances Jeschke had vanished without a trace. There was no son named Tommy, no husband lost on Coventry, no record of her adoption or of Galen Cox's father having sired a child out of wedlock. The woman who had so convincingly come asking for help last November had dropped from sight, and all computer records previously confirming her existence had been destroyed.

The only fact that remained from the whole curious incident was the match between the DNA of Galen Cox and Jerrard Cranston. And it was identical. The chances of another such match was one in four billion. If that weren't enough, superimposition of pictures of one man over another showed multiple points of correspondence. Voiceprints even matched.

The implications of all that were inescapable for Katrina and made her hearken back to her confrontation with Victor at their mother's grave. *He has learned a great deal. He sent the woman to me, then made her vanish to let me know he knows of my role in our mother's death. He may even have proof of it, but he didn't use it sooner because it would have shattered the Star League before we could revive it. He sent Jeschke to me for precisely the same reason I would have sent her to him were our roles reversed. He wants to torture me and make me fear his return.*

She allowed herself a sharp laugh. "Your problem, Victor, is that you have given me something to worry about and time to deal with it."

Ryan Steiner was dead, eliminating one third of the group of people who might know of her role in Melissa's death. The second was a man named David Hanau. She dimly recalled the portly man. He had been her agent in Ryan's camp and had served her faithfully. Now he resided on Poulsbo with his wife, on an estate, enjoying a lifestyle paid for by the Archon. She did not feel endangered because of him, but he was a loose end. *I can make the loss up to his widow.*

The only other person who could possibly know anything had been Ryan's personal secretary at the time of his death. Sven Newmark, a refugee from Rasalhague, had been present in the room at the time of Ryan's death. Various and sundry crackpot conspiracy theorists had decided, based on a tissue of coincidences spawned by ignorance, error, and wishful thinking, that Sven had actually murdered Ryan. Newmark, who had been cleared by authorities of any involvement, had endured infamy for a couple of months, then had disappeared.

*I cannot afford to take the chance that he might reappear. I must find him and make sure he can tell no tales.* Katrina smiled to herself. *Fortunately I have the resources of an entire government at my disposal to accomplish this end. Once he is gone, so is the axe Victor holds poised over my neck. Once that artificial restraint is lifted, only I will be able to restrain myself.*

She pressed her hands together. "And then, dear brother, when you come home, we will settle our differences once and for all."

### *Helspring Resort, Crescent Harbor*
### *New Exford*
### *Arc-Royal Defense Cordon*

The large dark sunglasses Francesca Jenkins wore allowed her to study Sven Newmark as she walked along, while making it appear as if she were reading the document in her hand-held E-reader. Long and lean, Newmark had stretched himself out on a towel-draped lounge chair beside the pool. He had dyed both his hair and his eyebrows a deep black, but his pale body hair kept its true color. She would have considered it an error that he had not dyed all of his hair, as she had, to disguise himself, but Newmark had established an identity as Reginald Starling, disaffected artist. As such, the contrasting hair color, as well as the two earrings in his right ear, marked him as a social rebel.

Francesca admired his audacity in choosing an identity that put him into something of the public spotlight, but that provided him just one more layer of armor between him and discovery. Most people looking to hide become virtual hermits, digging a hole and pulling it in after themselves. By becoming something of a public person—one with a reputation for being volatile, for being pathologically incapable of telling the truth, and for constantly reinventing himself—he became a caricature. Even if he had stood up and claimed to be Sven Newmark, no one would have taken him seriously.

Francesca would have rejected Starling as Newmark's new identity except for the very fact of his art. In researching Newmark she had caught a piece of an article from a gossip-diskzine on Solaris. Newmark's name was buried amid a list of people who had donated original works of art for a charity auction. After a week-long hunt she was able to find a copy of the catalog for the auction that included a digitized picture of Newmark's painting. Having nothing else to go on in her search for him, she had used a computer to analyze every aspect of the painting, and then started searching through news and art databases for any work that seemed similar.

She had plenty of hits in the area of color selection, subject, medium, and even name—a forger did a series of Newmark pieces showing Ryan Steiner's head exploding from an assassin's bullet—but only one was a good hit. The "S" he had used in signing his name on the charity piece and the "S" in Starling matched. This made her zero in on Reginald Starling—"Star" to his fawning admirers, "Reggie" to the critics who hated his work.

Those critics were few and far between. His art had a dark element that seemed to appeal to people who found living so close to the border with the Clans oppressive. His popularity had skyrocketed with the Jade Falcon advance to Coventry, and several of his pieces had been sold for tidy sums. Reginald Starling had become the toast of New Exford, which spoke more to its lacking anything above the most basic level of culture than it did his personal appeal or talent. He certainly was a good painter, but Starling could be abrasive and rude, so inviting him to a social gathering was an adventure in and of itself.

Everything she learned about Starling had some dim parallel to something having to do with Newmark, so she and Curaitis traveled to New Exford and closed in.

Francesca allowed her right foot to slip in a puddle of water at the foot of his chair. She fell backward, letting her thick, terry-cloth robe fall open as she went down. The E-reader slipped from her right hand and dashed itself to pieces right beside Newmark, tiny plastic fragments bouncing up to hit him along the flank. "Ouch!"

Newmark sat up, his attention initially riveted on her bare

breasts, then he blinked and swung his legs over the edge of the chair. "Are you hurt?"

"No, not really, but be careful. There's sharp plastic there under your feet."

"Right. Thanks." Newmark shifted around so he knelt on the chair and started to gather up the pieces of the shattered disk reader. He picked up the ejected disk and looked at it. "Breyers *Refugee's Folly*."

"Right. A little light reading." Francesca came up onto her knees and pulled the robe partially closed. "I'm very sorry about this. It's been a bad year."

Newmark brandished the disk. "It must have been horrible if you find *Folly* to be light reading."

She sat back on her haunches and gently adjusted the waistband of her bathing suit, brushing her fingers over a puckered scar on her left hip. "People in the Placement Agency said Breyer's book talked about the emotional problems displaced people have with trust and readjustments. I used to live on Zurich, but got caught in the fighting there and barely survived." She pointed to the scar beneath her breastbone and the one on her hip.

"After I got out of the hospital, I returned to my parents' home on Coventry. The Clans hit there, so I moved again." She gave him a warm smile. "I let my computer pick my new home at random, so I'm here."

Newmark handed her the disk. "How long?"

"Six months. I kept telling myself that if I could just get through the first six months I'd treat myself to a weekend at this spa. You know, time off for good behavior."

Newmark lay back in his chair and laughed. "Yes! Someone else who feels as if living here is a sentence!"

Francesca sighed. "Yes, well, now I've lost my E-reader, so it looks like the psych ward for me. Books have been the only thing keeping me sane."

He frowned. "You must have friends. From work, at least."

She shook her head, letting her white-blond hair lash her shoulders. "No, I'm a freelance researcher. I do bibliographical research. If an author or scientist wants to start a research project, I hunt down all the relevant material, then rank, cross-reference, and annotate a bibliography for her. It's interesting work, and pays pretty well. This is especially true since I've learned how to work old Star League-era search engines to check for new data from the Star League memory cores the Gray Death Legion keeps tripping over. Still it's very solitary work."

"If it pays well, you can buy another reader."

Francesca winced. "It's not like a real job. I get a small advance to begin my work, but I get the pay-off when I deliver. I'm in the middle of three projects right now and not close to finishing any of them. No product, no money."

Newmark nodded. "I understand. It's the same way with me."

"Oh, what do you do?"

"I'm a painter."

"Really?" Francesca gave him a friendly smile. "Maybe I could hire you to repaint my apartment. Cream, eggshell, and goldenrod just aren't my colors."

"I apologize for not making myself clear. I'm an artist." Newmark sat up again and extended his hand to her. "I'm Reginald Starling."

"Oh. I'm Fiona Jensen." She shook his hand, then ducked her head down. "Should I have heard of you?"

That question seemed to take Newmark back for a moment, then he smiled and shook his head. "Perhaps not."

Francesca injected enthusiasm into her voice. "Are your pictures on display somewhere? Could I go see them?" She frowned for a second. "I mean, I assume there are galleries here in Crescent Harbor. I like art, I really do, but I haven't . . ."

Newmark reached out and silenced her protests by touching an index finger to her lips. "You've been working too hard, so you've said." He watched her closely, his blue eyes holding her gaze steadily. "I tell you what, Fiona, I'm going to take you to one of the galleries. I have an opening tonight, and I wasn't going to show up—piqued patrons always buy so they can possess a piece of the artist who snubbed them. It's terribly feudal, with the unworthy and untalented thinking they can actually own the product of genius. We'll go and have fun."

Francesca hesitated. "A gallery opening? I'd like to go, but I don't know if I have anything to wear."

Newmark smiled carefully. "You'll be with me, sweet thing. Whatever you choose to wear will be suitable and you'll be praised for it." He slipped a hand past her left ear and swept her hair up and over to bare it. "Yes, perhaps a new 'do and some color just to make you outrageous, and you'll do wonderfully."

Francesca gently slipped her hair free of his grasp. "Am I going as your latest work, or a friend?"

Newmark pursed his lips and narrowed his eyes, then nodded. "Touché, Miss Jensen. Like you, I don't think I have a single friend on this rock. Perhaps it's time to make a change."

"A change for the better, I think." Francesca smiled up at him. "I can be a very good friend, but to be a good friend I need three things: trust, support, and honesty. With my friends there are no secrets from each other, only those we share between us. If you can't handle that . . ."

Newmark laughed lightly, and Francesca caught a hint of relief in the sound. "I have secrets you won't want to know."

"Let me be the judge of that, my friend." She touched the scar between her breasts. "Once you've survived what I have, there's not much that can surprise you."

"You keep thinking that, Fiona." Newmark gave her a broad grin. "If we become good friends, we'll test that hypothesis, sorely test it. Your new life in Crescent Harbor begins today, Fiona Jensen, and I promise you it won't be anything like whatever you have known before."

# About the Author

Michael A. Stackpole, who has written over twenty-two novels and numerous short stories and articles, is one of Roc Books' bestselling authors. Among his BattleTech® books are the *Blood of Kerensky* Trilogy and the *Warrior* Trilogy. Due to popular demand, the *Blood of Kerensky* has recently been republished, as will the *Warrior* Trilogy. Other Stackpole novels, *Natural Selection, Assumption of Risk, Bred for War,* and *Malicious Intent,* also set in the BattleTech® universe, continue his chronicles of the turmoil in the Inner Sphere.

Michael A. Stackpole is also the author of *Dementia,* the third volume in Roc's Mutant Chronicles series. In 1994, Bantam Books published *Once a Hero,* an epic fantasy. *The Bacta War,* the last of Stackpole's four Star Wars® X-wing® novels, was recently published.

In addition to writing, Stackpole is an innovative game designer. A number of his designs have won awards, and in 1994 he was inducted into the Academy of Gaming Arts and Design's Hall of Fame.

# Other books by Michael A. Stackpole
(* denotes available from ROC)

**BattleTech**
*Warrior Trilogy*
Warrior: En Garde
Warrior: Riposte
Warrior: Coupé

*Blood of Kerensky Trilogy*
Lethal Heritage*
Blood Legacy*
Lost Destiny*

Natural Selection*
Assumption of Risk*
Bred For War*
Malicious Intent*

*The Fiddleback Trilogy*
A Gathering Evil
Evil Ascending
Evil Triumphant

Once a Hero
Mutant Chronicles: Dementia*
Talion: Revenant
A Hero Born

**Star Wars® X-wing®**
Rogue Squadron
Wedge's Gamble
The Krytos Trap
The Bacta War

**The Twilight of the Clans series
continues with**

**THE HUNTERS**

**by Thomas S. Gressman
coming in December from Roc Books**

*Jerseyville, Defiance
Point Barrow Combat Region, Crucis March
Federated Commonwealth
27 January, 3059
1415 hours*

"Incredible." The single word, breathed out as though it were a curse, carried with it more meaning than a thousand profanities. "How can anybody live here?"

"I know what you mean," the portmaster said. "I've been stationed on seventeen worlds since I got hired by the Ministry of Commerce, and this is by far the ugliest, hottest, smallest, all-around nastiest post I've ever had."

Kasugai Hatsumi chuckled politely at the man's bitter humor as he accepted his travel documents back from the clerk.

"And what did you do to get yourself assigned to this garden spot?"

"Do? I didn't *do* anything. That was the whole problem. I *was* on New Syrtis. I was planning on being there until I retired. Then, two years ago, this little skinny guy comes up to me and offers me half-a-million C-Bills to let a couple of crates go through customs uninspected. At first, I turned him down. Then I got to thinking about it, y'know? I mean half a mil. I'd been pullin' freight for House Davion for twenty-three years, and what did I have to show for it? Retirement, a half-salary pension and two grand in the bank, so I figured, what the heck? I let the crates slip through."

Like the Ancient Mariner, the customs inspector seemed compelled to recount the tale of his transgression to any stranger who would listen.

"Anyhow, I got the cash, and thought that was the end of it. I found out later that the crates were full of guns and bombs for Liao terrorists. When they blew up that 'Mech plant, back in '49, there was an investigation, and the Fox Fives traced the explosives back to my part of the yard. Somebody had to take the blame, and I got picked. Suspension, probation, reduction in grade, the whole nine yards. Then, when I tried to bid up again, the big bosses shuffled me off here. And here I'll stay for the next four months, twelve days, two hours, and fifteen minutes. After that, Prince Victor can kiss my feet."

Hatsumi laughed again to cover the chill that ran down his spine. "Fox Fives" was a common slang term for the agents of M15, the counter-insurgency branch of the Federated Commonwealth's Department of Military Intelligence. So far the Davion agents had yet to develop a security net so tightly woven that Hatsumi or one of his comrades could not slip through. Still, no covert operative, no matter how well trained and proficient, could penetrate every safeguard, every time.

Picking up his carryall, Hatsumi headed for the terminal's main door. He hadn't gone three steps when the portmaster called out to him.

"Son? 'Less you like breathin' sulfur oxides, you'd better put on a respirator."

Hatsumi grinned sheepishly as he pulled a pyramidal device constructed mostly of rubber and metal from a pocket of his faded AFFC field jacket.

"I wasn't thinking. Thank you."

The portmaster waved once and turned back to the newsfax he'd been reading when Hatsumi entered the terminal.

Standing just inside the building's airlock-type double doors was a slightly built woman, wearing the stained jumpsuit and canvas jacket of a common laborer. Her plain appearance was relieved only by the slightly oriental cast to her features. A commercial-grade respirator mask hung by its neck strap below her chin. Her eyes flickered in recognition as Hatsumi approached.

"Ready?"

She jerked her head toward the doors. "What about your luggage?"

"This is it. The rest of our materials will be arriving in a few days."

Rumiko Fox shrugged, pulled her respirator over her nose and mouth, and stepped into the lock. Hatsumi followed her example.

It took only a few seconds for the outer doors to cycle open. Defiance suffered from a slight taint in her atmosphere, as the portmaster had warned Hatsumi, but the pressure was well within the so-called "normal" levels of human tolerance. Hatsumi was grateful for that. He was fully qualified in the use of pressure suits and other hostile environment equipment, but he loathed the restrictiveness of the suits.

A five-year old Gienah sedan sat next to the curb a few dozen meters from the door. Fox walked straight to the vehicle and climbed into the driver's seat without saying another word. Hatsumi followed silently. After tossing his carryall into the back seat, he settled down next to the silent woman.

Fox pressed the vehicle's starter, eliciting not the quiet roar of a well-tuned internal combustion engine, but a high-pitched, mechanical whine.

"It's the pollution," she said to the windshield, her voice muted by the mask. "The gunk in the air makes fuel-burners run rough. Most of the cars here are electric, even the heavy haulers."

Without another word, Fox put the vehicle in gear and pulled away from the curb.

The drive into Jerseyville took forty minutes. During that time, Fox never spoke again, leaving Hatsumi to stare at Defiance's scenery. As scenery went, it wasn't inspiring. The long stretch of macadam-paved highway ran, laser-straight, through rocky flatlands. Here and there, hardy bushes sprouted in clumps, giving refuge to whatever reptilian and avian life could tolerate the mephitic atmosphere.

From the data chips he'd reviewed while in transit, Hatsumi knew that the planet's main spaceport was located on the site of the original settler's first landing. The flatlands wedged in between on the Pearce Sea to the east and the Devil's Backbone mountain range on the west, would be some of the richest farming lands in the Inner Sphere, if not for the taint in the atmosphere. Though the sulfur content was not high enough to prevent plant life from growing, even flourishing, in the black, volcanic soil, it was sufficient to be absorbed into the crops, giving any foodstuff grown there an unpleasant, bitter taste. It was ironic that the volcanoes that provided the richness of the soil made it unusable.

That was not to say that Defiance was without economic value. The planet was rich in mineral wealth. The almost constant eruptions which had marked Defiance's early life had brought many rare earth elements up out of the young planet's core. Transuranic elements were especially common in the now (mostly) extinct volcanoes of the Devil's Backbone.

Jerseyville itself was only marginally more interesting to look at. A large cluster of small houses, shops, and office buildings, huddled in the foothills of the Backbone range, was the site of the first settlement, named for its founder, Malcolm Jersey. The settlers, most of them prospectors, came to Defiance during the early days of the Star League. They came seeking mineral wealth. Many of them found it. Over the years, the hundreds of small, independent mines were acquired by large corporations, until, eventually, the greatest portion of the planet was owned outright by Solar Metals Limited, who sold it to the Davion family in 2748.

Fox brought the car to a halt in front of a small single-family house in Jerseyville's northern suburbs. Hatsumi climbed out of the vehicle, retrieved his bag, and strode up the walk. At the door, he had to pause to allow Fox to tap in the proper access code.

As silently as ever, the woman punched a seemingly random series of buttons on the ten-digit keypad. The door rewarded her with a series of heavy thuds before swinging open.

It took a full minute for the residential model airlock to run through its cycle. It was the same story everywhere; bigger and faster meant more expensive. The designers of the house intended for it to be built cheaply. Thus, when the inner door began to swing open and Hatsumi removed his respirator mask, he could still smell the rotten-eggs odor of sulfur oxide.

"Kasugai!" The cry of greeting was laced with joy. Hatsumi looked up to see a small, powerfully built young man leaping out of an armchair. He, like Fox, was dressed in the clothing of a common laborer.

"Honda Tan. It is good to see you again."

"Stormcrow told me that I would be working with an old friend, but I had no idea he meant you." Tan threw his arms around Hatsumi in a crushing bear hug.

The man Tan called Stormcrow was the Jonin, the clan leader of the Amber Crags nekekami. Hatsumi knew as much of Stormcrow's reputation as any other of his clan. During the days prior to the Fourth Succession War, as a field operative, Stormcrow had slipped into the HQ of the Fourth Skye Rangers, rifled that regiment's secure rooms, and escaped undetected, leaving behind only confusion and a small origami cat. Later, as a chunin, a cell-leader, he had ordered the assassination of a nosy reporter who had written an exposé revealing the long-hidden secrets of the nekekami.

The nekekami, Hatsumi mused over the word, and what it had come to mean throughout the Inner Sphere. The word, roughly translated, meant "spirit cat." They were the indirect descendants of the ninja—the secret society of spies and assassins of feudal Japan. Like their predecessors, the nekekami had raised intelligence gathering, sabotage, and assassination to an art-form. All their lives, the nekekami trained, studied, and practiced their skills. A warrior would work all his life, honing himself into the perfect weapon, a weapon that might be expended in a single mission.

The legends about the Spirit Cats were many. It was said that they could walk through walls, breathe underwater, sink into the ground, and become invisible at will. Some of the more outrageous tales said the nekekami were apprenticed to Death himself, or to powerful necromancers who could kill with a glance.

When at last he released his grip, Tan nodded at Fox. "I see you've met our talkative Rumiko."

The woman glared at Tan, but never spoke a word.

Tan, unimpressed, flashed a toothy smile in return.

Hatsumi felt a certain relief at seeing Honda Tan again. He and Hatsumi had been together on a number of operations, including a few covert operations against the hated Smoke Jaguar Clan.

"You might as well get to know the whole team all at

once." Tan took his friend by the arm and ushered him into the house's tiny kitchen. There, seated at the table, was a handsome young man who was bent over a bundle of wires and circuit boards, a soldering iron in his left hand. A small, plasticized paper-wrapped bundle rested in his lap. Just enough of the parcel was visible for Hatsumi to read the lettering: "Block, Explosive, M26A1."

"Is it safe for him to have that stuff around a soldering iron?" Hatsumi had received only limited instructions in the handling of explosives in the course of his training, and treated anything with that much destructive capability with awe and respect.

"I don't know," Tan shrugged. "That's Kieji Sendai, our resident explosives expert. Kieji, this is Kasugai Hatsumi, our team leader."

The man looked up, nodded once, and went back to work.

"Is it safe for you to have explosives sitting in your lap while you're working with a soldering iron?" Hatsumi repeated his question for the demolitions man.

*"Hai,"* Sendai answered. Finishing the joint he was working on, he sat back and tossed the explosive to Hatsumi. "That's Davion-issue C-8. It's mostly Cyclonite, with a few stabilizing agents. The stuff is completely stable until it is initiated by means of a blasting cap. Then, it gives you a good high-speed explosion, somewhere around sixty-eight thousand centimeters per second."

The plastic explosive was stiff, gray-green putty, wrapped in olive drab paper. Hatsumi knew the stuff could be used for any number of applications. It could be used as is, or smoothed over the object to be destroyed. It could be molded into a shaped charge, or wrapped with chain to make an improvised fragmentation bomb. Rigged with a short fuse-type detonator, it could be bundled together in a satchel charge and stuffed into the vulnerable knee and ankle joints of a BattleMech. Only pentaglycerine was a more powerful blasting agent.

Returning the block to the table, he asked Sendai to be careful.

"It wouldn't do for us to get ourselves blown up before we started our mission."

"Pardon me for asking," Tan handed his team leader a cup of tea poured from the pot that had been warming on the stove ever since Hatsumi had arrived. "What *is* our mission?"

Hatsumi sampled the tea and nodded his thanks before answering.

"We are to link up with the Second Com Guards Division, posing as combat support personnel assigned to their second battalion.

"I have been assured that the Second will arrive on Defiance within the week. Places for us have already been established. When they arrive, we will report to the old Defiance Militia compound west of Jerseyville to take our places. We are to remain with the Second until our contact gets in touch with us. Once contact is made, we will receive all of our specific orders through this agent."

"That's all very good." Tan was unimpressed with the secrecy shrouding their mission. "What I want to know is, what is the specific nature of our mission?"

"I do not know, Tan-*san*. I have told you all I *do* know. The Amber Crags Clan was contacted indirectly, through a representative of our client. The client, who I have been told is very important, insists that there can be no connection between our team and himself. We are to hook up with the Second, and wait until contacted." Hatsumi took another sip of tea. "After all, waiting for our prey is a large part of being nekekami."

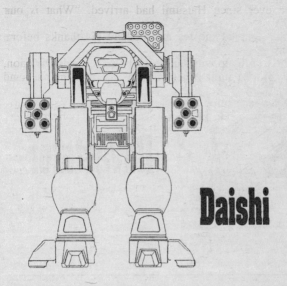

# Daishi

---

# Penetrator

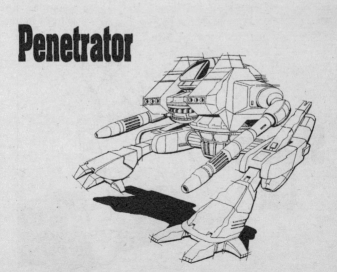

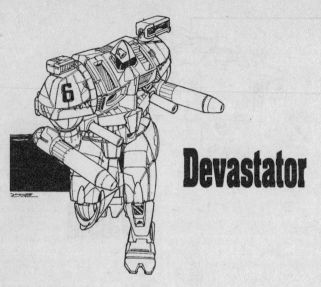

**Devastator**

**Shadow Cat**

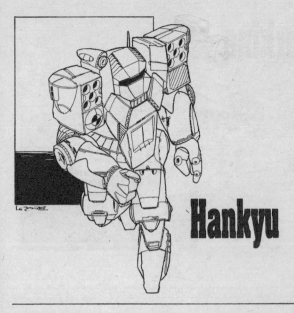

**Hankyu**

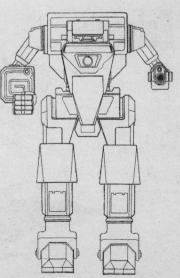

**Fenris**

# Turkina

# Falconer

# Kodiak

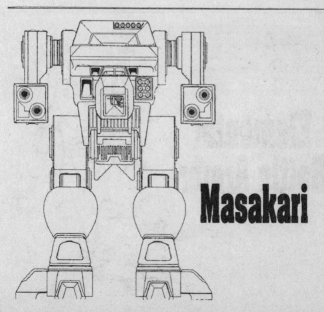

# Masakari

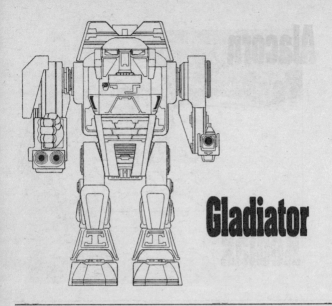

**Gladiator**

**Elemental
Battle Armor**

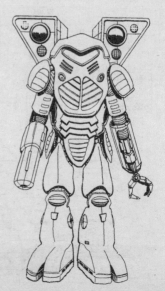

# Alacorn
# Tank

# Brutus
# Tank

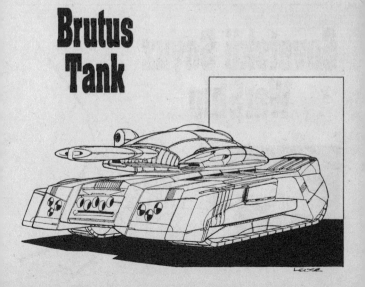

# Leopard Class DropShip

# Sovetskii Soyuz WarShip

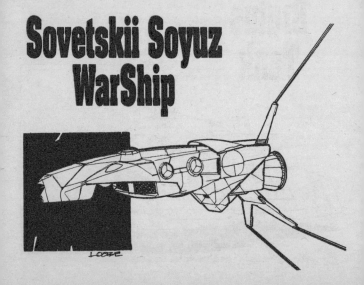

LOOZE

FASA

# RELENTLESS ACTION FROM BATTLETECH ®